M000275710

DUMBARTON OAKS
MEDIEVAL LIBRARY

Jan M. Ziolkowski, General Editor

YSENGRIMUS

DOML 26

Ysengrimus

Edited and Translated by

JILL MANN

DUMBARTON OAKS
MEDIEVAL LIBRARY

HARVARD UNIVERSITY PRESS
CAMBRIDGE, MASSACHUSETTS
LONDON, ENGLAND
2013

Library of Congress Cataloging-in-Publication Data
Nivardus, 12th cent.
    Ysengrimus / edited and translated by Jill Mann.
    pages. cm. — (Dumbarton Oaks medieval library ; 26)
    ISBN 978-0-674-72482-2 (alk. paper)
    1. Nivardus, 12th cent. Ysengrimus. I. Mann, Jill. II. Nivardus, 12th
cent. Ysengrimus. Latin. 2013. III. Nivardus, 12th cent. Ysengrimus.
English. 2013. IV. Title. V. Series: Dumbarton Oaks medieval library ; 26.
    PA8347.I8A2 2013
    873'.03 — dc23   2013007343

Originally published in slightly different form as Ysengrimus:
Text with Translations, Commentary and Introduction under
ISBN 978-90-04-08103-1, Copyright 1987 Koninklijke Brill NV,
Leiden, the Netherlands.

Contents

Introduction

The *Ysengrimus* is one of the most original and ambitious works of medieval literature. It is a Latin beast epic, over 6,500 lines long. It is the first work to give the now familiar names of Reynard and Ysengrimus to the fox and the wolf, and to make the antagonism between them into the main-spring of the narrative development. Most of the twelve episodes of the narrative recount the fox's repeated humilia-tions of the wolf, who is beaten, flayed (twice), mutilated, and finally eaten alive by sixty-six pigs. In true epic style, the narrative begins *in mediis rebus,* and recapitulates earlier events midway through. A detailed summary can be found at the end of this Introduction. Although some of these episodes have a recognizable source in beast fable or animal an-ecdote, they are extended and elaborated into highly origi-nal forms, mainly by the addition of lengthy speeches by the animals, heavy with rhetorical expressions of sententious wisdom. The style of the poem is highly sophisticated: the author had an assured command of the Latin language and was steeped in classical Latin authors, especially Ovid, whom he seems to have had by heart.[1]

Antecedents

Most of the narrative episodes of the *Ysengrimus* have no identifiable source; the others are linked with a varied assortment of antecedents (see accompanying table of Sources and Analogues).[2] The booty-sharing (and its variant, the bacon-sharing), the horse's kick, and possibly the field-division, stem from the Aesopic fable tradition. The fox's trick of "shamming death" is a staple of the medieval bestiary tradition. The "sick lion" episode, which contains the first flaying of the wolf, and the mutual outwitting of the fox and the cock, have parallels in independent Latin poems of the Carolingian period and later.[3] The motif of the wolf-monk also appears in some independent Latin poems.[4] But the only work to challenge *Ysengrimus*'s claim of being the earliest beast epic is the *Ecbasis captivi,* a full-scale narrative of over 1,200 Latin hexameters, which was probably written in the eleventh century. Like the *Ysengrimus,* this work portrays the enmity between the fox and the wolf (though they are not named), and both works have a monastic ambience. The "captive" of the earlier poem's title is a calf whose escape from confinement represents the author's own longing to be free from his "cloistered prison" (58), and the wolf into whose clutches he falls is also a monk. The "sick lion" story also appears in the *Ecbasis:* the wolf relates it to explain his fear of the fox. But the dramatis personae of the *Ecbasis* includes an unusual set of animals (for example, otter, hedgehog, leopard, panther, unicorn) that give the poem a fanciful and imaginative coloring that is quite different from the mordant satire of the *Ysengrimus.* The later poem is also much more tightly organized, held together by an overriding satiric motive, which determines its structure, its often grotesque physical cruelty, and its interminable rhetorical elaborations.

THEMES AND STRUCTURE

The satire of the *Ysengrimus* is directed against a quite specific target, represented in the figure of the wolf. Traditionally, the wolf is the embodiment of greed, but in this poem, his greed is associated with a specific social type. In the opening episode of the poem, Ysengrimus explains that since he became a monk, his natural greed has been doubled; a monk's greed far exceeds that of a wolf's (1.634–50). But the satiric focus is narrowed still further, as can be seen in the account of the wolf's entry into the monastery (5.335–1120), which forms part of the Inset Narrative. His decision to become a monk is motivated by greed (Reynard has given him a taste of monastic food), and once admitted, he gives a spectacular demonstration of it by opening all the taps on the monastic wine-barrels and drinking most of the wine. When confronted by the angry monks, Ysengrimus claims that his depredations were designed to prove his worthiness to become a monk-bishop. Bishops elected from the secular clergy are mere amateurs in the practice of rapacious greed, while monks who are elected bishops know how to devour everything (5.995–1040). The infuriated monks respond by promising him an immediate "consecration," which takes the form of a maelstrom of blows.

The real-life counterpart to the wolf's role as monk-bishop appears in Reynard's denunciation of his teeth for having failed to hold on to the cock (5.109–30). If only, he says, they had imitated the behavior of Anselm, bishop of Tournai. *He* is sure that the only thing wrong with plunder is that it has a necessary limit—that is, he can't take more than he finds (5.121–22). This "shepherd" shears his flock right down to the living flesh, so that the fleeces are unable to grow again (5.111–12, 119–20). Anselm was, at the time of his election as bishop, abbot of Saint-Vincent at Laon; he is thus one of those monk-bishops whom the wolf holds up as examples of unrestrained greed. The other historical figure who is made the object of a major satirical attack, Pope Eugenius III, is a monk-pope: before his election he was abbot of the monastery of Saints Anastasius and Vincent *ad Aquas Salvias* in Rome. Reynard's ironic praise of Anselm's rapacity is preceded by equally ironic praise of the pope's insatiable greed for money (5.99–108); at the end of the poem, this pope is identified as Eugenius by the accusation that he took a large bribe from Roger, duke of Sicily, to send the Second Crusade to the Holy Land by the land route, instead of by the sea route via Sicily (7.664–704). "One feeble monk has overthrown two kingdoms!" is the twice-repeated summary of this event (7.468, 672)—the "two kingdoms" being France and Germany, partners in the ill-fated Crusade.

In accordance with his role as the fictional counterpart to these real-life figures, the wolf is consistently referred to or addressed not only as a monk ("monachus") but more specifically as "abbot" ("abbas") and "bishop" ("praesul," "pontifex,", "antistes").[5] As already mentioned, the beating administered by his fellow monks is presented as a mock consecration. The same is true of the flaying of the wolf in Book 3, the climactic event of the first part of the Outer Narrative. After the bear's claws have sliced away most of his hide, a scrap of skin on his head is left behind, which the sheep Joseph jeeringly interprets as a bishop's miter (3.991–92). Up to now, he says, the wolf has been an abbot; is he now going to be made a bishop as well? Why should wolves have all the luck? (3.1001–2). The fox then mockingly interprets the stream of blood in which the wolf is enveloped as a scarlet robe that he has been concealing beneath his shaggy pelt —another feature that can be linked to the monk-bishops, who wore *two* sets of ecclesiastical robes, their episcopal garments on top and the monastic habit underneath. The flaying scene is also linked with the satiric praise of Anselm of Tournai by verbal echo: as the bear is about to make his onslaught on the wolf's skin, the fox hurls himself at his feet, begging him not to take more than he finds, since the wolf himself never took more than that (3.932–33; compare also 2.27). That is, the wolf, like Anselm, takes everything he can lay hold of, although, alas, it is impossible to take more. The verbal echo prompts the realization that the flaying of the wolf is the exact counterpart of Anselm's practice in "shearing" his flock down to the living flesh; the treatment that the real-life abbot-bishop metes out to his flock is here ruthlessly applied to his fictional counterpart. In real life, as the poet makes clear (6.325–26), such greedy "shearing" is counterproductive: a sheared fleece will grow again, but a flayed skin will not. In the cartoonlike world of the *Ysengrimus,* the wolf's skin *does* grow again, but only so that he may receive a repeated punishment when the lion removes it for a second time (6.201–3). The abbot-bishop's greedy fantasy comes true, only in order to form the basis of renewed punishment.

This punitive structure is also visible in the pilgrimage

episode, when the wolf gatecrashes the hostel where the animal pilgrims are spending the night, and is offered three wolf's heads for dinner. In fact, there is only one wolf's head, which is disguised by the sheep Joseph on its second and third appearances to make it look different. The first head, Joseph claims, is that of an old Angevin (4.272); the second, the head of an English abbot (4.279); the third, the head of a Danish bishop (4.302). Setting aside the geographical references as contributing to the playful differentiation, it becomes clear that the three heads represent the three fundamental characteristics of Ysengrimus himself: he is old (e.g., 1.75, 103, 115, 151, 180, 189), he is an abbot, and he is a bishop. Joseph "tonsures" the second head by tearing out its hair, and claims that the "hermit" Ysengrimus should find it acceptable, "since he was of a similar order" (4.287–88).[6] Following Reynard's instructions, Joseph props open the jaws of the third head with a stick, so that the terrified Ysengrimus is confronted with a mirror image of his own gaping jaws. The devourer is offered himself to devour; he is threatened by an image of his own rapacious greed.

The turning of the tables, predator becoming victim, is the structural principle that pervades the whole poem. It is of course evident in the repeated humiliations inflicted on the wolf by the fox, the sheep, the horse, and other animals whom he expects to make his victims. Only once does he triumph, when he successfully devours the bacon that he had promised to share with the fox. Even this fits the pattern of comic reversal, however: the poem opens with the wolf devouring bacon, and closes with him being devoured by pigs. The opening episode also fits the pattern of comic reversal in a different way, since in the light of the rest of the

poem we can see the usually triumphant fox being outwit-
ted. This is also the case when he is tricked by his natural
victim, the cock, in the sequel to the pilgrimage episode.
Similarly, the horse who tricks the wolf is himself outwitted
by the apparently feeble stork. The whole poem thus illus-
trates the satiric principle that the predator will become the
victim, the trickster will be tricked; "luditur illusor," as the
poet puts it (1.69).

Finally, it should be noted that this vision of a "world up-
side down" has a strongly apocalyptic character. Ysengrimus
evokes the "false prophets, who come to you in the clothing
of sheep, but inwardly are ravening wolves" (Matthew 7:15),
and whose appearance will mark the approach of the Last
Judgment and the end of the world (Matthew 24:11, 24). In
the final episode of the poem, Ysengrimus takes on the role
of a "pseudopropheta": seeing that he is about to suffer the
(alleged) fate of the prophet Mohammed in being eaten by
pigs (7.295), he asks leave to prophesy the future (7.297–98),
which is granted. He is then sardonically addressed as "do-
mine Ysengrime propheta" (7.371). The references in this
same episode to the disastrous Second Crusade also fit this
apocalyptic scenario: earthquake, eclipse of the sun, flood,
hailstorms, nation rising up against nation, Jerusalem sur-
rounded by an army—all these signs of the end of the world,
as foretold in the New Testament,[7] are paralleled in the po-
em's account of the Crusade. But it was not only disas-
ters that were supposed to herald the end of the world: the
Sybilline prophecies foretold that the final coming of Christ
would be preceded by a miraculous period of peace and
abundance. This universal peace would extend even to the
animal kingdom: as Isaiah had prophesied, the wolf would

lie down with the lamb and the leopard with the kid (Isaiah 11:6, 65:25). The *Ysengrimus* offers a comic travesty of this miraculous peace between predator and victim. The wolf habitually greets his intended victims with "Pax vobis" or "Pax tibi" (4.141–42, 6.56, 7.13). He offers to give the pig Salaura the "kiss of peace" given by the priest to the congregation at Mass (7.27). He purports to put an end to the strife between the four sheep by issuing a "bannus," a legally binding peace (2.525–28). Similarly, the fox tries to persuade the cock to trust in a legal "peace," which he says has been proclaimed by secular authorities (5.137–38). But the wolf's real attitude to such legal proclamations of peace is revealed in the court episode (3.163–70, 185–86), and his intended victims are not fooled by his sham offers of peace: Salaura's porcine companions retaliate by offering the wolf "just the same sort of peace as he had come to impart himself" (7.153–54; compare 4.714–15 and 6.60); the cock convinces the fox that the figures he claims to see coming to confirm the peace are a huntsman and a pack of dogs. And instead of lying down with the wolf, the sheep batter him to a pulp.

In the Old Testament, "false prophets" are frequently castigated for making deceptive promises of peace: "Peace, peace," they say, but "there is no peace" (Ezekiel 13:10–16; Jeremiah 6:13–14, 8:10–11). Saint Bernard of Clairvaux, whose preaching gave decisive impetus to the Second Crusade, ruefully echoed Jeremiah in addressing his disciple Pope Eugenius III after the Crusade's disastrous conclusion: "We have said 'peace,' and there is no peace; we have promised good, and there is confusion."[8] The contemporary annalist who speaks of "certain pseudo-prophets, sons of Belial, witnesses of Antichrist" who deceived Christians by "empty words" and persuaded them to attack the Saracens by "vain preaching" alludes only obliquely to Saint Bernard and Eugenius, but the identification is clear enough.[9] This probably explains not only the attack on Eugenius, but also the two glancing references to Saint Bernard, one of which implies that his greed is amateurish in comparison to that of Anselm of Tournai (5.126),[10] and the other seems to imply that he is a "bigmouth" (6.89). The wolf's proposal that his fellow monks should get rid of all church ornaments and spend all their money on sheep (5.665–88) is very likely a satiric hit at the Cistercians, who similarly rejected all superfluous ornament and who devoted themselves to sheep rearing, and this too may have arisen from, or given rise to, dislike of Bernard, monk of Cîteaux.

Despite its episodic nature, therefore, the *Ysengrimus* proves on close examination to be very carefully structured and organized around its specific satiric themes. The details of the narrative fiction are brilliantly designed to enact the punishment of the monk-bishop, whose insatiable greed leads him to shear his "flock" down to the living flesh. In the apocalyptic world-upside-down that the poem conjures up, it is the monk-bishop who is skinned by his usual victims, and his skin grows again, as if it were a fleece, only so that he may suffer renewed tortures.

DATE, PLACE, AUTHOR

The numerous allusions to real-life persons and events in the poem make it possible to locate it in time and place with a precision unusual in medieval literature. Chief among these allusions is the reference to Anselm, who was bishop of Tournai from 1146 to 1149. The account of the disasters that befell the Second Crusade (1147–1148), which are the subject of conversation between Reynard and Salaura the pig at the end of the poem (7.465–84, 665–76), also link the poem with this relatively brief time span. The crusaders traveled to the Holy Land in the second half of 1147, and news of the disasters that befell them probably began to circulate in the West from the end of the year onward. Eugenius III, who is blamed as having caused these disasters by taking a bribe to send the crusaders overland rather than by the sea route, was pope from 1145 to 1153, and it was in December 1145 that he issued the bull that urged King Louis VII of France and all the faithful in his kingdom to take up arms against the heathen in defense of the Holy Land.

The two abbots who are the subject of the poet's eulogy in Book 5 also fit naturally into this time span: Walter of Egmond, who is identified by name (5.459, 501), was abbot from 1130 to 1161; the abbot of Liesborn who is said to rival him in virtue must therefore be Balduin, whose abbacy lasted from 1131 until his death, in 1161.

Taking all these allusions together, it becomes clear that the *terminus post quem* for the poem is early 1148 (when news of the Second Crusade reached the West), and the *terminus ad quem* is August 1149 (when Anselm died).

Indications of place show a similar consistency, centering on the town of Ghent in the county of Flanders. When the wolf decides to become a monk, the monastery he enters is named as "Blandinia claustra" (5.447)—that is, the abbey of Saint Peter's, situated on the small hill known as Blandinium, just south of the main town-settlement of Ghent. Walter of Egmond was a former monk of Blandinium, and it was

Arnold, abbot of Saint Peter's from 1114 to 1132, who nominated him as abbot of Egmond. Anselm of Tournai visited Ghent in 1147, when he consecrated a leper chapel built on land belonging to Saint Bavo's, the other abbey of Ghent, and great rival of Saint Peter's. Another link with Ghent is Saint Pharaildis, who is credited with an entirely spoof history by the author of the *Ysengrimus* (2.71–94): her relics were in the possession of Saint Bavo's, and the chapel of the counts of Flanders, located beside their castle in Ghent, became the home of a chapter of canons dedicated to her. Saint Bavo himself is mentioned at 3.717, and other saints alluded to—Saint Brigid, Saint Giles, Saint Gereon of Cologne, and Saint Malo—all have their feast days recorded in the Saint Bavo's martyrology.[11] The river Scheldt, on whose banks Blandinium is situated, is twice referred to as if it were close to the scene of the narrative action (4.592, 5.551). When the poet thinks of a bishop, he thinks of the diocese of Tournai, to which Ghent belonged (5.109–12); when he thinks of an archdiocese, it is Reims, the province within which Ghent lay (1.467, 7.174). The wider horizons of the poem extend in the east to the cathedral city of Cologne (where the monks of Saint Bavo's bought their wine) and to the mighty rivers of the Rhine and the Elbe; in the west, to the monastery of Saint-Bertin at Saint-Omer (Sithiu; 4.285), which maintained a bond of confraternity with both Saint Peter's and Saint Bavo's; in the south, to the city of Arras (1.193) and its abbey of Saint-Vaast (4.286); in the north, to the abbeys of Egmond, in the diocese of Utrecht, and Liesborn in the diocese of Münster.

It is therefore relatively easy to locate the poem in time and place, but it is less easy to identify its author. He was long known as "Nivard of Ghent," but this identification rests only on the evidence of one late manuscript, a late thirteenth-/early fourteenth-century copy of the *Florilegium Gallicum,* in which the group of proverbial maxims excerpted from the poem is headed "magister Niuardus de Ysengrino et Reinardo."[12] The title "magister" has been taken to indicate that he was a teacher, and on this basis Voigt presumed that he was one of the canons of Saint Pharaildis, who had charge of the schools of Ghent; but it seems that both Saint Bavo's and Saint Peter's also exercised rights over teaching in their immediate vicinity,[13] and, in any case, "magister" may just mean someone who had studied at university. Furthermore, another copy of the *Florilegium Gallicum,* contained in a thirteenth-century manuscript, heads its series of excerpts from the *Ysengrimus* "Proverbia Bernardi," while two medieval references to a work that they call "apologya de actibus Ysengrini" or "de Ysengrino" attribute it to one "Balduinus Cecus."[14] In modern times, A. van Geertsom has proposed that the author himself indicates that his name was Bruno: when the lion asks to hear the earlier adventures of the wolf and the fox, he is told that Bruno the bear had put them into verse ("versus fecerat inde novos": 3.1194). This is an interesting and appealing suggestion, although impossible to prove. Less appealing is van Geertsom's further claim that the author is Simon, former abbot of Saint-Bertin, to which there are a number of objections, not least the fact that Simon died in February 1148, restricting the timescale of the poem's composition in a highly improbable, not to say impossible, way.

It must therefore be regretfully concluded that the author's name remains uncertain. But it seems highly likely that he was a cleric, and if not himself a monk, a member of the monastic *familia* of Saint Peter's or Saint Bavo's. His appeal to Walter of Egmond and Balduin of Liesborn to offer him "subsidium" (5.538), and to add him to the burden that their loaded necks already bear (5.539–40), suggests that he was looking for future employment or promotion. In this connection, it is highly interesting that Walter of Egmond was not only responsible for boosting the financial prosperity of his abbey, but also seems to have stimulated an extraordinary burst of literary and scribal activity at Egmond, embracing the acquisition and copying of books, the composition of new versions of the lives of local saints, the compilation of the records of the abbey's rights and landholdings known as the *Liber S. Adalberti,* and the overhauling and amplification of the *Annales Egmundenses*.[15] It is tempting, to say the least, to imagine that the author was putting himself forward for co-optation into this literary program.

Afterlife and Influence

Only five surviving manuscripts contain a complete (or once complete) version of the *Ysengrimus.* A further ten are florilegia containing proverbs excerpted from the poem.[16] But the *Ysengrimus*'s influence was far greater than this relatively restricted number of manuscript witnesses would suggest, by virtue of its role as a major narrative source for the French *Roman de Renart.* As Lucien Foulet convincingly demonstrated, no fewer than eight branches of the *Renart*—six of them among the earliest and most important—were modeled on episodes of the Latin poem.[17] The *Ysengrimus* thus played a key role in stimulating the major explosion of ver-

nacular beast literature that took place from the middle
of the twelfth century onward, including the Middle High
German *Reinhart Fuchs,* the Flemish *Van den Vos Reinaerde*
and its later adaptation *Reinaerts Historie,* Jacquemart Gelée's
Renart le Nouvel, the *Couronnement de Renard, Renart le Con-
trefait,* and the Italian *Rainardo e Lesengrino.*[18] The *Ysengrimus*
is not only one of the most brilliant and ingeniously crafted
literary works of the Middle Ages: it can also be said to have
invented a whole literary genre.

Narrative Summary

1. The Bacon-Sharing (1.1–528)

The wolf Ysengrimus captures the fox Reynard and threat-
ens to eat him, but is diverted by Reynard's offer to get for
him a piece of bacon carried by a passing peasant, if he will
agree to share it with the fox. Reynard pretends to be so ex-
hausted that he can hardly walk; the peasant, greedy for his
pelt, tries to catch him, and puts down the bacon so as to
have both hands free for this task. Behind his back, Ysengri-
mus makes off with the bacon, but when Reynard has es-
caped from the confused peasant and finally arrives at their
agreed rendezvous, he discovers that the wolf has already
eaten the whole bacon, and has left for the fox's share only
the willow rope by which it had been tied to the rafters.

2. The Fishing (1.529–2.158)

Reynard persuades Ysengrimus to go fishing, using his tail
instead of a net. Leaving him with his tail hanging hopefully

in the water, the fox goes to a nearby village and steals a cock belonging to its priest. Pursued by the priest and an angry crowd of villagers, the fox leads them back to the wolf, whose tail is by now frozen fast in the river. Forgetting the fox, the villagers fall on the wolf and beat him. An old woman tries to finish him off with an ax, but manages only to sever his tail from his body, by which he makes good his escape.

3. The Field-Division (2.159–688)

Reynard commiserates with Ysengrimus on the state of his skin after the beating, and suggests that he repair it with sheepskin. He explains that four sheep nearby are constantly quarreling over the division of their common field, and he suggests that Ysengrimus should offer to mark out their individual territories, and punish any sheep who crosses the boundaries by eating him. The sheep pretend to acquiesce in this plan, and they place the wolf in the middle of their field to act as a boundary marker. Retiring to its four sides, they then all charge at the wolf simultaneously, battering him to a pulp and making yet more rents in his skin.

4. The Court of the Sick Lion (3)

The lion, king of beasts, falls sick, and summons the chief representatives of the animals to his court to give him counsel. Only Reynard disobeys and stays away. Ysengrimus, pretending to have medical knowledge, advises the king that he will be cured if he eats the flesh of a sheep and a goat. In response, the sheep and the goat advise the king to send for

Reynard, and this time the fox obeys the summons. On arrival, he pretends to have been away on a journey to Salerno to seek medicine for the king, and produces six pairs of worn-out shoes (counting them out three times so that they appear to be eighteen) as evidence of his long journey. He recommends that the king, besides taking a potion of the medicinal herbs that he has acquired, should undergo a sweating cure inside the skin of a three-and-a-half-year-old wolf.

Ysengrimus's age then becomes the subject of debate, but he is finally flayed by the bear, and his skin is used to cure the lion. The king then asks to hear some of the previous adventures of the fox and the wolf, which have been referred to in the course of this episode; it is revealed that they have been put into verse by the bear, and the boar reads them aloud to the court.

The Inset Narrative

5. The Pilgrimage (4.1–810)

Bertiliana the roe, having set out on a pilgrimage, is joined by Reynard and six other animals. The company stops for the night at a hospice, where they are joined by the wolf. Pretending to welcome him, they offer him as food an apparent series of wolf heads (in fact only one, which is presented three times in different guises). Panic-stricken at this evidence of their "lupicidal" prowess, the wolf tries to leave, but is wedged in the doorway by the ass, and then pounded from inside and outside by the other animals. When he is finally allowed to leave, he goes off to collect eleven of his relatives, and then returns to the attack. The animal pilgrims take refuge on the roof, but Carcophas the ass, being less agile than the others, is still perched on a pile of hay next to it when the wolves arrive. Making a belated effort to heave himself onto the roof, he instead topples backward and falls on two wolves beneath him, squashing them flat. Reynard applauds this feat as if it was intentional, and the other wolves flee in terror.

6. THE FOX AND THE COCK (4.811–5.316)

The cock and the goose, afraid of the fox's cunning, steal away from the company. Reynard pursues and after some time finds the cock. He flatters him into crowing with his eyes closed, seizes him, and runs off with him, pursued by a large crowd. The cock tricks Reynard into putting him down so that he might explain to the pursuing crowd that he has a right to him. The cock then immediately flies up into a bush. Reynard tries to trick him a second time, by pretending that a piece of bark is a legal document proclaiming a general "peace," but the cock frightens him off by feigning that he sees a huntsman and his dogs approaching.

7. THE WOLF IN THE MONASTERY (5.317–1128)

Reynard is given a pile of cakes by a friendly cook. Keeping back eight of them, he shaves his head, and tells the wolf that he has become a monk and that cakes are the daily fare of the monastery. In search of such treats, the wolf enters the monastery of Blandinium, and is made guardian of the sheep. Meanwhile, Reynard has gone to Ysengrimus's house, urinated on his children, and lured his infuriated wife into chasing him back to his den, where she sticks fast in the narrow entrance. Reynard slips out by the back door and rapes her from behind.

Back in the monastery, the wolf totally disrupts the night office by breaking the rule of silence; then he demands a drink. Taken to the cellar, he opens up all the barrels and is soon swimming in wine. The indignant monks beat him and throw him out.

The End of the Inset Narrative

8. The Horse and the Wolf (5.1129–1322)

The scene changes to a marsh, where the horse Corvigarus encounters a feeding stork. The stork frightens off the horse by beating its wings loudly. Corvigarus then meets Ysengrimus, who claims the horse's hide in place of the skin he has lost. Corvigarus offers to renew Ysengrimus's tonsure with the razors that he says he keeps in his hooves. Called to show the wolf his razor strop, he displays his penis. As Ysengrimus approaches to verify the presence of the razors, the horse kicks him so hard that the horseshoe becomes implanted in his forehead.

9. The Sheep and the Wolf (6.1–132)

Reynard persuades Ysengrimus to make another try for a sheepskin. They visit Joseph the ram, who claims to be only too willing to be devoured by the wolf. Joseph persuades

Ysengrimus to sit with his back braced against a post and his jaws wide open, so that he may hurl himself straight inside them. Instead, the sheep charges at his head and prostrates the wolf once more. Ysengrimus crawls home.

10. THE BOOTY-SHARING *(6.133–348)*

The wolf's skin has grown again. Reynard falsely tells the lion that Ysengrimus has invited him to dinner. The wolf is stupefied with fear and surprise at their arrival, but agrees to Reynard's suggestion that they go hunting together. They kill a calf, and Ysengrimus is asked to divide the spoils. He makes three equal heaps, one for each of them. Enraged, the lion removes the wolf's skin for the second time, with one swipe of his paw. The lion then asks Reynard to make the division. He makes three piles: the first, of the fattest and fleshiest meat, is for the king; the second, slightly less good, is for the lioness; the third, of bony pieces, is for the cubs. The fox puts aside only one foot for his share, if the king approves. Very pleased with this, the king asks the fox who taught him to divide so well. Reynard answers that it was his uncle the wolf.

11. THE OATH *(6.349–550)*

Ysengrimus now once more needs a skin. Reynard tells him that his father was owed one by the father of the ass Carcophas, and he should press for payment of the debt. Carcophas insists that Ysengrimus should swear the truth of his claim on some "relics," which will miraculously immobilize him if he swears falsely. The "relics" are in fact a trap, and when Ysengrimus lays his foot on it, he is duly trapped. He escapes only by gnawing off his own foot.

12. THE DEATH OF THE WOLF (7)

Ysengrimus meets the great sow Salaura, and offers to give her a priestly kiss of peace. She insists that Mass must be celebrated first, and suggests that he bite her ear so that her squeals may summon her well-fed relatives, who can help her sing the office. A crowd of pigs then thunders to Salaura's rescue; they attack the wolf and devour him. Salaura laments the disaster of the Second Crusade. Reynard arrives and expresses hypocritical regret at his uncle's death. Salaura reverts to her lamentations on the state of the world and the signs of its approaching end. Reynard wishes his uncle were alive to defend the pope against her accusations.

As in my 1987 edition of *Ysengrimus,* my first and greatest debt is to the monumental edition by Ernst Voigt, which is the indispensable foundation for all subsequent work on the poem. As far as the present edition is concerned, I am grateful to E. J. Brill for giving permission to reproduce the text and translation of my 1987 edition. I must also thank Ross Arthur of York University, Toronto, for his invaluable help in producing a scanned version of the translation, and in processing both that and the Latin text to fit the spelling and punctuation norms of the DOML series. I am grateful to Jan Ziolkowski for suggesting that *Ysengrimus* be included in this series, and for his ready assistance with advice and guidance in bringing the project to fruition. Raquel Beglei-ter went through the typescript with scrupulous care and made numerous helpful suggestions.

Notes on Grammar and Syntax

These brief notes on grammar and syntax are designed to avoid repetitive explanations in the Notes to the Transla-tion. I list here only a few selected features of specially fre-quent occurrence, as an aid to understanding the relation between text and translation; the examples given for each are merely samples offered by way of illustration. A full anal-ysis of the language of the *Ysengrimus* is provided in the in-troduction to Voigt's edition, xxxviii–liii; it is reprinted in Alf Önnerfors, ed., *Mittellateinische Philologie: Beiträge zur Erforschung der mittelalterlichen Latinität* (Darmstadt, 1975), 192–211.

1. The distinction between cardinal and distributive numerals is not rigorously adhered to. The distribu-tive is used for the cardinal (*sena* for *sex,* 1.1048; *unde-nis* for *undecim,* 2.8), and the cardinal is used for the distributive (*duo* for *bina,* 2.15). Both can be used with-out discrimination in the same construction (1.1013, 3.22). Occasionally a distributive (5.1083) or a numeral adverb (3.635) is used in place of an ordinal.
2. Hypallage (interchange of cases) is frequent (*dabat densum gratior umbra nemus* instead of *dabat densum gra-tiorem umbram nemus,* 3.40; compare 3.159, 4.449).
3. In adjectives and adverbs, the comparative is often used for the positive (1.131, 284, 924; 2.458; 3.265;

4.843, 960, 1005) and the comparative is sometimes used for the superlative (2.297, 3.387).

4. The present subjunctive is often used in place of future indicative, especially with *ire* (1.225, 2.514, 7.383), but also with other verbs (3.392, 5.418, 6.462, 7.216).

5. In compound forms of the passive, *fui, fuerim,* etc., are often used in place of *sum, eram, essem, ero, esse,* etc. (1.397, 410, 851, 864).

6. The future tense is often expressed periphrastically by the future participle in conjunction with an appropriate form of the verb *esse* (3.292, 417, 440, 750, 1141).

7. The use of the present tense to express future time, characteristic of Germanic languages, is extremely frequent (1.249, 349–50). Similarly, the perfect is used in place of the future perfect (1.371).

8. The second-person perfect subjunctive is sometimes used for the imperative (a back-formation from its customary use in prohibitions—e.g., *ne dixeris* gives rise to *dixeris*) (1.186, 382).

9. The ablative form of the gerund is used (as in classical Latin) to express instrumentality (1.31, 905) and also (as commonly in medieval Latin) as the equivalent of a present participle (1.113, 303, 1043).

10. Conditional clauses without an introductory conjunction are frequent (1.176, 395, 547, 574); sometimes they are indicated by inversion of verb and subject, but by no means always (both forms are found together in 2.514).

11. Paired clauses with concessive force *(velis nolis)* similarly lack introductory conjunctions (1.230, 507, 985).

12. *ceperam* is used to form something approaching a narrative imperfect (4.265, 7.659).

13. *suus* is used nonreflexively, as equivalent to *eius* (2.108, 580).

14. *ipse* is used as equivalent to *ille, is* (1.379, 444).

15. *-ve* is used as a line filler (3.579).

NOTES

1 Space does not permit documentation in the notes to the translation of every echo of a classical Latin author; for a comprehensive list, see Voigt, lxix–lxxii.

2 For previous analyses of the sources, see Voigt, lxxix–lxxxv, and Knapp, *Das lateinische Tierepos,* 65–76.

3 See Ziolkowski, *Talking Animals,* 48–51, 61–66, and Mann, *From Aesop to Reynard,* 16–17, 238–43.

4 See Mann, *Ysengrimus,* 12.

5 3.1073: "abbas et episcopus"; 7.17–18: "antistes et abbas"; 7.445–47: "abbas . . . praesulque"; for other examples, see Mann, *Ysengrimus,* 13, 17–18.

6 This episode precedes the wolf's entry into the monastery in "real" time, and he is here pretending to be a hermit; but the Benedictine Rule (ch. 1) recognizes hermits as one of four types of monks, and this notion is here drawn on in order to assimilate Ysengrimus to an abbot.

7 See Matthew 24, Luke 21, Apocalypse of St. John the Apostle 16, and Mann, *Ysengrimus,* 134–37.

8 *De consideratione,* Lib. II, cap. I.1 (*S. Bernardi Opera,* ed. J. Leclercq et al., vol. 3 [Rome, 1963], 411), quoting Jeremiah 6:13, 8:11, 14:19.

9 See Mann, *Ysengrimus,* 141.

10 For a different view, see J. Berlioz, "Saint Bernard dans la littérature satirique, de l'*Ysengrimus* aux *Balivernes des courtisans* de Gautier Map (XIIe–XIIIe siècles)," in *Vies et légendes de Saint Bernard de Clairvaux, Création, diffusion, réception (XIIe–XXe siècles): Actes des rencontres de Dijon, 7–8 juin 1991,* ed. P. Arabeyre, J. Berlioz, and P. Poirrier (Cîteaux, 1993), 211–28, at 213–17.

11 See Mann, *Ysengrimus,* 163 n. 508.

12 Now Berlin, Staatsbibliothek zu Berlin, Preussischer Kulturbesitz, MS Diez B. Santen 60; the ascription to Nivard is on fol. 5v. See Mann, *Ysengrimus,* 157.

13 See Mann, *Ysengrimus,* 92 n. 240.

14 See Mann, *Ysengrimus,* 157; R. B. C. Huygens, ed., *Reynardus vulpes. De Latijnse-Reinaert-Vertaling van Balduinus Iuvenis* (Zwolle, 1968), 27 n. 2.

15 See Mann, *Ysengrimus,* 176–81.

16 Space does not allow identification in the notes of every one of the poem's many proverbs; for further details, see Singer, *Sprichwörter des Mittelalters,* 1:143–78, and Mann, "Proverbial Wisdom in the *Ysengrimus,*" 93–109.

17 Foulet, *Le Roman de Renard,* 121–39 (Branch 2); 239–45 (Branch 5); 282–88 (Branch 3); 316–18, 320–22 (Branch 14); 370–80 (Branch 10); 434–40 (Branch 8); 460–67 (Branch 16); 489–91 (Branch 20). See also Mann, "The *Roman de Renart* and the *Ysengrimus.*" Foulet's proposed chronological order for the various branches (according to which only Branches 16 and 20 are later than 1190) is conveniently reproduced in tabular form in J. Flinn, *Le Roman de Renart dans la littérature française et dans les littératures étrangères au moyen âge* (Toronto, 1963), 16–18.

18 Flinn, *Le Roman de Renart.*

BOOK ONE

Egrediens silva mane Ysengrimus, ut escam
    ieiunis natis quaereret atque sibi,
cernit ab obliquo Reinardum currere vulpem,
    qui simili studio ductus agebat iter,
5 praevisusque lupo non viderat ante videntem,
    quam nimis admoto perdidit hoste fugam.
Ille, ubi cassa fuga est, ruit in discrimina casus,
    nil melius credens quam simulare fidem,
iamque salutator veluti spontaneus infit:
10 "Contingat patruo praeda cupita meo!"
(Dicebat patruum falso Reinardus, ut ille
    tamquam cognato crederet usque suo.)
"Contigit," Ysengrimus ait, "laetare petisse,
    opportuna tuas obtulit hora preces.
15 Ut quaesita michi contingat praeda, petisti;
    contigit; in praedam te exigo, tuque daris.
Difficilis semper non est deus aequa petenti;
    te petere attendens aequa, repente dedit.
Te michi non potuit contingere gratior hospes;
20 non me hodie primum perfida vidit avis.
Unde venis, vesane Satan? Non curo rogare
    quo tendas, ego te longius ire veto.
Si quid adhuc exinde tibi procedere restat,
    huc tantum in fauces progrediere meas.

One morning, as Ysengrimus was leaving the wood to look for food for his hungry children and himself, he saw running across his path Reynard the fox, who had been led to venture forth by the same motive. Spotted first by the wolf, the fox had lost the chance of flight (his enemy being too near) before he perceived his observer. In a situation where flight was futile, he plunged into the hazards of chance, trusting to nothing better than a show of good faith. On the instant he produced what sounded like a spontaneous greeting: "May the prey he looks for fall in my uncle's way!" (Reynard used the inaccurate term "uncle" in order that the other might always put the trust in him that he would in a kinsman.)

"And so it has; be glad that you made the request!" said Ysengrimus, "a happy hour has brought the fulfillment of your prayers. You asked that the prey I sought might come to me, and so it comes about; I claim you as my prey, it's you who are bestowed on me. God is not always grudging to someone who asks for what is reasonable; perceiving the reasonableness of what you asked, he promptly granted it. A more welcome guest than you could not fall in my way. I wasn't seen first by the bird of ill-luck today. Where have you come from, you mad demon? As to where you're going, I don't bother to ask, since I refuse to allow your going any further. If any more forward movement remains for you, it will only be that you advance here into my jaws.

3

25 Hinc video duplicem nobis consurgere fructum:
   scilicet haec stomacho proderit esca meo—
phisicaque Obitio non haec michi lecta magistro est,
   dentibus inscripta est atque legenda meis—
cumque Camena meae te totum saepserit alvi,
30   nec via longa tibi est nec metuenda brevis.
Condoleo, quia saepe pedes lassaris eundo;
   sis faciam miles, nec gravia arma time.
Efficieris eques, sed non oneraberis armis,
   incumbet collo sarcina tota meo.
35 At ne forte cadas, equitabis more prophetae:
   non tibi sella super dorsa sed intus erit,
nec dedignor equus fieri—vellem ante fuisse
   cognatoque diu suppeditasse meo.
Nunc grator patiens pulsus et verba tulisse;
40   vulnera pensabunt, quod tacuere minae.
Insanit, quicumque minis efflaverit iram;
   hostem praemunit, qui timuisse facit.
Tutus it in clades, timidum sollertia servat;
   dissimulans odium promptior ultor erit.
45 Optatum fortuna diu te tradidit ultro—
   sic, quibus invideo, quotquot habentur, eant!
Quisne ego sim, nosti, siquidem tuus hospes ego ille,
   cui Sclava ante tuum potio sumpta larem est.
Ha, Reinarde, illa quam Brabas nocte fuisti!
50   Hic, nisi te Satanas glutiat, Anglus eris!
Quid mea, quid referam, quae natis probra meaeque
   feceris uxori? Nonne fuere palam?
Hospitium nostro tibi nunc in ventre paratur,
   incide!" (pandebat labra) "Sodalis, ini!

Hence I see a twofold profit arise for us: first, that is, this 25
food will do good to my stomach (a medicine which hasn't
been taught me by Professor Obitius, but which is inscribed
on my teeth for all to read). And second, when this singing
stomach of mine has enveloped you completely, you needn't 30
fear a journey of any sort, long or short. I'm sorry for you
because you often wear yourself out traveling on foot, so I'll
make you a knight. Don't be afraid of heavy armor. You'll be
made a rider, but you won't be loaded down with arms; the
whole burden will rest on my shoulders. But in case you fall, 35
you shall ride in the manner of the prophet: your seat won't
be on my back but inside me. I'm not ashamed to be a
horse—I wish I had been one earlier, and that I had long ago
offered such service to my kinsman. Now I'm glad that I
bore words and blows patiently; it's because threats were 40
not uttered that vengeance will be exacted by blows. The
man whose anger explodes into threats is a fool; whoever
makes his enemy afraid, forewarns him. Complacency walks
into disaster, whereas wariness preserves the fearful; the
one who dissembles his hatred will get his vengeance
quicker. You have long been wished for, and Fortune has 45
spontaneously handed you over—may all those I hate per-
ish thus, however many they are! Who I am, you know,
since indeed I am that guest of yours to whom the Slavic
drink was administered before your hearth; oh Reynard, on
that night you were as savage as a Brabanter! Here, unless 50
Satan swallows you up, you'll be as meek as an English-
man! Why should I repeat what shameful things you did
to me, nay, to my wife and children—they were public
enough, weren't they? Now a lodging is prepared for you
in my stomach; come on," (opening his lips) "enter, friend!

55   Sis collega licet pravus michi, nolo tibi esse.
      Deteris, ut debes; detere! Nolo sequi.
  Pando tibi hospitium, quamquam mereare repelli;
      incide iocunde, laetus adhisco tibi!"
  Dixit et admoto foris hostem dente titillans
60   leniter extremos vellit utrimque pilos;
  Reinardus tolerat, quod non tolerare libebat,
      et patienter adest, mallet abesse tamen.
  Sic alacer cattus, dum prenso mure iocatur,
      raptum deponit depositumque rapit,
65   ille silet raptus, nullo divertit omissus,
      tam fugere inde pavens, quam remanere dolens;
  denique si fidens obliquat lumina victor,
      oblitus fidei fit memor ille fugae,
  luditur illusor, mus absque vale insilit antrum,
70   observatorem non sibi deesse querens;
  liber ut evasit, non iret in oscula rursum
      ob quicquid fulvi rex habet aeris Arabs.
  Ha, rudis infaustusque, viae qui parcit et hosti!
      Ambiguum finem res habet usque sequens.
75   Incautus senior versutum circinat hostem,
      in pugno tutum fisus habere iocum.
  Suffocare metu mavult quam viribus illum,
      posse putans artes inter acerba nichil.
  Concutit inde quater dentes, sonuere coicti,
80   ut super incudem bractea tunsa sonat.
  "Ne vereare! Meo quos," inquit, "in ore ligones
      cernis ebent usu et tempore, nilque secant.

Although you're an evil comrade to me, I won't be one to 55
you. Criminal that you are, you get worse; well, get worse! I
won't follow your lead. I open up a lodging place for you, al-
though you deserve to be turned away; come in gladly—I am
happy to open up for you!"

Having spoken, he moved his teeth forward so that they
brushed his enemy's frame, and delicately he pulled at the 60
outermost hairs on both sides. Reynard endured what was
not very pleasant to endure, and patiently stood still, though
he'd rather have been somewhere else. So the nimble cat,
when playing with a captured mouse, lays him down when
caught, and catches him when laid down, while the prisoner 65
is silent, and when released, doesn't dart off anywhere, fear-
ing to run away as much as he regrets staying put. At last, if
the trusting victor turns his eyes aside, the mouse, oblivious
of loyalty, thinks only of flight, and the trickster is tricked;
the mouse, without a goodbye, dives into a hole, not com- 70
plaining that there's no one to watch him. Having got away
free, he wouldn't go back to those embraces for all the yel-
low gold of the king of Arabia. Ah, ignorant and ill-fated is
anyone who fails to trample down a path and trample down
an enemy! The subsequent course of events will lead to an
unsatisfactory conclusion.

The unwary old man encircled his cunning enemy, confi- 75
dent of having his bird well and truly in the hand, prefer-
ring to choke him by fear rather than by force, and think-
ing that cunning was powerless in tight corners. So he
clashed his teeth together four times, and they rang as
they clashed, just as a beaten sheet of metal rings on the 80
anvil. "Don't be afraid!" he said, "The mattocks you see
in my mouth are blunt with use and age and cut nothing.

Ostia (quid dubitas?) forsan non usque patebunt;
   nunc adaperta vides, quando vocaris, adi!
85 Ingredere, explora! Quid stas, vesane? Quid haeres?
   Intranda est propere ianua, quando patet.
Huc ergo cupide, ne sero intrasse queraris,
   gaudia cum gustu senseris illa, sali!
Si sapis, hoc fieri, quod praeformido, vetabis,
90 ne tibi propositas vendicet alter opes."
Hospita non audet Reinardus in ora salire;
   praecipites durum saepe tulere diem.
Vix quoque, quin quamvis passim iubeatur inire,
   ter mallet noctes octo cubare foris;
95 nam recolens olim mordendi gnara fuisse
   ora lupi, nondum credit ebere satis—
si nequeant mordere, putat quassantia saltem.
   Non ergo hospitii tactus amore refert:
"Leniter imprimis invita, patrue demens!
100 Nemo suae debet prodigus esse rei.
Sentio velle tuum; quid nostros scindis amictus?
   Desine paulisper, dum tria verba loquar—."
Iratus senior vocem interrumpit obortam:
   "Non est ante fores longa loquela decens.
105 Ingredere hospitium! Scito, nisi protinus intres,
   post intrasse voles sero; repente veni!
Ut socio praedico: semel fortasse rogabis,
   nec tibi pandetur ianua clausa quater.
Ergo lepor morum placeat, prius ibitur intro,
110 tunc tria sexque refer verba quaterque decem.

Why are you hesitating? Perhaps the gates won't always stand open. Now you see them thrown back, so come, when you're invited! Enter, explore! Why do you stand still, mad- 85 man? Why are you motionless? A door must be entered quickly when it's open. Jump in here eagerly, then, lest when you have tasted these joys you complain that you entered so late. If you are wise, you will prevent what I am afraid will happen: that someone else may claim the benefits of- 90 fered you."

Reynard did not dare to jump into the hospitable mouth (rash people have often had a nasty fate), and though he had just been and was continually being ordered to enter, he would rather have bedded down outside for four and twenty nights. For, reflecting that the wolf's jaws were once expert 95 in biting, he did not believe they had got blunt enough. If they couldn't bite, he thought they could at least squash him flat. So, unmoved by hospitable affection, he replied: "First make your invitation less forcefully, foolish uncle! No one 100 ought to be prodigal of his wealth. I understand what you wish; why do you tear the coat off my back? Leave off a little, while I speak three words —." The old one angrily interrupted the speech he had begun: "A long parley before the doors isn't proper. Enter the lodging! Know, that unless you 105 enter immediately, you will afterward wish too late that you had done so; come at once! I predict, as one friend to another, that perhaps one day you'll be making the request, and the door which has been four times closed shan't be opened. So get some polish into your manners; first enter, and then speak your three or six or forty words. Put up 110

9

Quassarique aliqua (pro caris multa feruntur)
    fer placide; patruus sum tibi, redde vicem!
Scis, ubinam biberim tua pocula lene ferendo,
    tu nunc exempli fungere lege mei."
115 Sic fatus senior non protinus irruit hosti,
    morsibus innocuis vellit et ambit ovans;
ergo, quod utilius nescisset, scire laborat,
    et tandem didicit, quod didicisse luit:
quaerat an arte aliqua redimi, qui saeptus in arto est?
120   Traditus an morti quid nisi morte premi?
Curane vivendi vel spes aliquanta supersit
    insano, suadens nolle repente mori?
At Reinardus itemque loquens "Proh patrue," clamat,
    "non Scitha, non Saxo sive Suevus ego!
125 En Reinardus adest, cognatum agnosce fidelem!"
    Ille refert: "Patruum tu quoque nosce bonum!
Ysengrimus adest, quo quando subire rogante
    negligis hospitium, vim faciente subi!"
Ille licet sermo multum pietatis haberet,
130   non placuit vulpi, taliter ergo monet:
"Patrue, tu posses aliquando urbanior esse;
    ambo sumus clara nobilitate sati,
at tu nescio quo iam rusticus omine dudum
    degeneras; patrii sanguinis esto memor!
135 Mane rubescit adhuc; more invitarer equestri!
    Me, velut ingruerent nubila noxque, trahis!

calmly with being jostled a little. Many things are put up with for the sake of those dear to us; I am your uncle, so give me my due! For you know that whereas I patiently put up with swallowing your punches, you are now to act by the law of my example."

At the end of this speech, the old man did not straight- 115 way fall on his enemy, but tugged at his hair with harmless bites, and exultingly circled round him. So he labored to be in possession of knowledge he would most profitably have been ignorant of, and at length received a lesson which it cost him dear to have learned: may the person who is trapped in a tight corner look to be saved by some cunning? Or, yielded up to death, should he look for nothing except 120 to be overwhelmed by death? May any care or hope to live survive in a fool, persuading him against a desire to die forthwith? But Reynard, speaking again, cried out: "Alas, uncle! I am not a Scythian, not a Saxon or one of the Suevi! See, it's Reynard; recognize your loyal kinsman!" The other 125 replied: "And you, recognize your kind uncle! It's Ysengrimus here; when you neglect to enter the lodging at his request, enter at his exercise of force!"

Although this speech had a great deal of kindness, it 130 didn't please the fox, so he admonished him as follows: "Uncle, I wish you could be more polite just for once; we are both the descendants of an illustrious nobility, but you, by some accident, have for some time been degenerating into a peasant. Remember your ancestral blood! It is still early 135 morning, so I should have been invited inside in a gentlemanly way. You drag me in as if night and fog were gathering! If, on this one occasion, I should refuse to enter your

Hospita tecta semel si iussus inire negarem,
 protinus alternum subsequeretur ave?
Gratia reddetur maior praestare volenti,
140 quam tibi praestanti restituenda fuit.
Huc potior michi causa viae est, patruique volebam
 discere ego eventus atque docere meos.
Quid dapis ergo tibi est hiberna in tempora partum?
 Qui tibi vita placet? Qui mea domna valet?
145 Qui spes magna mei patrueles? Obsecro, vivant!"
 "Ergo tibi curae," rettulit ille, "sumus?
Fors secus ac velles nostra est, hoc dico, cibique
 nil nisi te partum, frater, habemus adhuc."
Hospes ad haec: "Utinam ergo tibi satis esse valerem!
150 Nil nisi me exiguum sumptibus esse nocet."
Econtra senior: "Non est mea regula, qualem
 esse putas, aliter res ego tracto meas.
Iure caret magnis, qui sumere parva recusat;
 sufficere ut possint grandia, parva iuvant.
155 Grandia tota voro (michi tam patienter agenti
 gratia!), de modico nil superesse sino.
Gaude igitur, tam parva michi quam magna vorantur,
 nec parvum reputo, quicquid habere queo.
Purius elambi debet, quo parcior esca est;
160 fer patienter edi!" "Patrue, fiat!" ait,
"non michi sunt odiosa tui penetralia ventris,
 nec vereor fieri nobilis esca gulae.
Hospitio vellem numquam peiore locari,
 sed non hoc patria vendico sorte decus;
165 quolibet ut latro siccandus stipite pendi
 promerui potius quam cibus esse tibi.

hospitable roof at your command, should a very different kind of welcome be the immediate consequence? Greater thanks shall be given you for wishing to be of service than 140 would be your due if you actually served me. A stronger reason for my coming here was that I wanted to know what had become of my uncle, and to tell him what had become of me. What have you acquired in the way of food during the winter season? How does life please you? How is my lady? How are my cousins, those rising hopes? I pray that they are 145 well!"

"So we are of concern to you?" replied the other. "I tell you this, our luck is worse than you wish, and so far we have no food available except yourself." The guest responded: "Would, therefore, that I were enough to satisfy you! It's a 150 bad state of affairs when there's only little me for your meals." The old man replied: "My rule isn't what you think it; I handle my affairs differently. He who sniffs at picking up trifles is rightly deprived of big winnings. Little things play a part in the provision of big ones. Big things I gobble 155 up completely (thanks to my forbearance!) and of a little thing I leave nothing over. So be glad; little things as well as big are devoured by me, nor do I consider as a trifle anything I can get hold of. Where the food is scantier, it must be licked up the more cleanly—so allow yourself patiently to be 160 eaten!"

"Uncle, so be it!" he said. "The recesses of your stomach are not repugnant to me, nor do I fear being made a dish for a noble palate. I could wish never to be placed in a meaner lodging, but I don't claim this honor as my hereditary due. I have deserved to be hung up like a thief 165 to parch on the first tree rather than to be food for you.

Quod si fata michi decrerunt tale sepulcrum,
    laetor honore meo, sed tua probra queror.
Parvus ego et virtute carens, tu fortis et ingens,
170   et quidnam tituli mors tibi nostra dabit?
Ut caret obprobrio stratus miser hoste potenti,
    sic miserum sternens hostis honore potens.
Quin heu quanta meo tibi funere dampna parantur!
    Quis tibi consultor, qualis ego usque fui?
175 Ergo tibi dampnum mea mors et dedecus infert;
    vivam, consiliis prodero saepe tibi.
Exiguos artus cumulata peritia pensat;
    conciliant artes debilitatis onus.
Prodero—nunc equidem!" (cum "prodero" diceret, optans
180   addere, quo fieret lenior ira senis,
indicat hora viam: gestabat pone baconem
    rusticus, adiecit "nunc equidem" hospes ovans).
"Ecce baco hic coram tener est et crassus et ingens,
    et lentus morsu et parvus ego atque macer;
185 alteruter praesto est, neuter, si quaeris utrumque,
    pluris uter tibi sit, dixeris! Ille datur.
Detege continuo, quemnam praependeris esu;
    tempus adest epulis, pars bona lucis abit."
Subridens senior (dentes tamen extrahit) infit:
190   "Perna michi dabitur? Qua ratione, Satan?
Tu sic effugies forsan; promitte, quid obstat?
    Taliter haut hodie ludificabor ego!
Tam potes Atrebatum quam despondere baconem;
    da tibimet, frater, spe mea vota carent.
195 Laetificare solet stultum promissio dives;
    nescio promissis credere, credo datis."

So if the Fates have decreed such a sepulcher for me, I rejoice at my honor, but I regret your disgrace. I am little and lack strength, while you are strong and huge, so what glory 170 will my death give you? As a wretch overthrown by a powerful enemy suffers no disgrace, so a powerful enemy who overthrows a wretch wins no honor. Indeed, how many disasters, alas, will be brought on you by my death! Who shall be such a counselor as I have always been to you? So my 175 death will cause you both shame and harm, whereas if I live, I shall often make myself useful to you by my advice. Accumulated experience compensates for puny limbs; cunning makes up for the handicap of weakness. I shall be useful...this very moment!" (While he was saying "I shall be useful," wishing to add something by which the old man's 180 fury should be softened, the moment shows him the means: nearby, a peasant was carrying some bacon. So the exultant guest added "this very moment!") "See, this bacon in front of your eyes is tender, fat, and huge, and I am tough to chew and little and scrawny; one or the other is available, but nei- 185 ther, if you go for both. Say which is worth more to you, and it shall be given to you. Reveal quickly, which you'd rather have to eat; it's dinnertime, and a great part of the day has gone."

Smiling, but removing his teeth, the old man said: "The 190 ham will be given to me? On what grounds, devil? Perhaps you intend to escape by these means. Promise away—what's to stop you? I shan't be fooled like that, not today. You can promise me the town of Arras as easily as the bacon! Bestow it on yourself, brother; my wishes are without hope of fulfillment. It's usually a fool who's made happy by rich promises. 195 I don't believe in promises, I believe in gifts." Since the

Dentibus extractis audacior ille loquendi
    castigat patruum: "Sumere disce, miser!
Hoc solo impedior, quod nondum sumere nosti;
200   sumere si scires, perna parata foret.
Patrue, quis praesul, quis sumere rennuit abbas?
    Sumere lex media est, regula rara dare."
Ysengrimus ad haec: "Posses dare, sumere novi!
    Nunc castigor, eram sumere doctus heri.
205 Eia quid facies? Abiens tenet ille baconem,
    colloquimur stantes, ambulat ille procul;
et visi fortasse sumus, nostrique pavore
    ungue tenet quod fert, acceleratque viam."
"Quaeris," ait, "quid agam? Sublecto tramite passim,
210   quo te praecedit rusticus iste, veni,
et mea facta vide! Baco decidet, auguror, aude
    tollere depositum neve moreris ibi.
Si tibi furandi pudor est aut forte vereris
    peccatum furti, solvere utrumque potes:
215 collige desertum custos, latoris egentem
    fer miserans, insons et bene tutus eris.
Saepe ebetes magni, subtiles saepe pusilli,
    nunc animi dos est experienda mei.
At vero fieri lucrum commune paciscor;
220   iam pro dimidia non ego parte loquor—
parva deus fecit parvis, ingentia magnis—
    sit pars quarta michi, tres remanento tibi."
Ille coaequari iurabat; "Patrue, nolo;
    ut statui partes," ille reclamat, "erunt.
225 Quid cunctamur? Eam, scis vesci carne suilla?"
    Ille quasi iratus dicit, at intus ovat:

teeth had been removed, the other was bolder in speech and scolded his uncle: "Learn to take, wretch! I am hindered only by this, that you haven't yet learned to take. If you knew how to take things, the ham would be ready for you. Uncle, what bishop, what abbot has balked at taking? Taking is the general law, giving the exceptional rule." Ysengrimus replied: "Were you able to give, I know how to take! Although I'm admonished now, I was given a lesson in taking yesterday. Alas, what are you going to do? He's going away with the bacon in his grasp; we stand talking while he walks away. And perhaps we've been seen, and in fear of us he is hanging on tightly to what he's carrying and quickening his pace." "You ask," said he, "what I'll do? Follow, by a stealthy route, wherever that peasant leads you, and watch what I shall do! The bacon will fall to the ground, I prophesy; have the guts to take it up when it's dropped and don't hang about on the spot. If you're ashamed of stealing, or perhaps fear the sin of plunder, you can clear yourself of both. Take up what's been abandoned, as its safekeeper; have pity on its need for a bearer and carry it—you'll be innocent and quite safe. Big creatures are often dull witted, and little ones cunning; it'll now be seen how much brain I'm gifted with! But I stipulate that the profit should be shared. I don't now ask for a half portion; God made little things for little people, and large things for big ones. Let a quarter be for me, three-quarters remaining for you." The other swore that he should be made an equal partner. "No, uncle; the shares will be as I've stated," he replied. "What are we waiting for? I'm off—can you eat pork?" As if angry, but inwardly glad, the other re-

"Quid, Satan, insanis? Sine me pausare, liquaster!
    Dem pretium, ut vadas, scilicet? Anne rogem?
Graeca salix posses prius esse aut Daca sacerdos!
230   Ire, velim nolim, vis, ierisque feram;
nec veto nec iubeo, nec me minus ire vetante
    nec tu me cuperes praecipiente magis.
Esurio; nisi des pernam, te quaeso reverti."
    Evolat obliquo concitus ille gradu;
235 iuncta legens arbusta viae, citiore redemit
    circuitum cursu praeceleratque virum,
clamque fluens in plana praeit, qua perniger ibat,
    insectante lupo rustica terga procul.
Reinardus solitae temptans ludibria fraudis
240   fert tremulos clauda debilitate pedes;
in caput, in caudam, in costas titubatque caditque—
    rusticus insectans prendere certus erat.
"Mene mei valeant," ait, "explorabo velintque
    ferre pedes, istum destituere sui.
245 Unde huc cumque venis, iter est tibi paene peractum;
    ut nolis, ego te nunc reor esse meum.
Praestolare, nepos, donec tibi solvere talos
    vepribus elicitis, longius ire nequis;
solvo morae pretium, portaberis." Ista locutus
250   protendit dextram (laeva tuetur onus),
irrisumque sequens, pellem, magis anxius haeret,
    cui dare vellet herae, quam capere, unde daret.
Hic veluti prensurus erat, par ille prehenso,
    tam citus hic sequitur, tam praeit ille piger.
255 Spe vires augente celer villanus euntem
    urgebat passu mobiliore sequens.

plied: "What, you devil, are you mad? Let me stay here, you babbler! I suppose I'm to pay you to go, or beg you to do so! You could be a Greek willow or a Danish nun before that would happen! You want to go, whatever I wish, and I'll allow you to do so. I don't command or forbid; your desire to go would not diminish if I forbade it, nor increase if I urged it. I'm hungry; if you don't get me the ham, I require you to come back here."

Away flew the fox excitedly, on a devious route, passing through the trees by the side of the path. He made up for his roundabout route by a quicker pace, and overtook the man; stealthily issuing on to the level ground he preceded the bacon carrier in his course, while the wolf followed behind the peasant at a distance. Reynard, trying out the tricks of his habitual cunning, carried feet trembling with halting weakness. He tottered and fell on his head, on his tail, on his sides. If the peasant pursued him, he was sure to catch him. "I'll see whether my legs have strength and willingness to carry me," said he, "since this creature is let down by his. Wherever you've come from, your journey is almost over. Although against your will, I now adjudge you mine. Hold on, son, until I release your feet by pulling out the brambles. You can't go further, but I'll make up for stopping you by carrying you." So saying, he stretched out his right hand (the left was looking after his burden), and pursuing the object of his mockery, was more worried about which lady he'd give the fur to, than about catching the source of the gift.

The man was as if on the point of catching him, he was as good as caught—so quickly did the former pursue, and so sluggishly did the latter advance. With hope increasing his energy, the speeding peasant pressed on with a quicker pace,

Repplicat ille vices, et quam propiore sequentis
urgetur gressu, tam citiore fugit.
Villano clamante gemit, pausante resistit,
260   suspirante reflat, fit properante celer;
nec potior fugiente sequens, fugiensve sequente,
ambo pari gressum strennuitate ferunt.
Visus erat prensu facilis, si rusticus illum
impeteret cursu concitiore parum;
265 obstat onus voto, sapuit villanus, onusque
decutiens collo, tendit utramque manum,
tunc cursu manibusque simul strepituque iuvatur,
cogitat esse nichil post sua terga doli.
Reinardus solito venantem decipit astu —
270   at lupus arrepto lustra bacone petit.
Reinardus varia spatians ambage meandi
callidus irritat ludificatque rudem;
nam nunc multifido spiras curvamine tricans
anguis compliciti vincula cassa notat,
275 nunc obliquus ad hanc partemque incedit ad illam.
Non redit aut prodit lineolasque terit,
sed numquam venturus eo, quo creditur isse;
Daedalia fallax implicat arte chaos.
Ancipites tricas tenui discriminat hora,
280   longius oblongans ante parumque retro.
Nunc illuc obliquat et huc proditque reditque,
nunc aliquo giros ordinat orbe breves,
ignorante viro, per tot diludia cursus
tricantem dubios certius unde petat.
285 Ille fluit furtim lusa inter crura diuque
a tergo saliens ante putatur agi.

following him as he went. The fox retaliated, and the closer
he was pressed by the steps of his pursuer, the quicker he
fled. When the peasant shouted, he groaned; when the peas-
ant halted, he stood still; when he panted, the fox caught his   260
breath, and when he made haste the fox put on speed. The
pursuer did not outdo the pursued, nor the pursued the pur-
suer, but both followed their course with equal alacrity. He
seemed easy to capture, if only the peasant were to rush at
him with a rather livelier pace. His load was an impediment   265
to his wishes; realizing this, the peasant threw the burden
from his shoulder, and stretched out both hands. Then he
had the benefit of legs, hands and voice at once; it didn't oc-
cur to him that there was fraud behind his back. Reynard
eluded the hunter by his usual cunning—but the wolf had   270
snatched up the bacon and was making for the trees.

   Reynard, making constant zigzags as he ran, cunningly
exasperated and mocked the rustic. For at one moment, in-
terweaving loops with many a twist, he imitated the redun-
dant coils of a curled-up snake, while at another moment he   275
darted off at a tangent to this side or that. He went neither
backward nor forward in his little incursions, but he never
arrived at the point he seemed to have been making for;
with the art of Daedalus the trickster wove chaos. In a mo-
ment, he varied his labyrinthine confusions, striking ahead   280
for a long way, and turning back a little. Now he darted aside
one way and another, and ran forward and doubled back;
now he made little twists in a kind of circle, while the man
did not know where to look for him with certainty as he
wound about his baffling course through so many feints. He   285
stealthily jumped between the peasant's ridiculous legs, and
for a long time was leaping behind him while thought to be

Transposuere vices: qui fugerat, ille sequentis,
  quique sequens fuerat, par fugientis habet.
Erectis oculis absentem denique sentit
290 rusticus, ammirans attonitusque diu
haeret mentis inops, quando aut amiserit illum,
  aut amissus ubi delituisse queat.
Lumina trans humerum dextrum torquere parabat,
  explorare volens, qua latitaret humo;
295 Reinardus metuens, ne quatenus ille lupinam
  respiciens fraudem post sua terga notet,
prodiit, a laeva rediens, oculosque latentem
  quaerentis gemitu bis revocante praeit.
Rusticus ablatum tam se ignorante redisse
300 quam stupet ignaro se latuisse prius.
Hic fugere, ille sequi; persaepe extrema teneri,
  effluere et cassam linquere cauda manum.
Tunc quasi deficiens cadit expectatque iacendo
  prensorem, caudam dextera tuta tenet.
305 Vir "Mecum," inquit, "amice, manes!" Cultrumque sinistra
  expediens, misero demere vellus avet.
Acre gelu, ferrumne secans, an cautus utrumque
  horruerit, dubito, noluit ille pati;
ergo supersiliens dextram, qua cauda tenetur,
310 transfluit obliquam, pondere dextra labat.
Attonitus caudam dimittit, at ille paventis
  per scapulas saltans et caput ante redit.
Se cepisse videns et non potuisse tenere
  rusticus indignans cor sibi paene fodit.

driven in front. Thus they exchanged roles: the one who had
been running away acted as pursuer, and the one who had
followed acted as pursued. At length, raising his eyes, the
peasant realized he had disappeared, and, mentally para- 290
lyzed through surprise and astonishment, was for a long
time baffled as to when he had lost sight of him, or where he
could have hidden himself when lost sight of. He started to
look back over his right shoulder, wishing to investigate
where in the world he might be hiding, but Reynard, fearing 295
that he might on looking back somehow catch sight of the
wolf's deceit behind his back, went forward, coming back
on his left side, and, going in front of him, with a double
groan recalled the peasant's eyes from the search for his hid-
ing place. The peasant was as much stupefied by the unper-
ceived return of the missing fox, as by the fox's having previ- 300
ously hid himself unbeknown to him.

The fox fled, the peasant followed. Many times the tip of
his tail was grasped, but it slipped through and left the
empty hand. Then, as if faltering, he fell, and lay waiting for
his captor, whose right hand securely grasped his tail. "You'll 305
stay with me, friend!" said the man, and got out his knife
with his left hand, intending to remove the wretch's hide. I
don't know whether it was the biting cold or the piercing
steel, or both at once, that he prudently feared, but the fox
didn't want to put up with this, and so, leaping on to the
right hand, by which his tail was held, he hurled himself 310
crosswise, and the hand gave way under the weight. Be-
wildered, the peasant let go of the tail, but the fox jumped
over the head and shoulders of the frightened man and came
back in front of him. Perceiving that he had caught what he
couldn't hold on to, the angry peasant all but stabbed his

315　Ille iterum in faciem divolvitur atque retrorsum
　　　procidit, et misero vox morientis inest.
　　Rusticus accedens sensim ruiturus in illum
　　　mole sui tota "Si potes," inquit, "abi!"
　　Poplitibus pronis nutat tenditque lacertos
320　　et ruere incipiens paene beatus erat—
　　praefugit obliquo saltu vafer ille ruentem,
　　　nudaque suscepit terra ruentis onus.
　　Surgere conantis Reinardus colla caputque
　　　occupat et morsa concitus aure salit.
325　Vir vehemente ferox animo et gemebundus humumque
　　　pressa fronte legens acrius instat item.
　　Fidus erat prensu sed perfidus ille retentu
　　　et vix effugiens effugit usque tamen.
　　Linea currentes non intercesserat usquam
330　　ulnarum spatio longior acta trium;
　　ter tenuit caudam prensor, ter tenta fefellit,
　　　terque fere felix, ter miser esse tulit.
　　Sic pueris levis aura perit coeunte pugillo,
　　　lubricaque anguillae fallere cauda solet.
335　Ille igitur ioculans assueta fraude viarum
　　　fert tremere et labi, fert cadere atque capi,
　　taliter illudens, donec comitante rapina
　　　in saltus reducem novit abisse lupum;
　　protinus insultis obliqua per invia silvis
340　　tollitur ex oculis ut duce pluma notho.
　　Sustinet ille novi stupidus fantasmata monstri
　　　plus ammirari quam sua dampna queri.
　　"Unde," ait, "existi, redeas, illabere Averno!
　　　Non equidem vulpes, sed quater ipse Satan!"

own heart. The fox tumbled down again in front of his face, 315
toppling backward, and the noise of a dying animal was in
the wretch. The peasant, moving forward slowly so as to
rush on him with all his weight, cried: "Escape if you can!"
He fell on bended knees, stretched out his arms, and, begin- 320
ning his pounce, was almost lucky—but the crafty fox
eluded his grab by a sidelong leap, and the empty ground
rushed up to meet his weight as he fell. Reynard perched on
his head and neck as he tried to get up, bit his ear, and then
excitedly leaped off. Furious and in a raging temper, groan- 325
ing and picking off the soil in which his forehead had been
embedded, the man made a second, swifter approach.

The fox was secure to seize but treacherous to hold, and
although not quite escaping, continually escaped. The run-
ners had never been separated by a distance of more than 330
three ells; three times the captor had grasped his tail, and
thrice it had cheated him when grasped. Thrice he had al-
most been lucky, and thrice he had suffered failure. Just so
does the light breeze disappear from the grasping fist of
children; just so elusive is the eel's slippery tail. So the fox, 335
rejoicing in the well-worn deception of his twists and turns,
allowed himself to waver and fall, allowed himself to stum-
ble and be caught, playing tricks in this way until he knew
that the wolf, together with the plunder, had got away and
brought it back to the woods. Then, immediately bounding
through the impenetrable side paths of the forest, he was 340
snatched from sight like a feather driven by the wind.

The idiot was more concerned to marvel at the appari-
tions of this strange monster than to bewail his loss. "Go
back where you came from," he cried, "get down to hell!
You're no fox, but the devil himself, four times over!"

345 Ille gradu fixo villanum dulce salutans
    eminus exclamat: "Vado, sodalis, ave!
    Ut scires (etenim haerebas) cui mittere velles
       membranam dominae, tardius ire tuli.
    Inconsultus adhuc dubitas, custodio pellem;
350   cum scieris, cui des, trado libenter eam.
    Quam tua parta michi fuerat, si pellis egerem,
       tam mea nempe tibi est; nec, quia vado, dole —
    ut fuit abstractu te caudam prompta tenente,
       sic, quacumque soli parte morabor, erit."
355 Callidus ad pactam quaestor pervenerat aedem;
       circumfert oculos, stat reticetque diu.
    Cernit relliquias strophium restare salignum,
       quo fixum extulerant fumida tigna suem;
    ipsa senex tota cum carne voraverat ossa,
360   iam salicem rodens insatiatus adhuc.
    Incipit ergo prior vulpes atque eminus abstat,
       os patrui fidum non nimis esse ratus:
    "Patrue, paene michi tonsa haec pastura videtur,
       rodis enim, nondum crederis esse satur.
365 Pax est et requies de toto facta bacone —
       cur etiam non est esa retorta simul?
    Parva fere saturo defectum fercula supplent,
       unde capit nullam venter inanis opem.
    Cras iterum esuries (hic nulla refectio restat!),
370   prandia constabunt uberiore cibo.
    Adice relliquias, et non aliena vorasti;
       cui servas, operam conciliantis agens?"

The fox, halting his stride, called out from a distance in po- 345
lite salutation to the peasant: "I'm going, friend, goodbye! I
tolerated the postponement of my departure until you
should have made your mind up (for you were in doubt)
which lady you wanted to give my skin to. You're still waver-
ing undecided, so I'll look after my hide; when you know 350
who you'll give it to, I'll hand it over willingly. To the same
extent that your skin would have been at my disposal if I
had needed a pelt, so mine is, of course, available to you.
And don't be sad that I'm going—in whatever part of the
world I reside, my skin will be as speedily removable as it
was when you were holding my tail."

The cunning purveyor had arrived at the agreed rendez- 355
vous, and glancing around, stood for a long time silent, as he
observed that what was left was the cord of willow by which
the smoky rafters had once held up the tied pork. The old
man had devoured the very bones with all the meat, and, 360
still unsatisfied, was gnawing on the willow. So the fox began
first, standing at a distance (having decided that his uncle's
mouth wasn't trustworthy): "Uncle, this pasture seems to
me to be pretty well cropped, for you gnaw away, still not
thinking yourself full. We can read the funeral service over 365
the whole ham—why hasn't the rope been eaten up at the
same time? Tidbits from which an empty stomach would de-
rive no benefit fill up the corners when one is almost full.
Tomorrow you'll be hungry again (there's nothing to eat left
here!) and there'll be meals with richer food. Eat up what's 370
left over; you won't have devoured what's not yours. Who on
earth would you be keeping it back for by way of compensa-
tion?"

Repplicat haec senior: "Per canos hosce seniles!
   Parva animae est adeo non michi cura meae
375 et tunc unde tibi pars expectata daretur.
   Fraus inter socios crimine nulla caret;
tu quoque laturus, si me servante relictum
   nil tibi vidisses, impatienter eras.
Cerne, retorta vacat, servata fideliter ipsa est;
380   rosa quidem sed non est violata nimis.
Vix tamen hanc potui servare bacone comesto,
   sed scieris, non est unus utrique sapor:
lenius in lardo penetrabiliusque momordi,
   et fuit utilior fissiliorque caro.
385 Sume, tua haec pars est, et dic socialiter actum;
   non alii leviter sed tibi tanta datur."
"Patrue," quaestor ait, "cui competit, illius esto!
   Hic aliquid peius quam nichil esse puto.
Quod michi servasti, serva pendere volenti;
390   invenit arbitrium nulla retorta meum."
Offensus senior truculenta voce profatur:
   "Rebar amicitiam promeruisse tuam;
nunc ego deprendi, tua quo versutia vergat.
   Pars mea consumpta est, hic tua, sume tuam!
395 Quo funem traheres, praenovi: nempe tulissem,
   particula velles solus utraque frui.
Alliceres astu, quaecumque reperta fuissent;
   ut mus muscipula, vis solet arte capi.
Ergo ego praeripiens sperato cautius egi;
400   tundatur ferrum, dum novus ignis inest.
Res est forma rei, factis facienda notantur,
   et nichil est, quod non mentis acumen alat.

The old one replied: "By these old man's hairs! It's truly no small trouble to my mind from what source your ex- 375 pected share should be given in that case. Trickery between companions is always reprehensible. You also would have taken it badly if I had kept the remains and you'd seen nothing for yourself. Look, the rope is at your disposal, faithfully preserved; it's gnawed a bit but it isn't really harmed. It was 380 with difficulty that I could hang on to this when the bacon had been eaten, but you are to know that there isn't the same taste to both. My teeth sank more gently and with less resistance into the bacon, and it was the more nutritious and tender meat. Take it, this is your share, and say that the 385 action is that of a comrade! So much wouldn't lightly be parted with to anyone but you." "Uncle," said the purveyor, "let it belong to whoever it's fitting for! I think what's here is worse than nothing. What you've kept back for me, keep for someone who wants to hang; no rope ever met with my ap- 390 proval." Displeased, the old man answered in stern tones: "I thought I had earned your friendship; now I've discovered what your cunning is driving at. My part is consumed, this is yours, take it! I knew what you were driving at; had I only 395 permitted it, you would have enjoyed both shares all to yourself. Your cunning would have made you master of whatever was found; strength is trapped by skill as the mouse is by the mousetrap. For that reason I have antici- pated you, and acted more cleverly than expected; the iron's 400 best struck while the fire is hot. One event is the model for another; what is to be done is indicated by what has been done, and nothing exists which does not improve the keen- ness of the understanding. For if you were as well bred as

Quod si tam lepidus, quam vulgo diceris esse,
   et si, quam sapiens crederis esse, fores,
405 carpere te saltem, quamvis pietate careres,
   haec mea non sineret publicus acta pudor.
Ubertate tuus si tanta venter egeret,
   quanta non dubitas indiguisse meum,
pace mea potuit salvo michi virga bacone
410 cortice plus medio rosa fuisse tibi.
Sicut enim es prudens, rosae iactura retortae,
   non tibi maerorem perna comesta movet.
Sufficeret, si tota foret, tibi virga, meamque
   ingluviem nosti, turpiter ergo doles,
415 alvus cum tibi sit stricta et brevis, at michi late
   oblonga pendens in cavitate capax.
Si res ad synodum traheretur, nonne parasti
   materiam risus et pietatis ego?
Protinus ergo tuae completo fine querelae
420 cum peteres dampno ius synodale tuo,
redderet orator vera argumenta disertus,
   innocuum tali me ratione probans:
'Ysengrimus adest obiecti criminis insons —
   hoc rerum series indubitata docet.
425 Voverat hoc anno claustralis seria vitae,
   Reinardo laicos inter habente suam,
frater et in claustro, quoadusque abbate voracem
   formidante gulam iussus abiret, erat.
Iussus abit, verum quamvis et iussus abisset,
430 sacra verebatur frangere dicta patrum.
His igitur scriptis in sacrae codice normae:
   "Hunc, qui pluris eget, sumere plura decet"

you are popularly said to be, and as wise as you are thought
to be, even if you were devoid of family feeling, your sense of   405
public propriety at least wouldn't allow you to criticize these
acts of mine. If your belly were to need so great an abun-
dance as you know well that mine did, as far as I'm con-
cerned the gnawed willow twig, with still more than half its   410
bark, could have been for you, so long as the bacon was re-
served for me. Wise as you are, it's the loss of the gnawed
rope, not the eating of the bacon, that causes you sorrow.
The twig would be enough for you if it were whole. But
knowing my greed, you are churlish to bear a grudge, since   415
your belly is short and narrow, while mine is roomy and its
hollowness hangs lengthy and wide. If the case were brought
to the synod, haven't you provided matter for laughter, and
I, for leniency? So, when you sought synodal justice for your   420
injury, once the end of your complaint had been reached,
learned counsel would reply with just arguments, proving
me innocent on these grounds: 'Here is Ysengrimus, inno-
cent of the crime with which he is reproached, as is shown
by an unquestioned series of facts. He had consecrated   425
this year to the serious occupations of monastic life, while
Reynard led his life among laymen. And he was a cloister
brother until the abbot became nervous of his vora-
cious greed, and he was ordered to leave. He left as or-
dered, but even although he had left as ordered, he was still   430
afraid of breaking the sacred precepts of the Fathers.
For these things are written in the book of the holy Rule:
"It is fitting for the man who needs more to take more,"

et "Cum tinnierint veniendi cimbala signum
 fratribus, ad mensas coetus adesto celer."
435 Ysengrimus habens sacro super ordine curam
 vertere nolebat, quod pia secta iubet.
Obviat interea Reinardo, dumque vicissim
 rite vale faciunt, umbra baconis adest.
Clam loquitur fratri vulpes: "Hunc, domne, baconem
440 si mecum velles dividere, arte darem";
frater ait: "Communis erit," quo more iubetur
 claustricola "Est nostrum" dicere, quicquid habet.
His dictis abiit Reinardus, fratre relicto
 nil absens misit, nil dedit ipse redux.
445 Monachus inspecto fore comperit aethere tempus,
 cimbala quo fratres pulsa vocare solent;
incidit oblatum, nescit quo dante, baconem,
 debita sumendae venerat hora dapis;
hora facit neglecta reum, Reinardus et istum
450 praeter claustricolam quilibet alter abest.
Dona dei laudans, accedit frater ad escam,
 nil servat, dominum sic monuisse memor:
"Noli sollicitus fieri pro luce futura."
 Denique completis omnibus iste venit,
455 utque videt torquem, quo vinctum fumida tergum
 tegula sustulerat, "Pars mea," clamat, "ubi est?"
Clamanti monachus "Frater, temere exigis," inquit,
 "exige fraterne, debita solvo libens.
Ordinis est nostri, plus sumere pluris egentem;
460 pluribus indigui, plura proinde tuli.
Frater inexpleta si mensam liquerit alvo
 ultra dimidium, regula fracta perit.

and "When the bells have rung out the sign for the brothers to come, let the assembly gather quickly at the tables." Ysengrimus, out of concern for the sacred order, was unwilling to go against what the holy Rule commands. Meanwhile he meets Reynard, and while they are duly greeting each other, the shadow of a ham passes over them. The fox whispers to the monk: "I'll bestow this bacon on you by my skill, sir, if you are willing to share it with me." The brother says: "It will be common property"—in the same way as a monk is ordered to say "It's ours" about anything he has. This exchange over, Reynard went off, and sent the abandoned brother nothing while he was away, nor did he bring back anything to give him. The monk, after inspecting the sky, found that it was the time when the ringing of bells customarily summons the brethren. He stumbles on the offered bacon, ignorant of whose gift it is, when the hour devoted to taking a meal has arrived. To neglect the hour makes him guilty; Reynard and everyone else except this monk are absent. Praising God's gifts, the brother falls on the food, keeping nothing, since he is mindful that the Lord said: "Take no thought for the morrow." Finally when everything is over this fellow turns up, and as he sees the loop by which the smoky roof had held the tied-up haunch, he cries out "Where's my bit?" The monk replies to his cry: "Brother, your demand is rashly made. Ask in a brotherly way, and I'll willingly pay what's due. It's part of our order that he who needs more should take more. I needed more, so I took it. If a brother left the table with his stomach more than half empty, the Rule would be broken and void. Whoever was re-

A quocumque baco datus est, quod oportuit egi,
    haec superant, plus his non iubet ordo dari;
465   quod superavit, habe!" Monachus sic ista fuisse
    arbitrio synodi nec secus acta probat,
nec coram Remico metuit nec praesule Romae,
    sedis uter libeat sollicitetur apex.
Pendite, censores, causam!'—Sic, stulte, locuto
470   rethore quid synodus diceret esse tuum?
Si, quibus et quantis egeam, perpendere velles
    et gereres socia sedulitate fidem,
quamvis abrosus prope liber adusque medullam
    et comitata duas perna fuisset oves,
475   non culpandus eram, potius culpabilis essem,
    si michi mansisset mica pusilla super.
Desine conquestu modo, pars tua maior habetur,
    sed pietate cares et rationis eges.
Sanus adhuc ferme cortex lignumque remansit,
480   et non est morsu laesa medulla meo.
Perna michi iuxta modulum divisa videtur,
    fecissem fratri non meliora meo.
Cominus huc accede, miser, metire retortam,
    quam vice te socia prosequar, ipse vide,
485   et si non aliter, quam dico, probaveris esse,
    consulo, ne spernas hoc, quod habere potes.
Rode foris librum tenuemque exsuge medullam.
    Esu dura aliam pars tibi praebet opem:
cum fortuna aliquem dederit tibi prospera quaestum,
490   commodius poterit sarcina vincta vehi."

sponsible for giving the bacon, I have done what was right. This is left over; more than this, the order doesn't require should be given. Take what's left over!" Thus, and no other- 465 wise, does the monk prove that things happened, for the decision of the court. Nor does he quail before the bishop of Reims, or of Rome, supposing that the prelate of either see were appealed to. Judges, weigh up the case!'

When the lawyer's spoken like this, what, you fool, do 470 you think the synod will say is yours? If you'll only consider of what and of how much I was in need, and if you were to act loyally and with a friendly helpfulness, even if I'd gnawed away the bark to the core, and the bacon had been accompanied by two sheep, I wouldn't be to blame—in fact, I'd be 475 to blame if the teeniest crumb was left over. Stop moaning now; your share is even too big in proportion, but you have no consideration for others, and are devoid of good sense. The bark has survived almost whole up to now; the wood's still there, and the core isn't harmed by my bites. The ba- 480 con seems to me to be divided with scrupulous fairness; I wouldn't have done better by my own brother. Come close, wretch; take stock of the rope, and see for yourself in how comradely a fashion I'm proceeding with you . And if you 485 are satisfied that it's just as I say, I advise you not to scorn what you can have; gnaw the bark on the outside and suck the tender core. The part that is hard to eat offers another advantage: when benign Fortune bestows some windfall on you, the bundle can be carried more conveniently by being 490 tied up."

Reinardus patruum, si quicquam diceret ultra,
    irasci metuens fraude benignus ait:
"Patrue, te insontem iusta ratione probasti—
    sicut iustitiam mos hodiernus habet.
495 Peius agit, qui plura potest, luit omnia pauper,
    scit sibi fautorem dives adesse deum.
Ignorante deo est pauper; quod prodigus ardet
    fundere, quodque tenax condere, pendit inops.
Quod locuples, quod pauper habet, locupletis utrumque
    est;
500   divitis ex dono est pauperis omne parum.
Non igitur nostro quicquam de iure tulisti,
    tam mea quam tua res est tua, cuius eges.
Si minus edisses, stomachus tibi laxior esset;
    vestis et esca hodie cuncta licere iubent.
505 Nullius ignoscentis eges, vis imperat aequo,
    indulgente sibi divite, quicquid agit.
Accusatur inops, sit noxius ipse, sit insons;
    venalis venia est—ut mereatur, emat.
Iustus inops sine iure, reus sine crimine dives,
510   ipse sibi ignoscit pro pietate dei.
Ergo si locuples alibi indultoris egebit,
    nonne deus referet pro pietate vicem?
Conqueror ergo nichil, concordes simus ut ante!"
    Tunc senior blanda voce profatur ovans:
515 "Nunc sapis, impensumque tibi gratanter habeto!
    Scis bene, sic sociis partior usque meis.
Si tibi deterior, quam velles, portio cessit,
    et mea pars voto non fuit aequa meo.
Fer modo! Restituam, cum quid lucrabere rursum,
520   non quia debuerim, sed quia largus ego."

Reynard, fearing to anger his uncle if he said any more, spoke in the bland tones of deceit. "Uncle, you have proved yourself innocent on just grounds—as the modern fashion defines justice. The man with more power acts worse; the poor man pays for everything, and the rich man knows that God is on his side. God doesn't know of the poor man's existence; whatever the spendthrift wants to squander, or the miser to hoard, the poor man pays for. The possessions of rich and poor both belong to the rich; every mite of the poor is the gift of the rich. You haven't therefore plundered anything that was rightfully mine; what's mine is yours, as well as what's your own, if you need it. If you'd eaten less, your stomach would be too slack; the requirements of clothing and food make everything permissible these days. You need no one to pardon you; force rules over justice. The rich man is indulgent to himself in whatever he does; the pauper is held guilty, whether he has harmed anyone or is innocent. Mercy is venal, so let him deserve it by buying it. The poor man who is just is deprived of justice, while the rich man who is guilty is freed from blame, and pardons himself in exchange for God's mercy; so if the rich man needs someone to pardon him elsewhere, won't God repay his mercifulness? For these reasons I'm not complaining at all; let's be in harmony as before!"

Then the old man triumphantly spoke in honeyed tones: "There's a wise fellow; be glad to have what's given you! You know well that this is the way I always share with my friends. If a worse portion than you wish fell to your lot, well, my share wasn't equal to my wishes either. Be patient now! I'll pay you back the next time you get something—not because I ought, but because I'm generous."

Acrior idcirco Reinardum iniuria torquet,
    quod non reddiderat debita verba dolor.
Exspirata minis rabies cor lenius angit,
    interit erumpens, permanet ira latens.
525 Sed quia facta solet dictis praeponere prudens,
    declamare bonam noluit ante diem.
Non usurpat "agam," ne dicere perdat "ego egi";
    tuta mora spes est, anticipata perit.
Venerat ergo dies vindictae lectus, uterque
530 hostis agens hosti, non temere actus, obit.
Visa vulpe senex hilaris concinnat inanes
    blanditias, blaesa calliditate loquens:
"Tempore felici venias, cognate! Quid affers?
    Nunc, si quid dederis, partior absque dolo."
535 Cui vulpes: "Refer ergo fidem, quae, patrue, primam
    divisit, tibi si perna secunda placet.
Sicut prima fides suadet sperare secundam,
    sic fraus indicium prisca sequentis agit.
Dicitur hoc vulgo: 'Fraus acta minatur agendam';
540 divisus recte vix fuit ille baco.
At michi nunc merces illaesa retorta daretur,
    si vescenda tibi perna veniret item?
Te peccasse piget, desisti fallere frustra,
    et de perfidiae crimine sero doles.
545 Si michi servasses primam sine fraude retortam,
    venisset melior perna priore sequens.
Tendamus meliore via! Considero mores,
    cras hodieque sumus, quod fueramus heri.

The insult tortured Reynard the more keenly because his grief could not make the called-for reply. Fury which is breathed out in threats pains the heart less severely; anger dies as it bursts forth, but lives on when it is buried. But because a wise man prefers deeds to words, he didn't want to make speeches before the right time. He didn't resort to "I'll do such and such," in case he might lose the chance of saying "I've done it." With delay, hope is confident, but it vanishes when it is anticipated.

So the chosen day for vengeance had arrived, and both enemies met while in pursuit of each other, not led by chance. Catching sight of the fox, the old man jovially produced empty blandishments, speaking with tentative artfulness: "Blessings on your arrival, kinsman! What have you got with you? If you put anything in my way, this time I'll share it honestly with you."

The fox replied: "If a second ham takes your fancy, uncle, remember the good faith which shared out the first. The first example of good faith teaches one to expect a second of the same kind; thus initial deceitfulness acts as a sign of that which is to follow. It's popularly said that 'the trick that has been played is a warning of the one to come.' That bacon was hardly divided up fairly. And would you now give me as a reward the untouched rope, if you were to get the chance of eating the bacon over again? You regret having done wrong, but you have left off your cheating in vain, and it's too late for you to be sorry for your crime of treachery. If you had kept the first rope for me without cheating, a better ham than the first would have followed. Let's take a better course! If I consider our makeup, today and tomorrow

Non igitur tecum communia rursus habebo;
550   te, nisi solus edas, copia nulla replet.
Nonne querebaris vesanum ambabus abusum
    particulis uterum paene vorasse nichil?
Et nunc divideres socialiter? Immo videtur,
    ne pecces iterum, res facienda secus.
555 Non prohibet pisces tibi regula, tuque fuisti
    monachus, et non est semper edenda caro;
fac dapibus licitis insanum assuescere ventrem,
    cuius ob ingluviem noxia nulla times.
'Ius!' ubi ius non est, ubi ius 'Iniuria!' iuras;
560   in res externas irreverenter hias.
Res proprias, medias, alienas credis easdem,
    vivere vis rapto, carnibus usque frui.
Munditiae frenum ebrietas et crapula vendunt;
    qui mundus fieri quaerit, utramque cavet.
565 Heu te sexta dies nec quadragesima terret—
    Iudaeus siquidem, sicut opinor, eris.
Te minus est nequam Satanas quaecumque gerente;
    ille aliquid sed tu nil superesse sinis.
Nec lex moralis nec scripta leporve pudorve
570   aut timor aut pietas his posuere modum."
Aemulus econtra loquitur, spe laetus habendi:
    "Quid, cognate, adeo faris amara michi?
Parce, precor! Quicquid praeceperis, obsequor ultro,
    norim, quid iubeas, quid prohibere velis.
575 Exceptis parebo tribus quaecumque iubenti:
    nil do, sperno modum, devoveoque fidem.
Haec tria cur fugiam, quam congrua causa sit, audi,
    nam tribus his sapiens nemo carere dolet:

we are just what we were yesterday. So I won't have any
property in common with you again. No amount of abun- 550
dance fills you up unless you're eating alone. Weren't you
complaining that your raging stomach had devoured next
to nothing when it had eaten up both shares? And would
you now share out like a friend? Rather it seems that things
should be conducted differently, in case you're guilty a sec-
ond time. Your Rule doesn't forbid you fish; you were a 555
monk, and you shouldn't eat meat all the time. Accustom
your raging belly, on account of whose greed you fear no
crimes, to its lawful foods. You swear there's justice where
there's none, and that there's inequity where there's justice;
you insolently gawp after things that aren't yours. Your own 560
things, other people's, communal property—they are all the
same to you; you want to live on plunder, and enjoy meat all
the time. Drunkenness and excess yield up the reins of pu-
rity; he who wants to be pure, is wary of both. Alas, Friday, 565
or even Lent, doesn't put you off meat eating; you're a very
Jew, in my opinion. Satan is less wicked than you, in what-
ever you do; he allows something to escape, but you—noth-
ing! Neither moral nor written law, not politeness, nor de-
cency, nor fear, nor mercy, have acted as restraints on what 570
you do."

His rival, rejoicing in the hope of gain, protested: "Kins-
man, why do you speak so bitterly to me? Spare me, I beg
you! Whatever you order, I'll comply with willingly, if only
I know what you prescribe, and what you want to forbid. I'll 575
obey you in whatever you order except for three things: I
give nothing away, I scorn moderation—and to hell with
good faith! Hear why I shun these three things, how fitting
is my reason, for no wise man is pained by the lack of these

parta michi teneo, data non redduntur egenti,
580   et praeformido rebus egere datis.
Me rerum ignari nimis esse fatentur edacem—
    venter ubi impletur, nil superaddo cibi.
Partior, hoc stulti culpant, communia prave—
    sed non sufficerent dimidiata michi.
585 Quaeque michi desunt, nunc vi, nunc aufero furtim—
    pellerer aut captus penderer, illa rogans.
Cetera iussa geram, liceant haec; abdico carnem,
    si michi quid dederis carius, unde ciber."
Commentator ad haec "Leviter sanaberis," infit,
590   "Carne tibi excepta nil prohibere volo.
Pauca volo ut mutes, et cetera cuncta licebunt;
    ignosco vitiis, in quibus ambo sumus.
Diceris (et verum est) in me peccasse frequenter,
    cum dederim, ut nosti, commoda multa tibi;
595 tam fidus fido, quam concolor Anglicus Indo,
    quo michi plus debes, hoc minus usque faves.
Omne malum vice nemo mala nisi pessimus aequat,
    ergo, ne pereas, consiliabor item.
Piscibus innumeris vivaria subdita novi;
600   emoritur stricto plurima turba vado.
Piscibus ut reliquis laxetur copia nandi,
    gratus ibi hunc illo captor agente trahit.
Nec potior quisquam quam tu michi crederis esse,
    tot pressum monstris evacuare locum.
605 Sit quamuis in ventre tuo tam creber et amplus
    angulus, es numquam vel satiandus ibi."

three things. I keep my profits for myself because gifts aren't
returned when you need them, and I am afraid in advance of   580
needing what I give away. People who are ignorant of things
call me too voracious—but when my stomach's full, I don't
pile any more food on it. Some fools make the criticism that
I share out common property dishonestly—but if it was
halved, it wouldn't be enough for me. Whatever I lack I   585
carry off, now by force, now by stealth—but I'd be driven off
or caught and hanged if I asked for it. Your other commands
I'll carry out if these allowances are made; I'll give up meat if
you'll give me something better to feed on."

To this the plotter replied: "You'll be cured easily. Except   590
for meat, I don't want to forbid anything to you. I want you
to change a few things, and all the rest will be permitted. I
pardon faults which we both share. You are said (and truly)
to have sinned against me many times, while I have con-
ferred many benefits on you, as you know. You are as loyal   595
to a loyal friend, as an Englishman resembles an Indian in
color; the more you owe to me, the fewer good turns you do
me. However, no one but the vilest of men pays back every
evil done him with evil in turn, so I'll counsel you again in an
attempt to save you. I know of ponds, stocked with innu-
merable fish; the greater number die in the cramped condi-   600
tions of the stream. The fisherman is welcome there, and
draws in one fish which has been shoved toward him by an-
other, so that the fish remaining might be able to swim. Nor
do I think anyone is better equipped than you to empty this
place crammed with monsters; although the recesses of your   605
belly are so abundant and roomy, if you're not stuffed full
there, you never will be." The other cried out happily: "Are

Ille reclamat ovans: "Furimus, Reinarde? Quid istic
    figimur? Accelera! Mors, nisi piscer, adest!
Vis vivam, in pisces age me, carnem abdico prorsus.
610   Tu prisci sceleris ne meminisse velis;
perdideram lances, quibus exaequare solebam
    particulas, ideo solus utrasque tuli.
Quem nunc ergo dares, tu solus habeto baconem;
    pars tua quarta foret, par modo noster eris,
615 et veterem patruum capiendis piscibus induc."
    Praecedit vulpes subsequiturque lupus;
ambo pari cursu sed voto dispare tendunt,
    hic cupidus lucri, conscius ille doli.
Spe labor in seniore, fames stimulatur utroque,
620   his ergo stimulis instimulatus ait:
"Dic, cognate, etenim nimis expedit hoc michi nosse,
    piscatura vadi quam procul abstat abhinc?"
"Patrue, cur," inquit, "scitaris?" At ille subinfert:
    "Scitandi quaenam sit michi causa, rogas?
625 Quo tibi surreptu tam nunc industria simplex?
    Unde haec rusticitas—nonne facetus eras?—
ut, cur quaesierim, quaeras, quod et ante rogatum
    dicere debueras? Expediebat enim;
nam licet ipse nichil nosses (at fama fatetur),
630   quam natura meae sit furiosa gulae,
quam mordax in ventre meo luctetur egestas,
    nescis, quod cupidos segnia lucra necant?
Tarda magis cupidos quam perdita lucra molestant.
    Nonne fui monachus? Scisque, ita dicor adhuc.
635 Materia crescit crescente voracior ignis,
    res avidam mentem nulla praeire potest.

we mad, Reynard? What are we standing here for? Hurry up! I'll die if I don't go fishing! If you want me to live, take me to the fishes; I renounce meat straight away. Forget my old of- 610 fense; I'd lost the scales on which I used to measure out tid-bits, so I took them both myself. You can have all to yourself any bacon you might now give. A quarter was going to be your share, but now you'll be our equal; lead your old uncle 615 to the fish we are to catch."

The fox went ahead and the wolf followed, both advanc-ing with equal speed but different aims in view. The latter was greedy for gain, the former was plotting trickery. The old man's efforts were increased by his desire, and his hun-ger by both, and so, prompted by these stimuli, he said: "Tell 620 me, kinsman, for it's very important to me to know this, how far from here is the fishing at the shallows?" "Why do you want to know, uncle?" said he, and the other replied: "Do you ask the reason why I should know? Has your cle- 625 verness suffered some kind of diminution, to have become so naive? Whence this boorishness?—didn't you once have some savoir faire?—that you ask why I inquire after what you should have told me (for it was the right thing to do) before being questioned? For even if you yourself had known nothing (and yet gossip spreads it abroad) of how ravenous 630 is the nature of my greed, how gnawing is the desire that struggles in my belly, can you be ignorant that long-delayed gains are death to the greedy? Belated winnings vex the greedy more than lost ones. Wasn't I a monk?—And, you know, I am still called so. Fire grows more greedy as the fuel 635 to feed it increases; nothing can surpass the desires of the

Fax nativa meos satis incendebat hiatus,
    adiecit stimulos regula sancta suos.
Monachus oblatum cum viderit affore lucrum,
640   irruit ut pluvio fulgetra mota polo.
Sciret bina modum, cum nesciat una Caribdis?
    Hinc me sanctus agit, noxius inde furor.
Plus claustri pietas furit impietate lupina;
    dico satur 'Satis est,' monachus usque 'Parum est.'
645 Antea peccabam, quotiens violenter agebam,
    et veniam raptus non habuere mei;
sacra cuculla michi simul est accepta, suumque
    exemplum fratres edocuere boni,
protinus illicitum coepit licitumque licere,
650   et nichil est vetitum praeter egere michi.
Dic igitur, nostro quantum de calle supersit,
    ne pariat subitam dupla cupido necem."
"Patrue," ductor ait, "cum plena crepuscula mundum
    induerint, coeptum perficiemus iter.
655 Nocte fere media, si tendimus omine laeto,
    tanta trahi poterit sarcina, quanta vehi."
Piscaturus ad hec: "Tua nonne peritia languet?
    Nescio quid passa mente reduncus ebes.
Milibus octo super nubes extantis acervi
660   impositum dorso me superaret onus?
Sed facile est portare michi, quos occulit aequor;
    ni dicam 'Satis est,' abnatet oro nichil.
Si felix fortuna meis arriserit ausis,
    quot michi sufficiant in duo lustra, traham."

greedy spirit. An innate flame was already kindling my de-
sires to a fair height, but the sacred order added its own in-
citements on top. For when a monk sees any wealth on offer,
he falls on it like the flash of lightning produced by a stormy   640
sky. Should a twofold Charybdis acknowledge a limit, when
a single one doesn't? Holy ardor spurs me on from one side,
and my destructive urges from the other. A monk's kindness
is more savage than a wolf's cruelty; I say 'that's enough'
when I'm full, while a monk still says 'that's not much.' In   645
the old days I used to be guilty of sin whenever I commit-
ted violence, and my depredations were not granted pardon,
but once I had taken on the holy cowl, and the good broth-
ers had taught me their example, both lawful and unlawful
things were immediately permissible to me, and nothing is   650
forbidden me except that I should go without. So tell me
how much of our journey remains, lest my doubled greed
brings on sudden death."

    "Uncle," replied his guide, "when thick dusk has fallen on
the world, we shall complete the journey we're engaged in.
Round about midnight, if our journey is free of mishap, you   655
can drag away as large a sack as you can carry." The future
fisherman replied: "Hasn't your brain gone to sleep? Your
mind's had some sort of injury and you're not thinking
straight. Would the weight of a heap sticking up eight miles
above the clouds be too much for me if it were placed on   660
my back? On the contrary, it's easy for me to carry the crea-
tures that the waters conceal; I pray that none may swim
away until I say 'that's enough.' If kind Fortune smiles on my
attempts, I'll drag off enough to keep me supplied for ten
years."

47

665 Moverat algorem Februi violentia, quantus
   stringere Danubias sufficiebat aquas.
 Nacta locum vulpes dixit: "Sta, patrue dulcis,"
   (hiscebat glacies rupta recenter ibi)
 "Hic impinge tuam, carissime patrue, caudam,
670 rete aliud nullum, quo potiaris, habes.
 Utere more meo (quotiens ego piscor, eundem
   piscandi quovis sector in amne modum):
 utque experta loquar, si multum linea claudant
   retia, ter tantum cauda tenere solet.
675 Quod si consilium non exaudire recusas,
   hortor, ut hic sapiat dupla cupido semel.
 Salmones rumbosque et magnos prendere lupos,
   mole supernimia ne teneare, cave;
 anguillas percasque tene piscesque minores,
680 qui tibi sint, quamvis plurima turba, leves.
 Viribus aequa solet non frangere sarcina collum;
   obviat immodicis ausibus usque labor.
 Lucratur temere, qui perdit seque lucrumque;
   interdum lucris proxima dampna latent.
685 Ne capiens capiare, modum captura capescat;
   virtutum custos est modus atque dator."
 Retifer econtra: "Ne quid michi consule, frater,
   da tibi consilium, consule memet agor!
 Per caput hoc canum, si tam scius aequoris essem,
690 quam michi silvarum compita quaeque patent,
 sciret, ob hoc quod aquas nondum spoliare parabam,
   vindice se Ionas hac caruisse tenus.
 Praetulerim rumbo cancrum delfinave ceto?
   Non meus hoc fecit consuluitque pater.

The savageness of February had produced a cold so great 665
that it was sufficient to freeze the waters of the Danube.
When the place had been reached, the fox said: "Stop, kind
uncle"—just there the ice, recently broken, gaped open—
"here, dearest uncle, thrust in your tail; you have no other 670
fishing line with you. Follow my practice; whenever I fish, I
follow the same method of fishing in every river. And speak-
ing from experience, I say that if twine nets enclose a lot, a
tail usually holds three times as much. But if you don't re- 675
fuse to listen to some advice, I urge that your twofold greed
may show some wisdom for once; take care not to catch
salmon or sturgeon or huge pike, in case you're immobilized
by their excessive size. Take eels and perch and smaller fish
which may be light for you, even though they're a numer- 680
ous heap. A burden that's matched to one's strength doesn't
break one's neck, while extravagant attempts are always
frustrated by the effort involved. He makes a rash profit,
who loses his profit and himself as well. Sometimes losses
lurk next to gains. In case you are caught while you're catch- 685
ing, let your catch admit a limit; moderation is the bestower
and preserver of virtues."

The fisherman replied: "Don't give me any advice,
brother. Keep your opinion for yourself; I'm directed by
my own counsel! By this gray head, if I were as well ac-
quainted with the water as I am with all the crisscrossing 690
tracks of the woods, Jonah would realize that he had lacked
an avenger up to now only because I wasn't yet ready to
plunder the waters. Shall I prefer a crab to a sturgeon or a
dolphin to a whale? That isn't what my father did or advised.

695 Quo buccella michi minor est, hoc tristius intrat;
 res brevis est Satanae, copia plena dei.
 Vae michi, cum subito dentes ossa obvia laedunt!
 Immersis longe dentibus esca iuvat.
 Tunc primum me teste deus laudabilis extat,
700 cum nichil offendit libera labra diu.
 Pauper ovat modico, sum dives, multa capesco;
 tangit parva super paupere cura deum.
 Divitibus fecit deus omnia, servat et offert;
 dives qui sapiant scit bona, nescit inops.
705 Scit dives scitasque cupit quaeritque cupitas,
 quas sibi quaerendas praemeditatur, opes;
 quaesitas reperit, fruitur parcitque repertis
 ordine, proventu, tempore, lege, loco.
 Colligit ac spargit, colitur, laudatur, amatur,
710 cominus et longe cognitus atque placens.
 Infelix, qui nulla sapit bona, nulla requirit,
 vivat et absque bono, vivat honore carens.
 Nullus amet talem, nullus dignetur odire!
 Ergo ego piscabor, qua michi lege placet.
715 Proximitas quaedam est inter cupidumque deumque:
 cuncta cupit cupidus, praebet habetque deus."
 "Patrue," dux inquit, "moneo, non quaero docere;
 perfectus sapiens absque docente sapit.
 At timeo tibi, debet amans hoc omnis amanti,
720 vincula praeterea nos propiora ligant.
 Huc me igitur duce ductus ades lucrumque locumque
 indice me nosti—temet agenda doce.

The smaller a mouthful, the more unhappily it goes down. 695
Small portions are the devil's; full abundance is of God! How
miserable I am when my teeth are brought up with a jolt by
coming into contact with bones! I like food in which my
teeth sink deep—then, for the first time, is God to be
praised, in my opinion, when nothing jars against my unim- 700
peded jaws for a good long while. The poor man is happy
with a little; I'm rich, so I take a lot. Little concern for the
poor man affects God. God has made everything for the
rich man, guards it for him and bestows it on him; the rich
man knows what good things taste like, whereas the poor
man has no idea. The rich man knows what riches are; when 705
known, he desires them, and when desired, he strives for
them, working out beforehand which are to be striven for.
When they are striven for, he finds them, and once found,
he consumes or stores them, according to rank, income,
time, manner and place. He amasses and deploys; he is re-
spected, praised and loved, well known and popular far and 710
near. As for the wretch who doesn't get a taste of any good
things, he doesn't seek any, so let him live without wealth,
let him live without respect. Let no one love such a man—
let no one even deign to hate him! So I'll fish by whatever
rule I like. There's a certain similarity between the greedy 715
man and God: the greedy man wants, God has and gives, ev-
erything."

"Uncle," said his guide, "I'm giving a warning, not seeking
to instruct you. A completely wise man is wise without an
instructor. But I'm afraid for you; every friend owes that to
his friend, and in addition we are bound by closer ties. So 720
you have been brought here under my guidance, and I have
pointed out to you the place and the booty; instruct yourself

Sic studeas lucris, ne dampnum lucra sequatur;
    quid valeas, pensa, ne vide, quanta velis.
725 Perfeci, quaecumque michi facienda fuerunt;
    ire michi restat, cetera mando tibi.
Quid vel ubi faceres, dixi, facienda subisti;
    securus dixi—tu facis, esto pavens.
Fac bene! Dum piscaris, eo conquirere gallum;
730   sunto tui pisces, sufficit ille michi.
Dico iterum: si temet amas, piscare perite,
    consulo, si cuius consiliantis eges.
Improperanda puto commissa voraginis amplae,
    cum steteris fixus pondera magna super."
735 Emergente die Reinardus, ut arte ferocem
    eliciat turbam, proxima rura subit.
Iamque sacerdotis stantis secus atria gallum
    ecclesiam populo circueunte rapit,
intenditque fugae; non laudat facta sacerdos,
740   nec laudanda putat nec patienda ioco.
"Salve, festa dies!" cantabat, ut usque solebat
    in primis feriis, et "kyri" vulgus "ole."
"Salve, festa dies!" animo defecit et ori,
    et dolor ingeminat: "Vae tibi, maesta dies!
745 Vae tibi, maesta dies, toto miserabilis aevo,
    qua laetus spolio raptor ad antra redit!
Cum michi festa dies vel maximus hospes adesset,
    abstinui gallo, quem tulit ille Satan;
sic praesul doleat, qui me suspendere cantu
750   debuit! En galli missa ruina fuit.

as to what's to be done, only pursue your gains in such a way that harm doesn't follow them. Keep your mind on what you're able to do, instead of considering what you want. I've 725 done everything I was to do; it remains for me to leave, handing over the rest to you. I've told you what you should do and where, and you've undertaken to do it. It was safe enough for me to instruct you, but it's you who are to do it, so you should feel the trepidation. Good luck! While you're fishing, I'm going in search of a cock; that's enough for me, 730 the fishes are all yours. I say again: if you love yourself, fish wisely. That's what I advise, if you're in need of anyone to advise you. I think the transgressions of your huge stomach will call for criticism, when you stand rooted above a great weight."

As day was breaking, Reynard, with the intention of lur- 735 ing out a furious crowd by stratagem, made for a neigh-boring village, and seized the cock belonging to the priest, who was now standing near the door while the people were still processing round the church. The fox took to flight; the priest didn't express any praise of his action, nor did he 740 think it praiseworthy or to be borne cheerfully. He was sing-ing "Hail, festal day," as he always used to on Sundays, while the people chanted "Lord have mercy." "Hail, festal day" fal-tered in his heart and throat, and his grief issued in a moan: "Woe to you, day of mourning. Woe to you, day of mourn- 745 ing, wretched to all eternity, on which the ravager, elated with his spoil, makes off to his den! Despite the arrival of a feast day, or of the most important guest, I held back from the cock which that devil has carried off. May the bishop suffer the same anguish, since he ought to have suspended me from singing Mass!— for the Mass was the destruction 750

Non me missa iuvat sed vulpem, altaria iuro:
    malueram missas ter tacuisse novem!"
Protinus inceptum populo comitante relinquens
    clamitat: "O proceres, accelerate, probi!
755 Me quicumque volunt pro se meruisse precari,
    et qui fida michi corda deoque gerunt."
Arma omnes rapiunt, arma omnia visa putantur;
    "Hai! hai!" continuant, "hai!" sine fine fremunt.
Per iuga, per valles, per plana, per hirta sequuntur,
760 post hostem profugum milia mille rotant:
clerus vasa, crucum baculos, candelabra, capsas,
    aedituus calicem, presbiter ipse librum,
sacras deinde cruces, saxorum milia vulgus,
    presbiter ante omnes voce manuque furit.
765 Pertigerat gnarus, quo vellet tendere, raptor,
    qua piscaturum liquerat ante senem,
et procul increpitans, ut vix clamaret ad illum,
    turbat, ut ad furcam tractus, anhela loquens:
"Ibimus? Esne paratus adhuc? Rue, patrue, cursim!
770 Si cupis hinc mecum currere, curre celer!
Non equidem veni cum libertate morandi,
    si venies, agili strennuitate veni!"
Talia clamanti succlamans ille reclamat:
    "Audio! Quid clamas? Non ego surdus adhuc!
775 Desine bachari, nos nulla tonitrua terrent,
    nec tremor est terrae iudiciive dies.
Ad quid praecipitur via tam rapienda repente?
    Colligo nunc primum, captio coepta fere est;
dic tamen, an fuerit, si scis, michi pluris abisse
780 quam tenuisse moram." Turbidus ille refert:

of my cock. The Mass was not to my profit, but to the fox's.
I swear on the altar that I'd rather have missed twenty-seven
Masses!" And immediately, the people accompanying him,
he abandoned what he'd begun, crying "Honest worthies,
hurry! — those of you who wish to earn my prayers for them, 755
or who bear a heart loyal to me and to God."

They all seized weapons, everything they laid eyes on be-
ing deemed a weapon. "Halloo, halloo!" they cried uninter-
ruptedly; "halloo!" they roared out without ceasing. Through
hills, through dales, through thick and thin they pursued;
a thousand people hurled a thousand things after the fleeing 760
enemy. The clerks seized the vessels, the crucifix staves,
the candlesticks, the reliquaries; the sacristan, the chalice;
the priest himself the Bible, and then the holy crucifixes;
the people, thousands of stones. The priest led them all in
furious shouts and gestures.

The thief, well aware of where he wanted to go, had ar- 765
rived at the place where he had previously left the old man
to get on with his fishing, and calling out from a distance, so
that his cry just reached the other, he raved as if he'd been
dragged to the gallows, panting out: "Shall we go? Are you
ready yet? Fly, uncle, quickly! If you want to run away from 770
here with me, run fast! For I haven't come with the freedom
to linger; if you're to come, come with prompt alacrity!" The
other shouted back to this call: "I can hear! Why are you
shouting? I'm not deaf yet! Stop panicking! We're not fright- 775
ened by any thunderclaps, nor is there an earthquake, nor is
it the day of judgment. What's the sudden order to be on my
way for? I'm hauling in now for the first time, my catch is
hardly begun. But tell me, if you know, whether it's to my
advantage to leave rather than to stay." 780

"Nescio, suspendisse viam tibi prosit an obsit,
        dicturi veniunt post mea terga tibi.
Non michi dignaris, dignabere forsitan illis
        credere, sed prodest accelerare michi;
785   collige constanter, siquidem lucrabere, persta."
        Hic pavidus paulum repplicat ille precans:
"Ecce celer tecum venio, subsiste parumper!"
        Respondet patruo taliter ipse suo:
"Non ego pro septem solidis tria puncta morarer.
790   Ad tua sedisti lucra, morare satis!
Quod capere optabam, fors obtulit, haeret in unco."
        Serio formidans ille precatur item:
"Fige gradum sodes! Et quos fugis, eminus absunt;
        dux meus huc fueras, esto reductor abhinc!
795 Ne dicare dolo duxisse, merere reducens;
        pondus amicitiae tristia sola probant.
Pura fides etiam personam pauperis ornat,
        at fraus purpuream privat honore togam.
Non rebar captos, quantis fore sentio plures;
800   sarcina me praedae detinet, affer opem!
Auxiliare seni patruo! Scelerate, quid haeres?"
        Clamat ovans vulpes: "Ista profecto velim!
Subvenientis eges, non castigantis egebas,
        venit ad hoc: 'Vivum linquere velle nichil'!
805 Dedecus et dampnum piscatus es atque dolorem;
        qui queritur de te, perpetiatur idem.
Quid iuvit clamare: 'Modum servare memento'?
        Incidis aerumpnam transitione modi.

Excitedly the other replied: "I don't know whether it's a good thing or a bad thing for you to put off your journey. Those who are coming behind me will tell you; though you don't deign to believe me, perhaps you'll condescend to believe them—but I have to hurry. Carry on hauling in; since 785 you'll get profit from it, stay put." The other, rather afraid, in answer begged him: "See, I'm coming with you as fast as I can; wait a little!" He replied thus to his uncle: "Not for seven shillings would I wait three ticks. You sat down to 790 your profit, stay your time! What I was hoping to capture, luck offered me, and it's fast in my hand."

Seriously frightened, the other begged him again: "Stop, friend! Those you're running away from are a long way off. You guided me here, now guide me away again. Prove your- 795 self innocent of the accusation that you led me here through trickery, by leading me back. It's only misfortunes that test the weight of friendship. Simple faith is an adornment even to the poor man's person, whereas deceit robs even a purple gown of respect. I didn't think my catch would be so numer- ous as I feel it to be. My load of booty holds me back; help 800 me! Give a hand to your old uncle! You wretch, what are you waiting for?"

Gleefully the fox cried out: "Oh yes, that's just what I want! You need someone to help you, but you didn't need anyone to criticize you. So your 'wish to leave nothing alive' has come to this! You've fished up disgrace and in- 805 jury and grief; if anyone's sorry for you, may he suffer the same fate. What use was it to cry out 'remember to observe moderation'? You've fallen into trouble by overstepping

Captus es a captis, periit modus, hocque peristi,
810   et nunc operiar subveniamque iube!
Scilicet expectem mundo in mea terga ruente
    cum canibus, gladiis, fustibus atque tubis!
Fortunam misero non vult coniungere felix;
    differimus multum stans ego tuque iacens.
815 Stare recusasti, cum stares, sponte ruisti;
    vis modo restitui, si potes, omen habes.
Stantibus est facilis casus, grave surgere lapsis;
    quisque memento sui, dum meminisse iuvat.
Qui cecidere, monent stantes vitare ruinam;
820   quam sit stare bonum, scire ruina facit.
Stent igitur stantes, strati, si copia, surgant;
    surgere si nequeunt, qui cecidere, cubent.
Lene cubas et nocte parum dormisse videris;
    subsequitur parcus dulcia saepe sopor.
825 Leniter ergo cuba, donec pausaris, ego ibo;
    solus habe pisces, sat michi gallus agit."
"Ergo," inquit, "redies patruo, Reinarde, relicto?
    Tam consanguineae nil pietatis habes?
Si pietate cares, saltem cogente pudore
830   ibimus hinc pariter, me michi redde prius.
Nulla mei michi cura, tuo fac server honori!"
    Galliger econtra: "Patrue, nolo mori.
Non ego diffiteor curam pietatis agendam,
    si non pluris emit, quam valet, auctor eam,

moderation; you've been caught by your catch; moderation
has been destroyed and you've been destroyed with it—and   810
now tell me to wait and help! That is, I'm supposed to wait,
with the whole world thundering at my heels with dogs,
with swords, with cudgels and horns! A lucky man doesn't
want to link his fortune with a loser; there's a world of dif-
ference between us, I on my feet and you sprawling. You re-   815
fused to stand, when you were standing; you fell of your own
accord. Now you want to be set back on your feet again; if
you can make it, you're in luck. It's easy for those standing to
fall, and it's hard for the fallen to get up; everyone should
keep his mind on number one, so long as it's profitable to do
so. Those who've tumbled advise those who haven't to take
care not to fall; a fall makes one know how good it is to be on   820
one's feet. So, let those who are on their feet stand, and
those who are prostrate get up, if the ability is there. If those
who've fallen can't get up, let them lie. You're lying comfort-
ably, and you seem to have slept little during the night; it of-
ten happens that a scanty amount of sleep is the sequel to
enjoyments. So lie comfortably until you've rested enough,   825
and I'll go. Keep the fish all to yourself, the cock's enough
for me."

"So you'll go back and leave your uncle, Reynard?" he
replied. "Are you so devoid of family feeling? If you're with-
out affection, the dictates of decency at least will mean
we'll leave together. First restore me to myself; I'm not con-   830
cerned about myself, but for the sake of your honor make
sure I'm looked after!" The cock-bearer replied: "Uncle, I
don't want to die. I don't deny the obligation to show fam-
ily feeling, if the one who shows it doesn't pay more than

835 sed cum propositum superant conamina rerum,
       tunc est subsidio subiciendus honor.
   Tu, qui non dubitas vitam suspendere laudi,
       deposito turbas operiare metu.
   Nulla suo fructu res carior esse meretur;
840   bos ovis est pretio pluris equusque bovis.
   Singula praelibat sapiens pretioque laborem
       aequat, amans quanti quaeque valere videt.
   Venit honor nimio, quem leto comparat emptor;
       hunc hodie patiar solius esse tui.
845 Hic honor amborum nostri communiter esset,
       parte mea primum fungere, deinde tua.
   Parte mea te dono, tuum non curo favorem
       quam multo mercer, posse sinatur emi."
   Dixerat haec simulatque fugam subitoque recurrit,
850   et rea contundens pectora rursus ait,
   tamquam paeniteat se falsa fuisse locutum:
       "Patrue, ne metuas! Pondere dicta carent;
   irrita praefabar, quia te terrere volebam,
       nunc ego sum verax, nunc loquor absque dolo:
855 huc transmissus adest populo comitante sacerdos,
       cum crucibus librum relliquiasque ferens,
   et tibi neglectam pensat renovare coronam,
       discessusque tui vult abolere nefas.
   Quanta sit impietas hinc me fugisse, probabis,
860   cum fuerit capitis silva putata tui.
   Tunc vere, quia plena dei sit copia, dices,
       cum benedicta tuum sparserit unda caput,
   nec tibi tot pisces Satanas donasse feretur,
       iurabis captos dante fuisse deo.

it's worth. But when the difficulties of the affair are greater   835
than the proposed reward, then one's honor has to be sub-
jected to one's interest. You, who don't hesitate to sacrifice
your life for praise, can wait for the crowds with fear cast
aside. Nothing should be valued higher than its usefulness;
an ox is worth more than a sheep and a horse more than an   840
ox. A wise man inspects things beforehand and balances the
effort against the value, cherishing everything according to
what he sees it is worth. Honor is sold too dear when the
buyer pays for it with his death; so today I'll allow it to be all
yours. This honor would be common to both of us, but you   845
enjoy my part first, and then your own. I make you a present
of my bit; I don't care how much I pay for your goodwill, if it
is possible to buy it."

So he said, and feigned flight, but immediately ran back,
and spoke again, beating his wicked breast as if he was sorry   850
for saying something that wasn't true. "Uncle, don't be
afraid! My words have no weight. I was speaking frivolously
just now, because I wanted to frighten you. Now I'm tell-
ing the truth, now I'm speaking without guile. A priest has   855
come up and is nearby, and the people along with him. He's
carrying the Gospel and the relics, together with the cruci-
fixes, and he intends to renew your neglected tonsure, and
wipe out the crime of your desertion. You'll be able to gauge
my lack of family feeling in having run away, when the forest   860
on your head has been lopped. When the holy wave has
laved your head, then you'll say truly, that abundant is the
generosity of God. Nor shall it be said that Satan gave you so
many fishes; you'll swear that they were caught by the gift

865 Optatur temere, quicquid praestabile non est;
　　patrue, vado, mane, dicere nolo vale!
　Qui sapit, hic valeat; stultus se tradit, ut illi
　　nec deus auxilium nec dare curet homo."
　Dixit et absiliens iterum simulabat abire;
870　piscator revocat: "Quo, scelerate, ruis?
　Quo sine me properas?" Subsistens ille reclamat:
　　"Patrue, vis aliquid? Praecipe, nolo roges.
　Sed quia multa soles dominorum more iubere,
　　atque ego proposui singula iussa sequi,
875 una dies spatium iussis non aequat et actis;
　　tu iubeas hodie, cras ego iussa feram."
　"Perfide," respondit, "iubeo nichil, obsecro solvi!"
　　Galliger obstrepuit: "Patrue, nonne furis?
　Tu piscaris adhuc—et velle recedere iuras?
880　Esse nimis captum dicis—et usque capis?
　Absolvique petis? Simulas, per sidera caeli;
　　mens aliter versat, quam tua lingua sonat.
　Sublegeres sursum—tu laxas rete deorsum,
　　ergo discidium quam paterere libens?
885 Quid defixus, iners, haeres, velut inter Ianum
　　Februus et Martem, si tibi cura fugae est?
　Emolire loco piscosaque retia subduc,
　　et, nisi non egeas, auxiliabor ego."
　Captus ad haec captor: "Nescis, quid, perfide, dicas,
890　clunibus impendet Scotia tota meis.
　Undecies solvi temptans, immobilis haesi;
　　alligor, immota firmius Alpe sedens."

of God. It's rash to long for what's unobtainable. Uncle, I'm   865
off; you stay. I won't say 'farewell'; it's for someone with
common sense to fare well here. A fool just gives himself up,
so that neither God nor man bothers to help him."

Having said this, he made a bound and pretended to leave
a second time. The fisherman called him back: "Where are   870
you going in such a hurry, you wretch? Where are you rush-
ing off to without me?" Halting, he called back: "Uncle, do
you want anything? Just give the order, I don't want you to
have to ask. But since, in the way of masters, you usually
issue a lot of orders, and I've resolved to carry out each of
them, a single day won't provide enough time for the orders   875
and their execution; you give your orders today, and I'll carry
them out tomorrow."

"Traitor," he replied, "I'm not giving an order, I'm beg-
ging to be released." The cock-bearer protested: "Uncle,
aren't you mad? You're still fishing—and you swear you want
to leave? You say your catch is too big—and you carry on   880
making it? You ask to be released? You're dissembling, by
the stars of heaven. Your mind is thinking other things than
your tongue expresses. You should pull up your line, but you
let it hang downward—so how willingly would you put up
with leaving here? Why are you immobilized, rooted to the   885
spot, inert, like February between January and March, if
your concern is to get away? Get up from your seat and haul
up your fish-filled net, and unless you don't need me, I'll
help."

The trapped trapper replied: "You don't know what
you're saying, traitor. All Scotland is hanging on to my arse.   890
Eleven times I've stuck fast while trying to be freed. I'm
fettered, sitting more firmly than the motionless Alp."

Tunc ita lusor ait: "Semper tibi, patrue, prosum,
    econtra laqueos insidiaris agens.
895 Qua non ire potest, nequam versutia repit;
    si potero, sensum dicar habere semel.
Solvere te cupiens unum si retibus allec
    excuterem, fieret talio dura michi.
Non ego te dubito, si me abstraherere iuvante,
900   in prima synodo proposuisse queri:
rete diu iactum, bene te coepisse referres,
    capturum melius subveniente deo;
divitias nactum, si te perstare tulissem,
    me, quod eras felix, non potuisse pati;
905 me celerem ingessisse metum tibi cassa minando,
    teque supervacuam corripuisse fugam,
nec modo, quod capturus eras, quin prorsus id ipsum,
    quod captum fuerat, fraude perisse mea;
taliter egregiam messem victumque bilustrem
910   conquererere mea fraude perisse tibi.
Cur me odisse queas aut legitime unde queraris,
    nunc penitus causa conveniente cares.
Scis, quod scire doles, bene me meruisse frequenter,
    vim facere insonti lexque pudorque vetant;
915 quem non iustitia potes angere, niteris astu,
    defecit ratio, fraude nocere cupis.
Impius esse mea temptas pietate meisque
    sumis ab obsequiis in mea dampna viam.
Ergo prius fient duo sabbata Renus et Albis,
920   Cos prius Aprilis, quam tua lucra morer.
Collige constanter, collectis collige plures;
    nil nisi, quo condas, lar tibi parvus obest.

Then the joker said: "I'm always useful to you, uncle, while
you're plotting and setting traps; where wicked cunning 895
can't walk it crawls! If I can manage it, for once I'll be said to
have my wits about me. If, in my wish to set you free, I were
to shake out a single herring from your nets, a harsh revenge
would befall me. I don't doubt that if you were got out by my
help, you would decide to bring a complaint in the first 900
synod. You would say that your line had lain there for a long
time; that you'd made a good catch, and with God's help
were going to make a better one; that you'd found riches, if
I'd let you carry on; but that I couldn't allow you to be in
luck; that I instilled a rash fear in you by empty threats, and 905
that you needlessly took to flight, and not only what you
were going to catch, but even that which you had caught,
was lost by my deceit. So you would complain that a bumper
harvest, and food for the next ten years, was lost to you by 910
my deceit. As it is, you're completely lacking a suitable rea-
son why you should be able to hate me, or legitimately com-
plain. You know, and it irks you to know, that I have often
deserved well of you, and law and decency forbid that vio-
lence should be done to the innocent. You're trying to ha- 915
rass through cunning him whom you can't harass with jus-
tice; right has been suppressed, and you want to do harm by
fraud. You aim to be cruel by means of my kindness, and
through my services you create the way to my ruin. So the
Rhine and the Elbe can be turned into two Saturdays, and 920
the isle of Cos be turned into spring, before I wait for any
profit of yours. Keep hauling in; haul in more than you have
done so far. There's no obstacle, unless it's the smallness of
the house where you're to store them. Your net, your vessel,

Rete, ratis, pisces, locus, omen, tempus et aer
   riserunt voto prosperiora tuo;
925 piscandi tibi tuta repiscandique potestas.
   Dem tibi, si possim, scis, quia tollo nichil.
Quod lecturus eram, legi, tibi mando 'Tu autem';
   lectio perlecta est, dic, domine abba, 'Tu au.'"
(Ultima non poterat sermonis sillaba dici,
930   tam prope clamosae murmura plebis erant.)
Galliger iratum cernens incumbere vulgus
   maioresque moras posse nocere salit.
Impegisse adeo Remicae pro sedis adeptu,
   quam patruum norat, retia nollet aquae;
935 omnibus et patrui lapsis in retia rumbis
   gallus, quem tulerat, carior unus erat.
Serio festinat, iam non discedere fingit,
   tam laetus caudae quam levitate pedum;
neve diem festum spectandi perderet hostis,
940   iam sibi proviso caverat ante loco.
Colliculi costam terebrat rugosa crepido,
   ostiolo impendent densa filecta super;
formato maiore minor maiorque minore
   Reinardi credi forma fuisse potest.
945 Hanc adiens sollers latet aequicolore sub herba,
   spectandus nulli despiciensque procul.
Ut sibi sublatum penitus cognoverat hostem,
   sensibus excedit presbiter ille miser,
deficiensque sibi cadit ictus imagine mortis,
950   frigida quem reddit iactus in ora latex.
Tunc infestus arat maxillas unguis utrasque,
   largiter avulsas excipit aura comas.

the fish, the place, the conditions, the time, and the weather
have all smiled propitiously on your wishes. The power to   925
fish and fish again is safely yours; you can see that I make
over to you whatever I can, because I'm taking nothing
away. I've read my Lesson; I commend to you the final 'Lord
have mercy.' The reading's over, lord abbot; pronounce the
'Lord have mer—.'" (The last syllable of the speech couldn't
be got out, so near was the roar of the clamorous people.)   930

The cock-bearer, seeing the enraged populace rushing
forward, and that greater delays could be harmful, leaped
away. He wouldn't, for the bishopric of Reims, have thrust
his line as deep in the water as he knew his uncle had; the   935
cock which he had carried off was by itself worth more than
all the sturgeon which had fallen into his uncle's net. He
didn't, now, merely pretend to leave, he made haste in ear-
nest, happy in the lightness of *his* tail, as well as that of his
feet. And so that he would not lose the treat of watching
what happened, the wolf's enemy had already provided him-   940
self with a place marked out beforehand. A wrinkled crack
opened into the side of the hill, and thick ferns hung over
the entrance from above. Not bigger and not smaller in out-
line, you can believe it to be just Reynard's size. Reaching it,   945
the trickster lay hidden under the fronds of the same color,
visible to no one, but seeing a long way.

When the wretched priest realized that the enemy had
completely slipped from him, he lost consciousness, and fell
in a swoon, as if stricken by death. Water thrown on his cold   950
face revived him, and then his cruel nail furrowed both his
cheeks, and his hair, torn out in handfuls, was cast to the

Arguit inde deum male commendata tuentem,
    qui bona det miseris, ut data rapta gemant.
955 Omnibus hinc sanctis convicia debita fundit;
    praecipue domini noxia mater erat.
Nominat egregiam, quae tali merce rependat
    innumeras laudes obsequiumque frequens.
His tandem lacrimis maestis compassa querelis
960 solatur flentem turba sodalis herum,
neve nimis doleat, melior promittitur illi
    gallus et eximio femina iuncta viro;
dumque exacturus duplicis promissa repensae
    sponsor vel pignus poscitur illa valens,
965 cominus aspicitur miser Ysengrimus adesse.
    "Gaudia!" conclamat, "Gaudia!" coetus ovans.
"Quo, domine abba, paras nostros traducere pisces?
    Quo capti tibi sunt, hoc quoque vende loco!
Huccine piscator, dubium est, an veneris abbas —
970 si piscator ades, iura aliena rapis;
veneris huc abbas, ovium dare vellera quaeris
    fratribus et famulos carne cibare tuos.
Te quaecumque movens intentio compulit istuc,
    crederis hanc parva proposuisse fide.
975 Hanc privata nequit confessio solvere culpam;
    publica deprensos exigit ira reos.
Iudicium sinimus, si te peccasse negaris;
    proponit pulcrum gens tibi nostra iocum.
Candelabra, cruces, capsas et cetera sacrae
980 instrumenta domus attulit ista phalanx.
Sacra tibi his sacris dabimus, quae verbera si non
    senseris, esto insons; senseris, esto nocens."

wind. Then he accused God for taking such bad care of what was entrusted to him, and for giving good things to wretches only so that they might bemoan the gifts when they were snatched away again. Next he poured out well-merited insults to all the saints, the mother of God being especially culpable. He called her a fine one, who with such a reward repaid innumerable praises and constant service.

Having sympathized in these tears with melancholy laments, the friendly crowd consoled its weeping master, and so that he should not grieve too much, a better cock was promised to him, and a female added to the splendid male. Just as he was asking for a guarantor who would exact these promises of double compensation, or for some security equal to them in value, the wretched Ysengrimus was observed to be near at hand. "Oh, joy! Oh, joy!" cried the happy throng. "Where are you about to take our fish, lord abbot? Sell them on this same spot where you caught them! It's not clear whether you came here in your capacity as a fisherman, or as an abbot. If you're here as a fisherman, you're appropriating other people's rights; if you came here as an abbot, you want sheepskins to give to your brothers and meat to feed your servants. Whatever the compelling motive that brought you here, it's believed that there was little honesty in your resolve. This guilt cannot be absolved by private confession; apprehended criminals are claimed by public wrath. If you deny that you've done wrong, we'll allow you an ordeal; our people propose a fine game for you. This crowd has brought candlesticks, crucifixes, reliquaries, and other utensils of the sacred edifice. With these holy objects we'll give you holy blows, and if you don't feel them, you're innocent; if you do, you're guilty."

Quis dolor, o comites, in piscatore calebat,
  hanc legem populo testificante bonam!
985 Difficilem eversu, sit iniqua, sit aequa, tenendam,
  quam dederant legem, noverat, ergo silet.
Respondere pavor prohibet, gens stulta furebat;
  quid tamen audebat, qui nichil ausus erat?—
Volvere daemonibus decretum tale placere;
990   credere villano pravius esse nichil;
hoc opus edicto nullis abbatibus esse;
  se male piscatum scire nimisque diu;
pendere velle nichil, permitti liber abire;
  quamvis sacra forent verbera, nolle pati;
995 si sibi praescisset pisces hac merce parandos,
  non minus hoc cuiquam quam sibi velle lucrum;
scire sibi non esse malum, si nocte redisset,
  esset rete carens piscibus, esset habens;
quodque lupo mille inter oves sit tutior annus,
1000   quam cum villanis quattuor una dies;
quin etiam ad pastum legere et cantare diatim
  coram lanigero non dubitare choro,
denique cornutis tam cornua nulla vereri,
  ut non imprimeret basia corde bono,
1005 et nisi prima citus sequeretur ad oscula sanguis,
  iudice se furcae vindicis esse reus;
insuper eximium sua tergora ponere pignus,
  et gravidum cetis addere rete novem,
quod numerum serie conversim diceret acta,
1010   quo numquam recte vir numeraret oves.
(Nam sic: "una, duae, tres" rusticus ordinat amens,
  non aliter stultus scit numerare miser;

What misery, my friends, was kindled in the fisherman, when the people enunciated this good resolution! That the law they had laid down was difficult to overturn, and was to be kept whether it was just or unjust, he knew, so he kept silent. Fear forbade him to answer; the foolish people were in a mad rage. But what did he dare to think, though he didn't dare to say anything?—That he thought a decision like that would please only devils.— That he thought nothing was worse than a peasant; that this edict was unnecessary for abbots; that he knew he'd fished wrongfully and for too long, but he wanted to be allowed to go away free without paying for it, and although the blows were sacred, he didn't want to undergo them.— If he'd known beforehand that he'd have to make this payment for the fish, he'd have wished the profit on no one less than on himself.—He knew it was no bad thing for him to have gone home by night, whether his net were full or empty of fish.—That a year among a thousand sheep is safer for a wolf than a single day among four peasants—indeed, he didn't hesitate to celebrate Mass daily in front of the woolly choir at pasture, and finally was not so afraid of their horns as to fail to implant on the horned ones the kiss of goodwill, and unless blood quickly followed the first kisses, in his own opinion he was worthy of the vengeance of the gallows.—What's more, he'd lay his hide as a special pledge, and his net weighted down with nine whales in addition, that a peasant said numbers in reverse order, so that he never counted the sheep correctly. (For the stupid peasant counts in the order "one, two, three," and the foolish wretch doesn't know how to count any other way. The old man, on the other hand, used to go

985

990

995

1000

1005

1010

ex tribus ut binas, ex binis fecerat unam,
    sueverat extremum dicere "nulla" senex.
1015 Sic rudis ad quamvis summam villanus ab una
    orditur numero multiplicante gregem;
qualibet a summa sene grex numerante gradatim
    defluus ad nullam paucior usque foret.)—
Quid tot posse iuvat bona totque et plura cupisse?
1020   Villani captum posse cupita vetant.
Nil facere audebat, nil dicere, deinde rogatur,
    an prandere velit, plebe rogante tacet.
Pars optasse ferunt, pars dissensisse tacentem;
    dicat ut ipse, rogant, fatur itemque nichil.
1025 Poscere saepe pudet, quod sumitur absque pudore,
    scilicet hoc illum more silere ferunt.
Respondit dominus Bovo: "Causa illa silendi,
    quam versatis, abest, altera maior inest:
abbas ipse fuit, benedicite ruminat illud,
1030   quod solet astantes sanctificare cibos.
Plus sapit hic aliis, numquam benediceret alter,
    ni prius oblatas cerneret esse dapes;
ergo dicant alii praesentes, iste futuras
    divinans epulas appropiare sibi."
1035 Undique clamatur: "Verum est, speratque cupitis
    maiores epulas, spes bene cessit, edat;
maiores dabimus speratis"; ista locuti,
    expediunt dextras, prandia laeta parant.
Presbiter abbati dare fercula prima iubetur;
1040   "Nos," aiunt, "dabimus grandia liba dein."

from three to two, and from two to one, and to make the last number "none." So the uneducated boor begins with "one" and counts upward to any total, making the flock increase in number, while the old man counts downward from any number in stages to naught, so that the flock always dwindles in size.)—What use is it to have been able to say so many good things, and to have wanted to say even more? The peasants didn't allow their prisoner to accomplish his wishes.

He didn't dare to do anything, or to say anything; he was asked whether he wanted to eat, but remained silent in the face of the people's inquiry. Some of them claimed he assented by his silence, some that he refused; they asked him to speak himself, and again he said nothing. They said that there's often shame in asking for something that is accepted without shame, and it must be on this principle that he was silent. Master Bovo replied: "The cause of silence that you're thinking of is not involved here; it's another, more important one. He used to be an abbot; he's thinking about the 'benedicite' which usually blesses the food laid out. He's wiser than others; no one else would ever say grace before he'd first seen the food offered up. Let everyone else bless meals which are actually present; he blesses those that he divines are going to be put before him." The cry broke out on all sides: "That's right, he's hoping for a feast bigger than his wishes. Well, his hope has a happy conclusion; let him eat and we'll give him more than he hoped for." Having said this, they raised their fists and prepared for a happy banquet. The priest was asked to give the abbot an appetizer: "We'll give him a whopping dessert afterward," they said.

Presbiter assiliens crispat benedicite longum,
    crispanti tellus assonat icta procul.
Sic celebres disci in claustris (clamatur hiando)
    aut bonus abbatis visitat ora calix,
1045 tunc cum festa dies ventri promisit avaro
    solvendos cantus omnibus esse bonis.
Presbiter ergo gravi tundit cava timpora libro;
    verbera sena dabat, plura daturus adhuc,
praecipitem turbam laedit iactura morandi,
1050   inque senem unanimi sedulitate ruunt.
Heu quam dissimilis bellum fortuna gerebat!
    Tota acies uno vim patiente facit.
Hic caput, ille latus caedit, pars plurima dorsum,
    multicavi ventris mantica longa gemit.
1055 Qualiter argillae sordes fullone lavante
    icta sub incusso subtonat aura sago,
aut plumosa cadens in pulvinaria magnus
    asser, et admota timpana pulsa manu,
aut uterus tonnae saxi sub verbere mugit,
1060   taliter ad vastas bulga lupina sudes.
Vix ego crediderim, nisi quod scriptura fatetur,
    ferre flagra abbates tot potuisse decem.
Sic ego triticeis paleas extundere granis
    audieram in patulo tribula mille foro.

The priest, leaping up to him, struck up a long grace, and the earth, reverberating into the distance, echoed his tune. Thus, in monasteries, the numerous dishes, or the abbot's good old wine cup (called for with gaping throats), pass from mouth to mouth, when the feast day has assured the glutton that his masses are to be rewarded with every good thing. So the priest struck his hollow temples with the heavy Bible; six blows he gave them, and was going to give them still more, but the loss incurred by delay pained the impatient crowd, and with one accord they zealously fell on the old creature. 1045 1050

Alas, how unequal was the war Fortune was waging! A whole army was doing violence to a single victim. One man bashed his head, another his side, most of them his back, and the long bag of his many-hollowed stomach groaned. As when a fuller is washing out the dirt of clay, and the compressed air resounds underneath the trodden cloth, or like a great beam falling on to a feather bed, or drums beaten by a striking hand, or as the belly of a barrel rumbles under the stroke of a rock, so did the wolf's pouch to the mighty cudgels. I'd hardly have believed, without scripture relating it, that ten abbots could have endured so many lashes. Just so I've heard a thousand threshing sledges, in the public market, beating out the grains of corn from the chaff. 1055 1060

BOOK TWO

Iam laxare suas iteranda ad verbera vires
    sederat invita fessa quiete cohors.
Sola Aldrada furit, quamvis defessa recusat
    sidere, ni truncet praesulis ante caput.
5   Illa manu vastam vibrans utraque bipennem
    et misero capiti vulnera dira minans
semiloquas voces balbo stridore babellat,
    dentibus undenis dimidioque carens.
Efflua nascentes lingua feriente parumper
10 aera deformat spuma liquatque modos:
"Quam michi Gerardus creber bonus, improbe raptor,
    fraude tua periit, quam bona Teta frequens!
Parta tibi hic eadem est pietas, utinamque bis essent,
    quot michi dempsisti, colla secanda tibi!
15 Pro cuiusque anima Tetae duo colla darentur!
    Talio nunc meritis non redit aequa tuis.
Debueras nasci capitis deformiter expers
    et capitum innumera perditione mori,
dignus tot cupiens infectas pendere fraudes,
20 quot faceres ultro, si tibi posse foret.
Mens ubi persistit fallax et prona nocendi,
    nequior integro est truncus agente volens.

Now the exhausted crowd sat down, resting, albeit reluctantly, so as to recruit their strength for another round of blows. Only Aldrada raged on; although weary, she refused to sit down before she had sliced off the bishop's head. Brandishing a huge ax with both hands, and aiming terrible 5 blows at his wretched head, she driveled out half-formed words in a stuttering shriek (she was missing eleven and a half teeth). As her tongue struck the air, the dripping sla- 10 ver deformed and thickened the sounds at the moment they arose: "Wicked thief, how often has a good Gerard, how many times has a good Teta of mine perished through your treachery! The same kindness is on tap here for you; I just wish that the neck I'm going to cut for you were double the number you've taken from me! I wish you could give two 15 necks for each hen's life! As it is, my revenge doesn't justly meet your deserts. You should have been born deformed, without any head, or die by the loss of heads without number, since you deserve to pay for merely intending all the un- accomplished crimes which you would happily go on to 20 commit if you could! Where a treacherous mind still per- sists in its inclination to do harm, the one who has the wish but is physically unable to fulfill it is actually more wicked than the man who is fit enough to translate it into action.

Nil faciens Satanas plus omni peccat agente;
    sufficit omne deo iudice velle malum.
25 Nunc unum atque malum caput est tibi, multaque debes;
    una lupis melior Teta duobus erat.
Plus habito dare nemo potest, donabo, quod ultra est;
    quod potes hoc uno solvere, solve dato.
Non ego curarem, si quid prodesset habenti,
30   tollere, sed senuit, sed probitate caret,
et capite exempto levior fit sarcina trunci;
    non est, cur teneas amplius, ergo metam.
Ne crebro indigeat tonsore corona recrescens,
    rado tibi pariter colla caputque semel."
35 Dixerat et recto miserum caput impetit ictu,
    ausa in pontificem tam furiale nefas,
et mediam frontem plaga expectata fidisset—
    vertice subducto funditur ille retro.
Aut metuens demptum sero sibi, sicubi rursum
40   vellet eo fungi, posse redire caput,
aut ovium miserans, quae defensoris egerent,
    aut animo versans augure utrumque metum,
credere nolebat collum veniente securi,
    et peior sinoco visa securis erat.
45 In sua piscator transfusus terga rotatur,
    in glaciem longe mersa bipennis abit;
occipitis molem testatur bulla repente,
    spectari potior quam redimire sinum.

Satan sins more when he's doing nothing than anyone else when actually doing something; in the eyes of God, just wishing any wickedness is enough. Now you've got only one 25 head—and that a bad one—but you owe a multitude; one Teta was better than two wolves. Nobody can give more than he's got; I'll concede the rest, but make whatever compensation can be made with this single head by surrendering it. I shouldn't care to take it if it was any use to its owner, but 30 it's old and worthless, and the burden of your body will be lighter when the head is taken away. There's no reason why you should keep it any longer, so I'll cut it off. So that your tonsure, as it grows again, doesn't need the frequent ministrations of a barber, I'll shave your head and shoulders at one go."

Having said this, she attacked his wretched head with a 35 straight-aimed blow (such mad sacrilege did she venture against the bishop!), and the blow would have split his forehead in two if he had waited for it—but with his head pulled out of the way he threw himself backward. Either he was afraid that his head, if taken away, might be too slow in returning to him when he wanted to use it again, or he had 40 compassion on the sheep, who would be left without a protector, or he entertained both fears in his farsighted mind— whatever the reason, he was unwilling to trust his neck to the approaching ax; in fact the ax appeared to him worse than the plague. Tumbling on to his back, the fisherman 45 rolled over, and the ax missed him and plunged deep into the ice. A sudden protuberance testified to the weight of his head—a protuberance of the kind that is more fitted to catch the eye than to adorn a bosom.

Iam sursum senior plantas extenderat omnes,
50   poscere divinam more volentis opem.
Vult, ubi subsidunt brevioribus ilia costis,
      partiri miserum rustica saeva senem,
porro cohaesurum nodo vivace cadaver
      cogitat et prisco posse vigore frui;
55 utque puer ruptum prudens intermeat anguem,
      ne coeant partes atque animentur item,
sic reducem vitam coituris demere truncis
      trino intercursu provida versat anus.
Supplice tunc voto sanctorum multa vocantur
60   quae plebeius habet nomina nota canon:
scilicet Excelsis cum coniuge sanctus Osanna,
      dicitur a furca quem rapuisse deus,
et quam rex Phanuel de sura everrerat Annam,
      qua mater domini, sancta Maria, sata est,
65 et qua promicuit pennatus matre Michael,
      Alleluia Petro coniuge fausta diu,
Helpuara Noburgisque, bonae implorantibus ambae,
      et pecorum tutrix Brigida saeva lupis,
praecipue fidus Celebrant, ope cuius, ubi omnes
70   defuerant testes, est data Roma Petro,
traditaque iniusto Pharaildis virgo labori,
      sed sancti faciunt, qualiacumque volunt.
Hac famosus erat felixque fuisset Herodes
      prole, sed infelix hanc quoque laesit amor.
75 Haec virgo thalamos Baptistae solius ardens
      voverat hoc dempto nullius esse viri;
offensus genitor comperto prolis amore
      insontem sanctum decapitavit atrox.

82

At this point the old man had all his feet raised in the air, in the manner of one who wishes to beg for divine as- 50 sistance. The furious peasant woman intended to split the wretched old man in two, just where his ribs narrowed down into his groin, but she thought the corpse would reunite in a living bond, and be able to enjoy its former vigor, and so, as a clever child walks between the severed halves of a snake 55 to stop the parts joining together and coming to life again, this farsighted granny thought to hold off the returning life from his limbs before they recombined, by stepping be- tween them three times. Then with suppliant prayer, many well-known names of the saints in the popular canon were 60 invoked: namely, Saint Hosanna (whom God is said to have snatched from the gallows) with his wife Excelsis, and Anna, brought forth from the loins of King Phanuel, and of whom Saint Mary, mother of God, was begotten, and ever-benign 65 Alleluia, with her husband Peter, to whom was born the winged Michael; Helpwar and Noburgis, both ladies gra- cious to suppliants, and Brigid, fierce guardian of the flocks against wolves; and especially the faithful Celebrant, by whose aid, when all witnesses were absent, Rome was given 70 to Peter, and the virgin Pharaildis, given over to unjust suf- fering—but the saints do whatever they want. Herod was renowned for this daughter, and would have been blessed in her but that she, like others, came to grief through an unfor- tunate love. This girl, yearning for the bed of the Baptist 75 alone, had vowed to be no man's, if he were denied her. Her cruel father was angered by the discovery of his daughter's love, and beheaded the innocent saint. The grief-stricken

Postulat afferri virgo sibi tristis, et affert
80   regius in disco timpora trunca cliens;
mollibus allatum stringens caput illa lacertis
     perfundit lacrimis osculaque addere avet.
Oscula captantem caput aufugit atque resufflat,
     illa per impluvium turbine flantis abit.
85 Ex illo nimium memor ira Iohannis eandem
     per vacuum caeli flabilis urget iter;
mortuus infestat miseram nec vivus amarat.
     Non tamen hanc penitus fata perisse sinunt:
lenit honor luctum, minuit reverentia poenam,
90   pars hominum maestae tertia servit herae.
Quercubus et corilis a noctis parte secunda
     usque nigri ad galli carmina prima sedet.
Nunc ea nomen habet Pharaildis, Herodias ante,
     saltria nec subiens nec subeunda pari.
95 Hos anus atque alios, quos est mora dicere, sanctos
     pollicitis captat, voce fideque vocat,
bisque Pater noster sanctum et Credinde revolvit,
     quinque Dei paces et Miserele quater,
Oratrus fratrus, Paz vobas clamat et infert
100   Deugracias finem, quando ferire parat.
Tot periere preces, audacia cassa sine astu est,
     affectus factum praepedit arte carens.
Rustica praecipiti raptum nimis impete telum
     pollice non circum perveniente levat.
105 Dumque levat, clamat, quem nec mutire decebat,
     nescius hic monitu non opus esse suo;
terretur populus, qui circumquaque sedebat,
     ipsa etiam tonitru terrificata suo est.

maiden asked to have brought her—and the king's servant 80
brought, on a dish—his severed head; when it was brought,
she clasped it in her soft arms, drenched it with tears and
burned to imprint kisses on it. As she strained after its
kisses, the head backed away and blew at her, and she dis-
appeared through the skylight in the eddy of breath. Since 85
then, John's unforgettable hissing anger drives her on a jour-
ney through the empty heavens; he plagues the wretched
woman when dead and he didn't love her when he was alive.
Yet the fates don't allow her to perish completely; honor
softens her grief, and reverence lessens her punishment. A 90
third portion of mankind serves this melancholy lady, and
from the second part of the night until the black cock sings
Prime, she perches on oaks and hazel trees. Now her name
is Pharaildis, whereas before it was Herodias, a dancer nei-
ther preceded nor followed by anyone equal to her.

These saints, and others whom it would be too long to 95
enumerate, the old granny lured with promises and sum-
moned through the power of her faith and voice, and twice
she ran through the holy "Hour father" and the "I believe in
Cod," five "Cod's pieces" and four "Laws-a-mercy's"; "Let us
play," and "Bees be with you," she cried, and finished with 100
"Thanks be to Cod" as she prepared to strike. All her prayers
were lost; courage is fruitless without cunning, and desire
without skill prevents achievement. The peasant woman
lifted her snatched-up weapon with too hasty a violence,
and without circling it properly with her thumb; while she 105
was lifting it, the wolf shouted (since it wasn't an occasion
on which to mumble)—unaware that this encouragement
wasn't necessary. The people who were sitting round about
took fright, and she herself was terrified by his bawling. The

Coeperat ut fulgur ruere exaltata securis
110   (visa procul prope fit, res prope saepe procul);
intererat spatii bis, quantum vulnifer ictus
        transierat, iustum caedis adusque locum—
prensa male elusam liquere manubria dextram.
        Non tamen omnino vulnus inane fuit;
115   rete secat lapsa inter aquas clunemque bipennis,
        nec partes aequat, maior inhaesit aquae.
Pars servata tamen, quamvis minor esset, habenti
        carior est illa, qua viduatus erat.
Nec consistit anus magnoque inhibere nequibat
120   impete propulsas assequiturque manus.
Illa genu nondum clamante diacone flectens,
        qua dederat plagam, condidit acta labrum.
Oscula figuntur velut emplastrantia vulnus,
        inque cavo veniam podice nasus agit.
125   Rustica pontifici misero abmorsura putatur
        relliquias trunci retis, et ipse tremit.
Prima dolore carens fit plaga timore secundae;
        anus anusque pavent, sed magis anus anu.
Ergo abrupta simul sensit retinacula praesul,
130   nec rogat, an tempus fasve sit ire sibi;
corpore succusso sublatus in alta ruentis
        catti more super recidit ipse pedes.
Nec stetit (hoc dico) nec scissum rete refecit;
        rete diu carum vilius asse iacet;
135   quod de reticulo sibi, si quid inhaeserat, aufert.

uplifted ax was beginning to descend like lightning—but of- 110
ten something far off seems near, and what's near seems
far off. There still remained double the distance that the
wounding blow had already traveled to be covered before it
would arrive at the right place for murder, when the handle,
clumsily grasped, slipped from her cheated hand. But the
wound was not completely without effect; the fallen ax sev- 115
ered his fishing net between the water and his arse, although
not in equal parts, since the larger part remained fast in the
water. Yet the part he retained, although smaller, was more
affectionately regarded by its possessor than the part he had
lost. Nor did the old woman stop there. Unable to check the
mighty violence in the forward rush of her hands, she fol- 120
lowed after them; her knees bending (though the deacon
had not yet called for it), her mouth, in the place where she
had inflicted the wound, concealed what she had done. Her
kiss was glued to the wound like a plaster, and her nose
brought relief to the gaping arsehole.

The wretched bishop thought that the peasant woman 125
was about to bite off the remains of his mutilated fishing
net, and he trembled; the pain of the first blow disappeared
through fear of a second. The crone and the crotch were
both terrified, but the crotch more than the crone. So, once
the bishop felt his bonds cut, he didn't inquire whether it 130
was the right thing or the right moment for him to leave;
with a jerk of his body he rose in the air and landed on his
feet like a falling cat. Nor, let me tell you, did he stand still,
or repair his broken net. The fishing net which he long held
dear lay there not worth a ha'penny to him, and he took 135
away with him only what, if anything, he still had of the net
attached to him.

Pontificem tali miror abisse modo:
decepit miserum sperata remissio vulgus;
   non pungunt animos dogmata sacra rudes;
non banno vincire reos, non solvere curat,
140   nec sibi substratam surgere iussit anum;
non neglecta novat, non aspera iussa resignat;
   nec facienda iubet, nec bene facta probat.
Confirmare ferat? Nec fert benedicere turbae,
   nec socium ex tanta quem sibi gente legit,
145   nec, quoadusque semel posset benedicite dici,
   pro naso papae stare tulisset ibi,
nec meminit cantare brevem post prandia psalmum,
   nulla agitur populo gratia, nulla deo.
Presbiteri et plebis per colla et brachia saltans
150   immemor officii pontificalis abit,
dumque probat cursu se non sensisse citato
   verbera, quae tulerat, iusta fuisse negat.
Affectu maiore redit quam venerat illuc;
   nil nisi more alias esse volentis agit.
155 Nec reduci intendit piscatum nocte redire,
   nec, quos tunc pisces ceperat, inde vehit.
Nec placet electu nec displicet ulla viarum
   praeter ad has reducem, quas fugiebat, aquas.
Ysengrimus, uti quis rete indutus hiulcum,
160   corpore multiforo vulnera totus erat.
Iam discussa fere vix nervis ossa cohaerent,
   venarum penitus sub cute nulla latet;
sed non ille tamen tanta tam clade gravatur,
   quam de Reinardi prosperitate dolet.

I'm amazed that the bishop went off in that way. The wretched people were deceived of the hoped-for remission of their sins; their coarse souls weren't penetrated by sacred teachings; he didn't bother to subject sinners to excommunication, nor to release them from it, nor did he order the old woman prostrated before him to rise. He didn't make new provision for what had been neglected, nor rescind over-harsh orders; he didn't order what was to be done, or praise what had been done well. As for offering confirmation, he didn't even offer a blessing to the throng, nor did he choose anyone, out of so many people, as an escort for himself. Not for the pope's nose would he have endured standing there while even one blessing was said! Nor did he remember to sing a short after-dinner psalm; he gave no thanks to the people nor to God. Jumping over the shoulders and arms of both priest and people, the bishop made off, unmindful of his duties, and in so far as he proved by his rapid movement that he hadn't felt the blows he endured, he denied their justice. He retraced his steps with greater eagerness than he had come there; he just acted like someone who wanted to be somewhere else. He didn't intend to return the next night to fish, and he didn't even carry away the fishes he had caught; all roads were alike for his choice, except the one that led back to the waters from which he was galloping away.

Ysengrimus was, in his much-pierced body, a mass of wounds, like someone who was covered with a net gaping with holes. His broken bones were almost coming away from his sinews; not one of his veins remained hidden beneath his skin. And yet he was not so much oppressed by this great disaster as sore at Reynard's triumph.

165 Inscius ergo simul secus hostem colle latentem
    pervenit, his horret questibus atque minis:
    "Vivere me taedet, me taedet vivere!—quidni?—
    qui michi non esset profore dignus, obest—
    qui gaudere meo non esset dignus honore,
170   me sibi ridiculo non habuisse timet.
    Ergo in fata ruens evasa reverterer ultro,
    laedere nolentes velle precarer ego,
    usque adeo vitam penitus detestor et odi,
    spes nisi vindictae conciliaret eam.
175 Illa dies sperata pati me vivere cogit,
    qua latro calicem, quem dedit, ipse bibat.
    O si forte dies impleverit ulla, quod opto,
    hanc ego non distat qua nece laetus emam.
    Terribilem sancti Gereonis iuro columpnam,
180   cui nec Roma parem nec Ierosolma tenet,
    post quam nullus agens reprobus vestigia profert,
    momentum nulla conditione sequar.
    Planxerit ille dolos sive ostentaverit actus,
    sive roget veniam sive rogare neget,
185 donaque promissis superet promissaque donis,
    sive horum neutrum fecerit, unus ero."
    Cominus hanc recubans vocem Reinardus ut audit,
    coeperat ad tantas horripilare minas,
    neve excusandi praerepto copia desit,
190   prosiliens tamquam sponte coactus ait:
    "O deflende michi lamentis, patrue, longis!"
    (singultusque inter singula verba dabat).

So, unawares, he came up with his enemy, concealed on the   165
hill, as he bristled with these moans and threats: "Life! I'm
sick of it, sick of it!—why not?—when someone who isn't
worthy to help me, does me down—when someone who
wouldn't deserve to be made happy by my good fortune,
doesn't shrink from making me a laughingstock. I now hate   170
and detest life so utterly that I would voluntarily rush back
to the fate I have escaped, and beg for injury if they were
unwilling to give it, were it not that the hope of vengeance
made life bearable. That hoped-for day, when the thief shall   175
himself drink from the cup he has proffered, compels me to
endure living on. Oh, if by good luck any future day accom-
plishes what I hope for, I'll purchase it cheerfully with any
kind of death. I swear by the terrible column of Saint Ge-
reon, whose like isn't to be found in either Rome or Jerusa-   180
lem, and beyond which no criminal who has directed his
steps there leads them further, I shan't delay that moment
on any account. Whether he's sorry for his tricks or boasts
of what he's done, whether he asks for mercy or refuses to
do so, whether he outdoes his promises with his gifts or his   185
gifts with his promises, or whether he does none of these,
I'll be unalterable." When Reynard, lying nearby, heard
his voice, his hair began to stand on end at such threats,
but lest he might be forestalled and lose the chance to exon-
erate himself, he leaped out, and although under com-   190
pulsion, said as if spontaneously: "Oh uncle, how much
your case deserves to be wept over with lengthy lamen-
tations!" (and he sobbed between each word). "Who has

"Membra quis hoc scisso texit tibi regia sacco?
    Non habuit nostros talis amictus avos!
195 Amodo piscandi studium sectabere forsan,
    et piscatores frigora saepe gravant,
ergo gravesne ista ventos crebrosque cuculla
    assultus gelidae pellere credis aquae?
At tegitur Ioseph vervex meliore cuculla,
200   omne quidem frigus demeret illa tibi;
quae cum te deceat, quin et tua debeat esse,
    haec tibi cur gratis parta vel empta placet?"
Coeperat hoc senior paulum mansuescere verbo
    et non praemissis aequiperanda refert:
205 "Pessime seductor, loqueris quasi nescius acti,
    fraude tua cum sim ductus in omne malum.
Praeduce te in fustes venabulaque actus et uncos
    dissipor: hic scindit, pungit is, ille ferit.
Sic michi discussum est in mille foramina corpus,
210   te spectante, nichil subveniente tamen;
denique nescio quo caudam truncante recessi,
    nulla tamen gravior quam michi plaga famis.
Sic ego discissi nactus velamina sacci—
    daemonibus pisces annuo teque simul."
215 Fictor ad haec: "Meritum merces sua quodque coaequet!
    Da, cui vis, pisces, at michi iure faves.
Nil ego commisi, scis ipse; tibi tamen insons
    omnia debentis, dummodo placer, agam.
Te, quia poscebas, ad plena cibaria duxi,
220   ut posses avidam pacificare gulam,

covered your regal limbs with this torn sack? It wasn't a gar-
ment like this that clothed our ancestors! Perhaps you'll   195
take up fishing as a hobby from now on, and cold is often a
nuisance to fishermen; do you think, then, you will ward off
severe winds and frequent dousings of cold water with that
cowl? Joseph the sheep, now, is clothed in a better
cowl—that one would ward off all cold from you. Since that   200
would suit you, and really ought to be yours, why do you
bother with this one, whether you bought it or got it for
nothing?"

At this speech, the old one began to soften a little, and
replied with words that ill matched what he'd just said: "You   205
wicked seducer, you speak as if you're ignorant of what has
happened, although it was by your trickery that I was led
to utter disaster. Under your guidance, I was driven on to
sticks and spears and hooks, and beaten to pieces as they cut
and stung and struck in turn; so my body is torn into a thou-
sand holes, while you looked on, but did nothing to help. Fi-   210
nally, I got away, through someone or other cutting off my
tail, although I was worse afflicted by hunger than by any
wound. That's how I got a torn sack for clothing—and you
and the fish can go to the devil together!"

To this the deceiver replied: "Let everyone get what he   215
deserves! Give the fish to anyone you like; although it's right
that you should do me a favor. I've done nothing, as you
yourself know. Yet though I'm innocent, I'll do everything
a guilty man should do, until I'm granted reconciliation.
Because you asked me to, I led you to ample stores of food,
so that you could appease your ravenous greed, and I   220

et tibi, quos caperes, praedixi, quosque caveres,
    sperabas nullo pondere posse premi.
Ut suus est modicis, nimiis sic terminus ausis;
    quid gravidum rumbis rete fuisse querar?
225 Vivere non posses, nisi captus et ille fuisset
    cuius in ingenti ventre propheta fuit.
Hoc capto tu captus eras solvique petebas,
    abstulit officium turba maligna meum.
Tunc omnes claustri ratus actos daemones in te,
230   ut desertori vincula saeva darent,
direxi celerem sub tuta latibula cursum,
    ne iubear tecum claustra subire timens.
Malo, quod edidici, gallum explumare vel aucam,
    ducere quam rigida relligione chorum.
235 Cumque tibi irruerent secumque reducere vellent
    vestibus abscissis verberibusque datis,
laetabar fugisse procul; si pone fuissem,
    obsequium acturos nam michi rebar idem.
Denique credidimus caudam truncantibus illis,
240   quod fieres abbas claustra novena super,
ut tot praebendis, ne paupertate gravante
    rursus suffugeres, efficerere satur.
Quod si, cauda tibi cur sit mutilata, requiris,
    istius officii congrua causa fuit:
245 luxus opes sequitur, sibi quisque fit utilis abbas,
    sanctior est, quisquis pinguior esse potest.
Nunc ferrum, nunc flamma adimit, nunc potio morbum
    pinguibus, o tanti est promeruisse deum!
Qui sapit, est sapiens; tu pauper multa vorasti;
250   ingluviem dives prosequerere magis,

instructed you beforehand on which you should take and
which you should leave alone, while you flattered yourself
that no weight would be too much for you. As there's a limit
for small enterprises, so there's a limit for extravagant ones.
Why should I be sorry that your net was weighed down with
sturgeon? You couldn't live until you'd caught the fish whose   225
huge stomach had harbored the prophet Jonah! When it
was caught, so were you; you asked to be released, but the
malevolent crowd preempted my assistance. Then, imagin-
ing that all the devils of the cloister were let loose against
you, so that they might lay cruel fetters on a deserter, I   230
quickly made my way to a safe hiding place, frightened that
I might be ordered to enter the cloister with you. I prefer
what I've learned to do—defeathering a cock or a goose—to
leading the choir with strict piety. When they rushed on you   235
and wanted to lead you off with them, your clothes torn
from you and blows inflicted on you, I was glad I'd gone
a long way off; because if I'd been in the neighborhood,
I thought they'd have done me the same favor. Then I
thought, when they cut off your tail, that you were going to   240
be made abbot in charge of nine monasteries at once, so
that you would be satisfied with so many livings, and
wouldn't run away again under pressure of poverty. For if
you ask why your tail was mutilated, the proper reason for
the rendering of this service was as follows: self-indulgence   245
is the result of wealth, and an abbot looks after himself; the
more holy he is, the fatter he can be. At one time, the knife,
at another, fire, at a third, purges, relieve the sickness of
the bloated; so great a thing it is to have won favor with
God! The man with a good deal of *taste* is wise; you gobbled
down a lot when you were poor, and as a rich man you would   250

et crassus fieres abbatum more proborum.
    Idcirco utiliter cauda resecta tibi est:
cum non suppeteret prudens curator aventi,
    per certum efflueret noxius humor iter.
255 Inde ego plus metuens abbas quam monachus esse
    abscondebar, et est hinc michi culpa gravis?
At post tanta famem quereris tibi flagra nocere,
    tollitur haut ulla clade querela vetus.
Omnibus adversis praestat penuria ventris;
260   haec tibi praecedens, haec tibi causa sequens.
Et quando saturam semel esse fateberis alvum?
    Si sapis, hunc stimulum non patiere diu!"
Vocibus his senior reparato corde profatur:
    "Non sum tam sapiens, quin magis esse queam.
265 Sed tantum sapio sapiamque: oblata vorabo,
    malo quoque, ut quaeram, quam caruisse feram.
Et de nescio qua nobis paulo ante cuculla
    verbum sive dabas sive daturus eras;
exuviis sane non curo quis accidat heres,
270   quod vacuas fauces impleat, illud amo."
"Patrue, res melius quam speras accidit," inquit,
    "quattuor hic fratres iurgia longa trahunt.
Cursibus atque ortu fratres praeeuntis habetur
    quod recolis nomen me posuisse supra;
275 succedentis ei Bernardus, et ille priore est
    citerior cursu, robore vero prior;
proximus, intortis quod opertae cornibus aures
    vix pateant, nomen Colvarianus habet;
at nomen quarto dat vitrea lana Belino.
280   Quattuor his similes insula nulla tenet;

BOOK 2

follow up your greed to a greater extent, and you'd get fat in
the way that worthy abbots do. So it was useful for you that
your tail was cut off. Since a skilled doctor wasn't on hand to
provide what you wanted, the nasty pus had to find a safe
outlet. So I, even more afraid of being an abbot than a monk,   255
tucked myself away. Was that very bad of me? But after such
a beating you complain that hunger torments you, and the
old complaint isn't removed by any calamity. Your stomach's
emptiness takes pride of place over all misfortunes; it's your   260
first and last preoccupation. When will you ever acknowl-
edge that your belly is full? So if you have any sense, you
won't put up with this urging for long!"

With spirits revived by these words, the old fellow re-
plied: "I'm not so wise that I can't be more so. But I've got   265
this much sense, and always shall have: I'll devour whatever
comes my way, and I also prefer to seek something than to
tolerate being without it. A little while ago you were say-
ing something, or were going to say something, about some
cowl or other. I don't at all care who falls heir to the sheep-
skin; what I like is something to fill my empty jaws." "Uncle,   270
matters are in a better way than you hope," he said. "Four
brothers in this area are dragging out a long dispute. The
name of the one who precedes his brothers in swiftness and
age is that which you remember I gave him earlier. Bernard   275
is the name of the one next after him, and though inferior
to Joseph in swiftness, he surpasses him in strength. The
next, because his ears are hardly visible, being covered by his
twisted horns, is called Colvarianus. The fourth is named
Belinus because of his shining fleece. There's no isle that has   280
four like these; I know them and likewise I know how much

novimus hos certe, quantis et tota minores
    Fresia, vervecum maxima mater, alit.
Deliciae pausare vetant, accede sequester,
    lis ad iudicium pertinet ista tuum.
285 Quinque fere stadiis maiore colonia giro
    quattuor in partes his dirimenda iacet;
inde ubi quis spatium, citra quod habenda putatur
    regula processus, transmeat, arma movent.
His odium frustra collecto saepe suorum
290   agmine conata est demere turba rudis;
usque adeo non est aptus giometer in illis,
    qui mediam iusto limite signet humum.
I propere, aequatis tu partibus erige metam,
    ut tuus illorum patribus ante pater.
295 Piscatum redeas, si quid (nisi lana) superstes
    manserit (hac caedem conciliare potes).
In minus illorum pingui pinguedo bipalmis
    excedit costas!" Prosilit ille, meant.
Cornua bina ferunt caput insignisse Belini,
300   bis vero totidem, Colvariane, tuum;
amborum numerum Bernardi in fronte rigere,
    horrificant Ioseph munia bina quater.
Arma videns capitum pavet Ysengrimus et infit
    arma putans oris plus metuenda sibi:
305 "Aspicis o turres, Reinarde, in frontibus horum?
    Anne parum nobis ora timenda putas?
Dentibus iratis non est colludere tutum,
    et (fateor) piscis dens michi rete tulit.

lesser are the ones nourished by Friesland, the great mother
of sheep. These dainty morsels forbid you to hesitate; go to
them as a mediator! This dispute is for you to settle. An es-   285
tate which is all of five furlongs in circumference has to be
divided into four parts for them; so that when any of them
crosses over the space within which the regulation of his
movements is supposed to be confined, they do battle. The   290
untutored populace, collecting a band among themselves,
have often tried to put an end to their hostility, but in vain;
up to now, there's been no proper surveyor among them,
someone who might mark out the middle of the land with
an exact boundary. Go quickly, and set up a marker for the
equally divided parts, as your father did for theirs. If any-   295
thing is left over except the wool, you can go back to your
fishing (and with the wool, you can repair the damage done
to you). In the thinnest of these sheep, the fat covers the
ribs two hand-spans deep!" He leaped forward, and off they
went.

They say that twin horns distinguished the head of Beli-
nus, while twice as many, Colvarianus, distinguished yours.   300
The total of both numbers bristled on Bernard's forehead,
and twice times four were the battlements that turned Jo-
seph into a frightening figure. When he saw the weapons on
their heads, Ysengrimus was terror-struck, and, thinking he
ought to fear the weapons in their mouths even more, he
said: "Do you see the turrets on their heads, Reynard? Don't   305
you think we ought to be more than a little afraid of their
mouths? It's not safe to play around with savage teeth, and (I
admit) the tooth of that whale chewed off my fishing net.

Ire libet, certe non sum giometer, an essem,
310 si male metirer, te duce tutus ego?
Quattuor hic fortes, duo sunt exercitus uni,
 unius occubitu saeviet ira trium."
Reinardus monitis animum formavit inertem;
 praecedit timidus vulpe sequente senex.
315 Aspiciunt laetique parum viso hospite fratres;
 nil nisi "Quid fiet? Nescio," vocis habent.
Nec maior numerus tantum potuisset in hostem
 reddere securos: fortis egenus adest.
Aspera sors contra est, ubi vim comitatur egestas;
320 ingenium velox expedit atque sagax.
Fortis egens, quicquid valet, ut valet, optat et audet;
 Ysengrimus erat fortis egensque nimis,
pro pietatis habens decreto parcere nolle,
 dumque timet ventri, saepe timenda subit.
325 Consiliis spatium non suppetit hoste propinquo;
 alternant dubie, quae facienda forent.
Obvius it Ioseph, reliqui prope terga sequuntur,
 explorat primum foederis arma timor.
Eminus exclamant: "Frater, benedicite! Nullum
330 vidimus hic monachum, septima friget hyemps."
Frater ad haec: "Tanti fuerat maledicite dici!
 Credite nos alium proposuisse iocum.
Arma quid haec vobis? Vivumne quid orbis habebit?
 Quo genere et qui vos? Ad quid et unde sati?"

It's better to retreat; I'm certainly not a surveyor—or if I
were, supposing I made bad measurements, would I be safe   310
under your leadership? Two are as good as an army to a single
opponent, and there are four champions here. Even if one
were killed, the anger of three will still rage strong."

Reynard put his weak spirit into shape with exhortations,
and the frightened old man went forward with the fox fol-
lowing. The brothers caught sight of their visitor, and were   315
not very happy at the sight, but their only comment was
"What's going to happen? I don't know." Their greater num-
ber couldn't make them safe against such an enemy; a crea-
ture both strong and hungry was in their presence. Cruel
fate is unfavorable, when hunger is joined to strength; a   320
swift and shrewd mind is of great advantage. A strong and
hungry creature aims at and ventures on whatever he can, in
whatever way he can. Ysengrimus was both strong and ex-
tremely hungry. His idea of mercy was to be willing to spare
nothing, and while he feared for his stomach, he would un-
dergo many fearful things. There was no time for delibera-   325
tions, since the enemy was close; in perplexity they wavered
as to what should be done. Joseph went to meet him, and
the others followed behind him; fear led them to try out the
weapon of treaty-making first. From a distance, they called
out: "Blessings on you, brother! We've seen no monk here   330
for seven freezing winters."

The brother replied: "You might as well have said 'curses
on you!' Believe me, it's another game I have in mind.
What are you doing with these weapons? Is the world
going to see some action? From what family and who are

335 "Primus," ait Ioseph—venientia verba refringit
    monachus impatiens: "Sermo sit iste brevis!
    Sit sermo brevis iste, aliud quam verba requiro,
      quaerere nil aliud me nisi verba putant!
    Sit brevis aut nullus! Nullus michi sermo videtur
340   esse brevi melior." "Fer, domine," inquit, "erit.
    En ego sum Ioseph, si cognita nominis huius
      fama tibi," (et fratres nominat inde suos)
    "Obsequiisque tuis iussum ad portabile prompti,
      pacis amatores, vulgus inerme sumus.
345 Tuque licet parvas grates ductore merente
      ob causae quid in haec veneris arva, liquet:
    finibus ut medio signatis limite norit,
      qua sibi committat pascua quisque tenus."
    "Nomina," mensor ait, "novi, sed roboris huius,
350   quod video, vobis rebar inesse parum.
    Gratulor obsequiis, utinamque essetis inermes!
      Obsequium posset promptius esse michi;
    at nunc obsequium non tam michi ferre potestis,
      quam vos obsequio constat egere meo.
355 Taliter armati non conspirastis in aequas
      dividere hanc partes, si sineremus, humum.
    Conflictum dirimam, sed nunc pro ventre loquendum est:
      mando epulas." Contra Colvarianus ait:
    "Quas, domine, hic epulas mandas tibi? Vivimus herbis,
360   nec teneros dentes pabula dura decent.
    Mollibus his alimur, molles ad mollia nati,
      dentatos metuens grex sine dente fere."
    Respondit senior: "Sic vos ego dicere iussi?
      Vocibus his forsan ludificandus ero?

you? Whence and for what were you begotten?" "First," said 335
Joseph—but the impatient monk interrupted the progress
of his words: "Let this speech be a short one! A short one, I
say; I'm after something other than words (they think I'm
looking for nothing but talk!). Speak briefly or not at all; no
kind of utterance seems to me better than a short one." 340
"Give me a chance, sir," he said, "and it will be. Well, I'm Jo-
seph, if the name is known to you by report," (and then he
named his brothers), "ready to serve you in any command
that we can manage; we're peace loving, harmless folk. Al- 345
though the one who has brought you deserves little thanks,
it's clear for what reason you've come to these fields: so that
the boundaries may be marked out, and each of us may
know by a central limit the extent of the pasture granted
him."

"I'm acquainted with your names," said the surveyor, "but
I little thought that you possessed the strength I behold. I 350
thank you for your services, but I wish you *were* harmless!
Then your service could be a more immediate one; but now
you're not so able to do me a service as it's clear you need me
to do one for you. Armed with such weapons, you haven't 355
managed to agree (with my permission) to divide this land
into equal parts. I'll put an end to the dispute. But now it's
time to speak about my stomach: I want to order a meal."
Colvarianus replied: "What meal, sir, will you order here?
We live on grass, and hard food is no good for our weak 360
teeth. We're fed on soft things; we're born soft and for soft-
ness, an almost toothless herd, afraid of those with teeth."
The old one replied: "Is that how I ordered you to speak?
Perhaps you think you can fool me with that speech?

365 Dicite, quod vultis, non sic ego fallar, ut esse,
    cum michi sint dentes, vos sine dente putem;
non verbis sed credo oculis, ostendite dentes!"
    Ostendunt, visis obstupet ille diu.
Subter enim paucos cernit nullosque superne;
370   hic primum redeunt spes animusque lupo.
Sevocat exultans vulpem lenique susurro
    alloquitur: "Verum est, quod tibi dico, tene!
Miraris facinusque vocas, quod claustra reliqui,
    hos inter fratres vita beata foret;
375 certe si similes his essent fratribus illi,
    tam latera effusi, tam sine dente pii,
hanc et in usque diem durasset at unus eorum,
    me claustralis ibi norma teneret adhuc!"
Repplicat haec vulpes: "Dentes non esse timendos,
380   patrue, vidisti, viribus ora carent.
Litigium tollit praemissi cautio verbi;
    unde timor fuerat, pax tibi certa patet.
Sum super eventu liber, quicumque sequetur;
    cras nolo obicias: 'Tu michi causa mali.'"
385 Ille refert: "Quicquid facient michi quattuor isti,
    haec equidem ignosco, sed tibi grator ego."
Procedit trepidosque pio solamine fratres
    taliter ungebat: "Ne trepidate, precor!
Vos etenim, ut video, tristes, credebar abisse;
390   serio non abii, ponite, quaeso, metum!
Votivum refero rumorem, audite: revertor
    spectandus pleno dentibus ore bonis.
(Heu michi! Vos, fratres, sine dentibus estis, ego ecce,
    ut butirum culter, dentibus ossa seco.)

Say what you like, I won't be tricked into imagining that al- 365
though I've got teeth, you are toothless. I don't trust words
but my eyes—show your teeth!"

They opened up, and he was dumbfounded for a long
time at what he saw; he saw that they were small on the bot-
tom, and nonexistent on top. Now for the first time hope 370
and spirits returned to the wolf. He exultingly called the fox
aside and in a soft whisper, said to him: "What I tell you is
true, believe me! You express surprise, and call it a crime,
that I left the cloister; but among these brothers, life would
be blessed. Truly, if the other brothers were like these, so 375
broad in the belly, so gentle and toothless, and if even one
of them had lasted up to the present day, the monastic or-
der would still hold me there!" The fox answered thus:
"You've seen that their teeth aren't to be feared, uncle, and 380
their mouths lack any power. The precaution of a prelimi-
nary parley removes the need for conflict; from the quarter
where fear lay, it's clear to you that peace is to be relied on.
I'm not bound by the event, however it turns out; I don't
want you to cast up at me tomorrow: 'You're the cause of my
trouble.'"

The other replied: "Whatever these four may do to me, I 385
not only pardon you, but thank you for." He went forward,
and buttered up the flustered brethren with comforting
gentleness, in these words: "Don't be alarmed, I beg you! I
see that you're sad because you thought I'd gone away, but I 390
didn't really go away, so throw off your anxiety! I bring back
welcome news; listen! Back I come with a mouth full of
good teeth to show you. You, brothers—what a pity!—are
toothless, and look, I cut through bones with my teeth as a

395 Inspicite," (et rictus expanderat) "ecce videte!
　　Hos habeo dentes, ecce videte!" Vident,
exclamant visis, nec maior causa timendi
　　processisse fuit quam repedasse retro.
Sic suis et riguisse canis, quos pulte comesta
400　vis eadem et rabies induit, ora ferunt,
alterutrum longo donec fudere duello
　　sus, canis; icta canis viscera, morsa suis.
Dentibus inspectis amisso pectore Ioseph
　　clamitat, in cacabum protinus ire putans:
405 "O pater, hae falces ad quid tibi? Prata recusas
　　radere! Faenisecae, qui potiantur, emant."
Laetus ad haec senior: "Novi metere ipse metamque,
　　quae vos prata meti non timuistis heri.
His soleo lucos, quales in vertice fertis,
410　caedere, et hos veni; quod scio, sector opus.
Hinc et ab antiquis cognominor Ysengrimus
　　Corniseca, et mores apposuere 'Bonus.'
ut taceam carnes, his quaelibet ossa moluntur
　　dentibus." Irridens lene Belinus ait:
415 "Quid cum carne tibi? Tu scisso fictus amictu
　　cerneris ad normam!" Rettulit ille iocans:
"Vos miseret conscissa mei tegumenta ferentis;
　　vos, unde haec reparem, constat habere satis.
Maximus es fratrum, Ioseph, tua maxima pellis,
420　hanc michi praestabis, tu satis usus ea es.
Hac utriusque michi lateris reparabo fenestras;
　　tegmine Bernardi rete parabo novum

knife cuts butter. Look!" (he had opened wide his jaws), "See 395
here! These are the teeth I've got; see here!" They saw, and
they exclaimed at the sight. The idea of running away was
no less a cause of fear to them than the idea of advancing.
Just so, they say, did the jaws of the pig and the dog bristle
when they were seized by equal violence and fury over some 400
eaten porridge, until they hurled themselves at each other in
a long duel; the dog's guts were battered, and the pig's were
bitten.

When he'd seen the teeth, Joseph's heart sank, and think-
ing he was heading straight for the cooking pot, he cried
out: "Oh father, what are you doing with these scythes? You 405
don't want to mow the fields! Let the mowers buy them for
their own possession." The old one happily replied: "I know
how to mow, and I shall myself mow a few meadows whose
cropping you weren't afraid of yesterday. With these teeth
I'm accustomed to cut down forests of the kind you wear on
your head—and those I've come to cut down. I practice the 410
trade I know. For that reason, I was nicknamed Ysengrimus
Horn-mower by the ancients, and my virtuous qualities have
added the title 'the Good.' Any bones, not to mention meat,
are ground up by these teeth." Gently mocking, Belinus
said: "What have you to do with meat? With your torn 415
cloak, you look as if you were got up for monastic life!" The
other replied with banter: "You're sorry for me because I'm
wearing torn clothing; it's clear that you've got the materials
from which I can repair it. You're the biggest of the broth-
ers, Joseph, you've got the biggest fleece; you'll give it to 420
me—you've had enough use of it. With it, I'll repair the
gaps in both my sides. With Bernard's hide I'll make a new

(fors piscabor adhuc, aer post nubila candet,
  orbita fortunae ducit utroque rotam).
425 At mea sanguineo livore corona notatur,
  candeat exuviis illa, Beline, tuis;
Colvariane, tuo faciam michi tegmine saccum.
  Nec vos sollicitet, quid michi saccus agat:
si qua superfuerit, coriis inclusa voranti
430 pars michi; sin autem, postera lucra feram.
Hoc scio, non facile haec alii tegumenta daretis,
  ter quamvis solidos redderet ipse novem;
verum sponte michi datis haec, sed scitis, ut aiunt,
  'Non omnes homines convenit esse pares.'
435 Ergo prius viso miror non missa fuisse;
  haec pendenda gravi pondere culpa fuit.
Sed quia vos video non excusasse iubenti,
  ammissum probitas haec veniale facit.
Quod si (vera licet nil ausos dicere) vosmet
440 malle frui coriis quam dare nosco michi,
dissimulans animum, quia iussa veretur, ut ultro
  obsequitur domino verna iubente piger.
Sit pellis sua cuique, meum est, quod clauditur intus.
  Non mereor laudem tam mediocre loquens?
445 Sit deforme licet multo michi vulnere tegmen,
  non michi vestra facit tam placuisse decor.
Quin coriis caream, donate, quod intus habetur,
  non poteram salvo poscere honore minus;
vos quoque fortassis michi parva dedisse puderet,
450 patribus hoc vestri saepe dedere meis.
Cumque ego vos tractem socialiter atque paterne,
  nunc superest tantum danda repente dari.

fishing net—perhaps I'll go fishing again some time. (Bright weather follows clouds, and Fortune's course leads her wheel up as well as down.) But my tonsure is marked by a bloody 425 bruise; it will regain whiteness from your hide, Belinus. Colvarianus, from your hide I'll make myself a bag, and don't let it trouble you what use the bag will be to me. If there's any portion left over when I've eaten, it will be wrapped in the hide for me; if not, I'll carry my future winnings in it. I 430 know this, that you wouldn't lightly give those hides to anyone else, even though he were to give you three times nine shillings, whereas you give them to me of your own accord; but you know, as they say, 'It's not right that all men should be equal.' So, I'm surprised that they weren't sent to me be- 435 fore you saw me; this was a fault to be given serious weight. But because I see that you didn't make excuses when I issued the order, this plain dealing makes your former omission venial. But if (although you didn't dare to speak the truth) I know that you prefer to have the use of your hides 440 rather than give them to me, nevertheless a lazy servant will suppress his reactions and obey his master's commands as if voluntarily, because he respects orders. Let any one of you keep his fleece, but what's inside it is mine. Don't I deserve praise, when I speak so moderately? Although my 445 hide is made ugly by its multiple wounds, the beauty of yours doesn't please me so much as my own. No, I'll do without the hides; but give me what's contained in them. I couldn't ask for less and preserve my self-respect. Perhaps, also, you would be ashamed to give me something trivial, but this is what your ancestors often presented to mine. 450 Since I treat you like a friend and a father, this much remains: that what's to be given should be given immediately.

Omnibus efficiam vobis re taliter acta,
    iurgia ne moveat partificandus ager."
455 Audierant fratres, quod non audisse libebat,
    et stat raptor hians impatiensque morae.
Verba Belinus ad haec non multum territus audet
    talia, nimirum iunior atque rudis:
"Tu super his satis es, domine Ysengrime, locutus;
460   quidque velis, fuerat te reticente palam.
Sed nescimus adhuc, cui praeparet alea lucrum,
    fortuna varias distribuente vices.
Si fuerit fors fida tibi, potiere cupitis;
    dispositum nobis hoc super ire iube."
465 Ysengrimus ad hunc sermonem turbidus ore
    et vultu pariter talia dicta furit:
"Stulti, nonne satis, quicquid delibero, nostis?
    Quid modo consiliis est opus? — Ite tamen!
Et sit consilium, quod non audire recusem.
470   Currite dictatum, porro redite citi,
terminus est horae cunctos urgentis ad escam,
    inque meis hora est faucibus acta diu."
Stant trepidi fratres. Ioseph, quid suadeat, haeret,
    poscebatur enim, denique fatus ita est:
475 "Non bene perpendi, fratres, quid congruat actu;
    sub grave discrimen concidit iste dies.
Causa levis fit saepe gravis sub iudice pravo,
    iudicis hic causa est improbitate gravis.
Auribus in vestris habeat mea suasio pondus,
480   iam vereor nostrae tempus adesse necis.
Expedit ergo bonis illiso pulsibus hoste
    non impune mori vel meruisse fugam.

When the business is done in this way, I'll ensure for all of
you that the dividing of the field won't cause any disputes."

The brothers had listened to what they'd rather not have 455
heard, and the plunderer stood with jaws open, impatient
of delay. Belinus, not greatly frightened, ventured to rejoin
with these words, being very young and untutored: "You've
said enough on these topics, Dom Ysengrimus. What you 460
wanted was obvious without you opening your mouth. But
we still don't know who is going to win in this dice game,
since Fortune doles out varying strokes of luck. So long as
chance stays on your side, you will enjoy what you wanted.
Give us the O.K. to step aside and talk this over." At this 465
speech Ysengrimus, his face and voice both contorted,
spluttered out the following: "Fools, don't you know well
enough what I have in mind? Then what need of delibera-
tion now?—But get on with it! Let there be consultation,
which I may not object to listening to; run off for your chat- 470
ter, but come back again quickly. It's just verging on the hour
which calls everyone to their food—and indeed, in my jaws,
that hour has long passed."

The brothers remained in perturbation. Joseph hesitated
about what to advise, but at their request he finally said this:
"I haven't been able to consider very thoroughly what might 475
be appropriate for us to do, brothers. This day hangs in great
peril. A trivial lawsuit often becomes a serious one under a
bad judge; so this case is a serious one because of the judge's
dishonesty. Let my advice have weight in your ears, because 480
I'm afraid that the time of our death has now come. It's
therefore necessary that we batter the enemy with hearty
blows, so that we either put up a fight before we die, or else

Finis tetragoni medius lupus ipse sit agri,
　　aequale ut spatium portio quaeque trahat;
485 iamque interposito partes aequante quaternas
　　　motus ab opposito cardine quisque ruet,
　　sic tamen, ut stadium (gravis est emenda sub isto
　　　iudice) praesumat nullus adire prior.
　　Vaticinor, sospes non emendaverit ausum,
490 qui prior irruerit; quisque timeto sibi!
　　Dentatum est stadium, mordebit meta, cavete,
　　　nos sibi, non nobis dividere arva cupit.
　　Mensorem mora longa gravat, breviemus oportet,
　　　sic igitur nobis assiliendus erit:
495 frontem ego; tu caudam, Bernarde; Beline, sinistrum
　　　incute; tu dextrum, Colvariane, latus.
　　Cornibus ex rigidis prima et bona fercula demus;
　　　si plus optarit, postea nosmet edat.
　　Utere vi, Bernarde, tua, tu fortis ut ursus;
500 irrue, si nescit dividere arva, doce.
　　Qui minimus nostrum est, uno pertunderet ictu
　　　tres clipeos, tantis fortior unus erit?"
　　Voces "nosmet edat," "prior emendaverit," istas
　　　hauserat arrecta callidus aure senex;
505 gratatur fratresque vocat, venere vocati,
　　　monachus astantes hac ratione fovet:
　　"Consultum satis est, fratres! Facietis honeste.
　　　Plurima dixistis, quae placuere michi:
　　'emendaturos et edendos' nescio quosnam—
510 credite, non fallo, praemeditabar idem.

manage to escape. Let the wolf himself be the midway
boundary of the four-sided field, so that each section covers
an equal space. And when he's placed in the middle, dividing   485
up the four sections equally, let each of us rush from the cor-
ners facing him, but in such a way that no one ventures to
approach the boundary before the others; with this judge,
the penalty for it will be a heavy one! I predict that anyone
who rushes out ahead of the others won't survive intact to
pay the penalty for his rashness; let everyone look out for   490
himself! The goal has teeth, the post will bite; take care! He
wants to slice us up for himself, not the field for us. The long
delay is irritating the surveyor, and we need to cut things
short, so this is how we'll make the attack: I'll take the head,   495
and you, Bernard, the tail; Belinus, strike at the left side, and
you, Colvarianus, the right. Let's give him some nice appe-
tizers from our hard horns, and let him eat us afterward if
he wants any more. Put your strength to good use, Bernard,
you have the strength of the bear. Rush at him, and teach   500
him how to divide up fields, if he hasn't learned. The least of
us would burst through three shields with one charge, and
shall a single creature be stronger than so many?"

The words "let him eat us" and "ahead of the others . . .
he'll pay the penalty"—these, the wily old man had taken
in with pricked-up ears. He was overjoyed, and called the   505
brothers, who came when called. The monk encouraged
them with the following speech as they stood before him:
"There's been enough consultation, brothers! You'll do the
right thing; you said some things which pleased me. You said
that some people or other 'were going to pay the penalty
and be eaten'; believe me, I'm not kidding, that's just what I   510

Nil igitur restat nisi fractam nectere pacem,
　　pauca tamen vobis ante iubere velim:
tres aut unus eat de vobis gramina carptum;
　　tres ierint, unum, tres, eat unus, edam.
515　Scilicet hoc facto partibor pascua recte,
　　praeter enim sibimet non studet alvus egens."
Primus ad haec fratrum: "Melius providimus," inquit,
　　"lis fremeret medio forsitan orta cibo—
quid si deciderent collisis cornibus astra?
520　　Iurgia quapropter sunt dirimenda prius.
Neve tibi illicitae patiare cibaria mensae;
　　quod fueris frater, te meminisse decet.
Tu medius nobis distans abeuntibus aeque
　　quattuor ad prati climata limes eris.
525　Tunc bannum statues, ne nostrum quilibet ausit
　　iudice te metam transiluisse datam;
et cum nos, cupidi partes extendere, bannum
　　fregerimus, dabimur legitima esca tibi.
Fercula tot, ne plura velis habuisse, dabuntur,
530　　si tibi sufficiet quinque vorasse quater."
Ysengrimus ovans medii fit terminus agri,
　　spectandique avidus dux senioris adest.
Frontibus oppositis fratres extrema tuentur;
　　inde gravi bannus conditione sonat.
535　Assiliunt fratres, Ioseph caput incidit amplum,
　　Bernardus fortis posteriora subit,
irrumpunt alii costas. Heu stulta timendi
　　improbitas quotiens utile perdit opus!
Si probitas animi vires aequasset eorum,
540　　illa lupo potuit summa fuisse dies.

was planning. So nothing remains but to patch up the broken peace. But first I want to give you a few orders. Either three of you or one of you can go away and nibble the grass; if three go away, I'll eat one, if one goes away, I'll eat three. Of course, when this is done, I'll divide the fields correctly; but a hungry stomach has no concern for anything besides itself." The first brother replied: "We've made better plans. Perhaps a quarrel would start raging in the middle of the meal, and what if the stars were to fall at the shock of our clashing horns? On this account, the dispute must be cleared out of the way first. Nor should you permit yourself the food of an illicit table; you ought to remember that you were a monk. We shall retire to the four parts of the field, and you, in the middle at an equal distance from us, shall be the marker. Then you'll issue a prohibition: that none of us should dare, while you are in charge, to cross the given limit. And if we, greedy to enlarge our share, break the prohibition, we'll be granted to you as legitimate food. You'll be given so many dishes you won't wish to have more—if it'll be enough for you to have gobbled down four times five." 515 520 525 530

The jubilant Ysengrimus became the boundary marker of the field's center, while the old man's guide was also present, eager to watch. The brothers occupied the edges of the field, facing each other, and then the prohibition, with its heavy restriction, sounded forth. The brothers attacked; Joseph struck the broad head, the mighty Bernard assailed his back, the others rushed at his ribs. Ah, how often has a useful achievement been spoiled by the foolish weakness of fear! If their resolution of spirit had been equal to their physical strength, that could have been the wolf's last hour. 535 540

Debita sed magnae servantur fata Salaurae,
    egregiamque manent tanta trophaea suem.
Machina Bernardi tanto ruit acta tumultu
    obvia, si Ioseph continuasset opem
545 obvius, aut fratri media Bernardus in alvo
    cornua fregisset cornibus acta suis,
aut certe cupidas ad fauces usque volasset,
    per longum ventris raptus inane cavi.
At citior cunctis Ioseph licet afforet, insons
550   emendare timens, praecelerasse cavet,
os avidum metuens, obliquus dextra peregit
    timpora, nec cerebri portio parva fluit;
et nisi cessissent prae vasto timpora pulsu,
    plaga penetrasset timpus utrumque simul.
555 Sed temere cautum est, Ioseph perfregerat aurem
    timporaque, et quinae dissiluere molae.
At fratres medii praeter discrimina cordis
    obvia per vacuum cornua pectus agunt.
Si foret in planis echo, iam cardine ab omni
560   cornibus oblisis assonuisset ager.
Cornua subducunt impulsus ausa secundos;
    Bernardusque obiter posteriora petit,
impete sub cuius primo, dum fratre secundum
    ocior opposito Colvarianus agit,
565 excussere lupum, veluti fortissima mittit
    machina quassuram moenia firma petram.
Sed nisi succussum Bernardus in alta rotasset,
    dum simul a dextris Colvarianus adit,

But the destiny due to the great Salaura was reserved for her, and so mighty a victory was left to the noble sow. Bernard's battering ram rushed forward on its course with such violence that if Joseph had carried through his assistance on the same trajectory, Bernard would either have broken his brother's horns with his own as they met in the middle of the wolf's stomach, or he would, for sure, have been impelled through the long void of the hollow belly and hurtled on as far as the greedy jaws. But although Joseph was on the scene, and quicker than all of them, the innocent creature, afraid of paying the penalty, was wary of outstripping the others. Afraid of the greedy mouth, he pierced the right temple sideways on; and no small part of the brain spilled out. Had not his temples drawn back before the mighty onslaught, the blow would have penetrated both temples at once—but boldness was mingled with caution; Joseph shattered his ear and temple, and five teeth sprang out. And the brothers assigned to the middle drove their opposing horns through the hollow part of his chest, missing the danger area of his heart. If there were an echo on plains, the field would now have resounded from every corner at their clashing horns.

They withdrew their horns to venture on a second series of attacks, and without delay Bernard made for his hindquarters. With his first charge, and while Colvarianus, swifter than the brother opposite him, made his second, they bowled the wolf over, as a powerful siege engine catapults a rock to batter down strong ramparts. But when he was knocked off his feet, if Bernard had not tossed him up high in the air while Colvarianus was simultaneously doing

pressisset miserum moles onerosa Belinum,
570 qui volitante lupo paene reversus erat,
nec rapidos cursus potuit compescere, donec
 oppositum fratrem praecipitavit agens.
Limes in obliquum cedens orientis et austri
 decidit, ut spatium transiit octo pedum.
575 Ut subito victum videt immotumque iacere,
 Bernardus tumido clamitat ore iocans:
"Trans medium signas, domine Ysengrime, nimisque
 trans medium signas, fit male limes ibi!
Istorsum redeas! Ego sum Bernardus, et audes
580 iure suo fratres expoliare meos?
Sospite me Ioseph sua detrahis atque Belino?
 Non aliter quam sic dividere arva soles?
Parte mea potiar, fratres fraudare refuto;
 est potior frater quam spatiosus ager."
585 Tunc Ioseph: "Bernarde, sapis? Quid inaniter horres?
 Aptius hic limes, quam stetit ille, iacet.
O quam stante iacens, quam stans est pluris eunte!
 Sic iaceat certe, sic iacuisse velim!
Lene feram mea dampna, velit sua ferre Belinus;
590 visne, Beline, pati?" "Nolo," Belinus ait,
"Cur ego iacturam paterer? Mea iura tuebor;
 qui vult, dampna ferat, non michi ferre libet."
Pulsibus ergo hostem validis aggressus in usque
 praecipitat partem, Colvariane, tuam.
595 "Sic statuendus," ait "tibi, Colvariane, videtur
 limes an est aliter? Sic ego pono, vide.
Sic ego, non aliter, didici signare; resigna,
 signari melius sicubi posse putas."

his bit on the right, the weighty mass would have squashed poor Belinus, who had almost got back to the middle as the wolf took his flight, and was unable to check his rapid strides before he crashed into the brother on the other side. The boundary mark himself, retreating diagonally southeast, fell after traversing eight feet in the air. When all at once he saw him lying defeated and motionless, Bernard elatedly cried out in jubilation: "Your sign's not in the middle, Dom Ysengrimus, your sign's way over the middle! That's a lousy place to put a boundary post! Get back there! I'm Bernard—do you dare to deprive my brothers of their right? Do you leave me untouched, and take away the property of Joseph and Belinus? Is this how you usually divide up fields? I'll enjoy possession of my share, but I refuse to cheat my brothers; a brother is worth more than an extensive estate."

Then Joseph said: "Bernard, have you any sense? Why are you making such a fuss about nothing? This boundary post is more convenient lying down here than it was when it stood up. Oh, how much better it is lying than standing, and better standing than in motion! Assuredly, let it lie like this, this is how I'd like it to lie. I'll bear my injuries with mildness, if Belinus is willing to bear his—won't you put up with them, Belinus?" "I won't," said Belinus. "Why should I suffer loss? I'll defend my rights. Anyone who wants to, can suffer injury, but it doesn't suit me to suffer it." So he attacked the enemy with powerful shoves and pushed him right into your section, Colvarianus. "Do you think, Colvarianus," he said, "that this is how the boundary mark is to be fixed, or differently? This is how I place it, look! This, and no other way, is how I've learned to set the mark; reposition it, if you think it can be placed anywhere better."

570

575

580

585

590

595

Colvarianus ad haec: "Temere in mea pascua venit.
600   Per tibi quam frater debeo care fidem,
in mea iura nimis cecidit; nisi fugerit ultro,
    vivam, alias illi tutius esse foret."
Tunc bis quinque pedes Bernardi in pascua pulsans
    non dubitat miserum praecipitare senem.
605 "Dic," inquit, "Bernarde, bene est hic limes?" at ille:
    "Nescio, Reinardum consule, novit enim.
Corniseca hic fieret fortasse, secare solebat
    cornua." Tunc clamat Colvarianus ovans:
"Huc accede, miser Reinarde! Quid eminus abstas?
610   Morsibus an nostris terrificatus abes?
Nec patrui dentes metuas, mansuesse videntur.
    Te siquidem Ioseph poscit adesse, veni!
Colvarianus et hoc, non gens externa precatur;
    accelera sodes, consiliator ades!
615 Circumfertur enim limes, tu siste vagantem,
    si melius nosti; nos dubitamus, ubi."
His nisi ridiculis Reinardus et ipse quid addat,
    finditur aut moritur, prosilit ergo celer;
qui patruum tam velle videns quam nolle perire
620   sermonis talem fertur inisse modum:
"Sic bene, sic, fratres, operaminor, approbo factum;
    iurgia nunc vobis non placuisse liquet.
Quam bene mensorem vestri satiastis agelli!
    Pro hoc epulo vobis gratia debet agi;
625 fercula viginti large promissa dedistis,
    promptior idcirco, quando voletis, erit."
"Non alias grates hac pro dape poscimus," aiunt,
    "dividat hic nobis iugera sicque cubet."

Colvarianus replied: "He entered my land rashly; by the 600
faith which I owe you, dear brother, he's infringing on my
rights. Unless he goes away of his own accord, as I live, it
would be safer for him to be somewhere else." Then he
didn't hesitate to hurl the old man with a blow ten feet into
Bernard's meadow. "Tell me, Bernard," he said, "is the 605
boundary mark all right here?" But the latter said: "I don't
know; ask Reynard, he knows. Perhaps this one would like
to become a horn-mower; he used to mow down horns."

Then Colvarianus called out in jubilation: "Come here,
Reynard, you wretch! What are you standing off at a dis-
tance for? You're not keeping away because you're terrified 610
of our bites, are you? And don't be afraid of your uncle's
teeth either; they seem to have softened up. Since it's Joseph
who asks for your presence, come! Colvarianus, not some
outsider, asks for this too. Be a friend and hurry up, be our
adviser! The boundary mark, you see, is pushed around; you 615
put a stop to his wanderings, if you know better. We're in
doubt about his position!" Reynard was about to burst or
die if he couldn't add something to these witticisms, so he
jumped forward quickly, and seeing his uncle as glad to die
as not, is said to have begun the following manner of speech: 620
"This, brothers, is how you should dispense charity; I ap-
prove of what you have done. Now it's clear that quarrels
aren't your line. How thoroughly you've stuffed the surveyor
of your little field! You ought to be thanked for this banquet.
You've given the twenty courses you so generously prom- 625
ised, so he'll be the readier to help you in future, when you
want him." "We ask no other thanks for this meal," they
said, "than that he lie like that and so divide up the acres for

"Insanitis," ait, "michi terminus iste videtur
630   iurgia non dirimens, immo dirempta novans.
Impingendus erat, vos expegistis et illum,
       signaret mediam cum bene limes humum.
Nunc ubi sistatur, toto perquiritis arvo,
       praeteritae lites exorientur item.
635 At minus in vosmet quam me peccastis in ipsum:
       adduxi patruum dividere arva meum;
scissuras sarcire miser sperabat hiantes
       exuviis vestris, spes caret illa fide,
nam maiora patent et plura foramina primis,
640   praecipitem toto deinde rotatis agro.
Indubie dici vos rustica turba potestis:
       lusibus aptatam creditis esse pilam.
Consilium sapiens et quaerit et audit et implet;
       indocilem turbam nil docuisse iuvat.
645 Scire, quid inscitum, qui discit scita, monetur;
       qui caret ingenio, non erit arte vigens.
Vivit adhuc spisso tutus sub cortice limes,
       et nimium vestri vendicat ille soli.
Ibit adhuc, quo non praeformidatur iturus,
650   atque aliquid pacis, quod doleatis, aget.
Tollatur cortex, ut inutilis areat arbor,
       cortice detracto fit minor atque iacet.
Ite, genus fatuum, capita inclinate iacenti,
       et dulci patruo pocula ferte meo!
655 Quisque parem numerum: quot pocula maximus illi
       intulerit, minimus tot pietatis agat!
Non aliter vobis placor." Sic fatur et ipse
       dilectum patruum decoriare parat.

us." "You're mad," he said. "To me this signpost seems not   630
to remove trouble, but to re-create it when it's already re-
moved. The marker should have been hammered in, but
you've jolted it out, when it would have marked out the cen-
ter of the ground very well. Now you're hunting through the
whole field for somewhere it can stay, and the quarrels of the
past will start up again. But you've committed less of a fault   635
against yourselves than against me. I brought my uncle here
to divide up the fields. The wretch hoped to patch up his
gaping slits with your hides, and that hope was illusory, for
the holes gape bigger and more numerous than before. And   640
now he's prostrate, you roll him round the whole field.
Without doubt you can be labeled a bunch of louts, since
you think he's a ball designed for games. A wise man seeks
advice, listens to and follows it; it's no good teaching the in-
educable hoi polloi. Anyone who learns what is known, is   645
advised to know what he doesn't know; someone lacking in
brains won't do well at learning. The boundary marker is still
living inside his thick skin, and he's taking up too much of
your ground. He'll go somewhere where there'll be no warn-
ing fear of him, and he'll do something to contribute to   650
peace that you'll suffer for. Let the bark be removed, so that
the fruitless tree withers up; when the skin is taken away,
he'll take up less room as he lies there. Go on, you stupid
race, bend your heads to him as he lies, and administer some
toasts to my dear uncle! Each one an equal number; how-   655
ever many loving cups the eldest serves up to him, let the
youngest show him an equal amount of affection! This is the
only way I'll be reconciled to you." So saying, he himself got
ready to skin his beloved uncle, biting with savage rage, so

Morsu saevit atrox, ingentia frusta trahuntur,
660   morderet siquidem lenius ipse Satan.
Assiliunt prompti fratres pulsantque vicissim;
    inter pulsandum verba benigna volant.
Ter feriens Ioseph proclamat: "Pocula grates
    redde propinanti prima, propino tibi,
665 accipe, cor miserum refove!" Quater actus in illum
    proxima Bernardus pocula largus agit:
"Quod licet," inquit, "ago, non ut desidero possum.
    Sunt dentes rari, cornua densa michi;
quod minus est in dente boni, bona cornua supplent."
670   Bis vicibus ternis Colvarianus adit:
"Plus tibi, frater," ait, "cupio praebere vetorque,
    Reinardus vetuit pocula plura dari.
Si brevis offensam cenantis cena meretur,
    addere plus cupiens non luat, immo vetans."
675 Bis senis adiens hac fatur voce Belinus:
    "Offer ave, sodes, ecce Belinus adest!
Ultimus hic crater, sed non vilissimus idem,
    iste calix offert vina Boema tibi!
Quis tibi potus in hoc veniat cratere, ligurri,
680   ditius hoc alios nil habuisse reor,
ultimus iste calix, hunc, si potes, ebibe totum!"
    Tunc vulpes: "Cuncti," clamat, "adite simul!"
Fortiter inde omnes adeunt, quo more feruntur
    in cacabo duram frangere pila fabam.
685 Monachus ille volens credi quandoque fuisse
    omne pie suffert dedecus atque silet.
In sua defesso redituri robore demum
    atria, seminecem deseruere lupum.

that huge pieces came away, and even Satan himself would   660
bite more gently.

The brothers promptly charged, and struck in turn, while
friendly words flew round between blows. Striking three
times, Joseph proclaimed: "Thank the one who offers you
the first round of drinks; this lot's on me! Take it, and revive   665
your poor spirits!" The generous Bernard, impelled against
him four times, offered the next round: "I do what's al-
lowed," he said, "I can't do as much as I want. My teeth are
sparse, and my horns thickly set. What's lacking in my teeth,
my good horns make up for." Colvarianus came up six times: 670
"I want to offer you more, brother, and am forbidden," he
said. "Reynard forbade that more drinks should be given. If
the scanty dinner incurs the diner's displeasure, let the pen-
alty not be paid by him who wants to add more to it, but by
him who forbids it." Coming up twelve times, Belinus spoke   675
with these words: "Say hello, friend, Belinus is here! This is
the last glass but not the most contemptible; this glass of-
fers you Bohemian wines! Whatever drink comes to you in
this glass, drink up; I'm sure the others had nothing fuller   680
than this. This is the last glass; drain it all, if you can!"

Then the fox cried: "All charge together!" Then they all
charged vigorously, rather as pestles are said to crush beans
in a bowl. The monk, wanting it to be believed that he *had*   685
been a monk at one time, meekly suffered the whole out-
rage and was silent. At last, when their strength was worn
out, they went back to their homes, leaving the wolf half
dead.

BOOK THREE

Ut miseros fortuna premit, mansuescere nescit,
    multatos multis pluribus illa ferit.
Nec super addendi metam mox provehit ullum,
    nec quemquam subita proterit illa manu,
5 impia namque pie, mala leniter et male lenis
    posse perire vetat, velle perire facit.
Materiam servans irae non prorsus inhorret,
    impatiens pacis convaluisse vetat,
et minus in quosquam est probitatis nacta iuvandos,
10   quam super angendos improbitatis habet.
Scilicet aeternum laedit fidissima quosdam,
    cum penitus nulli faverit absque dolo,
nam maiora solent miseris adversa nocere,
    prospera quam felix ullus habere potest.
15 Vidi ego felices, quos saltem infamia laesit,
    porro quibus miseris defuit omnis honor.
Sospite felices vita plerosque repellit,
    sed raros humiles erigit ante necem.
Cum multis bona pauca malis ulciscitur inde,
20   conciliat paucis hinc mala multa bonis.

When Fortune is oppressing the wretched, she knows no re-lenting, so that to those whom she has already punished, she deals out yet more blows. Similarly, she is not quick to push anyone beyond the limits to any increase in their suffering, and does not annihilate anyone with one swift stroke. Mercilessly merciful, kindly malicious, and mali- 5 ciously kind, she forbids the possibility of death, while she creates the wish for it. She broods long over matter for anger, and doesn't bristle up immediately; yet she is so im-patient of peace that she prevents it from getting properly established. And she has less benignity toward those whom she is to favor, than malice toward those whom she is to 10 torment. That is, there are some people whom she is utterly invariable in injuring to the end of time, but there is no one to whom she shows unqualified favor, without any trickery. For the disasters which beset the wretched are usually greater than the strokes of good fortune that a lucky man can come by. I myself have seen men who were prosper- 15 ous but wounded by slander, while on the other hand, I have seen wretches who were deprived of any mark of honor. She casts off many of the fortunate before their life is over, but she raises up few of the downtrodden before they die. Although she takes payment for a few benefits with many evils, she makes up for many wrongs with only a few 20

Ysengrime miser, numquam haec tibi candida gratis;
 pensavit colaphis oscula bina decem.
Nunc pellem scidit illa tuam, nunc prorsus ademit;
 non tamen, ut penitus destruerere, tulit,
25 donec continuos misere miserata labores
 viribus est totis in caput acta tuum.
Ergo quid eventus prodest aut quaerere laetos
 aut vitasse graves? Nemo futura fugat.
Nam miser in campo, miser Ysengrimus in aula,
30 hostibus in mediis usque et ubique fuit.
Contigit arreptum forti langore leonem
 nec refici somno nec potuisse cibo.
Nomen ei Rufanus erat, matrisque Suevae
 et patris Ungarici filius ipse fuit.
35 Alea iudicium vitae mortisque trahebat,
 spe timor ut fieret spesque timore minor.
Materiam morbi sors tempestatis alebat,
 solarem Cancro tabificante rotam.
Iusserat idcirco rex stratum valle sub alta,
40 quaque dabat densum gratior umbra nemus,
scilicet ut morbi geminatus et aetheris ardor
 temperiem caperet commoditate loci.
Porro animique ferox rex indocilisque ferendi
 ipse suae stimulus debilitatis erat.
45 Regius hinc praeco non omnia, regis ad arcem
 primatum regni nomina pauca vocat.
Quisque sui generis princeps accitur ad aulam:
 Berfridus capris, Grimmo tribunus apris,
Rearidus cervis et Bruno praeditus ursis,
50 Carcophas asinis dux sobolesque ducis,
vervecum Ioseph tuque, Ysengrime, luporum,

benefits. To you, poor Ysengrimus, she's never been favorable without exacting payment for it; she's balanced two kisses with ten blows. At one moment she split your skin, and the next, she took it away completely. But she didn't allow you to be utterly destroyed until, with a pitiable pity on your continual sufferings, she came down on your head with full force. So what advantage is it to aim at happy outcomes, or to have avoided sad ones? No one can fend off the future. For wretched in the field was Ysengrimus, and wretched in court; always and everywhere he was in the midst of enemies.

It happened that the lion was seized by a serious illness, and could find no refreshment in food or in sleep. His name was Rufanus, and he was the son of a Suevian mother and a Hungarian father. The dice had not yet fallen for a sentence of life or death, so that fear was lessened by hope, and hope by fear. The condition of the weather was adding fuel to the illness, since Cancer was scorching the chariot of the sun. For that reason the king had ordered a bed to be placed in a deep valley, and where a thick wood gave soothing shade, so that the twin heat produced by the illness and by the weather would be tempered by the amenity of the place. Besides, the king, being spirited in temper and not submissive to suffering, was himself an aggravation of his own infirmity.

Because of this, the royal herald summoned to the king's castle, not everyone, but a few named barons of the kingdom. Each leader of his kind was called to the court: Berfridus from the goats; Grimmo the chief of the boars; Rearidus from the deer and Bruno, who was in charge of the bears; Carcophas from the asses, a duke and a duke's son; and you, Joseph, leader of sheep, and Ysengrimus, of wolves; and

Reinardus rector stirpis honorque suae,
Bertiliana super capreas et Gutero velox,
   dux leporum; hos proceres regia carta iubet,
55 ut saltem, si nulla malum medicina levaret,
   officium pietas exequiale daret.
Rex quoque disposito praecidere iurgia regno
   cogitat uxori pignoribusque dari.
Regia turmatim petitur domus, hostis ab hoste
60   securus, veniens et rediturus, erat;
regius edicto mandaverat horror ubique
   pacem sub capitum condicione datam.
Nec nisi Reinardum vulpem fiducia quemquam
   impavidum iussae fecerat esse viae;
65 ille secus meditans frigus pulsura nivosum
   munia, quid comedat, providet ante famem.
Talia tunc secum: "Tibi te sapere," inquit, "oportet;
   quem tangat sibimet cura negantis opem?
Curia mandavit locupletes atque disertos,
70   qui ratione valent obsequioque iuvant;
vivere quos nescit, decerneret aula vocandos?
   Non curant proceres, absit an assit inops.
Desipiat sapiat, vivat moriatur egenus,
   nescit; si scierit, tradit id aula notho.
75 Ergo aut vilis inops aut est incognitus aulae,
   se dignam servo paupere gaza putat.
Pauperis obsequio est merces servisse licere,
   et post obsequium vilis ut ante manet.

Reynard, governor and glory of his race; Bertiliana, head of the roes, and swift Gutero, leader of the hares. The king's letter commanded these nobles, so that, if there was no 55 medicine that might alleviate his illness, their dutiful affection should at least provide a funeral service. Also, the king had it in mind to avoid future strife by bestowing the kingdom on his wife and children.

Troops of people made their way to the king's house; all enemies had a safe-conduct to protect them against each 60 other, going and coming. Fear of the king had imposed a universal peace by edict, on penalty of death, and none of them was so bold as to be careless of taking the journey he was ordered to. None, that is, but Reynard the fox, who had 65 his thoughts occupied instead by his own castle and how it would repel the cold of snow, and what he could eat so as to ward off hunger beforehand.

Then he said this to himself: "You ought to be wise on your own behalf; who can be touched by concern for someone who refuses to help himself? The court has summoned the rich and the eloquent, who are useful through their 70 counsel or helpful through their services. Would the court decide to summon those of whose very existence it is unaware? Nobles don't care whether a poor man is there or not; the court doesn't know if a pauper is wise or foolish, if he's alive or dead. If it does know, it casts the information to the winds. So the poor man is either despised or unknown 75 at the court, and wealth thinks it deserves to have the poor man as a slave. It's reward enough for the poor man's service that he's been allowed to serve, and after the service, he

Quaeritur officio si gratia, cogitet auctor,
80   quid, quando, quantum, qui, quibus, ad quid, ubi.
Utile iussus opus promptu, gratumque morando
    iniussus faciat, qui placuisse cupit.
Ut veniam, iubeat rex nomine, pareo iussus;
    ingratis probitas officiosa perit.
85 Ursus, aper, lupus (hos proceres, quos gaza timendos
    efficit et tumidos, curia mandat) eant;
accipiens reddat, timeat, quicumque timetur.
    Nullus amat miserum, nemo timere solet.
Quid sub rege michi nisi vivere? Pauper et (illud
90   pauperis ut ius est) omnibus aequus ero.
Nec cuiquam faveo nec quem michi credo favere,
    nec quemquam metuo nec metuendus ego."
Ysengrimus ovat Reinardum illudere regi
    dum reliqui proceres moenia iussa petunt;
95 seque tulisse putans non tot tormenta, quot esse
    ulturum, reduci vix cute tectus abit,
praeceleransque alios subit atria regis et intrans
    solus clamat ave, cetera turba pavet.
Murmur erat nullum, vix fortem rege gemente
100   rugitum suffert terrificata phalanx.
Ille amens queritur super aegro, cumque tacendum
    innuerint omnes, clamitat ille magis.

remains despised as before. If the provider of any service
wants thanks for it, let him give thought to what, when, how   80
much, who, for whom, wherefore and where. When some-
one is given an order, let him perform the service promptly,
if he wants to please; if, however, he's not been given an or-
der, let him make his service agreeable by holding it in re-
serve for a while. Let the king order me to come by name,
and I'll obey when I'm ordered; punctilious dutifulness is
wasted on the thankless. Let the bear, the boar, the wolf,   85
go (the court summons those princes, who are given conse-
quence and awesomeness by their wealth); let those who re-
ceive make return, and let those who are feared feel fear
themselves. No one loves the poor man, and no one, cus-
tomarily, fears him. What is there for me to hope for in the
king's service besides just staying alive? I'll be poor and (as is
the rule for a poor man) of equal interest to everybody; I'm   90
on nobody's side and I don't think anyone's on mine. I don't
fear anyone nor does anyone fear me."

Ysengrimus was glad that Reynard was showing con-
tempt for the king, while the other nobles made their way to
the castle as ordered, and thinking that the number of tor-   95
tures he had undergone was outweighed by the vengeance
he was about to take, he set off, barely covered by his new
growth of skin. Outstripping the rest, he entered the king's
halls, and as he went in, he alone (the rest of the crowd being
afraid) uttered a greeting. There was no hubbub; the ter-   100
rified company could hardly endure the mighty roar from
the groaning king. The stupid wolf lamented over the pa-
tient, and although everyone nodded at him to keep quiet,

Ordine discumbunt, iussique utrimque superne
 primates, infra coetus utrimque minor.
105 Vendicat iniussus rudis Ysengrimus et urso
 praeformidatum regis ad ora thronum,
rege vetante tamen non est compulsus abire.
 Rex inquit: "Dubito, spesne sit ulla mei."
Econtra archiater: "Rex, assum (iussus, at ultro
110 venissem) ut videam, quis tibi morbus agat.
Discutere edidici morbos interprete vena
 (haec saltem claustro dona docente tuli);
mox video, quisnam status exundaverit aegro,
 et quis debuerit creticus esse dies.
115 Exere tangendam!" Rex exerit, ilico venam
 tangit et exclamat: "Rex, michi vena placet!
Si, tibi quae superet complexio, quaeris, ego edam:
 contuor in primo te calidum esse gradu.
Talibus esse solet langor fortisque brevisque;
120 fit status hinc simplex et diuturna salus.
Te quoque non alio vexat discrimine langor,
 tertia lux huius cretica febris erit."
Aeger ad haec: "Minime rebar, quod phisicus esses.
 Sed velut hac factus iunior arte venis,
125 quod nisi tu praesens verbis habituque probasses,
 non faceret plenam nuncia fama fidem.
Nam lanugineae iuvenescere pellis amictu
 cerneris; hac quoque me, si potes, arte iuva."

he shouted all the more. They lay down in order of rank on both sides, the princes in the higher positions, and the less important group in the lower, as they were ordered. The 105 boorish Ysengrimus, unbidden, claimed a seat before the king's face, and one which the bear had previously rejected out of fear; but he was not compelled to leave it by the king's prohibition.

The king said: "I am in doubt as to whether there's any hope for me." Up spoke the master medic: "King, here I am (at your command, but I'd have come of my own accord), so 110 that I can see what disease is making itself felt in you. I've learned to diagnose illnesses from the evidence of the pulse (this gift, at least, I got from my monastery education), and I can see what kind of a pitch the illness will reach, and which day is the critical one. Put out your pulse so I can feel 115 it!" The king thrust it forward and he immediately took his pulse, and cried out: "King, I'm pleased with your pulse! If you ask what condition you're laboring under, I'll explain. I see you to be suffering from a category-one fever; in such cases the illness is usually violent and short, hence the crisis 120 is a single one and recovery is lasting. The illness doesn't threaten you with any other danger, and the third day will be the critical one for this fever." The patient replied: "I little thought that you were a doctor. But you come here as if you've been made young by this art; the report that an- 125 nounced this wouldn't serve to make it fully credible, unless you in person had proved it by your words and clothing. For you seem rejuvenated in the covering of your woolly hide. Give me, too, the benefit of this skill, if you can."

Phisicus econtra: "Iubeas te sospite facto
130   experiar, quam sit phisica nota michi.
Quid facias, dicam; tamen hanc, quam cernor habere,
    Reinardus speciem, non medicina dedit.
Haec atque his adversa tuli graviora per illum;
    cerne cicatrices, sic renovatus ego.
135 At me clade mea tua plus iniuria laedit:
    iusserat huc omnes praeco venire tuos;
ursus Bruno potens et Grimmo tribunus aprorum
    (nil ego sum) iussu contremuere tuo.
Hi proceres aliique omnes terrentur, et ille
140   imperii spreta mole superbus abest.
Non impune sines hunc ausum tanta fuisse,
    ut modo respires, det deus atque dabit!
Tu vervece hodie, cras hirco vescere, mandat
    talibus hos aegris phisica nostra cibos.
145 Mandere, si posses, pariter praestaret utrumque;
    vis dapibus largis est reparanda tibi.
Te michi per capitis discrimina certa iubente,
    farcirem ut cameras ventris utroque simul,
quamvis alteruter quater esset, quantus uterque est,
150   si meus est hodie, qui fuit uter heri,
me faceret miserum minima ungula dempta, nec, illam
    qui raperet, leto solveret absque suo.
At tibi servandus si cras caper usque videtur,
    nunc occide, caro caesa recenter obest.
155 Non quia sit praesens quisquam, cui tale quid optem,"
    (ast aderant pariter laniger atque caper;
oderat Ysengrimus eos, odisse negabat,
    ut tegeret dempta suspicione dolum.

The doctor replied: "If you command me, I'll prove how 130
familiar I am with medicine by curing you. I'll tell you what
to do. But it was Reynard, not medicine, who gave me the
appearance I can be seen to possess. These misfortunes, and
even greater ones, I suffered through him; look at my
wounds—that's how I was rejuvenated! But the insult to you 135
wounds me more than my own injuries: your herald ordered
all your vassals to come here. Bruno the bear and Grimmo,
the chief of the boars (me, I'm nobody!) trembled at your
command. They and all the other nobles are struck with
awe, but he, arrogantly scorning the force of your command, 140
stays away. You won't allow him to get away with such im-
pudence, may God only grant that you recover—as he will!
You shall eat mutton today, and goat tomorrow; these are
the foods my medicine prescribes in such cases. It would be 145
beneficial to eat both at once, if you can; your strength must
be restored by hearty meals. Were you to command *me,* on
pain of the certain loss of my life, to stuff the vaults of my
stomach with both at once, even though each of them were
four times the size that either is, if my stomach is today the 150
same as it was yesterday, the loss of the smallest hoof would
make me miserable, nor would the one who took it pay for
it with less than death. But even if you think the goat
should be kept until tomorrow, kill him now; freshly slaugh-
tered meat is harmful. Not that there's anyone present for 155
whom I'd wish such a fate." (But in fact, both sheep and goat
were there; Ysengrimus hated them, and denied that he
hated them so that he might avert suspicion and conceal his

Ergo ait): "Hos omnes, quos implet curia praesens,
160   diligo, meque etiam, sicut opinor, amant.
Verveces alii per rura vagantur et hirci;
      saepe tamen sapiens proxima prima rapit.
Si te sollicitant pacis decreta tuendae,
      stultus ego ostendam, quid sapienter agas:
165   ut multi valeant, paucos cecidisse ferendum est;
      gloria te regni tota ruente ruit.
Non violas pacem, maiori munere vendis;
      praestat uter, vervex et caper anne leo?
Si quid in hoc peccas, monachus feror atque sacerdos,
170   peccati moles in mea colla cadat.
Non semel in claustris fuit utile gratius aequo;
      praecedit merito crimina rara timor.
Non eris exemplar, si lucro vendis honestum;
      exemplum reperis atque relinquis idem.
175   Tenta diu secta est, rebus suspendere rectum,
      et veniam faciunt mutua probra levem.
Parva quis extimeat magno constantia lucro?
      Saepe fit ob fructum maxima noxa brevem;
ut scelerum iudex, sic excusator habundat;
180   si 'Scelus est' alter, 'Profuit' alter ait.
Utere non propria, sed consuetudine mundi;
      omnia te metuant, tu nichil ipse time.
Raptorem comitatur honos et commoda rerum,
      pauper et infamis iuris amator erit.
185   Nec si pascha foret, pacem violare vererer,
      cum michi profectum pax violata daret.

trickery.) So he said: "I love all those with whom the present
court is thronged, and they love me too, I think. Other 160
sheep and goats roam the countryside—although a wise
man often takes the first things that come to hand. If the
laws about keeping the peace bother you, I, although a sim-
pleton, will show you what would be wise for you to do. It's 165
to be accepted that a few should perish so that the major-
ity might benefit. If you fall, the whole glory of the king-
dom falls with you. You're not violating the peace, you're
exchanging it for a greater benefit; which is more useful, the
sheep and goat, or the lion? If you sin at all in this, I'm
known to be a monk and a priest—let the weight of the sin 170
fall on my shoulders! More than once in the cloister was
the profitable preferred to the just; fear is (rightly) felt only
before crimes that are rarely committed. You won't consti-
tute a precedent if you sell what's right for gain; you find an
example already there and you leave one of the same kind
behind you. The school of thought which is for sacrific- 175
ing right to expediency has long been maintained, and the
wrongs on both sides make forgiveness easy. Who would
fear a little outlay for a great profit? Enormous injury is of-
ten endured for a little reward. Just as there's many a cen-
surer of crimes, so there's many an excuser of them; if some- 180
one says 'it's a crime,' someone else says 'it did a lot of good.'
Follow the custom of the world, not your own; everything
fears you, so you should be afraid of nothing. The exploiter
is accompanied by status and material advantages, while the
lover of the law is poor and of no reputation. Not even if it 185
was Easter would I fear to break the peace, if the breaking

Alligat ac solvit leges secura potestas;
    nemo suis debet legibus esse minor.
Nam non, ut metuantur, agunt praecepta, sed auctor;
190   non gladius — gladium qui tenet, ille ferit.
Lex igitur domino, legi non subiacet ipse;
    ergo quod ipse iubes, quid variare times?
Rusticus est princeps, qui rustica iura tuetur;
    plebs procerum cibus est, utpote prata gregum.
195 Utilitas ergo per fasque nefasque petatur;
    saepius esuriet, qui minus aequa fugit."
Incipit interea rex circumvolvere corpus,
    nec veluti spreto repplicat ulla seni;
at plus verba doli regem dampnasse recenset
200   curia, subiectum quam doluisse latus.
Praescierant facilem stratis mansuescere regem
    laniger et socius prosiliuntque citi,
inque vicem, quid agant, praefantur, protinus ambo
    vocibus his stultum corripuere senem:
205 "Hinc, domine archiater, domine Ysengrime sacerdos,
    hinc fuge, tu nimium regis in ora sedes!
Non modo proposuit sua rex peccata fateri,
    presbiter aut medicus, quicquid haberis, abi!
Presbiter es sapiens regique assidere dignus,
210   foedera qui violas et violanda doces!
Ipse tuae legis, nisi nos reverentia regis
    terreret, primo supprimerere iugo."
Verborumque bonis numerum suppulsibus aequant,
    hocque sine officio sillaba nulla perit.

of the peace were to bring me some profit. Power enforces
and relaxes the laws with confidence; no one ought to be in-
ferior to his own laws. For it's not the laws that make them-
selves feared, but the author of them; it's not the sword, but   190
the man who holds it, that strikes. So the law is subservient
to the ruler, not he to the law; therefore why are you afraid
to change the order you yourself give? The prince who keeps
peasants' laws is himself a peasant; the masses are fodder
for princes, as fields are for sheep. So let right and wrong be   195
mere stepping-stones to profit; the one who least evades jus-
tice will be the one who suffers most from hunger."

Meanwhile, the king began to roll his body from side to
side, and answered nothing to the old man, as if scorning
him. But the court reckoned that the deceitful speech did
more harm to the king than his suffering flank gave him   200
pain. The sheep and his friend knew that the king soft-
ened easily toward those who were prostrate. They quickly
jumped up, and first discussing together what they were go-
ing to do, they then immediately attacked the silly old man
with these words: "Get out of here, Reverend Doctor, Dom   205
Ysengrimus the priest, out of here! You're sitting too close
to the king! The king hasn't planned to confess his sins at
this moment; however you're defined, priest or doctor, go
away! You're a wise priest, and worthy of sitting by the king,
you who violate treaties and advise their violation! If respect   210
for the king didn't hold us in awe, you yourself would be the
first to bow under the yoke of your own principle!" They
matched their words with an equal number of hefty thumps,
and not a syllable died away without the performance of this

215 Frontibus oppositis pronum quacumque retundunt,
    ne regem moveat mole cadentis humus,
  sed pellem lacerare cavent; pius ille tacebat,
    ad laudem meditans omnia ferre dei.
  Iamque ter hoc iterant: "Nisi rex metuendus adesset,
220   primitus in temet pax violanda foret!"
  Hoc aper, hoc ursus laudant; aper "Urse, vide," inquit,
    "quam placide tractent hi sua iura duo!"
  Ursus ad haec: "Meditabar idem te, Grimmo, rogare,
    quando duos minus his videris esse truces.
225 Contuor ac stupeo non ausos qualibet hostem
    tangere, nimirum regia iussa pavent.
  Ut dicunt, monachus meruit bona flagra, nec illum
    tractarent aliter, quam meruisse putant.
  Sed satis apparet, metuunt offendere regem;
230   rex statuit pacem, iussaque regis agunt."
  Hircus ovisque per haec paucis novere placere
    profectum medici sicque minantur item:
  "Iussimus, ut fugeres, domine Ysengrime, sedesque,
    irrita sumpsisti pectore vota tuo—
235 scilicet expectas, ut nostris rege refecto
    carnibus, ex nobis quod superarit, edas.
  Vis cadere in regem? Regi incidit iste, videte!
    Noscis, ubi sedeas, infatuate Satan?"
  "Ysengrime," (etenim nondum Ysengrimus abibat)
240   "effuge! Paene nimis lusimus," ursus ait.
  "Ni celer abscedas, ibi te sedisse pigebit,
    pluribus ad regem convenit esse locum."

service. Facing each other, they pounded the wolf as he reeled from side to side, so that the ground didn't jar the king with the weight of the wolf's fall; but they avoided scratching his hide. He was meekly silent, thinking to endure everything for the glory of God. Now they repeated three times: "If the king wasn't here to inspire fear, the first violation of the peace would have to be against you!"

This the bear and the boar applauded. The boar said: "Bear, see how peaceably these two talk about their rights!" The bear replied: "I was thinking likewise of asking you, Grimmo, when you'd seen two less ferocious than these. I observe with amazement that they don't dare to touch their enemy in any way, since they fear the king's commands too much. The monk, as they say, deserves a good scourging, and they wouldn't treat him otherwise than they think he deserves. But it's clear enough that they're afraid of offending the king. The king has instituted a peace, and they fulfill the king's command."

The goat and the sheep recognized by this that the doctor's departure would be pleasing to some people, and they threatened him again in this way: "We've ordered you to go away, Dom Ysengrimus, and you stay seated. You've conceived vain wishes in your heart. You must be waiting so that when the king has been restored by our flesh, you can eat anything of us that's left over. Are you aiming to fall on the king? Look, he's falling on the king. Don't you know where you should sit, you stupid devil?—Ysengrimus," (for Ysengrimus still didn't go away) "get out! We've played enough games," said the bear. "If you don't go away quickly, you'll regret having sat there; several of us have a claim on the place

Praecipitemque lupum magno rotat impete vervex;
    obvia non audet reddere verba miser.
245 Rex autem versa facie non viderat acta,
    tunc victus senior sustinet ire retro.
Dispositae fuerant sedes, sua quemque tenebat;
    stultus summa petens occupat ima pudens.
At caper et vervex pulso sene cominus astant,
250   Berfridoque prior laniger orsus ita est:
"Hinc fuge, sum potior regi, scabiosus es, hirce;
    sufficiam regi solus ego, aeger enim est.
Tu siquidem putes quasi luce ter ebrius abbas."
    Lanigero reddit dicta iocosa caper:
255 "Immo tu fugias, quem pessimus inficit ydrops;
    putri ventre tumes ut lutulenta palus.
Rex ergo ipse probet, quem nostri mandere malit;
    hoc scio, nos esu non sumus ambo boni.
Paene nichil studuit medica Ysengrimus in arte,
260   hunc quoque non recte dividere arva refers.
Phisicus unde modo est? Utinam Reinardus adesset,
    ille nichil iactat sed tamen arte valet!
Scilicet hic regi bene distinxisset edendas
    (novit enim) innocuas pestificasque dapes!
265 Si regi, Ysengrime, faves, hunc ocius adduc,
    et medicum credi te voluisse nega.
Hoc praesente quidem si posses muris in antrum
    repere, momentum non paterere foris!"

near the king." The sheep knocked the wolf flying with great force, and the wretch didn't dare to give back any words in answer. The king, with his face turned away, hadn't seen what was going on; so the old man, defeated, gave in and retired.

The seats were allotted, each one held its occupant, and the fool who aimed at the highest now shamefacedly took the lowest position. But the goat and the ram, after the old man's beating, stood near the king, and thus the sheep began to speak first to Berfridus: "Get away from here, I'm better for the king; you're mangy, goat. I alone will be enough for the king, since he's ill, because you stink like an abbot who gets drunk three times a day." The goat returned these bantering words to the ram: "No, you go away; the worst kind of dropsy has infected you. You swell up like a muddy swamp with your stinking stomach. So let the king himself judge, which of us he prefers to eat; I know this, we're not both good for eating. Ysengrimus has not advanced very far in his medical studies; you report that he was also unable to divide fields properly. How does he now come to be a doctor? I wish Reynard were here; he doesn't boast about anything, but he is well endowed with skill! Truly, he would successfully have distinguished (since he's learned to) which foods were harmless and must be eaten by the king, and which would bring trouble. If you've any concern for the king, Ysengrimus, bring him here quickly, and give up wishing to be thought a doctor. When he's here, if you can creep into a mouse's hole, you shouldn't stay a moment outside it!"

Rector ad hanc vocem se circumvolvit, at illi
270   regali properant accubitare thoro.
Regia nobilitas stratis ignoscere gaudet;
    surgere prostratos et residere iubet.
Curia collaudat vervecem tota caprumque,
    at peiora lupum promeruisse ferunt.
275 Iamque locuturi grave regis habentia pondus
    in vulpem Bruno mitigat ante minas:
"Rector, in absentem noli crudescere servum;
    forsan agit causa conveniente moras.
Si vero veniens non excusaverit apte
280   tardandi culpam, legibus ange reum.
Gutero, curre celer! Reinardum (namque moratur
    ut fatuus demens) huc properare iube."
Paruit ille urso; tunc multae carnis acervo
    Reinardum pinguem luxuriare videt.
285 "Quid facies, Reinarde miser?" clamabat, at ille:
    "Stulte lepus, miserum non comitantur opes!
Ergo quis est felix, si sum miser?" Ille reclamat:
    "Ut taceam, non hoc experiere parum.
Delatus prodente lupo, vix rege rogato
290   tempora, dum veniens ipse loquaris, habes."
Ille refert: "Ha, dicor ob hoc miser? Ista profecto,
    ne miser existam, causa datura michi est!
Rex nisi me nosset, non regius hostis haberer;
    gaudeo, quod vel sic sum manifestus ibi.
295 Qui non est odio, non est dignandus amore,
    nam, quibus irasci, quisque favere potest.

At this speech the ruler rolled himself over, and they hurriedly lay flat before the royal couch. Royal nobility was 270 pleased to pardon the prostrate, and he bade the stretched-out pair to rise and sit down again. The whole court praised the sheep and the goat highly, and said the wolf had deserved to be treated worse. And now Bruno softened the king's 275 threats against the fox before they were made (since the king was about to say something of serious consequence): "King, don't be harsh to your absent servant; perhaps he has a good reason for taking a long time. If, indeed, when he comes, he doesn't have a fitting excuse for his fault in delay- 280 ing, then bring the laws to bear on the criminal. Gutero, run quickly! Bid Reynard hurry here, since he is dawdling like a silly fool."

The hare obeyed the bear; then he saw a bloated Reynard gorging himself with a great heap of meat. "What are you 285 going to do, wretched Reynard?" he cried, but the latter an-swered: "You stupid hare, a wretch isn't surrounded with good things! So who is happy, if I'm wretched?" The other replied: "Never mind what I say, you'll be able to put it to the test in a big way. You've been accused by the treacherous wolf, and you've hardly got time, as the result of a request to the king, to come and put your own case." He replied: "Ah, is 290 that why I'm called wretched? Truly, this is a case which will give me the chance of *not* being wretched! Unless the king had known who I was, I wouldn't be accounted an enemy of his. I'm happy to be brought into prominence with him, even in this way. Anyone who isn't thought worth hating, 295 isn't thought worth loving, for someone can also be well

Obsequiis, quibus ira subit dampnumque negatis,
    exhibitis merces provenit atque favor.
Hinc michi pace lupi fit gratior ira leonis;
300   nobile plus odium quam miser ornat amor.
Sed nec sollicitor, quia me gravis oderit hostis;
    it sapiens liber, quo perit artis inops.
Astuto plus ira solet prodesse potentis,
    gratia quam stulto; neutra manere potest.
305 Vade relaturus nusquam tibi me esse repertum,
    neve michi timeas, porto quid artis adhuc.
Saepe sui dorsum caesoris virga cecidit,
    pocula pincernae sunt reditura suo.
Ysengrimus ibi nunc temporis esto tribunus,
310   non ierit quartum vespera praetor ero."
Reinardus solium lepore ad regale reverso
    multimodas species colligit atque bonas.
Tunc multas soleas nec hiantes vulnere pauco
    ad sua suspendens colla prehendit iter,
315 qui vix prae nimia poterat pinguedine, quamquam
    fasce carens alio, ferre suimet onus.
Quid tibi de tanta referam pinguedine? Frustra
    aestimo dicta quidem, non habitura fidem.
Cernitur a costis costas diffundere, quantum
320   cauda oriens medium corpus ab aure trahit.
Mollior in macris quam dorsum venter habetur:
    Reinardi dorso durior alvus erat.
Aeris hunc pleno folli talpaeve carenti
    ossibus impresso dixeris ungue parem.
325 More globi teretis volvi, non ire videtur,
    atque utero verrit, non pede signat humum,

disposed toward those with whom he gets angry. If the same services which are followed by anger and harm when denied, are actually produced, rewards and favor blossom. Hence, the lion's anger pleases me more than the wolf's friendliness would; the hatred of the aristocracy is a greater honor than the affection of scum. But I'm not worried that an important enemy hates me. The wise man treads freely where someone devoid of cunning comes to grief. The anger of the mighty is usually more use to the shrewd man than their favor is to the fool; neither can last long. Go and report that you haven't found me anywhere, and don't be afraid for me, I still carry some cunning with me. The rod has often fallen on the back of the one who cut it, and drinks are administered to the one who poured them out. Ysengrimus can be jury there for the time being, but before the fourth day is out I'll be judge."

When the hare had gone back to the king's throne, Reynard collected many sorts of efficacious herbs, and then, hanging lots of shoes, gaping with huge slits, around his neck, he started his journey. He was barely able to carry his own weight, let alone any other burden, because of his excessive fatness. Why should I describe such corpulence for you? Truly I think my words are useless, since they won't be believed. One of his flanks was seen to be as far spread apart from the other as the distance between the base of his tail and his ear. In thin people, the stomach is softer than the back, but Reynard's belly was harder than his back. You'd have said he was, to a T, like a ball filled with air, or a boneless mole. Like a smooth ball he seemed to roll, not walk, and instead of imprinting the ground with his foot, he swept

pendula quippe pedes totos exhauserat alvus.
   Reinardus talis moenia regis init;
terque salutato nec respondente tyranno
330   proiecit soleas cum speciebus humi.
Mox, velut ulteriore via prodire nequiret,
   deficere incipiens concidit atque iacet,
suspiratque diu; sessurus denique surgit,
   tamquam pausando membra refecta levans.
335   Iamque locuturam praestolans curia vulpem
   pendet, et illud idem rex manet ipse tacens.
Ille suam spatio vocem interstante perornat
   et ter suspirat; denique fatus ita est:
"Adduxere novos semper nova saecula ritus,
340   et veteris populi despicit acta rudis.
Res rebus subeunt, mutatur tempore tempus,
   nec caeli facies est modo, qualis heri.
Mens rationalis vertigine cetera vincit,
   moribus et citior quam fuga rebus inest.
345   En malus est hodie, cras peior, pessimus ultra,
   qui fuit hesterno vespere paene bonus;
cum fuerit peius faciendi pessimus impos,
   moribus hinc standi, non prius, ordo datur.
Plenior officiis primum, post aequa dabatur,
350   inde minor merces, denique nulla quidem;
gratia magna dehinc, tunc parvula, nullaque nuper.
   Nunc utinam liceat promeruisse nichil:
obsequiis redit ira! Cadit bene calculus istic!
   Proficit egregie tempore pauper in hoc!

it with his stomach, for his drooping belly had swallowed up the whole of his feet.

In such a condition did Reynard enter the king's castle. When he had greeted the king three times and got no reply, he threw the shoes, together with the spices, to the ground; then, as if he couldn't advance any further, he tottered, fell, and lay sighing for a long time. At length he rose to take his seat, as if raising limbs which had been strengthened by the rest. And now the expectant court was in suspense to hear what the fox would say, and the king himself waited in silence for the same thing. He increased the importance of his speech by interposing a pause, and sighed three times. Finally he spoke as follows: "Modern times have always brought modern customs, and the boor despises what was done by those of bygone days. Things succeed each other, season is varied by season, and the face of heaven is not today what it was yesterday. The human mind outdoes all the rest in its revolution, and transience in behavior is even swifter than that in material things. See—someone who was, yesterday evening, almost a good man, is today bad, tomorrow worse, and after that, evil through and through; and the order to halt is given at this point, and not earlier, in matters of morals, only because someone who is worst, is incapable of acting worse. Originally, the reward for a favor used to be given in the shape of greater services, next by ones that matched it, then by ones that fell short of it, and finally by nothing at all. Next, effusive verbal thanks, then perfunctory ones, and most recently, none. And now, would that it were permissible to be of no service at all, since anger is the response to favors! Accountancy's in a fine state here! A poor man does really well for himself these days!

330

335

340

345

350

355 Si, quod ego, quisquam locuples pro rege tulisset,
    obvia tota illi iam domus isset ovans,
rexque salutasset prior hunc, a rege secundus
    sideret, hic potum sumeret atque cibum.
Sed, quia nos inopes, servisse impune vetamur,
360   nimirum sors haec pauperis esse solet."
Fertur in hanc vocem rex subrisisse parumper.
    "Quid pro me tuleris, dic, ego grator," ait;
ille morans iterum suspensa voce parumper
    responsum tali calliditate linit:
365 "Rex, dubium facturus iter per compita quaedam
    insidiatores esse verebar ibi.
Vespere praecedente viam dum sidera rimor
    et reseraturum fata futura polum,
stella minax subito, mutandis regibus index,
370   crinali visus occupat igne meos.
Dirigui cecidique, tuum caput illa volebat;
    devoveo stellas, consulo quasque tamen.
Altera lucebat, quod adhuc medicabilis esses;
    spes michi cor coepit reddere, membra vigor.
375 Spes michi res, spes sola comes, mox curro Salernum,
    et volat in collum phisica tota meum.
Vi propero, mora parva odio est quasi dira cometae;
    artibus huc raptis fulminis instar agor.
Curia multifidos speculatur tota coturnos,
380   usus ego quibus hinc hucque agor inde redux."
Sexque coturnorum trisono paria explicat ore,
    Ungarice, Turce grammaticeque loquens,

If any wealthy man had endured what I have for the king's 355
sake, the whole court would have gone to meet him in cele-
bration, the king would have greeted him first, and he would
sit next to the king, he would be offered food and drink. But
because I'm poor, I'm not allowed to be useful without suf-
fering for it; this is only too often the fate of a poor man!" 360
    It is said that a smile flitted over the king's face at this
speech. "Tell me what you've endured for my sake," he said,
"and I'll thank you." The other, delaying once more with his
answer suspended for a little while, colored his reply with
cunning, in this way: "King, I was about to make a dangerous 365
journey by some crossroads, and I was afraid that bandits
were in the locality. On the evening preceding the journey,
while I was examining the stars, and the sky which would
reveal what fate was in store, a menacing star, sign of a
change in kings, suddenly filled my vision with its trailing 370
fire. I stiffened and fell; it claimed your life. I cursed the
stars, but nevertheless scrutinized them all for guidance.
Another one made clear that you were still curable. Hope
began to give me back my spirit, and energy my limbs. Hope 375
was reality to me, hope my only friend; immediately I
rushed to Salerno, and every medicine was hurled on my
back. Energetically I made haste; the slightest delay was as
hateful to me as the disasters of the comet. With the skills
I had hurriedly picked up, I rushed here like lightning. The
whole court can see the much-torn shoes I've used going 380
and coming back."
    Six pairs of shoes he displayed, with trilingual commen-
tary, speaking in Hungarian, Greek and Latin, counting

terque ea dinumerans, semel omnia quaque loquela,
   non hisdem numeris ad numeranda redit,
385 sed repetens eadem veluti restantia, vocem
   mutabat numero posteriore suam.
Finiturus eo, quo rex magis utitur, ore,
   expedit Ungarico tertia sena sono.
Adiecitque: "Fame tumeo, rex, aspice, rumpor!
390   Quid verbis opus est? Mors tibi nostra patet.
Vix, dum parta tibi sumatur potio, vivam,
   nec medicina michi quae tibi praestet opem.
Ne morereris, in haec vitae discrimina veni,
   terque salutatus non michi reddis ave!
395 Has autem species summus michi dona magister,
   sub cuius didici traditione, dedit."
Tunc sparsas in vasa legit, quibus undique motis
   moenia perfundens tota replebat odor.
Ysengrimus ubi medicas dimiserit ollam
400   servantem species, ursus aperque rogant.
"An, Berfride, tibi servandas tradidit?" aiunt,
   "Quane illas ergo temperet arte caret?"
Hircus ad haec: "Proceres, aliter, quam noscitis, actum est:
   artis adhuc medicae permanet ipse memor,
405 sed desunt species. Transcendere sueverat Alpem,
   mercari species more sagacis avi,
nostra sed arva super Gallae commercia vocis
   perdidit; idcirco stat vacua olla domi."
Tunc sibi Reinardum propius considere rector
410   praecipit, herbarum captus odore bono,
porro suas sumptu species aptare repente;
   incipiebat enim febris adesse tremor.

them all three times, once in each language, and returning
to count them with different numbers, picking up the same 385
ones again as if they'd been there all the while, and changing
language every time he got to the last one. Finishing in that
language which the king made most use of, he dispatched
the third half-dozen in Hungarian, and added: "I'm blown
up with hunger, king; look, I'm going to burst! What need 390
is there for words? My death is plain for you to see. I shall
hardly live until the medicine prepared for you has been
taken, and the medicine which will help you won't do me
any good. I've incurred this risk to my life to prevent you
from dying, and yet, although you were greeted three times,
you don't say hello to me! However, the excellent teacher 395
under whose instruction I was trained gave me these herbs
as a gift." Then he collected the scattered herbs in a bowl,
and as they were stirred from side to side, a pervasive odor
filled the entire palace.

The bear and the boar asked where Ysengrimus had left
his bowl containing medicinal herbs: "Did he give it to you, 400
Berfridus, to keep?" they said, "Or does he lack the skill to
blend them?" The goat replied: "The case is other than you
think, princes. He still remembers his medical skill, but the 405
spices are lacking. He used to cross the Alps, like his wise
grandfather, to buy spices. But in our fields he lost his capac-
ity for transactions in the Romance languages, and so his
jar stands empty at home." Then the king, attracted by the 410
pleasant smell of the herbs, ordered Reynard to sit closer to
him, and to get his spices ready to be administered at once,
since the trembling of his fever was beginning to make itself
felt.

In faciem patrui medicus nunc lumine verso,
    nunc repetens regem, talia verba refert:
415 "Quid species trivisse iuvat, nisi feceris illam
    rem prius acquiri, cuius egemus adhuc?
Potio tarda tuam non est motura querelam;
    en aliud nobis, unde queramur, obest.
Potio, quam primum fuerit confecta, bibenda est,
420 ne defraglascat vim minuente mora.
Exige rem propere, cuius defectio laedit;
    herbarum modicum conficit hora brevis.
Rem, dixi, propera—sed quid properasse iuvabit?
    Impingas, vellas, denegat illa sequi."
425 "Improbe!" rex inquit, "Quid apud mea regna, quid usquam
    invenies, quod non mox habuisse queam?"
Respondit medicus: "Non, sicut credis, agendum est;
    multa potes, sed non omnia solus habes.
Saepe fit inventu res prima novissima quaestu,
430 raraque quaerenti sponte aliquando venit.
Ungue quidem sua quisque tenet, sua quoque tenente
    in varios casus plurima vota ruunt.
Quod quaero, invenies et contemplabere forsan,
    quid tamen hoc prodest? Ungula prava tenet.
435 Omnia fingantur, praesentia servat avarus;
    subripit externas res, dabit ille suas?
Argue, posce, iube, da, sponde, tunde, minare,
    semper in obliquam nititur ille viam.
Non hunc aut venus aut pietas aut foedera tangunt,
440 vi cogente dabit, si qua daturus erit.

The doctor, with his eyes now turned toward his uncle's face, now turning back to the king, replied with these words: "What use is it to have pounded herbs, unless you've first 415 made sure of the acquisition of that thing which we still lack? A potion administered so late isn't going to get rid of your trouble, because, you see, there's another obstacle for us to worry about. The potion should be drunk as soon as it's made, in case it loses its aroma and the delay lessens its 420 force. Quickly, send for the item whose lack is causing trouble; a short space of time will be enough to get ready a little bit of herbs. Hurry up with this item, I said—but what will be the use of hurrying? You can rush off and make a grab, but it will refuse to come."

"Impudent creature!" said the king, "what will you find in 425 my kingdom, what will you find anywhere, which I'm not capable of obtaining without delay?" The doctor replied: "It can't be done the way you think. You have a lot of power, but you don't possess everything all for yourself. Many times, the thing which is the first to be thought of is the last to be obtained, and it's a rare one that comes, on occasion, of its 430 own accord to the one who wants it. A man holds on to his own possessions with tooth and nail, and when he does so, the desires of others often come to grief. Perhaps you'll find and inspect the thing I'm looking for, but what use is that? A wicked claw holds it tight. Whatever case is concocted, a 435 greedy man keeps what he's got; he appropriates everyone else's goods, and is he going to give away his own? Reprove, ask, command, give, promise, strike, threaten, he still tries to dodge. He is not affected by decency, nor compassion, nor by social bonds; if he's going to give at all, he gives under 440

Oblatis donec sua pluris pendit avarus,
  feceris hunc nulla conditione probum."
Rex iratus ait: "Quantocius assere, quidnam
  desit! Ego experiar, quis neget, ede palam."
445 "Cedo ego mox, domine," ille refert, "Utinam ille precando
  flectatur, qui rem, cuius egemus, habet!
Pelle lupi, qui dimidium tribus addidit annis,
  si cupis, ut subito potio prosit, eges.
Illius aetatis corium natura lupinum
450 tam mira medicae dote beavit opis,
ut, si tectus eo sumptis sudaveris herbis,
  mox priscus repetat membra fovenda sopor;
utque rapax cremiis elambit Mulciber unctum,
  desiccata semel sic tibi febris abit.
455 Perfice, quod superest, ego quaeque salubria dixi.
  Hic ergo species hicque parator adest,
eia nunc subito pilam pilumque parandis!
  Incipit instanti rex trepidare malo,
et reliqua interea sic provideantur oportet,
460 ut tempus teneant—en ego tardo nichil.
Cetera festinet nobis quicumque daturus,
  confestim species en ego frico meas.
Eia quisne dabit pilam? Rue, profer!"—at illi
  quisque alium cursu praecelerare parat.
465 Ysengrimus ad haec condensae irrepere turbae
  enitique foras cogitat esse bonum.
"Quamvis," inquit, "agant nullum haec michi verba
    timorem,
  infortunatis multa nocere queunt.

160

pressure of force. While a miser values his possessions more than what's offered him, you'll not make him do the decent thing under any circumstances."

The king, in a temper, said: "Declare at once, what it is that's lacking! I'll see who'll deny it; speak openly." "I give in 445 straightway, your majesty," he replied. "Would that the one who has the thing we lack may be swayed by entreaty! If you wish the potion to be of immediate benefit, you need the skin of a wolf who is three and a half years old. Nature has blessed the hide of a wolf of that age with so wonderful a 450 gift of medicinal power that, if you sweat under its covering when you have taken the herbs, sleep will quickly invade and refresh your limbs as of old. Just as greedy Mulciber licks up fat on kindling wood, so your fever will disappear when burned out. Do what remains; I've told you what's good for 455 you. Here are the herbs, and the one who can prepare them; make haste and get ready the mortar and pestle! The king is beginning to tremble at the approach of his illness. And meanwhile, it's necessary that the other things should be seen to, so that they are in time. You see *I'm* not holding 460 things up! Let someone hurry up and give us the rest, and I'll pound my spices without delay. Well, who'll provide the mortar? Come on, out with it!"—and they were all ready to outstrip each other in getting to him.

At this, Ysengrimus thought it a good idea to steal into 465 the dense crowd and make his way outside. "Although," he said, "these words don't cause me any fear, many things can inflict injury on unlucky people, and as a lucky man is apt to

Ut felix metuenda solet contempnere tutus,
470   sic etiam debet tuta timere miser.”
Senserat et tussit Reinardus, taliter horrens:
     “Quo via iurata est? Ibitis omne, quod est?
Octo valent pilam bene ferre!” (tot absque sene ibant)
     “At nonus sedeat, quo parat ille viam?
475 Ille manere potest ausumque ignosco sedendi.”
     Non dubitat de se dicier ista senex;
nescit, quid faciat, sed, quo processerat, haeret,
     tam migrare timens, quam remanere dolens.
Anxius interea rex volvit multa, diuque,
480   quid faceret, dubitans, nomina pauca vocat:
“Quid faciam, Bruno? Quid dicis, Grimmo? Quid omnes
     dicitis? Hic sapiens expedit atque favens.”
Ursus ad haec: “Longa non est ambage vagandum.
     Nos sumus ancipites, unde cupita petas;
485 Ysengrimus adest gnarus quarumque viarum,
     et tribus a denis hinc sua claret avis.
Alloquere hunc; si rennuerit, ne quaere, quod optas;
     non aliquis si non consulere ille potest.
Obsequeris, Reinarde, michi?” Cui repplicat ille:
490   “Inficior quaedam, quae, domine urse, refers,
et quaedam memoras constantia testibus aptis:
     consiliis, regi si favet ille, valet,
sed scio paucorum, nisi forte recensita sacris
     linea sit libris, hunc meminisse retro.”
495 His lupus auditis nusquam se mallet abesse,
     et nimis absentes devovet ipse fores.

scorn dangers from a position of security, so a wretch ought 470
to fear even what's quite safe." Reynard perceived this, and
coughed; then spoke as follows in a threatening tone:
"Where have you vowed a pilgrimage to? Is everyone here
going on it? Eight are quite enough to carry the mortar!"
(This was the number moving forward if you didn't count
the old wolf.) "Let the ninth sit down; where does he think
he's going? He can stay behind, and I pardon him for daring 475
to stay seated." The old man was in no doubt that this
speech referred to him. He didn't know what to do, but
stopped in the place he had reached, as much afraid to de-
part, as unhappy to stay put.

Meanwhile the king anxiously pondered many things, for
a long time hesitating as to what he should do. He called on 480
a few by name: "What shall I do, Bruno? What do you say,
Grimmo? What do you all say? A shrewd friend is needed in
this situation." The bear replied: "It's not necessary to go
through a great rigmarole. We're uncertain as to where you
should look for what you want, but Ysengrimus is here, and 485
he is acquainted with all the forest paths; his clan has been
famous for this for ten generations. Speak to him; if he says
no, give up looking for what you want. No one can advise
you if he can't. Do you agree with me, Reynard?" And he re-
plied to him: "I disagree with some things you say, Sir Bear; 490
other things you call to mind are attested by competent wit-
nesses. He is capable of advising the king, if he's well dis-
posed to him. But I know that he remembers few of his pre-
decessors, unless perhaps his family tree has been reckoned
up in the sacred books."

When the wolf heard this, he would rather have been 495
anywhere else, and cursed the excessively distant exits. So

Ergo sic fugiens, ut non fugisse putetur,
    dissimulare nova nititur arte fugam:
versus enim in socios, alio spectantibus illis,
500   retrorsum properat, visus itemque redit,
    sed minus usque redit passu, quam fugerat, uno,
    dum se furatur limen adusque fere.
Viderat hoc vulpes, oculorum cuius in herbas
    dexter erat, profugi laevus in acta senis.
505 "Patrue," clamabat, "numquam tam mira notavi,
    si, quae cerno, facis—sed michi credo parum.
Somnio, vel properas extrorsum introrsus eundo;
    quo plus huc properas, hoc mage limen adis.
Extrorsum properas, vel ianua nititur intro.
510   Huc potius, grates ut mereare, veni:
quaerendis regi super expedientibus aegro
    informa dubios sollicitosque iuva!"
Tunc lupus accedens itidem rectore iubente
    diffiso cassum corde reliquit iter.
515 "Utquid consiliis," ait, "applicor? Omne luporum
    ut vos me sic vos nosse ego dico genus.
Quaerite vos pellem regique impendite bimam
    seu libeat trimam—non ego curo quotam.
Grates nolo dati, quaerendi nolo laborem;
520   vos meritum expectat, vos labor ille vocat!"
(Saeva loquebatur, delato dulcia coram
    principibus norat profore verba parum.)
Archiater iurans caput ungui tangit et infert:
    "Hoc rufum, proceres, ecce videte caput!

he tried to disguise his departure by a new trick, making his getaway in such a way that he should not be thought to have done so. He was turned toward his companions, but while they were looking elsewhere, he hastily backed away, and while he was watched, he retraced his steps, but always did so with one step less than he had taken in the direction of flight, until by stealth he had almost gained the door. 500

The fox had seen this, with his right eye on the herbs, and his left on what the restless old man was doing. "Uncle," he cried, "I've never observed anything so remarkable, if you're really doing what I see—but I don't believe my eyes. I'm dreaming, or else you're actually hastening out all the time you're coming in. The more you hurry in this direction, the closer you get to the door. Either you're hastening out, or the door is moving in. Come over here instead and earn some thanks; give information to those who are uncertain about the things which are to be sought for as necessary for the sick king, and assist those who are concerned for him!" Then the wolf, as the king commanded the same thing, came up, and with a despondent heart abandoned his unsuccessful run for it. "What am I brought into consultation for?" he said. "I declare that you know the whole family of wolves as well as you say I do. Look for a skin yourself, of a two-year-old or three-year-old—I don't care how old—and give it to the king. I don't want thanks for the gift. I don't want the job of looking; the merit of it awaits you, and it's you who are called to the task!" (He spoke fiercely, unaware that honeyed words do more good to those who are accused in the presence of princes.) 505 510 515 520

The master medic, making an oath, touched his head with his paw and said: "Princes, you see this red head!

525 Per rufum caput hoc! Et nos quaesivimus aptum
    servitio regis repperimusque lupum.
Dicere quem nolo; praesens habet aula valentem,
    hic si nos audit, novit, an ipse sit is.
Terga laborando dabit aut vix absque labore;
530   gratia pro quaestu sit, quibus aequa venit."
Ysengrimus ait: "Delirat rusticus iste!
    Quis lupus hic sine me est? Me sine nullus adest;
utilis hic utinam lupus esset!" Id hoste locuto
    laetitiam Ioseph dissimulare nequit:
535 "Ysengrime, tene ferulam! Tu iure tenebis,
    per sanctum Aegidium, sume! Locutus enim es."
Laetus ad haec Bruno: "Scola, quae componere versus
    te docuit, Ioseph, scit bene velle lupis!
Ergo aliquis cum sit lupus hic nullusque nisi iste,
540   regis ad officium qui bonus esse queat,
his positis, Reinarde, doce, quid deinde sequatur.
    Concilium puncto non dirimetur in hoc."
Sevocat hic patruum vulpes et in aure profatur:
    "Patrue, quid nobis conferet iste dies!
545 Nonne patres nostros operum proventus opumque
    praeposuit nobis? Vix sumus umbra patrum.
Quis tamen illorum meruit donare leonem
    pellicio? Ut cuperet tanta, quis ausus ita est?
Ecce tibi hunc nostra deus arte paravit honorem;
550   quam faveam patruo, notificabo semel.
Ex hoc ergo tribus quotiens recitabitur, abs te
    linea principium nobilitatis habet.

By this red head, we have indeed sought out a wolf who is 525
suitable for the king's service and have found him. I won't
say whom, but this hall contains one who'll do. If he hears
us, he knows whether he's the one. He'll give us his skin, ei-
ther under pressure or under virtually none. Let the grati- 530
tude for the search be given where it's due." Ysengrimus
said: "This peasant is raving! What wolf is there here but
me? Except me, there's none. I wish there were a usable wolf
here!" When his enemy had said this, Joseph was unable to
hide his joy: "Ysengrimus, go to the top of the class! It's 535
right you should, by Saint Giles, since you've hit the nail on
the head!" Bruno merrily chipped in: "The school that
taught you to compose verses, Joseph, knows how to appre-
ciate wolves! So, since there is a wolf here who can suffice 540
for the king's service, and none other than this one—given
this, Reynard, tell us what should follow. The council won't
be divided in opinion on this point." The fox called his uncle
over and whispered in his ear: "Uncle, what this day will
bring us! Are not our ancestors set above us because of the 545
success of their deeds and abilities? We are hardly the
shadow of our fathers; but which of them was found worthy
of bestowing a skin on the lion? Which of them dared even
to dream of such a thing? See, God has prepared this honor
for you, by my contrivance; I'll make known once and for all 550
how warmly I feel toward my uncle. Because of this, as often
as our family tree is recited, the line will take its source of

Gloria tanta hodie tibi suppetit, omne priorum
  obscuras una prosperitate decus.
555 Tu caput augustum generis signabere nostri,
  et te posteritas tota vocabit avum,
et tibi subnascens extrema superbiet aetas,
  in nomen titulo tale profecta tuo!"
Ille retro saliens hoc se solamine tantum
560 roborat: "Exiero, mansero, nonne peri?
Quaevis poena minor fit tamquam sponte ferenti."
  Archiater residens "Mors," ait, "ista mora est.
Patrue, Brunonem nosti paulo ante locutum:
  'Sufficit ambages hac tolerasse tenus.'
565 ut video, regi non auxiliaberis ultro;
  cauda piri semper respicit unde venit.
Perdere rem pravi malunt quam vendere honesto;
  dantibus invitis gratia resque perit.
Dum nimis infixo res ungue tuetur avarus,
570 pro stipe saepe brevi maxima dampna tulit.
Testor herum foliis vescentem et frondibus (isti
  crede sacramento, perficietur enim):
non ultra patiar regem caruisse lupino,
  cum pateat praesens, tegmine, cuius eget.
575 Dicere tardabam, sperans te sponte daturum,
  ut foret officio gratia digna tuo.
Assero nunc, quoniam tibi inest, quae congruit illi
  aetas pellicio, quod medicina petit.
Vera favore metuve tacens et falsa loquensve
580 vel prece vel pretio dedecus omne ferat.

nobility from you. So great is the glory in store for you today, that you will obscure all the honor of your predecessors with a single triumph. You will be designated the venerable head of the family, and all your posterity will call you their progenitor, and the most distant offspring to be born of you will glory in you, being advanced to such a name by your renown!" The other, jumping backward, supported himself with this consolation: "Whether I go or stay, I'm a dead man, aren't I? Any suffering becomes less if one endures it as if one willed it."

The arch-physician said as he seated himself: "This delay is fatal. Uncle, you know that not long ago Bruno said 'We've put up with enough rigmarole.' As I see, you won't help the king of your own accord. The pear stalk always points back to where it came from. Mean people prefer to lose something rather than sell it for a decent price. Those who give unwillingly forfeit both thanks and repayment. While the miser keeps his claws on his property, he often endures great losses for the sake of hanging on to a little ready cash. I call to witness the king, who is reduced to eating leaves and foliage (have faith in this oath, because it will be fulfilled), that I won't allow the king to be without the wolf skin he lacks any longer, since it is evidently at hand. I was putting off speaking in the hope that you would give it of your own accord, so that gratitude would be due for your service. Now I assert that you are of the age which is right for the skin that medicine demands. May he who suppresses the truth for fear or favor, and speaks falsehood for love or money, incur utter

Phisica cum fuerit tibi tam percursa frequenter,
  res michi quae patuit, non tibi nota fuit?
Unde medela foret supplenda, sine indice nosti,
  sed tibi cor longe, quod bene vellet, erat."
585 Has veluti nollet voces audisse, videtur
  respondisse senex, talia namque refert:
"Rex credat: curabis eum, si tanta medendi
  quanta meae pelli vis speciebus inest.
Proditur, ut taceam, canis mea testibus aetas;
590 lustra supergredior temporis octo quater.
Auspicium, Reinarde, tuum nimis omnia turbat;
  optimus est nactis immoderata modus.
Fila trahis libito, quidni? Pro regibus oras.
  Vespere laudari debet amoena dies;
595 scorpio blanditur vultu, pars postera pungit—
  forsitan in campo conveniemus adhuc!"
Ursus ait: "Quod vis, loquere, Ysengrime sodalis;
  canities multos occupat ante diem.
Accidit albedo, nec temporis usque fit index,
600 et nova nix albet vixque triennis olor."
Obviat archiater, dulci violenta locutum
  responso patruum pacificare volens:
"Patrue, cognatum terres, qui nulla minantem
  te timet et, quamvis oderis, ipse favet;
605 pone minas, precor, ut cupio tibi prospera cedant.
  Sed gravis offensae te tenet aula reum:
nam libertus adhuc debere thelonea regi
  diceris et retinens usque latere modo.

disgrace! Since medicine has been studied so thoroughly by you, wasn't the information which was clear to me, well known to you? You knew, without it being pointed out, where the cure was to be got from, but a well-wisher's heart was far distant from you."

The old man seemed to reply as if he had heard these 585 words unwillingly, for he answered as follows: "Let the king believe what I say: you'll cure him, if there's as much power of healing in your spices as there is in my skin. Even without my speaking, my age is betrayed by the evidence of these gray hairs; I've passed four times forty years. Your control 590 of affairs, Reynard, is throwing everything into confusion; moderation is best for those who have already acquired immoderate profits. You spin yarns as you like. Why not? You're a royal spokesman. A day ought to be praised as beautiful only in the evening; a scorpion welcomes one with its 595 face, but its back part stings. Perhaps one day we'll meet in the field!" The bear said: "Say what you wish, friend Ysengrimus, gray hairs attack many prematurely. Whiteness is an accidental attribute, and isn't always a sign of age; snow is 600 white when it's new, and a swan when it's just three years old."

The master medic, wishing to pacify by a gentle response the uncle who had uttered such violent remarks, countered: "Uncle, you're frightening your kinsman, who is in awe of you even when you're not uttering threats, and will do you a favor even if you hate him. Lay aside your threats, I beg, and 605 may good fortune befall you, as I wish. But the court holds you guilty of a serious offense; for it is said that you, a freedman, still owe tax to the king, and that up to this very moment you are skulking around with it in your possession.

Computat exactor pluris, quam possumus ambo
610   solvere, iacturam, debita deinde iubet.
Rem tibi cum dampno (rex hoc, si spondeo pro te,
    annuit) impensa solvere pelle licet.
Solvere dimidium, si succurrentis egeres,
    promptus eram, at pellis sat tua sola facit.
615 Quod si canitie pellem defendis inani,
    convinci propria proditione potes:
annus enim est hodie, nec nox super una nec infra,
    ex quo nos eadem ceperat octo domus;
nec mora, nonus ades. Viso tibi plausimus omnes,
620   praeside te nobis prospera quaeque rati.
Poscimus, ut tamquam gravis aevo et praeditus astu
    dictator nostro praeficerere choro,
at tu te perhibens semi minus esse triennem
    excusas annis et ruditate iugum.
625 Unde tibi veniunt tot nunc quinquennia, quando
    dimidium lustri non superaris ibi?
Fallere si dicor super his, procedite, testes!
    Surge celer, Ioseph, testificare michi,
tuque, asine, atque caper! Vos tres coeratis ibidem.
630   Testibus externis non adhibebo locum;
vos, quibus ille favet quique ipsius estis amici,
    eligo, vos verum dicite, nostis enim."
Dissimulant testes, iussi prodire morantur;
    se referunt rerum non meminisse satis.
635 Bis iussi prodire sedent, quasi "Numquid amicum
    possumus aut dominum prodere sive patrem?"
Tertio clamati tardant; Reinardus "In ipsum
    peccastis regem, ni properetis!" ait.

The tax collector reckons the debit at more than both of us together can pay, and what's more, he demands what's due. 610 It's possible for you to pay the sum and the interest (the king allows this, if I stand bail for you), with the gift of your hide. I was ready to pay half, if you'd been in need of anyone to help you, but your hide alone is sufficient. And if you defend 615 your skin by your worthless gray hairs, you can be refuted by your own declaration: it's a year today, not a day more or less, since the same house took in eight of us, and before long you made a ninth. We all expressed our pleasure at seeing you, envisaging advantages of all sorts from your patron- 620 age. We asked that you, as one who was mature in age and gifted with cleverness, be appointed leader of our company. But you, declaring yourself to be less, by half a year, than three years old, refused the responsibility because of your age and lack of experience. Where have you got so many 625 quinquennia from, when you hadn't passed half five years at that time? If I'm accused of lying about this, step forward, witnesses! Rise to your feet quickly, Joseph, and testify for me; you, ass, and you, goat! You three were there with us. I 630 won't take up space with unfriendly witnesses; I choose you, with whom he is on good terms, and who are his friends. Tell the truth, for you know it."

The witnesses put on a show of reluctance; ordered to step forward, they hung back, and said they didn't remember things well enough. Ordered for the second time to step 635 forward, they sat still, as if to say "can we really betray a friend, a lord, or a father?" Called for the third time, they hesitated. Reynard said: "Unless you hurry up, you've committed an offense against the king himself." As if afraid of

Hoc tamquam veriti surgunt, properare iubentur,
640   segniter accedunt, curia tota silet.
Ursus "An hos," inquit, "qui ter quoque surgere iussi
    vix parent testes, dicere falsa rear?"
Ordo datur fandi; vulpes "Secedite paulum
    vos duo, tu proceres, laniger," infit, "adi!
645 Hos superas aetate duos meliusque loquacem
    rethoricam nosti, vox tibi prima datur."
Ille susurranti similis senioris in aurem
    clamat, ut audiri possit ubique loquens:
"Ecce, patrine, vides, testari cogimur in te;
650   res tibi proficuo, si sapis, ibit adhuc.
Ut grates mereare datis, quae debita tamquam
    non debens peteris, da sine teste libens.
Nil nisi vile lupi corium rex postulat abs te;
    si tam parva negas, grandia quando dares?
655 Alba solet cornix affectum scire tacentis;
    ecce taces — taceas, ast ego nota loquar:
Ysengrimus ibi quidam fuit illius aevi,
    quod Reinardus ait; non ego testor in hunc,
non habet hic caudam, velut Anglicus alter habebat.
660   Nam, nisi qui coram est, tunc quoque nullus erat.
Insuper addo parum, quod vulpes nescit, at omnis
    curia cum magno rege fatetur idem:
si quis pellicii dampnum Ysengrimus adempti
    senserit, ammisso pax violata caret;
665 hic monachus praesto est omnem indulgere reatum —
    sic certe socii crimina celo mei!"

this, they rose, and were ordered to make haste, but ap-   640
proached slowly; the whole court was silent. The bear said:
"Shall I suppose that those witnesses who hardly obey when
they have thrice been ordered to rise, will tell falsehoods?"
The order to speak was given; the fox said: "You two stand
back a little, and you, sheep, come here by the nobles. You   645
surpass those two in age, and have learned better the art of
eloquent rhetoric. You can take the witness stand first."

The sheep, pretending to whisper into the ear of the old
man, actually made so much noise that he could be heard
speaking on all sides: "Well, godfather, you see we're forced
to bear witness against you, but the affair will still go to your   650
advantage, if you're wise. So that you may deserve thanks
for the gift, give willingly, and without being convicted by a
witness, that which is due and yet is sought as if you didn't
owe it. The king asks nothing of you but a measly wolf skin;
if you refuse such a triviality, when would you give anything
impressive? Only a white crow knows what's in the mind of   655
someone who says nothing! Well, you say nothing; say noth-
ing, but I'll say what I know. There *was* an Ysengrimus there
of that age which Reynard mentions; I don't testify against
this one—he doesn't have a tail as the other one, being an
Englishman, did. But it's also true that there wasn't any wolf   660
there apart from the one who's here. I'll add a little more,
of which the fox is unaware, but all the court, together with
the mighty king, will acknowledge: if any Ysengrimus feels
it's an injury to have had his skin peeled off, the peace can
be violated without crime; this monk is ready to grant indul-   665
gence to every offense.—Truly, this is how I cover up for the
misdeeds of my friend!"

Finierat vervex, subiecit talia vulpes:
   "Tu bene celasti, gratia magna tibi!
Foederis alterni signum est, quod cominus astas;
670   sic faceres, tecum fors ubicumque foret,
si duo privatim quovis staretis in agro,
   in natis pietas esset aperta patrum.
Eia nunc, caper, huc! Quod amas, testare loquendo."
   Prodiit excusans atque locutus ita est:
675 "Actus ego in testem, quod dicere debeo, dicam;
   Reinardi cogor non reticere metu.
Cognita quod dixit Ioseph, non eloquor ultro,
   sed scio quod sciri dico necesse nimis.
Quod foret abscondi dampnosum, sponte fatebor:
680   luna hodierna bona est, crastina vero nocens;
pellis ob hoc cuiusque lupi, cras usque senescens,
   optima quae nunc est, absque vigore foret."
Tertius accitur Carcophas testis asellus,
   concutiebatur voce rudentis humus:
685 "Ysengrime, senex iuvenis, laetare! Quod isti
   finxerunt testes, obice casso brevi.
Scis, quis sim? Stanpis oriondus ego esse magister
   Carcophas inter pascha Remisque feror.
Artis ego arridens, Carcophas dicor ab artem
690   allatrante Petro, littera totus ego.
Tam rudis intrasti forsan quam iunior istuc,
   ergo discipulis associare meis.
Grammaticam nosces; age, dic, cum scribitur n. c.
   supposito titulo, sillaba qualis erit?
695 Non loqueris?" (reticebat enim) "Fur, exue, nequam!
   Caedite! Quis virgas? Decoriabo canem!

The sheep had come to an end, and the fox threw in the following: "You've covered up very well, many thanks to you! It's a sign of mutual friendship, that you stand near together. Were you to do so wherever he happened to be with you, if the two of you were standing on your own in some field, the affection of the fathers would be manifest in their children. Well now, goat, come here, and testify to your love of the wolf in what you have to say." Making excuses, he came forward and spoke thus: "I'm forced into being a witness; I'll say what I must, compelled to break silence through fear of Reynard. Unwillingly I declare that Joseph has stated what is well known; but I know that what I say is only too necessary to recognize. I freely acknowledge what it would be harmful to conceal: the moon is favorable tonight, but tomorrow it will be malignant. Because of this, the skin of any wolf, if allowed to grow a day older, would be without effectiveness, while at this moment, it's at its best."

Carcophas the ass was summoned as third witness; the ground was shaken by the voice of the braying animal. "Ysengrimus, elderly youth, be happy! I'll demolish what these witnesses have invented, with a brief objection. Do you know who I am? I'm master Carcophas, said to be of Étampes, between Easter and Reims; I'm a patron of learning, and I'm called Carcophas, from a fusion of 'Cephas' and 'art,' with a kind of a bark in front of it. I am scholarship personified. Perhaps you've come in here as untutored as you're young, so you can be counted among my pupils. You'll know grammar; so come, tell me, when 'nc' is written with a mark above it, what syllable does that indicate? . . . Aren't you answering?" (for he was silent) "You wicked rogue, take off your skin! Beat him! Who has the canes? I'll skin the dog

670

675

680

685

690

695

Collige litterulas, 'nunc' sillaba nascitur, hoc est,
    quod nunc pellicio despoliandus ades.
Indico, non testor, villos spectate recentes!
700   Iunior est dicto, praebeat ergo cutem.
Rusticus hic Ioseph versus facit atque b. e. b.
    colligit, at tu 'nunc' sillabicare nequis?
Grammaticae minimum nescis, medicusque videri
    appetis atque etiam claustra subisse refers?
705 Quam bene cantata est hodie tibi prima! Solesne
    sic sapere in claustro sicut agenda foris?
Psallere qui monachus non novit, consulo pellem
    exuat, exuta pelle peritus erit.
Quam procul hinc velles, si sors favisset, abesse!
710   Sed prius, ut scieris psallere, nosse velim;
horarum series causa est brevitatis agendae,
    quando dabis tunicam, tota canenda simul.
Exue, fur, saccum! Rex noster primitus illo
    utetur, tribulis serviet inde meis.
715 Contempnit parere michi; Berfride, iubeto!
    Te citius forsan praecipiente facit.
Per sanctum Bavona! Nichil pietate lucramur;
    mos suus est monacho, vi capit, ungue tenet."
Desierant testes, monachoque petita negante
720   intulit haec Graeco phisicus ore vafer:
"Testibus auditis reus, Ysengrime, subire
    cogitur emendam suppliciumve pati.
Ne tamen hinc aut tristis eas aut actus in iram,
    rex facere intendit, tu prout ipse sinis,

alive! Put the letters together, and the syllable 'nunc' appears
— that is, that *now* you're here to have your skin removed. I
don't bear verbal witness, I simply point to the evidence:
look at his new-grown coat! He's younger than he said, so let   700
him offer his skin. This simpleton Joseph makes verses and
can put together long and short to make 'bă-āā-bā,' and you
can't even produce the single syllable 'nunc'? You know next
to nothing of grammar, and you want to be taken for a doc-
tor, and furthermore, claim that you entered the cloister?
How well you've sung Prime today! Do you usually know   705
your duties inside the cloister as well as you do those outside
it? I advise, that a monk who doesn't know how to sing his
psalms, should lay aside his fur coat; once that's off, he'll be-
come learned. How far away from here you would like to
be, if only luck was on your side! But first, I'd like to know   710
how you can chant psalms. For the sake of brevity, when you
hand over your tunic, you must sing the whole sequence of
hours at once. Take off your hair shirt, thief! Our king will
have first use of it, and then it'll come in handy for my
leather straps. He is scornful of obeying me; Berfridus, you   715
order him. Perhaps he'll do it quicker if you tell him to. By
Saint Bavo! we get nothing by being kind to him. A monk
has his own way of doing things: he takes something by force
and hangs on to it with tooth and nail."

The witnesses had ended, and the monk still denied
what was requested, so the cunning doctor made the fol-   720
lowing remarks in the Greek tongue: "When the witnesses
have been heard, Ysengrimus, the criminal is forced to
make reparation or to suffer punishment. And so that
you don't leave here despondent, or driven into a rage,
the king intends to act just as you yourself will permit,

725   te potius pietate trahens quam viribus angens.
      Poscit permodico rex sua iura modo:
    si dare te taedet pellem, praestare memento;
      rex, ubi sudarit, mox tibi reddet eam.
    Dixeris haec contra quicquam, ter noctibus octo
730   non repetes punctum commoditatis idem!—
    Quid, miser, usque taces? Non est tibi cura pudoris?
      Fac, si quid facies, potio frixa fere est.
    Nunc calida est aestas, nec eges hoc pellis in aestu;
      quin huc miramur traxeris utquid eam,
735   tam gravis est tamque inspectu deformiter horret.
      Cur, vesane, tibi larva lupina placet?
    Talibus in media visis hyeme octo nec una
      dignarer scapulas dedecorare meas!
    Paene tamen dubitas, servare an tradere malis
740   pellicium, et quid si stricta rigeret hyemps?
    Quod si dimidiam petereris ponere pellem,
      exemplum Turoni tu sequerere patris?
    Tergora nec certe decimare paratior esses,
      persica quam myrtus fragave ferre salix!
745   Ut praestes, rex ipse petit, porro omnis agendas
      aestuat ad grates curia, vixque voles?
    Ergo michi pellem donares sero minanti,
      quam praestare parum rege rogante negas?
    Non dare (quid, demens, dubitas?), praestare rogaris,
750   et pellis domino mox reditura suo est!
    Nec tu praestiteris villano sive quiriti
      plebigenae, pellem rex petit ipse tuam!

coaxing you by kindness rather than constraining you by 725
force; he asks for his due in the most moderate manner pos-
sible. If you don't like the idea of giving your skin, think
about lending it. When the king has been through the
sweating process, he will give it straight back to you. Say
what you like against this, you won't find such a degree of 730
complaisance for a month to come!—What, wretch, are you
still silent? Don't you have any concern for decency? Do
something, if you're going to; the medicine is almost ground.
The summer heat is now blazing; you don't need a fur coat in
this temperature—indeed we wonder why you've lugged it
all the way here. It's so heavy, and it's so shaggy and horrible 735
to look at. What is it you like about this lupine outfit, you
lunatic? If I'd seen eight such things even in the middle of
winter, I wouldn't deign to disgrace my back with one of
them. And are you almost doubtful as to whether you prefer
to keep your skin or give it away? What if we were in the 740
iron grip of winter? What if you were asked to take off half
your skin, would you follow the example of the patron saint
of Tours? No, indeed, you wouldn't be any more likely to
yield a tenth of it than the myrtle is to bear peaches, or the
willow strawberries! The king himself asks you to lend it; 745
moreover, the whole court is eager to express its thanks, and
you can't bring yourself to consent? So, would you belatedly
make me a gift of your skin because of my threats, when you
refuse to lend it for a little while at the king's request? You're
not asked to give it (why are you hesitating, idiot?), but only
to lend it, and the skin will soon return to its owner! What's 750
more, you won't have lent it to a peasant or a bourgeois gen-
tleman; the king himself requests your skin! On a day like

Nonne domi fugeres hodie ter nudus ad umbram?
  Quis vetat hic Satanas ponere terga semel?
755 Non sine pelle potes tantillum vivere? Numquam
  pro nichilo vidi sic trepidare probum.
Si saperes, certe tu regem sponte rogasses,
  quod praestare negas, hoc licuisse dari.
Me miserum, quod iniqua michi natura negavit
760 obsequio domini congrua terga mei!
Aegocero fundente nives, incendia Cancro
  non, ut praestarem, sollicitandus eram;
non praestare michi plus quam praebere liberet—
  sed te nulla tuae laudis opella trahit!"
765 Hinc sperans patuisse sibi Ysengrimus asilum
  non profectura callidus arte refert:
"Decipis incautum, vulpecula perfida, regem,
  certius antidotum sum meditatus ego:
Francigenae est longe potior membrana senisque
770 quam iuvenis corium Teutonicique lupi.
Me fore Teutonicum nostis iuvenemque probastis,
  sed non et medicam vim mea pellis habet;
rex suspendat opus, pergam subitoque revertar,
  Francigenam regi quaerere vado senem."
775 Callidus archiater, quid possit dicere contra
  non dubitans, monacho leniter infit item:
"Patrue, quid si pelle tua minor illius esset,
  regis opus quando est omnia membra tegi?
Nec senis aut iuvenis praeter tua novimus usquam
780 tergora, quae regem totum operire queant."
Repplicat haec abbas: "Vanus timor iste videtur,
  si regis curam, quam profiteris, habes;

today wouldn't you three times rather run away home naked in the shade? What devil stops you taking off your skin just once! Can't you live skinless for just a little while? I've never 755 seen an honest man dithering about nothing in this way. If you had any sense, you'd certainly have asked the king of your own accord that you be allowed to make a present of this thing that you refuse to lend. Alas, that cruel nature denied me a skin suitable for my master's service! Whether 760 Capricorn was shedding snow, or Cancer heat, I wouldn't have to be begged to lend it, and giving it would be no less a pleasure than lending—but you're not attracted by any little effort toward your own glory."

Ysengrimus, in hopes that an escape route might be 765 opened for him, replied with cunning (but a cunning doomed to failure): "Deceitful fox, you're misleading the trusting king. I have more reliable ideas about the antidote. The skin of an old French wolf is far more potent than the 770 hide of a Germanic youth. You knew I was Germanic, and you've proved me to be young, and so my hide has no curative power. Let the king suspend the business; I'll go away and come straight back—I'll go to look for an old Frenchman for the king." The crafty master medic, in no hesitation 775 as to what he might reply, mildly spoke again to the monk: "Uncle, what if his skin were to be smaller than yours, when it's essential that all the king's limbs should be covered? We've never known a hide, whether of an old man or a young one, which is capable of covering the king completely, ex- 780 cept yours."

The abbot answered as follows: "This fear seems an idle one, if you have the concern for the king which you profess.

si brevior iusto fuerit quam legero pellem,
    adde tuam, fieri pilleus inde potest.
785 Sufficient binae; si vis captare tyrannos,
    fidere non debes calliditate diu.
Non procul a vivo debes urgere favorem;
    effectum probitas in probitate capit.
Gratia primatum brevis est, nisi semper ematur;
790 ne meritum perdas, usque merere sequax.
Maxima vilescunt avidis maiora parandi;
    omne bonum impendit pro meliore bonus.
Perdere nil metuat nisi regem regis amicus;
    me penes agrestes sufficit esse lupos."
795 "Patrue," respondit Reinardus, "ydonea suades,
    ista sed unicolor potio tegmen avet.
Non igitur curanda putes discrimina fandi.
    Proderit hic Galli mentio nulla lupi,
tam nos Sarmaticum quam commendamus Yberum;
800 unde sit, haut refert, sit lupus, ipse valet.
Fidus in hoc certe es 'senior plus proforet aegro';
    dico lupum iuvenem, dico valere senem.
Quemlibet esse bonum stat testibus, ore duorum
    laudatur senior, quattuor ore tener.
805 Nescio, praestet uter, iuvenis seniorne, medelae,
    dum, quis sit potior, iudice pelle probem.
Ergo senem iuvenemque simul vellemus adesse,
    praestaret regi tegmen uterque suum.

If the skin which I shall get is smaller than is appropriate, add your own! You can make a cap out of it; the two of them will be enough. If you want to win the favor of monarchs, you shouldn't rely on your wits for long. You ought to follow up a favor until you're bled dry; kindness needs to be followed by more kindness in order to get results. The gratitude of princes doesn't last for long, unless it is continually being won. If you don't want to lose your deserts, take care to be continually deserving. Great services are held cheap by those who are eager to be furnished with greater ones. A good fellow gives every benefit for the sake of a better one. Let the king's friend fear losing nothing except the king. I'm content to take my place among the simple wolves of the country."

"Uncle," replied Reynard, "you argue plausibly, but this medicine needs a covering which is all of one color. So don't think that linguistic distinctions need be worried about. Mentioning a French wolf won't do you any good; we recommend indifferently a Slav or a Spaniard. It's of no importance where he's from; if he's a wolf, he'll do. You're quite certain of this, that 'an older wolf would do the patient more good'; *I* say that a young wolf will do him good, and an old one too. It's clear from the witnesses that any wolf is good enough, an old one being recommended by two, and a young one by four. I don't know whether a young one or an old one will provide the cure, until I test which is more efficacious, with the skin as the basis for the decision. For this reason we should like both an old and a young one to be here together, so that each might offer the king his hide. However,

785

790

795

800

805

Proposuit iuvenem fortuna senemque negavit;
810   parcimus absenti praeripimusque datum.
Venandi indociles partis infigimus unguem;
    una avis in laqueo plus valet octo vagis.
Nullorsum ergo abies; si digrederere, reverti
    undecies nono non paterere die.
815 Si prorsus iuvenem prodesse negaveris aegro,
    esto senex potius quam potiare fuga;
te vetulum fingi malim quam pergere quoquam.
    Ante ego te novi tuque valere senem.
Vis ergo, iuvenis; vis, canus; es utpote pelvis,
820   quicquid habes aevi, te valuisse liquet.
Nunc age, da tunicam, ne rusticus esse feraris;
    fingeris, ut valeas te quoque teste, senex.
Si te nec formido potest nec gratia regis
    flectere, da saltem motus amore meo!
825 Nunc te gratanter, nisi desipis, arbitror esse
    facturum, quicquid te facere hortor ego,
praesertim, ut te semper amem, cum noveris, utque
    nunc quoque, me sanum consulere usque tibi."
Surdior ille piro glandes producere iussa
830   effluere in ventos mitia verba sinit.
Tunc primum effremuit medicus patruique tenacis
    duritiam increpitans probra favoris agit:
"Proh! Dubitas et adhuc? Et quando velle valebis?
    Nunc certe nimium te scio parva peti!
835 Ergo pelle tua regem vestire recusas?
    Cui procerum tantus non placuisset honor?

Fortune has offered the youth and refused the old man; so   810
we'll skip the one who's not here, and grab what's offered. I
don't know anything about hunting, so I lay hands on what's
available; a bird in the hand is worth eight in the bush. So
you won't go anywhere; if you were to leave, you wouldn't be
willing to return even after ninety-nine days. Of course, if   815
you're going to deny that a young wolf is any use to the pa-
tient, you can be an old one, rather than take to flight. I'd
prefer that you were supposed to be an old man, rather than
that you should go anywhere. Earlier on *I* was sure that you
could do it, and *you* were sure that an old man could. Be what
you want, therefore, old or young, seeing that you're like
a basin, capable of being useful however old you are. Now   820
come on, hand over your tunic, lest you're said to be churl-
ish. We'll pretend you're an old man, so that, by your own
testimony, you'll fit the bill. If neither fear nor favor of the
king can move you, at least give it under the influence of
love of me! *Now,* unless you've lost all sense, I believe that   825
you'll cheerfully do whatever I urge you to, especially since
you know that I am always your friend and that I always ad-
vise you for your good, as I do now."

Deafer than a pear tree ordered to produce acorns, he al-   830
lowed these gentle words to float away on the winds. Then
for the first time the doctor raised his voice, and rebuking
the harshness of his obstinate uncle, he reproached him
with the kindness shown him: "Well! Are you still waver-
ing? When are you going to be able to assent? Now, indeed, I
recognize that you've been entreated too much for a trifle!
Do you refuse to clothe the king with your skin? Which   835
of the nobles wouldn't have been proud of such an honor?

Villano temere piperatus pavo paratur!
   Sponte tibi occurrit gloria, tuque fugis?
Patrue, si fieret pellis michi causa petendae,
840   ut tua nunc regi, sic michi praesto foret?
Magna michi de te fiducia suppetit, a quo
   impetrare nequit terga lupina leo!
Audio, quod verum est, 'Paterae pix cassa madenti est,'
   clava velut stulto, pellis amata tibi est.
845 Quis cuiquam credat? Sumus una stirpe creati,
   nec tibi me sentis consuluisse probe.
Non captantis heros delato paupere ritum,
   immo tui curam fidus honoris ago;
nam sine pelle tua poterit rex vivere forsan,
850   tu, nisi praestiteris, manzer avarus eris.
Amodo res, ut oportet, eat sino; feceris illud,
   feceris hoc, sine me sat facienda sapis.—
Rex, claret probitatis adhuc tibi secta lupinae?
   Tredecies dixi: 'Nil dabit ille tibi,'
855 nec michi credebas, donec tibi prodidit ipse;
   credis adhuc saltem me tibi vera loqui?
Aspice, quo iactes! Non hic tibi sensio cessit;
   diligit et regno plus sua terga tuo.
Emorerere quidem citius, quam vile tibi illud
860   exueret saltem, quo sua terga tegit.
Non super externo moveor, carissime regum,
   confundor patrui rusticitate mei—
praesertim summi cum me sciat ipse magistri
   inter pellifices obtinuisse locum,
865 nec dubitet nostra regaliter arte novatum
   se prius huc quinto posse redire die."

It's pointless to put spiced peacock in front of a peasant! Glory comes of her own accord to meet you, and you run away? Uncle, if *I* were to ask for your skin, as the king does now, is this how you'd put it at my disposal? Great is my reliance in you, when the lion can't even get a wolf skin out of you! I've heard, and it's true, that pitch is no good to the basin that's already dripping wet. You're as fond of your hide as a fool is of his stick. Who can trust anybody? We're born of one family, and yet you think I haven't given you honest advice. I'm not acting like someone who wins the favor of his betters by accusing a poor man—rather I'm looking after your honor like a true friend. For the king could perhaps live without your skin, but you, unless you give it him, will never be anything but a greedy son of a bitch. Henceforth, I'll allow matters to take their own course; whether you do one thing or another, you'll know well enough what's to be done without my help.—Your majesty, is the nature of wolfish generosity clear to you by now? Thirteen times did I say 'he won't give you anything,' and you didn't believe me until he himself provided the evidence; now at least do you believe that I was telling you the truth? You see what you have to boast of! The old man hasn't given in to you here; he loves his own skin more than your kingdom. In fact you would die before he'd merely remove that vile covering from his back for your sake. It's not a stranger I'm making such a fuss about, dearest of kings, it's the boorishness of my own uncle by which I'm put to shame, especially since he knows that I have reached the position of supreme master among furriers, and is in no doubt that he can be renovated royally by my art and return here before five days are out."

Frivola longa suae medico complente loquelae
    rex breviter solvit talibus ora modis:
"Qua, Reinarde, licet, studet Ysengrimus honesto,
870   moeniaque intravit nostra cliente carens;
detrahere exuvias ipsum sibi dedecet ecce.
    Detrahat has aliquis, non negat ipse michi.
Tu, Bruno, alterutrum facies: vel detrahe nostro
    abbati tunicam, vel michi trade tuam."
875 Clamat ad haec vervex: "Utrum eligis, urse? Seorsum
    provisurus, utrum sit tibi pluris, abi!"
Reddidit haec Bruno: "Ioseph collega, quid horum
    praetulerim, memet consule nosco satis:
laetior exuerem regi mea terga daturus,
880   esset enim utilius commodiusque michi,
sed ne forte meo ferar invidisse sodali,
    nolo mala externam subripere arte vicem.
Impleat ergo suum, cui sors est prospera, munus,
    et regem trabea vestiat ille sua."
885 Non haec dicta lupus laudi putat esse, iocove
    nec risu studium dissimulantis agit;
sed nec consilium Bruno vocemque rogandam,
    quod de propositis eligat, esse putat.
Prosiliens ergo quasi fulgetra mota ruebat—
890   praecipitis vulpes volvitur ante pedes.
"O patrui miserere mei, Bruno inclite!" dixit,
    "Nescierat regem pellis egere suae,
huc ideo pellem non attulit ipse nisi unam.
    Unius est heres datque libenter eam,
895 incolumes ungues dumtaxat habere sinatur;
    cetera praestantis pace meaque feras.

As the doctor brought to a close the lengthy trifles of his speech, the king opened his mouth briefly to the following effect: "Ysengrimus is anxious for propriety at all costs, Reynard. He came into our castle without any servants, and, you see, it's not fitting for him to take his coat off himself. Let someone else remove it; he doesn't deny me it. You, Bruno, shall do one of two things: either remove our abbot's tunic, or give me yours." At this, the sheep called out: "Which do you choose, bear? Go away and consider which of them is of greater value to you!" Bruno gave this answer: "Colleague Joseph, I know well enough which of these, in my own mind, I would prefer. I'd more cheerfully remove my own skin to give it to the king—indeed it would be more useful and convenient for me. But lest perchance I should be said to have been envious of a companion, I am reluctant to rob someone else of his chance by devious means. Let him whom chance has favored discharge his office, and let him clothe the king in his robe."

The wolf didn't think there was anything praiseworthy about this speech, nor did he take any care to dissemble this fact by a laugh or a joke, but Bruno, not thinking it necessary to take counsel or to speak in favor of the option he should choose, leaped up and was falling on the wolf like a flash of lightning. The fox tumbled in front of his rushing feet: "Oh pity my uncle, noble Bruno!" he said. "He didn't know the king needed his fur coat, so he only brought one here with him. He possesses only one, which he is willing to give, so long as he is allowed to keep his claws intact. The rest you can have, as far as the donor is concerned, and me

870

875

880

885

890

895

Non nimis urgeri debet, qui commodat ultro;
   creber in os largae ne speculeris equae."
Arguit iratus poscentem talia Ioseph:
900   "Ha, Reinarde, tui nunc patuere doli!
Idcirco patuli satiabitur alveus Orci,
   implebuntque malos corpora multa lacus!
Tu quoque nimirum quanto livore gravaris,
   quod patruus potior te foret atque prior!
905 Maiorum et parium successibus usque secundis
   carpitur et languet callidus atque potens.
Plus, quamvis doleas, prior est fore dignus eritque!
   Reinardus prava calliditate viget;
ut favet, hortatur, non ut sapit, invidet ergo,
910   abba bone, auspiciis emoriturque tuis.
Qui meritum minuit, laudem rarescere cogit.
   Semari tunicam perfidus ille rogat!
Ysengrime, fave tibimet! Tuus aestimor hostis,
   sed tibi dogma meum non ut ab hoste datur:
915 serviat ad plenum, qui serviet, integra reddat
   obsequia, aut certe prorsus habeto sibi.
Suadeo, sicut amo: si quaeritur integra facto
   gratia, servitium dimidiare cave!
Unguibus amissis quid prodest cetera pellis?
920   Fervida per portas quattuor aura subit,
et sub quadrifora rex sudans pelle liquescit—
   sic tibi, sic regi phisicus iste sapit!
Da, domine Ysengrime, tuos radicitus ungues,
   da corium et carnem, nil retinere velis.
925 Praemoneo, minimum ne perdant tergora villum,
   nam si perdiderint, irrita prorsus erunt!"

too! Someone who makes a gift of his own accord shouldn't be nagged too much. Don't look a gift horse too often in the mouth!"

Joseph angrily attacked this request: "Ah, Reynard, now your schemes are clear—on whose account the hollow of wide Orcus will be filled, and a multitude of bodies will cram the sinister pools. You're overcome by so much envy because your uncle would be more distinguished and important than you! Someone shrewd and powerful is always wounded by, and grieved at, the good successes of his equals and betters. Even though it pains you, he's worthy of taking precedence over you, and he shall do so! Reynard is full of malicious shrewdness; his advice is dictated by self-interest, not by wisdom, and he's dying with envy, worthy abbot, at your good fortune. Whoever lessens anyone's merit, is also abstracting from his praise. The traitor is asking for the tunic to be halved! Ysengrimus, do yourself a favor! I'm reckoned your enemy, but my directive to you isn't issued as from an enemy: let anyone who is to perform a service, perform it fully. Let him do the favor without stinting, or keep it to himself! I advise you as I love you: if you want the thanks for an action to be complete, don't offer only half the service! What's the rest of the skin worth when the claws are left behind? The hot air will pass through the four openings, and the king's sweat will run away through the four holes in the skin. That's how wise this doctor is for you and for the king! Give, Dom Ysengrimus, give your claws in their entirety; give skin and flesh, and don't wish to keep back anything. I warn you that your hide shouldn't lose the tiniest tuft of hair, because if it does, it will certainly be ineffectual!"

Dixerat haec Ioseph, laudabat curia dictum,
    nec fore sic quisquam, qui reticeret, erat.
Tunc gemebundus ait specifer: "Bruno, optime consul,
930   publica quandoquidem contio censet, adi!
At peto pauca . . . locus fuerit . . . concede . . . merebor:
    amplius invento ne rapuisse feras!
Non plus ille quidem, quam repperit, abstulit usquam;
    fas habita est, habitis tollere plura nefas."
935 Annuit oranti miseratus itemque volabat,
    pontifici vetulo demere terga parans;
Berfridus tumido sic clamans obstitit ore:
    "Bruno, miser Bruno, siste parumper adhuc!
Testificor sanctum, quem saepe requiro, Botulphum,
940   pro vacua pulicem non ego pelle darem.
Detrahe plus toto! Nisi plus quam tota trahantur
    tergora, lumbrico deteriora facis.
Postulat archiater stulte, meritoque negantur
    munera, quae violant ius superantque modum."
945 Ursus ad haec paucis (et non revocabilis ibat):
    "Quod tribui, tribui, quodque paciscor, ago.
Tu vero Latiam nescis, domine abba, loquelam;
    tergora ne fiant deteriora, iuvo.
Tu submitte caput, tu membra extende, docebo,
950   qui tunicam Franco ponere more queas."
Desuper ergo ac subtus et hinc atque inde relectum
    grandaevi iuvenis restrofat ursus ephot;
unde altum medias discriminat occiput aures,
    postremas calces mensus adusque metit.
955 Horrida non alio falx pervolat impete faenum;
    non alio candens unguina crassa calibs.

Joseph's speech was over, and the court approved of what he had said, nor was there anyone who failed to say that it must be so. Then the spice importer said, groaning: "Bruno, noblest counselor, since indeed the public assembly has de- 930 cided, approach! But I make one small request—let there be room for it—grant it—and I'll show myself deserving: that you shouldn't take more than you find! He himself never took more than he found. It's right to take away what some- one has, but wrong to take away more than that."

Out of pity, the bear acceded to the suppliant, and was 935 on the move again, getting ready to remove the old prel- ate's hide, when Berfridus held him up by crying excitedly: "Bruno, wretched Bruno, still, wait a little! I swear, by Saint Botulph, whose devotee I am, I wouldn't give a flea for the 940 empty skin. Take more than everything! Unless you take more than the whole hide, you're just nibbling like a tape- worm. The master medic's request is foolish, and gifts which controvert what's right and exceed moderation are deserv- edly refused."

The bear replied briefly (and moved on inexorably): 945 "What I've granted, I've granted; what I agreed to, I per- form. Now you, my lord abbot, are ignorant of the French language; I'll help you so that your skin doesn't get shabby. Bend your head, and stretch out your limbs, and I'll teach you how you can take off your tunic in the French way." So, 950 having read off the priestly robe of the aged youth up and down and from side to side, the bear sheared it off, tak- ing the measure and slashing from where the middle of his skull separated his tall ears, right down to the heels of his back feet. With just such a swoop does the fierce scythe 955 slice through hay, or glowing-hot steel through thick fat.

Anteriora tamen restant suralia nec non
    aure tenus tegmen frontis ab aure patens,
porro super nasum caudale ut tortilis ibat
960   nervus ab exortu frontis adusque labrum.
Unguibus incussis citra nimis, ursus utrimque
    liquerat haec, nimia mobilitate volans.
Clamavitque alacer: "Comites, haec lectio lecta est;
    nunc melius, cui non complacet ista, legat.
965   Sed sic Teutonicae membrana est nescia linguae,
    tamquam Pictavi corpore rapta lupi.
Carcophas, quid ais? Videor legisse venuste?
    At tu dic, vervex, et caper!" Ambo tacent.
Reddidit haec asinus: "Peream, nisi legeris apte,
970   hactenus et placide sustinet ille legi.
Legeris ulterius, iam sentiet; ecce pusillum,
    quod modo legisti, senserat ipse fere."
Tunc iratus aper sic frenduit ore minaci:
    "Ysengrime, nichil convenienter agis.
975   Quam sit Bruno diu phanaticus aut ubi, miror,
    scit iuvenem papam detunicare probe.
Tam bene si casulam posuisset cappifer albus,
    ter tria mox surgens mala vorasset Abel.
Huic tamen officio grates ut honoris inani
980   ac fructus—animum nescio—voce siles.
Insipiens dici poteras, nisi norma vetaret;
    cautius at posthac utiliusque geras.
Dic super impenso famulatu gratus honorem;
    dedecet acceptis abnuere usque vicem.
985   Et ne despicias accire diacona talem,
    quocumque eligeris presbiter esse loco."

But there remained behind the socks on his forepaws, and also a covering for his forehead, visible between his ears — or rather a ribbon, like a crooked sinew, ran over his nose from 960 the swelling of his forehead as far as his mouth; the bear had plunged his claws in too much to each side, and had left this behind in the excessive haste of his rush.

He called out cheerfully: "Comrades, this Lesson has been read; now anyone who doesn't like it can read it better. But this vellum is as innocent of the Germanic language as 965 if it were torn from the body of a Poitevin wolf. Carcophas, what do you say? Do I seem to have read pleasantly? You at least, sheep and goat, speak up!" They were both silent, but the ass replied as follows: "Let me die if you didn't read excellently. And so far, he has patiently borne being read. If 970 you read further, he'll soon feel the effects; you see he's hardly felt the little bit you've just read."

Then the angry boar threatened with gnashing teeth: "Ysengrimus, you're not acting properly at all. I wonder 975 how long, or where, Bruno has been in orders, so well does he know how to unrobe a young bishop. If the white-robed surplice-wearer — the sheep — had removed a chasuble as well as that, he would have got nine apples to munch the minute he rose from his knees. But you express no thanks verbally (as for what's in your mind, I don't know) for this 980 service, as if it gave you neither honor nor benefit. You could be called a fool, if the Rule didn't forbid it. You should act more carefully and profitably in future. Be grateful and express appreciation for a service rendered; it's shameful always to refuse any return for things you've accepted. And 985 don't hesitate to summon such a deacon to the place, wherever it may be, where you're elected priest."

Laniger obiecit: "Potius michi Bruno videtur
  officio grates non meruisse suo.
Nil coepisse minus quam coepta refringere laedit;
990   officium grates integritate trahit.
Detrahe, Bruno, mitram! Si non detraxeris illi,
  glabrio dicetur; detrahe, Bruno, mitram!
Parcius abrepta grator, quam parte relicta
  anxior, et grates Bruno sibi optat agi!
995 Quod canis ambesa fertur meruisse placenta,
  hoc meruit Bruno nec meliora ferat.
Balnea laudarem, si rasa corona fuisset;
  nunc monachus credi protinus esse nequit.
Rex ubi pontificem fieri deliberat illum?
1000   Ampla ad utrasque aures infula tendit adhuc!
Hactenus est abbas, statuatur denique praesul?
  Unde lupis tanta est gloria tamque frequens?
Sic ego revera (nec sum robustior urso)
  obsequii grates non meriturus eram;
1005 expilarem oculos et demolirer ego aures,
  sin aliter nollet rapta tyara sequi.
Curandum paucis praeter michi credo tibique,
  O caper, expertem luminis ire lupum.
Si duo nos illi lumen pateremur abesse,
1010   auribus avulsis nulla querela foret;
scilicet abstracto penetralia libera peplo
  auditum traherent liberiore via."
Dixerat haec vervex; eadem Berfridus et illi
  dicere se iurat proposuisse diu,
1015 et poenam triduana iubet ieiunia culpae,
  saepius inculcans, post caveatur idem.

The sheep objected: "On the contrary, it seems to me that Bruno hasn't earned any thanks by his service. It's less harmful not to have begun, than to interrupt something that's been started; a service wins thanks when it's been performed to the full. Take off the miter, Bruno! If you don't take it off him, he'll be called a fop; take the miter off, Bruno! I'm less glad about what's been removed than concerned about what's left—and Bruno wants to be thanked! What a dog is said to deserve for gnawing a cake, that's what Bruno deserves, and he won't get anything better. I'd approve of the anointing, if his crown were shaved. Right this moment he can't even be thought a monk; to which bishopric is the king thinking of appointing him? His broad miter still stretches from ear to ear! Up to now he's been an abbot; is he going to end up by being made a bishop? What's the reason for such great and repeated honor being given to wolves? Truly, I wouldn't earn thanks for the service in this way (and I'm no stronger than the bear); I'd gouge out his eyes and rip off his ears, if the miter wouldn't be torn off and come away by any other means. I don't think many besides me and you, goat, would mind if the wolf were deprived of his eyes. If we two were to bear him losing his sight, there'd be no complaint about ripping off his ears; in fact when the covering is taken away, the exposed inner parts will be open for hearing with freer access." This is what the sheep said; Berfridus swore that he had long intended to say the same to Bruno, and ordered a three-day fast as punishment for his fault, frequently impressing on him that it should be guarded against in future.

Iam lupus abstracto fundebat tergore rivum
    sanguinis, ut denso defluit imbre latex,
rubrior et stilla fluvii currentis ab alto
1020   agnini iuguli vulnere totus erat.
Clamat ovans medicus: "Per totum venimus istuc
    delecti regnum ius agere atque loqui,
et quia lactificare caper, vel mingere ceram
    Carcophas didicit, contio nostra dolet;
1025 degrassetur enim cum tanta iniuria regem,
    vos aliud miror depuduisse queri.
Non detrans Tanaim plus fulgurat edita syndo,
    nec situs annosum tam rubefecit ebur,
quam poderis bis tincta rubet, de qua iste superbit,
1030 ante quidem, non nunc, patruus ipse michi.
Quis consanguineus miser audeat esse potentis?
    Dispariter funem dives inopsque trahunt.
Donec visus erat pauper, velamine vili
    obsitus, hunc poterat non puduisse mei;
1035 nunc fortasse pudet, postquam detecta vetatur
    purpura sub corio delituisse lupi.
Institor hanc Tyrio iam nunc extraxit aeno,
    stillat adhuc croceo tinctio rore recens.
Vos agite, o proceres, per vestrum et regis honorem,
1040 cernite fulmineae vestis herile iubar!
O quam pauperibus dives splendere videtur!
    Sed quid opes prosunt, cum sit avarus habens?
Divite commendor patruo, confundor avaro;
    prosperitas simplex est, ubi taeter olor.
1045 Dives avaritia est melior vix paupere largo.
    Solvis egestatis, patrue, probra meae;

Now the wolf was pouring forth a river of blood from his lost skin, just as rain flows from a thick cloud, and he was redder all over than a drop from the river that flows out of the deep wound in a lamb's throat. The doctor jubilantly cried: "We've been chosen throughout the whole kingdom to come here, to pronounce on and execute the law; and this whole assembly regrets that the goat has learned how to give milk, and Carcophas to piss honey, because when the wolf casts up such an insult against the king, I'm surprised that you have the effrontery to complain about anything else. There's no greater sheen on the silk produced beyond the Don, nor does disuse give a deeper blush to old ivory, than there is in the red glow of the double-dyed tunic which he flaunts—he who used to be, but is no longer, my uncle. What wretch can dare to be kinsman to one of the powerful? Rich and poor don't exert the same degree of leverage. While he seemed poor, covered with a nasty cloak, it was possible for him not to be ashamed of me. Now perhaps he is ashamed, since the purple revealed beneath his wolf's hide is not allowed to remain hidden any longer. The merchant has only just taken it out of the Tyrian vat; the fresh dye still drips with a golden dew. Come, you princes, by your own and the king's honor, look at the lordly splendor of his shining robe! How resplendent a rich man seems to the poor! But what use are riches, when it's a miser who has them? I am honored by my uncle's riches, but shamed by his greed; unqualified good fortune is found about as often as black swans. Wealthy avarice is hardly better than generous poverty. You remove the shame of my poverty, uncle; my

1020

1025

1030

1035

1040

1045

te mea non adeo laedit penuria, quantum
  constat avaritiae me puduisse tuae.
Visere quis cupiens regalem providus aulam
1050 tegmina gestasset deteriora foris?
Tu super inducens pellis tegumenta lupinae
  caesaris ad nudum cultus ad instar eras!
Quam decuit tali Tyrius sub tegmine murex,
  clara sub hirsuta purpura pelle lupi!
1055 Sed teneo, pellem cur non donaveris ultro:
  texta verebaris ditia posse peti,
sordidus idcirco venisti pelle lupina,
  ornatum celebrem dissimulare volens.
Vix precibus longis extorsimus, improbe, tandem,
1060 ostendi cultus ut paterere tuos.
Purpura si saltem gestata forinsecus atque
  interius pellis, culpa ferenda fuit.
Curia si mecum sentit rectumque tuetur,
  rege super laeso iudicat atque dolet.
1065 Contemptus regis pensandus honore coaequo est,
  excessus queritur regia causa duos:
potio suspensa est monacho retinente cucullam,
  induvias turpes horruit aula videns.
Praesumptum temere est, nec inemendata manebit
1070 aut non praeteriet sospite culpa reo."
Has medici voces confirmat curia clamans:
  "Emendare reum vel luere ausa decet.
Tam reus hic quater est abbas et episcopus idem,
  quam lupus esse solet laicus atque rudis —
1075 poena coaequa nefas aut emendatio penset!"
  Clamabant proceres, et grave murmur erat.

neediness hurts you less than my shame at your avarice hurts
me. What prudent man, when intending to visit the king's
court, would have worn his worst garments outward? You 1050
put the covering of a wolf skin on top, but disrobed, you
were adorned like an emperor! How fitting was the Tyrian
purple under such a covering, the splendid purple under the
hairy wolf skin! But I understand why you didn't give the 1055
skin voluntarily; you were afraid that your rich cloth might
be asked for. That's why you came here scruffily in a wolf
skin, wishing to hide your festal array. With long entreaties
we only just wrested from you in the end, you villain, that 1060
you should allow your splendid clothes to be revealed. If at
least the purple had been worn outside and the hide inside,
the fault could have been tolerated. If the court agrees with
me and cares for what's right, it will grieve for the injury
done to the king, and pass judgment on it. The contempt 1065
shown to the king is to be paid for by an equal amount of re-
spect. The royal suit makes complaint against two crimes:
the medicine has been held up while the monk hung on to
his cowl, and the court has been offended by the sight of his
ghastly clothes. This is a case of rash presumption, and the
fault won't remain without amendment, or pass by without 1070
the criminal suffering."

The court cried out corroboration of this speech from
the doctor: "The right course is that the criminal should
make reparation, or pay for his impudence. This wolf,
who's abbot and bishop together, is four times as guilty as
an uncultured lay wolf usually is. Let the crime be paid 1075
for by punishment or by equivalent compensation!" — So
the nobles shouted, and there was a great hubbub. At last

Denique sedati postquam tacuere peracto
   barones strepitu, phisicus inquit item:
"Patrue, non audis procerum decreta? Quid abstas?
1080   Protinus emenda, si tibi cura tui est!
Stulte, quid emendes, ignoras?" (namque rogabat)
   "Nonne, quod ammissum est, diximus ante satis?
Regis ad offensam gestatum intrinsecus ostrum,
   palliaque oranti praestita sero nimis!"
1085 Irato similis multum nec adesse volenti,
   stabat adhuc abbas, nec temere acta querens.
Turbidus archiater fremuit: "Quid, patrue, versas?
   Me, nisi ter iurem, dicere vana putas?
Patrue, per pennam sancti Gabrielis herilem,
1090   quam septena boum vix iuga ferre valent,
ni subito emendes, tunicam post pallia tollo;
   si vis, imperium transgrediare meum."
Iamque emendatum, fata et nocuisse recordans
   et nocitura timens, coeperat ire senex;
1095 ammonet hircus eum: "Sic tu, monache improbe, coram
   rege putas magno principibusque loqui?
Hoc quod in usque tuum pendet nasale labellum
   detrahe, ne balbo semiloquare sono.
Labra tibi nasale vetat ne libera claudas;
1100   (iudice sub cauto retia mille latent,
incolumes causas exilis scrupus iniquat!)
   Detrahe, supposita ne capiare plaga."
Laniger exclamat contra: "Berfride, quid erras?
   Desipit, indocilem qui sapere alta docet.

when the noise was over, and the barons had calmed down and were silent, the doctor said once more: "Uncle, don't you hear the sentence of the princes? What are you standing over there for? Make reparation at once, if you have any 1080 concern for yourself! Fool, don't you know why you should make atonement?" (for he was asking) "Haven't we just described very thoroughly what the crime is? The purple cloth, worn inwardly, in insult to the king, and the cloak bestowed too belatedly on the one who asked for it!"

Very much like a man in a temper, and unwilling to be 1085 there at all, the abbot still stood there, showing no regret for his rash action. The chief physician roared violently: "What are you deliberating about, uncle? Do you think that, unless I swear it three times over, I'm talking nonsense? Uncle, by the mighty wing of Saint Gabriel, which seven yokes of oxen 1090 are hardly capable of carrying, unless you make reparation immediately, I'll take the tunic after the cloak. Now ignore my command if you wish."

The old man, remembering that fate had harmed him in the past, and fearing that it would harm him in the future, was setting about atonement, when the goat admonished 1095 him: "Is this how you think you should speak, wicked monk, before the great king and the nobles? Take off that nosepiece which hangs down to your lip, so that you don't stammer out your words in a mumble. The nosepiece stops you closing your mouth freely. (A thousand snares lurk un- 1100 der a wily judge, and a very little difficulty is enough to make cast-iron cases go against you!) Take it off, in case you're betrayed by the laying of a trap." The sheep cried out in answer: "Berfridus, why are you going off the rails? It's a fool who teaches knowledge of profundities to an unteachable.

1105 Sit licet exiguum nasale, putasne, quod ipsum
        tam vilescat ei, quam mea lana michi?
     Tam fuit ille diu retinendae pellis avarus,
        assibus hoc ternis non pateretur emi."
     Emendantis agens ritum, lupus utraque tendit
1110   brachia, regalem cernuus ante thorum,
     obnixusque caput, placantia supplice gestu
        emendatoris dicere verba parat.
     Cautus ut archiater videt emendare paratum,
        corripiens duris vocibus acre furit:
1115 "Sic! sic! O Satanae, sic, patrue, patrue demens!
        Curre procul, Satanae patrue, curre procul!
     Egregie est factum, sic te facere obsecro semper,
        emendas lepide, iam tua facta probo!
     Quod si te velaret adhuc clamis hispida, numquid
1120   horroris tanti versus ad ausa fores?
     Emendaturum rebar—regemque duello
        impetis! Est peior culpa priore sequens.
     Purpura cor pretiosa tibi mutavit et artus.
        Provideat peltam rex citus atque pedum!
1125 Ysengrimus avet solio depellere regem;
        impetit o dignus regia colla pugil!
     In regem, o proceres, hoc dedecus isse sinetur?
        Heu michi, quos fastus ostrifer iste gerit!
     Dignus erat furca, tamen emendabile crimen
1130   baronum meritis extitit atque meis;
     nuncque duellarem ciroteca et pilleus arram
        proponunt! Proceres, probra quis ista ferat?
     Haeccine signa putas iram compescere, demens?
        His potius signis saevior ira subit.

Although the nosepiece is small, do you think it's of as small 1105
account to him, as my wool is to me? He was so greedy about
holding on to his skin for so long, that he wouldn't allow the
nosepiece to be bought for three ha'pence."

The wolf, going through the motions of atonement, sank 1110
to the ground before the royal couch, and with his head
pressed against it, stretched out both his arms and prepared,
in this suppliant attitude, to utter the placatory words of a
penitent. When the wily arch-physician saw him ready to do
penance, he attacked him with harsh words in a violent rage.
"So that's how it is! Uncle of the devil! So that's how it is! 1115
Madman-uncle! Get away from here fast, devil's uncle, get
away fast! This is acting admirably; I beg you always to act in
the same way! You make splendid reparation; now I really
approve of what you're doing! If your hairy cloak were still
enveloping you, I bet you would repeat your shocking impu- 1120
dence! I thought you were about to make atonement, and
you challenge the king to single combat! Your second fault
is worse than the first. Your costly purple has transformed
your heart and your limbs. Let the king quickly provide
himself with a shield and a staff! Ysengrimus wants to thrust 1125
the king from the throne; he attacks—oh worthy adver-
sary!—the king's life. Shall this insult to the king be allowed
to pass, princes? Ah me, what arrogance this wearer of pur-
ple shows! He was worthy of the gallows, but his crime could
have been atoned for, by virtue of my exertions and those of 1130
the barons. And now his glove and his hat offer the pledge
for a duel! Princes, who can bear these insults? Do you think,
madman, that these signs appease anger? Rather, anger

1135 Quis tibi persuasit Satanas prodire, priusquam
    consule me nosses, quae facienda forent?
    Consule me haec stulti praesumptus pignera certe
    debueras longe deseruisse foris;
    tunc tibi rex forsan precibus mansuescere posset,
1140   qui vix nunc aliquo conciliante potest.
    Dic michi, rex, quidnam super hoc iussurus es ausu?
    Ingenium magnae nobilitatis habes;
    parce precor stolido, patruus michi dicitur esse,
    et licet invitus serviit ipse tibi. —
1145 Regis more gerens, rex haec tibi, patrue, dicit
    (rex etenim iussit me sua verba loqui):
    'Debitor ignoscentis eget, sibi consulit insons,
    nec veniae nisi sit criminis auctor erit.
    Fortior est feriente ferens, nec saecula pulcrum
1150   tam fecisse deo quam scelerata pati.
    Ergo metu cessa, perge, Ysengrime, redique;
    Reinardo culpam dono rogante tuam,
    tam quia me aegrotum caestu grassaris iniquo,
    quam michi quod fuerit praestita sero clamis.
1155 Nec, quia non poscas veniam, inficiorve mororve;
    gratia non gratis, quando rogatur, adest.
    Parco, licet nolis, ingrato parcere grator;
    cum redies sensu, gratia pluris erit.
    Sive igitur tardas seu vis properare, cavebo
1160   ne quicquam hic fieri triste querare tibi:
    si vis ferre moram, postquam sudabo, resumptis
    protinus exuviis regrediere domum;

becomes fiercer at these signs. What devil persuaded you to 1135
advance before you were instructed by my advice as to what
you should do? According to my advice, you ought certainly
to have left these pledges of foolish rashness a long way out-
side. Then perhaps the king might be able to soften at your
entreaties, as he can hardly do now, even if someone acts as 1140
mediator.

Tell me, king, what will you direct as to this act of pre-
sumption? You have a temper of great nobility; spare this
dolt, I beg. He's said to be my uncle, and he's been of use
to you, although against his will. —Acting in royal fashion, 1145
the king says this to you, uncle (for the king ordered me to
speak his words): 'The sinner needs someone to pardon him,
while one who is guiltless is not in need of help, and will not
be the author of mercy unless he is the author of wrongdo-
ing. The sufferer is stronger than the one who strikes, and
God takes less pride in having made the world than in suf- 1150
fering its crimes. So leave aside your fear, Ysengrimus, de-
part and go home. At Reynard's request, I forgive your fault,
which consists not only in the fact that you challenge me, a
sick man, with your wicked glove, but also in the fact that
the tunic was given me too tardily. Nor do I refuse or delay 1155
mercy because you don't ask for it; grace is no longer gratu-
itous if it's requested. I spare you, although you don't want
me to; I take pleasure in sparing an ingrate. When you re-
turn to your senses, the favor will be better appreciated. So
whether you stay or whether you want to hurry off, I'll take
care that you don't complain of anything unpleasant being 1160
done to you here. If you want to stay a little, after I've done
the sweating you can put your clothes on again immediately

si properas, quacumque die remeaveris istuc,
    praestita servabo restituenda tibi.'"
1165 Regia finierat medicus mandata suumque
    ad patruum pro se talia versus ait:
"Patrue, me rursum tibi subvenisse negato,
    regia quem propter desiit ira, patet."
Repplicat ille nichil nec tam sibi praestita gaudet
1170   tergora servari, quam tribuisse dolet;
quin tardare recusat ibi foribusque nefandis
    approprians iterum cogitat inde gradi.
Cervus, aper, vulpes, vervex, caper, ursus, asellus
    quisque sua profugum voce valere iubent:
1175 "Eia nunc commendatus, nunc, dulcis amice,
    nunc commendatus, dulcis amice, deo!"
Respondet nichil ille salutantesque relinquens,
    hospitium tamquam non placuisset, abit.
Rex Rufanus ubi sumptis sudaverat herbis
1180   tegmine sub calido, pristina pausa redit.
Poscitur et capitur cibus, alternantque repente
    hinc natura valens, inde medela potens.
Mox animi compos rerum narramine dulci
    tempora Reinardum tollere longa rogat:
1185 ut lupus exierit claustrum aut intrarit, et hospes
    ut fuerit capreae transieritque redux,
factaque mutua, verba data atque relata vicissim,
    aut cur aetatem dissimularit ibi;
addit et, ut gallus Reinardum luserit ipsum,
1190   rex subridendo, scire quoque illud avens.
Difficilis Reinardus erat, nam multa loquentem
    sermo fatigarat continuatus eum,

and return home. If you hurry away, I'll keep what you've given, to return to you whenever you come back here.'"

The doctor had finished the royal commands, and turning to his uncle, said on his own behalf: "Uncle, though you once again deny that I've been of any help to you, it's clear on whose account the king's anger has dissipated." The other replied nothing, and was not so much glad that the skin he had given would be kept for him, as sorry to have presented it. Indeed, he refused to stay there any longer, and making for the cursed doors for the second time, he aimed to get out of that place. The stag, the boar, the fox, the sheep, the goat, the bear, the ass—all of them said goodbye to the fugitive in their own voices: "Now, God be with you, now, sweet friend; sweet friend, now God be with you!" He answered nothing, and leaving the chorus of well-wishers, as if he didn't like their hospitality, departed.

When King Rufanus had eaten the spices and sweated under his warm covering, his former repose returned. He asked for food and received it, and soon his vigorous nature and the powerful remedy supplemented each other. In a little while, he was calm in mind and asked Reynard to while away the long hours with a pleasant tale of adventures: how the wolf left the cloister and how he entered it, how he came to be the roe's guest, and went away again, what they had done together, what was said and what was replied, and why he had there dissembled his age. The king smilingly added that he also wanted to know how the cock tricked Reynard himself.

Reynard was reluctant, because his prolonged speeches had tired him out with so much talking, but he asked

sed Brunona rogat sibi saepe relata referre;
   at Bruno versus fecerat inde novos—
1195 quos ubi rex, an vellet eos audire, rogatus
   mandat, it allatum Gutero moxque redit,
datque urso, dedit ursus apro, legit ille, silebat
   dulcisonum auscultans curia tota melos.

Bruno to repeat those things that had often been related to him. However, Bruno had already made new verses of them, and when the king was asked if he wanted to hear them, he gave the order. Gutero went to fetch them; he quickly returned and gave them to the bear. The bear gave them to the boar; the boar read, and the whole court was silent, listening to the melodious lay.

BOOK FOUR

Orandi studio loca visere sacra volebat
    caprea cum sociis Bertiliana suis,
incomitata prius, septem post nacta sodales,
    officiis quorum nomina iuncta vide:
5 Rearidus cervus, suspectum ductor in agmen,
    horrida ramosi verticis arma gerit;
Berfridus caper et vervecum satrapa Ioseph
    praesidium armata fronte tuentur idem;
Carcophas asinus, portandis molibus aptus,
10   nomen ab officii conditione trahit;
dictatum Reinardus agens prohibetque iubetque,
    ut clavus facilem torquet utroque ratem,
nimirum sapiens senioque illectus, an artem
    tempore, an aetatem vicerit arte, latet;
15 actitat excubias anser Gerardus et hostes
    nocturnos strepitu terrificante fugat;
horarum custos Sprotinus gallus et index
    tempora tam lucis quam tenebrosa canit,
luce viae tempus cantat pausaeque cibique,
20   nocte deo vigiles solvere vota monet.
Hos ubi quove modo comites sortita sit, edam,
    caprea, res cunctis non fuit acta palam.
Sola domo exierat sanctos aditura peregre,
    visere quos crebro voverat ante diu,

Bertiliana the roe, together with her companions, was eager to visit some places of pilgrimage, out of a desire to pray there. At first unaccompanied, she later acquired seven companions. Here are their names, together with the duties they performed: Rearidus the stag, the leader against a dangerous enemy, wore bristling armor on his many-branching head; Berfridus the goat, and Joseph, leader of rams, offered the same protection to the band with their weapon-bearing foreheads; Carcophas the ass, fit for bearing burdens, took his name from the nature of his duty; Reynard had the leadership, gave orders and prohibitions, as a rudder turns a responsive boat to one side or the other—his great quickwittedness had been sharpened by the passing of time, although it's not clear whether his experience amounted to more than his cunning, or his cunning was greater than his years; Gerard the goose, whose function was to keep watch, and to put nocturnal enemies to flight with his dreadful cry; Sprotinus the cock, timekeeper and time signaler, chimed the hours of day and of darkness as well, by day crowing the time for travel, for rest and food, and by night admonishing those who were awake to offer prayers to God.

Where and how the roe acquired them as her companions, I shall relate; the business wasn't initiated in the presence of all of them. She had left home alone, to go abroad to the saints' shrines she had many times and over a long period

25 praecipue sancti Gereonis in aede columpnam,
  dispariter stantem sontibus atque piis.
Compita contigerat densis umbrosa frutectis
  caprea, cum coeptum dimidiasset iter;
per tribulos illic dominae sentesque vaganti
30 occurrit vulpes, edit et audit ave.
Tunc ait: "Unde soli? Quorsum? Cur sola? Quid actum?
  Singula (consulte sciscitor) ede michi!"
Domna refert: "Cur ista roges, ignoro, sed audi
  (forsitan exemplis instituere meis):
35 a laribus digressa meis pausantia Romae
  sanctorum atque aliis pignora viso locis.
Neve sacrum minuat circumflua pompa laborem,
  sola vior, turbae non famulantis egens."
Reinardus capream sollers dementer euntem
40 corripuit verbis commonuitque bonis:
"Cara soror, servire deo sanctisque placere
  non, nisi discurras incomitata, potes?
Iob si vera docet, fit numquam ypocrita felix;
  perfidius nichil est quam simulata fides.
45 Quisque, quod est, pateat: paupertas pauperis esto,
  divitias comites divitis esse decet.
Pauper nescit opes moderari, nescit honorem;
  subtrahe, confer opes, pauper utroque perit.
Pauper honore dato tumet, intabescit adempto;
50 aufer opes, exspes, redde, petulcus erit.
Optima sors misero est numquam feliciter esse;
  directo teritur semita nota gradu.

vowed to visit, especially the column in the church of Saint   25
Gereon, which operates differently on the guilty and the in-
nocent. Having begun her journey, the roe had got halfway,
when she reached a crossroads shaded by thick shrubs.
There the fox met the lady as she wandered through the
thistles and the brambles, and gave and received greeting.   30
Then he said: "What part of the world have you come from?
Where are you going? Why alone? To do what? Tell me all
the details (I ask advisedly)!" The lady replied: "I don't know
why you ask these things, but listen (perhaps you'll be in-
structed by my example). I have left my home and am visit-   35
ing the relics of the saints resting in Rome and other places.
No accompanying retinue impairs the sacredness of my un-
dertaking; I travel alone, without needing a crowd of ser-
vants."

The crafty Reynard spoke sound words of scolding and   40
admonishment to the roe on her foolish manner of travel:
"Sister dear, can't you serve God and please the saints with-
out running about unaccompanied? If Job teaches us the
truth, no hypocrite is ever blessed. Nothing is more dishon-
est than pretended piety. Let everyone appear what he is: 45
let poverty belong to the poor man, but it's only right that
wealth should accompany the wealthy man. The poor man
doesn't know how to manage riches, he doesn't know what's
decent; whether you give him riches or take them away, in
either case the poor man goes under. When he is given dis-
tinction, he becomes swollen headed; when it's taken away,
he pines. If you take away his wealth, he'll be desolate; if   50
you give it back, he'll be bumptious. The best thing that can
happen to a wretch is that he should never have any good

Perdere res nescit, quisquis non novit habere;
    instabiles animos mutat uterque color.
55 At dives, quem plena animi prudentia firmat,
    perdere tam suffert quam sapienter habet.
Collegasque domi, collegas diligit extra.
    Aufer honestatem, probra merentur opes.
Tu quoque vive probe, comitatu fungere pulcro;
60   esto larga domi, largior esto foris.
Non cassat meritum pomposi gloria coetus,
    cor vigeat pura simplicitate pium.
Forsitan et latitat carectis hospes in istis,
    vespere cui nolles incomitata loqui.
65 Cervus, ego et vervex, gallus, caper, anser, asellus
    sumpsimus eiusdem vota gerenda viae;
accipe fortunam socios per utramque fideles,
    viribus insignes consilioque sumus."
Dicta placent, comitesque vocat Reinardus, et omnes
70   alternum feriunt foedus euntque simul.
Ysengrimus eo vafer auscultarat et ictum
    foederis audierat, cominus inde cubans.
Hic lupus octo quater lustrorum traxerat orbes,
    qua comites illos caprea nacta die est;
75 qui cum vix prae fasce asinum reptare trahentem
    infertas bulgis intueretur opes,
angitur eximiae tactus dulcedine praedae.
    Quid faciat? Celeris mens erat, alvus iners.

fortune; you don't stumble along a path you know. Someone who never learned the art of possessing wealth doesn't know the art of losing it; both conditions unbalance unstable minds. But the rich man, who is fortified by a mind of mature understanding, can bear the loss of his possessions with the same wisdom that he shows in enjoying them. He loves to have companions, both at home and in the world at large. It's when you take away a decent manner of living that riches incur reproach. So you, too, should live decently, and maintain a splendid household. Be generous in your home, and more generous out of it. The dignity of a splendid retinue doesn't take away your merit, if only the devotion of your heart flourishes in pure simplicity. Perhaps, also, there might be lurking in these marshes some inhabitant with whom you'd be unwilling to speak, alone and after dark. The stag, the sheep and I, the cock, the goat, the goose, and the ass, have taken a vow to carry out the same journey. Accept us as companions, loyal in good or bad fortune; we are well endowed with both strength and wisdom." This speech won acceptance, and Reynard summoned his companions. They all came to a mutual agreement, and set off together.

The crafty Ysengrimus, lying nearby, had been eavesdropping in this spot, and had heard the making of the agreement. On the day when the roe acquired those companions, this wolf had passed through the revolutions of four times four decades. When he saw that the ass, who was carrying the valuables stuffed into bags, could hardly crawl along because of the weight, he was tormented by the preciousness of this extraordinary booty. What was he to do? His mind moved fast, but his belly was immobilized. He had

Ederat et biberat plus iure et largius usu,
80   ut gravido illisam ventre cavaret humum;
vertebro costisque super surgentia palmum
     ilia praeduro durius utre rigent,
sicque urgente cutis stomacho superaverat, ut non
     tota licet densis esset operta pilis.
85   Elicit inde omnes ex toto corpore vires,
     et ter conatur surgere terque cadit.
Ingemit et mortis species sibi mille precatur;
     "Proh dolor! Hic," inquit, "mors patienda michi est!
O quale hospitium nunc perdo miserrimus exul!
90   Ibo, queam nequeam, qualibet arte ferar.
Subsequar anguino saltem vestigia reptu,
     more suis volvar; sin comes, hospes ero!"
Ergo alvum dorso dorsumque reciprocat alvo;
     vim spes, spem generat vis, opus urget amor.
95   Dictator latitare sagax in saltibus illis
     noverat et paucis profore velle lupum;
digrediens igitur Ioseph comitante seorsum,
     frigida suspensi sustulit ora senis,
et docuit Ioseph, quid agat, si venerit hospes,
100   cui nomen lupus est, canus at absque fide.
Nox obiter surgit, Sprotino deinde canente
     hospitium subeunt et sua seque locant.
Carcophanta vocat Ioseph domuique tuendae
     praeficit. "Hoc," dixit, "stabis, aselle, loco!
105   Ianitor hic instar solidi defigere pali;
     appulit externo nostro carina solo.

eaten and drunk more than he should, and more generously
than usual, so that he was making a hollow in the ground un-   80
der the impact of his laden belly. His flanks, rising a span's
width above his hip bone and ribs, were even harder than his
drum-tight belly, and his skin, under pressure from his stom-
ach, had expanded to such an extent that it was only par-
tially covered by his hairs, even though they were thickly
set. Then he summoned up all his strength from his whole   85
body, and three times he tried to rise and three times he fell
back. Groaning, he called down on himself a thousand kinds
of death. "Ah, misery!" he said, "I'm fated to die here! Oh,
what hospitality I'm losing at this moment—wretched out-
cast that I am! I *will* go, whether I'm able to or not; I'll be   90
carried along by some stratagem or other. At the very least,
I'll follow their steps by crawling like a snake or by wallow-
ing like a pig; if not their traveling companion, I'll be their
guest!" So he made his stomach take the place of his back,
and his back take the place of his stomach; hope produced
energy, and energy produced hope, while desire increased
his efforts.

The wily leader of the band knew that the wolf was lurk-   95
ing in those woods, and was up to no good. So, going off
with Joseph, he gave him the lifeless head of an old wolf,
which someone had strung up, and told him what he should
do if an old and treacherous visitor by the name of wolf   100
were to turn up. Night drew on apace, and at Sprotinus' si-
multaneous crowing, they entered a hospice and disposed
themselves and their baggage. Joseph called Carcophas and
put him in charge of guarding the house. "You'll stand in
this spot, ass!" he said. "Here you'll be fixed, as doorkeeper,   105
like a sturdy post; our boat has come to land on foreign soil.

Tutior esse putas, quod non nunc arma minentur?
    Hamus inescatur, qui capit agmen aquae;
oblatus quandoque calix suspectior ense est;
110   scis, quibus ingeniis prodita Troia fuit?
Saepius extorres provincia blanda fefellit,
    dum vetuit fallax ante timere quies.
Quod si pravus in hoc quis repserit advena saeptum,
    hoc verbum cella posteriore tene:
115   fac, quaecumque iubebo tibi, contraria iussis."
    Ille libens iussas substitit ante fores.
Siditur ad mensas, asinum furor urget edendi,
    fertque suam stolida rusticitate famem,
neglectisque focum foribus petit inque repostos
120   discursat discos sparsaque frusta rapit.
Arguit hunc Ioseph: "Repete ostia, rustice demens,
    congruit officiis sollicitudo vigil!
Utilitas ingens perit utilitate pusilla;
    negligitur vitae cura favore gulae."
125   Ianitor insano tantum succurrere ventri
    anxius, ut didicit, serio cassa refert:
"Quid michi commendas servanda nisi ostia, sodes?
    Fas impune michi sit tua iussa sequi!
Mastico non oculis, committo dentibus escam;
130   os vacuat discos, ostia vultus habet."
Ire lupus laxa paulatim coeperat alvo,
    praecelerans vires sedulitate suas,
cumque reluctantem Ioseph ferus urget asellum
    pollicitis, precibus, pulsibus atque minis,

Do you think you're the safer, because no weapons are threatening you at this moment? The hook which catches the watery shoals is a baited one; sometimes a proffered wine cup is more dangerous than a sword. Do you know by what engine of war Troy was betrayed? The serenity of a colonial country often deceives those far from home, when a false calm lulls early suspicions. So if any malevolent intruder worms his way into this enclosure, keep this message firmly in your memory cells: whatever I order you, do the opposite of my commands." The other willingly took up his stand in front of the door as he was ordered.

They sat down at the table, and a ravening desire to eat tormented the ass. Reacting to his hunger with peasant obtuseness, he moved over to the hearth, leaving the door unattended, and rummaged among the abandoned dishes, grabbing the scattered leftovers. Joseph scolded him: "Go back to the door, stupid peasant; what's needed for your job is constant watchfulness! A major benefit is lost for the sake of a trivial one; concern for life itself is neglected in the interests of gluttony." The doorkeeper, concerned only to relieve his raging stomach, made a flippant reply to this earnestness, as he had learned to do. "What did you commit to my charge except to look after the door, friend? Just don't tell me off for following your orders! I don't chew with my eyes, I commit my food to my teeth . My mouth is emptying the dishes, but my eyes are kept on the door."

The wolf, as his belly gradually slackened, was beginning to walk, outstripping his strength by his eagerness, and while the fierce Joseph was urging the reluctant ass with promises, with entreaties, with blows and threats,

135 perfidus hospes adest; inventis laeta precatur,
　　non oris meditans verba animive loquens.
　　Propositum nequam pulcro sermone colorans,
　　　obnubit ficta relligione dolum,
　　nocte soporatos pensans iugulare lucroque
140　conciliare moram; limen ubi intrat, ait:
　　"Pax vobis! Heremita iubet, benedicite, fratres!
　　　Pax iterum vobis! Haec heremita iubet."
　　(Primitus horruerant, veluti fit, quando repente
　　　auribus aut oculis res inimica subit;
145 mox, simul obstandum est, uno, non pluribus, hoste,
　　　viribus et numero vis animosa redit.)
　　Addidit hospes: "Ego ad fratres heremita monendos,
　　　ut teneant pacem iustitiamque, vagor.
　　Me, quibus est post terga fides, praesente sit horror?
150　Vos super ingressu ne trepidate meo.
　　Mansuevit rabies, perstant michi forma sonusque;
　　　exigit hoc vitiis debita poena meis,
　　sum lupus aspectu, mens est mansuetior agno;
　　　voce lupum testor, sed probitate nego.
155 Ergo est vana soni, vana est acceptio formae;
　　　moribus et factis est adhibenda fides.
　　Pravus in insontes olim et truculentus habebar,
　　　tam bene nunc vivo, quam malus ante fui.
　　Nec michi tam quosquam quam vos invisere dulce est;
160　plus quibus offeci, plus pietatis ago.
　　Huc quoque me vestri traxit fiducia voti;
　　　usque precor Romam vester ego esse comes.

the treacherous visitor appeared, and wished all happiness 135
on those he had come upon, although he didn't mean the
words that came from his mouth, nor speak those that were
in his mind. Painting his wicked plan with fine speech, he
veiled his cunning with assumed piety, intending to murder
them in their sleep during the night, and to compensate for 140
the delay by the profit he would make. As he crossed the
threshold, he said: "Peace be with you!—a hermit entreats.
Blessings on you, my brethren! Again, peace be with you!—a
hermit utters this prayer." Initially, they had shuddered, as
happens when something threatening is suddenly presented
to the eyes and ears, but soon, once they had understood 145
that the enemy to be resisted was only one, and not several,
a bold confidence in their strength and number returned to
them.

The visitor added: "I wander about as a hermit to ex-
hort my brethren to keep peace and justice. Are those who
are confident in my absence to tremble in my presence?
Don't be alarmed at my arrival. My fierceness has softened, 150
although my shape and voice remain the same; this is de-
manded as the due penalty for my vices. I am a wolf in
appearance, but my spirit is gentler than a lamb. My voice
testifies to my being a wolf, but I contradict it by my gen-
tleness. So a judgment based on my voice and my shape is 155
misleading; reliance is rather to be placed in my behavior
and actions. I was once held to be fierce, and cruel to the
guiltless; now I live as virtuously as I was previously wicked.
Nor is it so pleasant for me to visit anyone as it is to visit
you; those whom I have injured most, I do most good to. 160
Reliance on your vow has brought me here; I ask to be
your companion as far as Rome. I want to search out the

Opto Palaestini patriarcham inquirere templi —
  da michi votivam, compater hirce, crucem!"
165 (Namque is praecipua figebat fronte loquentem,
  artis enim sociae non recolebat opem.)
Parturiunt antiqua novum peccata ruborem;
  dampnavit primus vota lupina caper.
"Quemlibet hic," infit, "non custodita fuisse
170 ostia gaudentem crastina furca levet!
Excipitur solus (non novimus omne cor) anser;
  noluerint alii, forsitan ille velit.
Qui pubem in vitiis contraxit, canet in hisdem,
  in quibus et canet, convenienter obit.
175 Credidero mansuesse lupum spirare valentem,
  hic me sive abbas sive heremita voret.
Ergo sit anachorita lupus, sit papa, sit abbas,
  non habeat dentes, aut eat, unde venit,
unde fugax abiit, repetat sua claustra crucemque
180 (nam caret hic coetus praesule) poscat ibi.
Dentato nostras heremitae claudimus aedes,
  nec vulpi aut asino dens michi carus inest.
Nullus habens dentes adeo mansueverit umquam,
  quin hunc sub terra meque velim esse super.
185 Nil habet hac heremita domo dentatus agendum.
  Dic, asine, et cur non ostia claudis adhuc?
Quaeris adhuc nobis heremitas addere plures?
  Absque alio officium scit satis iste suum."
Annuit his anser, neve excipiatur ab illis,
190 ostia qui cupiunt clausa fuisse, iubet.
Ysengrimus in hoc sensit sermone duorum
  introitum paucis complacuisse suum,

bishop of the Palestinian church. Goat, my father in Christ, give me the votive cross!" (For the goat, forgetting the assis- 165 tance of the social arts, was transfixing the speaker with an intense stare.)

Old misdeeds are ever the cause of fresh shame, and the goat was the first to pour scorn on the wolf's vows. "May the 170 gallows take tomorrow anyone who is happy that the doors were unattended!" he said. "I except only the goose—we haven't seen into every heart. Although the others were unhappy about it, he perhaps doesn't mind. Whoever has grown up in vices, will grow old in them, and in the vices in which he grows old, it's appropriate that he should die. If I 175 believe there's a strong and healthy wolf alive who's grown tame, may this one, whether abbot or hermit, eat me up! So, whether the wolf is an anchorite, or a bishop, or an abbot, let him be toothless or else go back where he came from; let him return to his cloister, which he left as a deserter, and ask there for the cross. We don't have a bishop to give it to him 180 in this company. We close our doors against a hermit with teeth. I don't like teeth even in the fox or the ass. No one with teeth shall ever grow so tame that I shan't wish him to be under the ground while I'm above it. A hermit with teeth 185 has no business in this house. Ass, why do you still not shut the door? Speak up! Do you want to add still more hermits to our number? This one knows his job well enough without any others." The goose agreed to all this, and asked not to be excluded from those who wished that the door had been 190 closed.

Ysengrimus perceived from the words of these two that his entry hadn't pleased many of them, and now, fearing that the others had similar or worse things ready for him,

iamque alios eadem vel deteriora parasse
formidans, fictae praevenit arte fugae.
195 "Ysengrimus abit, fratres, in pace manete!
Non quales," inquit, "cernimur esse sumus.
Ingresso ne fratre aliquis succenseat, oro;
si iubeor, maneo, si minus, ire libet.
Denique, si qua michi dicta est iniuria, dono,
200 et nobis fieri rite paciscor idem.
Discedo, Reinarde, vale, cunctique sodales,
quos ego me miror plus placuisse tibi!"
Aspicit optantem Reinardus abire vetari
et cogi inscissis posse redire pilis.
205 "Patrue, quo," dixit, "pergendum est nocte profunda?
Intempesta via est, ostia nulla patent!
Stulta piget dixisse caprum, revocabilis esto
nec mala te propter dicta fuisse putes!
Nostra putabatur tecta assiluisse quis alter,
210 quem nobis alio carius isse foret;
at tibi devoto servit chorus iste favore,
inque tuos usus optima nostra vacant."
Ysengrimus ovans sedit gratesque rependit;
mandabat subitas Bertiliana dapes,
215 atque ait: "O Ioseph, nescimus, an ederit iste
frater adhuc hodie, fac properare cocos!"
"Ha, domina," ille refert, "pisces pulmentaque desunt,
nec quis in his lucis invenit ova duo;
mandere si carnem sit fas, heremita rogetur!"
220 "O utinam carnem," cogitat ille, "dares!"
Caprea Reinardum, veluti vereatur ab ipso
quaerere, quae liceat talibus esca, rogat;

anticipated them by the stratagem of pretended departure. "Ysengrimus is going, brethren, rest in peace! We are not 195 what we seem to be," he said. "I beg that no one should take offense at the entry of a Christian brother. If I'm entreated to, I'll stay; if not, I'm happy to go. Finally, if I've been insulted in any way, I pardon it, and duly accept it being in- 200 flicted on me. I'm going, Reynard; goodbye to you and all your companions, whom I'm surprised you prefer to me!"

Reynard saw that he wanted to be told not to go, and to be forced to turn back without having his coat torn off. "Uncle," he said, "where are you going to in the middle of the 205 night? It's an unseasonable time for traveling; no doors are open! The goat is sorry for having said silly things; allow yourself to be called back, and don't think that harsh words were spoken on your account. Someone else was thought to have gate-crashed our house—someone whom we would 210 have preferred to go elsewhere. But this company is at your service with wholehearted goodwill, and the best we have is earmarked for your enjoyment."

Ysengrimus happily sat down and returned thanks. Bertiliana gave orders for a meal instantly, and said: "Oh, Jo- 215 seph, we don't know whether this brother has eaten yet today; make the cooks hurry up!" "Ah, madam," he replied, "there's no fish or vegetable stew, nor can anyone come across two eggs in this neck of the woods. Let the hermit be asked whether he is allowed to eat meat." "Oh, that you 220 would give me meat!" thought he. The roe asked Reynard what food was permissible for such as the wolf, as if too much in awe to inquire herself. A thief is less afraid of

fur pendere minus, quam vulpem dicere praesul
    illicitam carnem talibus esse, timet.
225 Affectum patrui dictator corde perito
    atque suum retinens taliter inquit herae:
"Domna, nichil nisi sola fames abdicitur illis;
    esse docet mundis omnia munda liber."
"Dic, pater," infit hera, "est, ut vulpes dicit? In isto
230   ordine vescuntur carnibus? Ipse refert."
Has voces scitantis amans heremita sibique
    non dubitans credi lenia fatus ita est:
"Vescimur appositis, nil exigo nilque recuso;
    dona dei fiunt et tua grata michi.
235 Sanctis sancta suis sanctus deus omnia fecit;
    nil comedit Satanas et malus usque manet.
Regula praecipua est peccato claudere pectus;
    sontibus iniunctum est saepe carere cibo.
Nil igitur iustis praeter peccare vetatur;
240   maxima libertas suppeditare deo est."
Tunc domina inquit ovans: "Ioseph, carne utitur hospes;
    nunc precor apponas optima quaeque potes!"
Ille refert paulum prius acto murmure, quale
    quoslibet ad iussus verna rebellis agit:
245 "Nil, domina, hic certe praeter capita alba luporum;
    hic cibus est simplex simpliciterque sapit.
Ne nimium iubeas! Gratanter parta ministro;
    si michi suppeterent, et meliora darem.
Scit michi Reinardus non his potiora vacasse;
250   omnia Reinardo nota aliisque reor."
Reinardus subicit: "Delirat domna iubendo;
    quid velit, ignorat, dat, quibus ipsa caret!

hanging than the prelate was that the fox might say that
meat was forbidden to his like. The leader of the company, 225
with cunning heart following his uncle's inclination as well
as his own, spoke to the lady as follows: "Madam, nothing
but hunger alone is denied them; the good book teaches
that to the pure all things are pure." "Tell me, father," said
the lady, "is it as the fox says? Do they eat meat in that or- 230
der? He says so."

The hermit, pleased by these words of inquiry, and not
doubting that he'd be believed, answered mildly as follows:
"We eat what's put in front of us; I demand nothing and I
refuse nothing. God's gifts and yours are welcome to me; the 235
holy God has made all things holy to his holy men. Satan
eats nothing, and he is in a continual state of wickedness.
The principal rule is to close one's heart to sin; going with-
out food is something imposed on sinners. So nothing is for-
bidden to the upright except sinning; God's service is per- 240
fect freedom." Then the lady gladly replied: "Joseph, our
visitor eats meat! Now, I entreat, bring the best you can!"

He first emitted a bit of a murmur, as a refractory servant
does at any commands, and then answered: "There's noth- 245
ing here, madam, truly, except white wolf heads. This is
plain food, and tastes plain. Don't ask for too much! I will-
ingly serve up what I've got—if I had better ones, I'd give
them. Reynard knows that nothing better than these is
available to me; I think Reynard and the others know the 250
whole situation." Reynard rejoined: "The lady's orders are
foolish; she doesn't know what he wants, and she gives him
what she hasn't got! Just let her give enough orders, and

Imperet ipsa satis, nos montem insidimus altum,
  salmones Reni porrige sive Mosae!
255 Ecce lupina tibi capita esse fateris habesque —
  porrige confestim, porrige, nonne valent?
Quod sapiunt, sapiunt, et nosmet vescimur hisdem.
  Haec quoque praesenti competit esca loco:
silva lupos, pelagus pisces habet, ergo lupinum
260 tam caput hic estur quam bene piscis ibi.
Da, quod habes, bone frater, adest heremita modestus;
  pauperibus pietas sufficit ante deum."
It Ioseph profertque caput, quod habebat, et alte
  ante sui saltans hospitis ora levat.
265 Coeperat intuitu capitis substringere caudam
  cruribus atque alias malle fuisse lupus.
Inter saltandum dapifer clamabat: "Herilem
  notitiam, quisquis donat ovanter, habet!
Arripui primum caput hoc, Reinarde, videto
270 an gustu placeat; convenienter olet,
sicut olet, sapiat, laudabitur! Unde sit, haeres?
  Hoc caput Andegavi credo fuisse senis;
cis Romam melius nullum vacat." Ista locuto
  dictator veluti felle citatus ait:
275 "Stulte, quod hoc caput est? Ede ex maioribus unum!"
  Ille redit velox et referebat idem,
porro hoc notitia viduaverat atque coronam
  desuper avulsis finxerat ante comis.
"Hoc," ait, "abbati nuper detraximus Anglo.
280 Non hoc obtulerim fratris ad ora mei!
Hoc carum nichil est, quo carior hospes habetur;
  aedis herus stramen plumeaque hospes habet.

although we're perched on a high mountain, you can bring some salmon from the Rhine or the Meuse! So, you say, you've got some wolf heads—bring them at once! Bring them—they're good enough, aren't they? Whatever they taste like, we'll eat them. What's more, this food is suitable for the place we're in. The wood is the home of wolves, the sea of fish, so wolf head is as appropriately eaten here as fish is there. Give what you've got, good brother; it's a modest hermit we've got here. Compassion is all the poor need be given to satisfy God."

Joseph went and brought the head which he had, and prancing about, held it up high in front of his guest's face. At the sight of the head, the wolf began to pull his tail between his legs, and to wish to be somewhere else. As he pranced about, the butler cried: "Whoever gives joyfully, has his mistress's approval! I snatched up this head first, Reynard; see whether it suits your taste. It smells all right; just let it taste the way it smells, and it'll meet with approval. Are you wondering where it came from? I believe this was the head of an old Angevin. There isn't a better one on this side of Rome."

When he had said this, the leader of the company, as if stung with annoyance, said: "Fool, what head is that? Bring one of the bigger ones!" He went back quickly and fetched the same one—but first took the distinguishing marks off it and made a tonsure on top by tearing out the hair. "This," he said, "we took the other day from an English abbot; I wouldn't have offered this one to my own brother! But its worth pales into insignificance beside the greater worth of our guest; the master of the house gets straw and the guest

255

260

265

270

275

280

O caput hoc, Reinarde, vide, quam pingue teresque,
  quam sint personae congrua quaeque suae!
285 Huic gravidi paribus capitones Sithiu nutant,
  Atrebas in claustro talia sanctus alit.
Laetius hoc heremita aliis admittere debet,
  non de dissimili relligione fuit."
Iussor acutus ad haec: "Sub pravo parca ministro
290 mensa iuvat paucos, et perit hora dapum.
Nec caput hoc laudo; melioribus alter habundat
  angulus, ad laevam digrederere parum,
grande illic caput abdideram, cui fuste colurno
  panditur os, esu praevalet illud, abi!"
295 "Quis caput," ille refert, "unum inter mille requirat?
  Quod prius ignoro posteriusve legam.
Visne, quod ablinxit, cum vellere crederet herbam,
  Gerardus coram quattuor anser heri?
Dacus in hoc denso pausabat gramine praesul,
300 pars visu facilis nulla cubantis erat;
gramen ibi vellens improvidus incidit anser
  pontificis Daci subripuitque caput.
Concitus eventu, nulla formidine rerum,
  efflavit villos auriculasque simul,
305 et valido flatu caput est huc inde rotatum—
  cervus id, id caper, id vidit asellus, ego id."
Ille ait: "Hoc vere est, cui stipes labra colurnus
  separat, hoc nobis sufficit, ede celer!"
Omnes ille pilos digressus demit et aures,
310 ne pateant ulla cognitione doli;
laxat et impacto distentam pungile buccam,
  horrifico rictu labra reducta patent.

236

the featherbed. Look at this head, Reynard, how fat and smooth it is—how everything about it is just like his reverence! The bigheads at Sithiu nod under the weight of ones like this; such are the ones nourished in Saint Vaast's cloister at Arras. The hermit ought to accept this one more gladly than the others, since he was of a similar order."

The quick-witted governor replied: "Not many people derive good entertainment from a niggardly table under the attentions of a bad waiter, and the dinner hour is passing. I don't give approval to this head either. The other corner has plenty of better ones; go a little to the left. I put away a huge head there, with its mouth propped open by a hazel stick. That is the best to eat; off with you!" "Who can look for one particular head among a thousand?" he replied. "I don't know which I should pick out first, and which later. Do you want the one that Gerard the goose bit off yesterday, in front of the four of us, when he thought he was plucking up grass? A Danish bishop was resting in this thick grass, no part of him easily visible as he lay. The thoughtless goose, plucking the grass there, struck the Danish prelate's head and tore it off. Excited by what had happened, and unabashed by what he had done, he blew off its hair and ears at one go, and with the mighty blast, the head rolled all the way here. The stag saw it, the goat saw it, the ass saw it, and so did I." "That's right," said the other, "the one whose lips are separated by the hazel twig; that'll do for us. Bring it quickly!"

Away he went and tore off all the hair and the ears, in case his tricks might become obvious through its being recognized, and he stretched its yawning cheeks by thrusting in a stick; its drawn-back lips gaped in a horrible grin.

Diriguit visis senior vultumque retorsit;
　　excutitur forti pulsa timore fames.
315　Tunc primum patuit fortunam nolle iocari;
　　haut umquam similem pertulit ante metum.
　　"Quis me," inquit, "Satanas lupicidas traxit ad istos?
　　Heu michi, quo tardat fune ligata dies?
　　Quid cornuta acies? Gerardus et iste refertur—
320　porro parum infaustos est iugulasse lupos—
　　quin efflasse pilos auresque rotasseque flando
　　huc caput! Hoc sensu sospite ferre queam?"
　　Anser ad haec: "Hoc ergo novum, Ysengrime, recenses?
　　Non michi res equidem contigit ista semel.
325　Si vellem, capita octo lupis maioribus illo
　　efflarem atque ipsi, domne heremita, tibi!
　　Mene fuisse putas materno semper in ovo?"
　　Et dabat ingentem gutture flante sonum.
　　Audito ter clamat "atat" lupus atque repente
330　sensibus amissis in sua terga cadit,
　　efflatumque diu caput amisisse putavit
　　atque illud Geticas transiluisse nives.
　　Semianimem rapta cognatus mente iacentem
　　erigit et dicit: "Patrue, surge, sede!
335　Patrue, ni fallor, dormitas, vade quietum!
　　Excessit morem cena favore tui."
　　Ille nichil dictis intendit, cetera versat,
　　terribilis turbae tecta subisse gemens.
　　Nec prius intrandi qui tunc erat ardor eundi;
340　spes minus oblectat, quam metus angit edax.
　　Tunc ita dictator: "Quid, patrue, volvis?" At ille:
　　"Quid pensem, rogitas? Maxima monstra quidem!

The old man stiffened at the sight and turned his face aside; his hunger was shaken off, driven away by great fear. Then for the first time it was obvious that Fortune wasn't playing games; never before had he experienced fear to the same degree. "What devil," he said, "led me to these lupicides? Oh, misery, is the day tied by a rope, that it drags so slowly? Why this horned army? This Gerard—not content with having murdered unfortunate wolves—is said to have blown off his hair and ears and to have rolled his head here with hissing! Can I endure this without losing my mind?" The goose replied: "Do you reckon this is something new, Ysengrimus? Truly, this has happened to me more than once. If I wanted, I could blow eight heads from wolves bigger than this one—and yours too, sir hermit! Do you think I haven't come out of my mother's egg yet?"—and he emitted an enormous noise from his hissing throat. When he heard it, the wolf cried "Aagh!" three times, and suddenly losing consciousness, fell flat on his back; for a long time he thought his head had been blown off and he had lost it, and that it had bounced away over the snows of Germany.

His kinsman raised him as he lay lifeless, his senses gone, and said: "Uncle, get up, seat yourself! Uncle, if I'm not mistaken, you're taking a nap; go and get some rest! In your honor, the dinner has gone on longer than usual." He paid no attention to this speech, having other things in mind—lamenting that he had entered the house of this desperate crew. His previous eagerness to enter bore no comparison with his present eagerness to leave; the allurements of hope were less powerful than the torments of gnawing fear. Then the leader said: "What are you meditating on, uncle?"—to which he replied: "Do you ask what I'm thinking? Of the

315

320

325

330

335

340

Quis Satanas umquam vidit loca sacra petentes
    tot capita in sumptus ferre lupina suos?
345 Nonne bovina forent esu potiora suumque?"
    Orator contra callidus ista refert:
"Patrue, nec sapiens sub relligione videris;
    nec fueras, pravum cum sequereris iter.
Quae michi, quid Scithicae vulpi, quidve egeris Indae?
350   Et, quid ego Hispanis, quae tibi cura, lupis?
Cum tua sedulitas nobis et nostra tibi assit,
    hostibus haec nostris, non tibi, poena venit.
Ansere meque times coram et vervece caproque?
    Gensne alii genti faverit ulla magis?
355 Graece allec loquitur, trans Alpes biga fritinnit,
    tam canere hoc, quam nos extimuisse potes.
Tolle dapes, Ioseph, refer in cellaria cursim.
    Provenit officio gratia pulcra pio:
obsequiis iras, impensis dampna lucramur!"
360   Ille caput raptum condidit atque redit,
sicque gemit dicens: "Heu pallet episcopus iste!
    Concolor infirmo est; langueat oro parum.
Aut habet aut fingit quintanae frigora febris;
    commodius posset forsitan esse domi."
365 Repplicat orator: "Io, quanta peritia Ioseph!
    Quam bene formatus matris in aede suae est!
Pergere vult abbas, ideo fortassis abibit?
    Optat sic asinus, tendit agaso secus.
Fas viget optandi, languet proventus agendi;
370   optato paucis suppetit usque frui.

greatest horrors! Who the devil ever saw travelers to holy places carrying so many wolf heads for their food? Wouldn't 345 cows' or pigs' heads be better for eating?"

The crafty pilgrim had this to say in reply: "Uncle, you don't seem to be a wise man, despite your religious order— nor were you one in the past, when you were following the paths of wickedness. What is it to me, what you might have done to a Scythian or an Indian fox? And why should it 350 worry you what I do to Spanish wolves? Since your services are at our disposal, and ours at yours, this vengeance falls on our enemies, not on you. Are you afraid to be with me, with the goose and the sheep and the goat? Has any bunch of people ever been friendlier to another? If you should be ter- 355 rified of us, then a herring chirping Greek, or a wagon squeaking its way over mountains, is singing! Take away the food, Joseph; quickly, take it back to the larder. Fine thanks we've got for our kind service; we get anger in return for our efforts to please, and injuries in return for our outlay!"

He snatched up the stolen head, hid it away, and came 360 back. Groaning, he said: "Alas, this bishop is pale! He's the color of a sick man; I hope he's not ill. He either has, or pre- tends to have, the chills of a five-day fever. Perhaps he might be more comfortable at home." The pilgrim replied: "Good- 365 ness, Joseph, what *savoir faire!* How well you've been brought up in your maternal home! The abbot wants to travel on— and so perhaps he'll push off? The ass might have something in mind, but the ass driver has other ideas. Anyone can hope all right, but success in execution is harder to come by; few people manage to have any lasting enjoyment of what 370

Vis permissus eat gratis bona nostra vorasse?
  Consiliis saltem comparet illa suis!"
Cetera dicturum vehemens intercipit hircus,
  ut qui doctorem nollet habere lupum:
375 "Non habet haec iustam, Reinarde, calumpnia causam;
  vastavit nostrum non nimis ille penu.
Res minuit sparsas communis abusio, ritum
  hospitii tota testificata domo.
Hospitibus mos est animoque manuque gerendus —
380   nostras atque suas solveret iste dapes?
Hospitis adventu densatur sumptus in omnes,
  pectoris affectum vox faciesque notant.
Egimus hoc isti rursumque libenter agemus,
  nimirum ut patruo sedula turba tuo.
385 Hactenus ergo illi scio nos servisse decenter;
  effice nunc summum, quaerit abire, iube!
Velle rogandus erat, quod nos rogat; ergo rogatum
  cum non obtineat, turba perita sumus?
Insipiens perdit parvis data magna negatis;
390   prisca perit probitas deficiente nova.
Cur remeare vetes, cui non intrare negasti?
  Ingressum decuit te vetuisse magis!
Consilium potius non experiamur euntis,
  quam nimis incumbat consiliantis onus.
395 Quid si consultor se paverit, ut tibi malles
  impastum reducem consuluisse nichil?

they've longed for. Do you want him to be allowed to go away scot-free, after he has eaten up our provisions? At least let him give us some advice which is their equivalent in value."

The goat, as if he didn't want to have the wolf as an adviser, impetuously interrupted the fox as he was about to say more: "This slander has no just cause, Reynard; he hasn't 375 made any great inroads into our provisions. It's the communal consumption that has caused our ransacked stores to dwindle; the whole household has given sign of the customs of hospitality. Guests should be properly treated, in spirit and behavior—and should he have paid for our food 380 and his own? At the arrival of a guest, the food for everyone is increased, and words and looks express the feelings of the heart. We've done this for him, and we'll willingly do it again, as a company only too attentive to your uncle. Up to 385 now, I know, we've treated him properly. Now put the finishing touch: he wants to leave, so tell him to do so! We should have asked him to concede the thing he is asking of us; so are we as a group showing wisdom if his request is not granted? A fool loses great rewards by refusing trifles; initial 390 kindness loses its effect if it isn't followed up by new kindness. Why should you forbid him to go, when you didn't refuse him entrance? It would have been more proper for you to have forbidden him to enter! We'll do better to be deprived of his advice by his departure than we would to endure the burden of having him present to give it. What if the 395 counselor should feed himself in such a way that you'd rather he had gone away, unfed, without having given you any advice?

Consulit, ut reditum concedas; quando retentus
   consulet utilius? Ter pluet ante trabes!
Discidio pensat cenam gratesque meretur;
400   eventus tantum suspicionis habent."
Providus obiecit qui norat fallere rethor
   nec poterat falli calliditate levi:
"Quemque loqui prohibes, nec cui tua grata loquela est!
   Inter grandaevos plus sapit iste senes;
405 consultor quaestorque bonus, quem dico patenter
   tot cumulasse artes quot senuisse dies.
Non equidem nobis hoc consultore carendum est;
   plus nobis dominae proderit iste meae.
Porro recedendi sit fas et tempus, et ipse
410   rennueret certe, si bene nosco fidem.
Creditis huc longo dignatum calle venire
   tam cito cognatos linquere velle suos?
Foedera per nostri generis rogo, sicubi malles,
   patrue, quam caros hic penes esse tuos."
415 Ruminat ille diu, quidnam respondeat apte,
   et perhibet tandem, quae sibi tuta putat:
"Quem fore me reris? Cur nominor, haut quod inique
   aspernor? Vellem patruus esse tibi!"
Intulit ille: "Mei frater patris aestimo cum sis,
420   dicere te patruum debeo iure meum.
Agnosco speciem, si vis, profitere, sonumque,
   nec, quia me miserum conspicis esse, neges."
Rettulit ille: "Quod est falsum, Reinarde, negabo.
   Eliciunt mentem forma sonusque tuam.
425 Vocibus et formis non semper credere debes;
   sunt multi similes vultibus atque sono.

The advice he gives you is that you should allow him to go away; if you were to keep him here, when would he give you advice that was more profitable? It'll rain tree trunks first! He pays for his meal, and earns our thanks, by his departure; only his arrivals are met with suspicion." 400

The far-seeing orator, who was skilled in deceiving and couldn't be deceived himself by any nimbleness of wit, objected: "You prevent everyone else from speaking, and your speech is acceptable to no one! Among the men of ripe old age, this one is the wisest. He's a good counselor and a good 405 steward, and I maintain that he has clearly built up as many skills as he has lived through days. We mustn't be deprived of this counselor; he'll be more use to our mistress than we are. Moreover, even if it were right, and it were time for him to go, he himself would certainly refuse, if I know true 410 friendship. Do you think he'd have done us the honor of making such a long journey here just to leave his kinsmen so quickly? By our family bonds, uncle, I ask you where in the world you'd rather be than here among your own folk."

He pondered a long time on what he might suitably re- 415 ply, and at length came out with what he thought safe for himself: "Who do you think I am? Why am I given a name I rightly reject? Would that I were your uncle!" The other replied: "Since I judge you to be my father's brother, I ought 420 by right to call you my uncle. I recognize your face and voice—admit it, if you will, and don't deny it just because you see me in poverty." He replied: "What is false, Reynard, I'll deny; my appearance and voice lead your understanding astray. You oughtn't always to trust to voices and 425 appearances; many people are alike in face and speech. I'm

Non ego sum, quem me ipse refers, vice falleris ista;
    nomen idem teneo, sed lupus alter ego.
Nominor Ysengrimus, ut is, quem reris adesse;
430   nomine sum compar, sed probitate minor.
Huius filiolum me glorior esse, sed ipsum
    ipsius aut prolem non potuisse queror.
Plaudo tamen fatis, quod nomine donor eodem,
    quod similem vultum porto sonique decus.
435 Elige consiliis, quemcumque probaveris aptum;
    annis praependet sarcina tanta meis,
partita est hodierna quidem michi vespera lustrum.
    Aetas consilii pondere parva caret;
vox iuvenum vento, seniorum traditur archae.
440   Ire sinar, nulla est hic michi causa morae;
nolo inopes sumptu socios onerare diurno,
    quos nequeo sensu provehere atque fide."
Taliter annosi iuvenis sermone peracto
    subiungit placida voce magister ovans:
445 "Huc subito, huc socii, vervex et cerve caperque!
    Filiolus patrui cogitat ire mei.
Mando tribus vobis, ut conducatis euntem;
    nos quamvis inopes diligit atque colit.
Ultimus hospitium tenor expleat: hospes iturus
450   degustet dominae pocula quaeque meae.
Non hic tractetur peius, quam creditis ipsum
    vos lare tractandos proposuisse suo.
Gratia reddatur, quia nos dignatus adire est,
    utque iterum veniat, poscite, quando volet!"
455 Ysengrimus ad has voces haec verba subinfert,
    pocula dulcorem non habitura timens:

not who you say I am; this time you're deceived. I have the
same name, but I'm a different wolf. I'm called Ysengrimus,
as is the wolf you think is present—I am identical in name, 430
but inferior to him in virtue. I boast of being his godson, but
I'm sorry I'm unable to claim to be himself or his real child.
Yet I thank the fates that I'm endowed with the same name,
that I have a similar face and the honor of a similar voice.
Select anyone you find suitable for your consultations, but 435
such a burden is too great for one of my years; this evening,
indeed, gets me halfway to my fifth birthday! Tender years
lack the authority for giving advice. The opinion of old men
is treasured up, but the opinion of young men is consigned
to the winds. Let me be allowed to go; there's no reason for 440
me to stay here. I don't want to burden with my daily keep
friends who are not well-off, and whom I am unable to help
with my wisdom and friendship."

When this speech of the aged youth was over, the ju-
bilant ringleader answered serenely: "Come here at once, 445
friends, sheep, stag and goat! My uncle's godson is thinking
of going. I order you three to escort him on his way. Al-
though we're poor, he loves and honors us. Let our hospital-
ity run to the end of its course; let our guest taste some 450
of our lady's parting cups before he goes. Let him not be
treated in this house worse than you imagine he would have
planned to treat you in his own home. Let him be given
thanks for condescending to visit us. Ask him to come again
when the mood takes him!"

Ysengrimus, fearing that these cups wouldn't have nectar 455
in them, replied to this speech with the following words:

"Nosco vias, venio satis inconductus eoque;
  ante satis biberam, non modo plura bibam.
Res perdit, quicumque suas nolentibus offert;
460   nil opus est addi praeter abire michi."
Talia poscentem dictator mulcet amica
  voce monens: "Oro, dulcis amice, tace!
Patrinusne tibi est patruus meus? Eius amore,
  quae fuerant illi, sunt facienda tibi,
465 ut, cum compererit, si nos ipse hospes adisset,
  non eadem dubitet parta fuisse sibi."
Ductores praeiere, sequique heremita iubetur.
  Quid faciat? Gemino stringitur ipse malo:
ire pavet, venisse dolet, promissa daturos
470   pocula pone videns, limen abesse foris.
Incipit ire tamen paulatim saepe reflexis
  huc illucque oculis itque reditque diu.
Ostia Carcophas obiter servanda subibat,
  clamitat infido laniger ore minans:
475 "Bulgifer, ausculta, quid, si vis vivere, mandem!
  Magnanimus Ioseph praecipit, ergo pave!
Per sanctos, quos quaero, nisi mea iussa sequaris,
  non erit exitio culpa redempta tuo!
Totas pande fores, tener Ysengrimulus ibit,
480   tramite ne stricto transeat, aeger enim est.
Ardalio demens, tu si qua strinxeris illum,
  te prius exocula, quam videare michi!"
Ianitor econtra: "Blandiri desine, frater!
  Sponte mea facerem qualia iussus agam!

"I know the way, I come and go quite well without a guide. I drank enough before; I won't drink any more now. Anyone who offers his goods to those who don't want them is chucking them away. All that needs to be granted me is to go away." The gang leader responded to his request with appeasement, rallying him in friendly tones: "Please be quiet, dear friend! Isn't your godfather my uncle? For love of him, whatever should have been done for him, is to be done for you, so that when he learns of it, he won't be in any doubt that the same things would have been lavished on him if he himself had arrived as our guest." 460 465

The escort led the way, and the hermit was told to follow. What was he to do? He was caught between two evils. He was afraid to go, he was sorry he had come; he saw that those who were about to give him the drinks they promised were near at hand, while the doorway was a long way off. Yet he began to move off gradually, casting his eyes this way and that many times, and for a long time he both advanced and retreated. 470

Immediately Carcophas went over to the door he was supposed to look after, and the sheep called out threateningly (but misleadingly): "If you want to stay alive, baghumper, listen to what I tell you! The noble Joseph issues an order, so tremble! By the saints I seek, unless you follow my orders, you won't be able to make up for the fault even by your death! Little Ysengrimikins is going; open the whole door, in case his path through is restricted, for he's not well. Stupid guzzler, if you crowd him at all, you'd better put out your own eyes before you come into my sight!" The doorkeeper replied: "You can turn off the charm, brother! I'd do of my own accord just what I'll do at your orders. 475 480

485 Multa iubes clamans, clamandi sentio causam —
    proficies ista calliditate nichil —
scilicet alliciens hac hospitis arte favorem
    insignire mea te probitate cupis.
Nil veter aut iubear, sapiens facit absque iubente
490   quod prodest; quod obest, absque vetante cavet.
Si plus serviero, meus ut tuus extitit hospes;
    ut maior tibi sit gratia, nolo pati.
Tu bonus absque fide, solo clamore laboras;
    nil ego clamo, fidem sedulitate probans."
495 Credidit haec praesul dixisse fideliter illos,
    et magis audaci coeperat ire gradu.
Ianitor interea laxaverat ostia paulum,
    "Hic," ait, "hic transi concitus, ista via est!"
Inter dicendum bis pulsans poplite dextro
500   currere grandisono ter iubet ore senem.
Ille supersiliens veloci limina saltu
    transierat medium tutus adusque femur.
Carcophas onerosus erat, sex Fresidos orae
    mole boves aequans et tria grana salis;
505 tanta mole fores adigens incumbit adactis,
    atterit attritis artius usque premens.
Abbas ut laqueo canis allidente tenetur
    aut quam viscosum rete cohercet avem.

You bawl out a good many orders, but I understand the rea-   485
son for your bawling. You won't get anywhere by this cun-
ning—you want to win the favor of our guest by this trick,
and get prestige for yourself by my faithfulness to duty. I'm
not to be forbidden or ordered to do anything; anyone with
sense does the right thing without being told, and avoids the   490
wrong thing without being warned against it. If I prove to
be of more service to him, I won't put up with your getting
more thanks than me, since he was my guest as much as
yours. Your kindness is only a show—the only effort you put
in is in the noise you make. I don't make a song and dance
about it; I show my reliability in my services."

The bishop thought their conversation was genuine, and   495
was moving forward with a more confident step. Mean-
while, the doorkeeper had opened the door a little. "Here,"
he said, "quickly, pass through here; this is the way out!" As
he spoke, he twice nudged the old man with his right knee,
and three times gave vent to his echoing voice, as a signal to   500
him to hurry up. Bounding over the threshold with an agile
leap, he had got safely through as far as the middle of his
thighs. Now, Carcophas was heavy, the equivalent of six
oxen from the coast of Friesland, with three grains of salt
thrown in. With this great weight he rammed into the door,   505
and pressed on it after he'd rammed it—leaned on it and
kept on leaning, continually pressing harder. The abbot was
caught, like a dog in a clashing trap, or a bird tangled in a

Non redit aut prodit, manet hac immotus et illac,
510   mobiliorque inter marmora iuncta foret.
Ilia non stabant, intus compressa coibant,
      sic forium inflictu stringitur ille gravi.
Eohe quam vincto non curat credere vinctor!
      Quam concordat inops cum locuplete parum!
515 Scit deus affectum vincti, scit vinctus et ipse!
      Quam mora non animo grata morantis erat!
Hunc quasi nolentem procedere ianitor asper
      voce urget, pulsat poplite, calce ferit.
"Ostia," dicebat, "socii, patefacta videtis,
520   nullorsumque gradi vult bonus iste cliens.
Quid moror hic? Alio compellor, abire rogate!
      Ianua, si scissem, non patuisset adhuc;
nullius hic causa peregrini stare tulissem,
      seria me rerum talia totque trahunt.
525 Nec petit hic standi veniam, nec stare quod ipsum
      hic patior, grates, quas michi debet, agit.
Restituit pretium nutrita monedula merdam;
      gracculus et cuculo, quem fovet, hoste perit.
Dedo tibi officium, Ioseph, da nescio sane
530   nec curo cuinam, quilibet illud agat.
Cuius ob insignes oculos ego ianitor essem,
      limen ubi semper, qui redit itque, tenet?"

sticky net. He moved neither backward nor forward; he re- 510
mained without motion in either direction. He'd have had
more freedom of movement sandwiched between two
blocks of marble. His flanks couldn't hold up under the pres-
sure, but caved in on one another, so severely was he
squeezed by the onslaught of the doors. Ah, how little does
the shackler care to give weight to the feelings of the shack-
led! How little do the rich and poor have in common! God is 515
the only one besides himself who knows how the fettered
wretch feels, or how unpleasant the standstill was to him
who was standing still! The cruel doorkeeper admonished
him verbally, as if he was unwilling to move on, pushing him
with his knee, and striking him with his hoof. "Friends," he
said, "you see the doors are thrown open, but this servant 520
of ours is so faithful he won't step out of the house. Why am
I kept waiting here? I'm in demand elsewhere. Tell him to
go. If I'd known what would happen, I wouldn't have opened
the door this far, and I wouldn't have put up with stand-
ing here, for the sake of any traveler—such and so many are
the important matters of business which call me away. He 525
doesn't request the favor of standing here, nor does he give
me the thanks he owes me for allowing him to do so. The
jackdaw, as a reward for its upbringing, gives shit, and the
crow dies by the enmity of the cuckoo it fosters. Joseph, I
resign my office to you! Give it to anyone—I don't know and 530
I don't care who; anyone can do it. Should I act as a door-
keeper out of the mere goodness of my heart, when he's
continually blocking up the doorway by coming and going
at the same time?"

Laniger obiecit: "Praecepi tota patere
    ostia, nec curas providus esse semel.
535 Offero pignus, ut es nequam, quia, quasseris illum
    parte sui quavis, perfide calo, lues!"
Ianitor "Absit!" ait, "Tu nempe patentia cernis
    ostia; non oculis credis, inepte, tuis?
Absit eum me astante quati! Scit enim ipse, rogetur,
540   non ultro hoc facerem, quin prius ipse michi!
Tu saltem, Berfride, vide!" Tunc hircus asello:
    "Nonne," inquit, "video? Si velit ire, potest.
Nescio, cur maneat, spontaneus ire recusat;
    ianua laxari latius ista nequit—
545 hoc vere speculor. Ioseph quoque ridet iniquus,
    ostia contemplans laxa fuisse diu,
invidet exprobratque tibi pravoque favore
    segnitiem spectat praesulis atque tacet.
Delirare liquet monachos iuvenesque senesque:
550   primitus ingressi claustra verentur, amant;
Regula vilescit vix cognita, cumque gerendum
    quid foris audierint exierintque semel,
vel nimis inviti vel numquam claustra revisunt.
    Hos sequitur ritus hic heremita piger.
555 Nescio, sis abbas an tu patriarcha, quid haeres?
    Ostia cum pateant, utquid abire negas?
Carmina nunc stares ad completoria iuste;
    quid tardas, demens? Hinc, heremita, sali!
Quo tu, cerve, paras?" (etenim fingebat abire)
560   "Expecta, sodes, dum patriarcha bibat!"

The wool bearer objected: "I ordered the whole door to be opened, and you don't, even for once, take the trouble to pay attention to my order. I guarantee that in so far as you're culpable, you'll pay for it, treacherous drudge, if you've jostled any part of him." "Heaven forbid!" said the doorkeeper. "Don't you see the wide-open doors? Don't you believe your eyes, idiot? Heaven forbid that he be jostled while I'm standing by! He knows very well (just ask him!) that I wouldn't be willing to do such a thing—rather, he should first do it to me. Berfridus, you take a look, at least!"

Then the goat said to the ass: "I'm looking, aren't I? If he wants to go, he can. I don't know why he's still here; he refuses to go of his own accord. This door couldn't yawn more widely—this I see clearly. Wicked old Joseph, moreover, is making fun; observing that the door has been open for a long time, he's envious and reproaches you, seeing the prelate's laziness but keeping quiet about it from a nasty toadyism. It's quite clear that monks, both young and old, are giddy creatures. When they first enter the cloister, they revere and love it. But before they're barely familiar with the Rule, its attractiveness wears off; when they hear what goes on outside, and when they've once been out themselves, they go back to the cloister either very unwillingly or not at all. This lazy hermit is following their practices. You—abbot or bishop, I don't know which you are—why are you sticking around here? When the doors are open, why do you refuse to leave? You ought by rights to be singing Compline at this moment—what are you waiting for, fool? Come on out, hermit! Where are *you* making for, stag?" (for he was pretending to move off) "Wait, friend, until the bishop drinks!"

Cervus ad haec: "Nondumne bibit? Cur ergo venire
   incipit? Utque abeat me duce, pergo prior.
Ioseph, nonne venit? Michi velle venire videtur."
   Repplicat ille: "Tibi quando libebit, abi!
565 Ille manebit adhuc; cur hinc impotus abiret?
   Grandibus est pateris ante abigenda sitis."
Cervus "Itemque bibat rebibatque antistes, ego," inquit,
   "ambulo, maiorem non tolerabo moram.
Esuriens et sola domum mea cerva tuetur;
570 si venies mecum, nunc, domine abba, veni!
Transiit hora, sali! Non stabo diutius istic;
   hic michi non tota nocte manere vacat.
Tu bene transieris, sed id ausus penderet alter,
   at tibi vim Ioseph nemo tuente facit."
575 Obviat his Ioseph: "Si debet, pendat et iste;
   dic, caper, estne reus? Dixeris esse, luat."
Hircus ait: "Non peior erit me iudice, quamvis
   perdiderit totum, quod probitatis habet."
Ingeminat Ioseph: "Tacui satis, abba, recede!
580 Otia sectari nos tua posse putas?
Aut intro redeas aut egrediaris oportet;
   elige mox, quid agas, optio dicta viget!
Crede, cito aut abies aut te tardasse pigebit!"
   O quales gemitus tunc dabat ille miser!
585 Irridens gemitus exclamat degener hircus:
   "Hic missam media nocte heremita canit!
Laniger, ausculta, quam dulciter organa fundat;
   tam bene, ni fallor, vix modularer ego!"

The stag replied: "Hasn't he had the parting cup yet? Then why is he beginning to leave? I'm going ahead first, so that I can escort him on his way. Joseph, surely he's coming? He seems to me to want to come." He replied: "Go whenever you want to! He'll stay a bit longer; why should he go away untoasted? First his thirst is to be slaked with great cupfuls." The stag said: "Let the bishop drink over and over again, but I'm going; I can't take any more delay. My doe is looking after my house, hungry and alone. If you're coming with me, come now, lord abbot! The hour of divine service has gone by—leave! I won't stand here any longer. I have no time to stay here all night. You can go on your way all right, but if anyone else had the nerve to do this, he'd pay for it. But nobody harms you, because Joseph is protecting you." 565 570

To this Joseph replied: "Let him pay for it too, if he's guilty. Tell me, goat, is he guilty of offense? If you say he is, let him pay the penalty!" The goat said: "In my opinion, he couldn't be worse were he to lose all the virtue he has." Joseph continued: "I've been quiet enough, father abbot; be off! Do you think we can imitate your idleness? You must either go out or come back inside. Make up your mind quickly which you'll do; the choice I've specified is the only one you've got! Believe me, you'll either go away quickly, or you'll be sorry you stayed!" 575 580

Oh, what groans the wretch then uttered! The brutish goat, in mockery of his moans, cried out: "This hermit is singing his Mass in the middle of the night! Listen, sheep, how sweetly he pours forth his music; if I'm not mistaken, I myself could hardly sing so well!" "Is that 585

"Sic tibi missa solet cantari?" laniger infit,

590   "Nunc scio te psalmos non bene nosse tuos.

Affirmat verbum ille quidem—missamque putasti!

   Esse supra Scaldum vult catigeta Remis."

Rearidus dixit: "Vos tortum dicitis ambo,

   doctus in hoc ego sum carmine vosque rudes.

595 Pluribus offensis cecidit, nunc illa fatetur,

   scire volens, quo sint ipsa pianda modo."

Tunc caper: "O Ioseph, vera est sententia cervi,

   postmodo quae nobis sint facienda, vide!

Excessusne suos exponet funditus omnes,

600   insimul ut positos indita poena lavet?"

"Stultitia haec nobis," respondet laniger, "absit!

   Quid faciam, satis est absque monente ratum.

Suppetat assensor, qui sicut ego omnia penset,

   non patiar culpas hunc recitare diu.

605 Quis scit, an in saltus vox transeat alta remotos

   et possit scelerum paenituisse pares?

A tribus absolvi nobis fortasse nequibit,

   quae veniet mores turba referre malos.

Absolvatur ab his, Brabantes cetera gaudent

610   corrigere, at nobis ista piare datum est."

Tunc caper oblongum variumque trifurculat amen,

   concinnat bifidum furcula quaeque melos:

ista velut bubo macer et rota putrida bigae,

   haec ut Arabs daemon gallicaque orca sonat,

615 scansilis exiles bis crispat tertia tongos,

   ut vox alta tubae summaque corda gigae.

how you usually sing Mass?" said the sheep. "Now I know 590
that you aren't very familiar with your psalms. Really he's re-
hearsing a lecture—and you thought it was a Mass! He wants
to be a theologian at Reims, far away beyond the Schelde."
Rearidus said: "You've both got it wrong. I'm an expert in
this kind of music, and you're mere laymen. He has fallen 595
into numerous sins, and is now confessing them, wanting to
know how they are now to be expiated." Then the goat re-
plied: "Oh Joseph, the stag's opinion is right. You see then,
what we have to do afterward! Isn't he going to reveal all his
misdemeanors, from beginning to end, so that when they 600
have been reckoned up he can purge them all at once by
means of the penance imposed on them?"

"Heaven forbid we be so foolish!" replied the sheep.
"What I shall do is quite certain without anyone instructing
me. If there's anyone present who agrees with me, and con-
siders the whole thing as I do, I won't let him rehearse his
sins for long. Who knows if his loud voice might not pene- 605
trate the distant woods, and whether others like him might
not repent of their crimes? Perhaps it will not be possible for
the three of us to absolve the crowd that will come to make
report of their bad behavior. Let him be absolved from these
offenses; the Brabanters can have fun putting the rest to 610
rights, but it falls to us to impose penance on this lot."

Then the goat sounded from her three horns a long and
variegated amen, each prong producing a twofold melody—
the first screeching like a hungry owl or a rusty wagon wheel,
the second booming like an Arabian devil or a French barrel,
while the third, at a high pitch, twice quavers out its shrill 615
tones like the high voice of a trumpet or the top string of a

Undique deinde "Feri!" nec vox sonat ulla nisi illud,
    excipiunt plena tunc pietate senem.
Cervus agit costas, caper armos, guttura vervex,
620   atque inter calices verba benigna volant.
"Has ego," cervus ait, "costas adigoque ligoque,
    quas abigit positu macra iuventa suo."
"Incute tu costas; armis," caper infit, "adactis,
    ne nimis, ut timeo, succutiantur, agam."
625 Laniger "Arto," inquit, "fauces nimis hactenus amplas;
    patribus hoc memini vix placuisse meis."
Ha quotiens cervus, pulsans benedicite, clamat:
    "Explora, frater, quid ferat iste calix!"
Ha quotiens hircus: "Non sum caper, immo sacerdos;
630   accipe quaesitam, sancte heremita, crucem!"
Ha quotiens vervex: "Si mecum pergere Romam
    appetis, hic peram do baculumque tibi!"
Ha quotiens omnes: "Satanas haec pocula magnus
    sanctificet famulo multiplicetque suo!"
635 Iam non exterius convivae talia caro
    pocula pincernas continuare piget.
Sed quid pauca iuvant? Dormitur forsitan intus?
    Non curant famulas inservisse manus?
Infra velle (licet non ultra nolle) sodales
640   non queritur dantes intus adesse senex.
Gallus terga, marem vulpes, caudam occupat anser;
    vellit is, hic mordet, calcitrat ille furens.

fiddle. Finally from all sides issued the call "Strike up!" and no other sound but this was heard as they addressed themselves to the old man with the utmost of loving care. The stag attacked his ribs, the goat his shoulders, the sheep his throat, and friendly words flew about during each round.   620

"I'm pulling in and corseting these flanks," said the stag, "which the old man's embonpoint has displaced from their proper position." "You attack his ribs," said the goat, "and I'll see to the firming up of his shoulders, in case they're too violently shaken about, as I fear they may be." The sheep   625 said: "I'll narrow his jaws, which have hitherto been a bit too wide. I remember that my ancestors weren't too pleased about that." Ah, how often the stag, pounding out a blessing, cried: "Have a taste, brother, of the medicine in this glass!" Ah, how many times did the goat cry: "I'm no goat, but a priest; take the cross you've been seeking, holy her-   630 mit!" How many times did the sheep cry: "If you want to travel to Rome with me, I give you this scrip and staff!" Ah, how often did all of them cry: "For what you are about to receive may great Satan make you truly thankful, and may he rain such blessings on his servant!"

The cupbearers outside the house showed no reluctance   635 in continuing such libations for their dear guest—but what good are a few drinks? Were those inside the house asleep perhaps? Didn't they want to lend a helping hand with the serving? The old man had no need to complain that the   640 friends within gave him less than he wanted (or indeed, that they failed to go past the point where he wanted no more). The cock attacked his back, the fox his balls, and the goose his tail. One pecked, the other bit, the third kicked

Non cuiquam monuisse vacat, se quisque monebat,
   ne, si quem moneat, non sibi forte vacet.
645 Qualiter astringit ferrum sub verbere forceps,
   sic angit caudam, sic premit anser ovans.
Astulat ut plancam bene mota dextra dolabra,
   sic cum carne pilos gallus ad ossa rapit.
Non tamen ille potest tantos sentire furores,
650 Reinardi feritas tam rabiosa furit.
Hospitii calices ut praesul sumpserat istos
   roboreque exhausto turba resedit ebes,
tunc Ioseph claudi iubet ostia, paret asellus,
   auribus instillans murmura pauca lupi:
655 "A caris sociis huc tu conductus es usque,
   nunc, si quid pedibus fidis, amice, sali!
Nunc intende salire! Sali, si quando salisti!
   Iam matutinum convocat hora chorum.
Ne tamen hinc salias, nisi grates egeris ante;
660 grandibus est meritis gratia parva satis.
Annuimus gratis discos paterasque dedisse—
   proventu medio pascua ventris eunt—
exigimus grates, quia te conduximus omnes.
   Offensam nobis materiare cave;
665 imprimitur pollex palmae redeunte petitum
   hospite, qui gratus non fuit ante datis."
Supprimit ille minas et nobilitate silendi
   fungitur, in tempus servat agenda suum.
Quid stulto concepta semel prudentia confert?
670 Post sapere exiguum stultior usque manet.
Bis reticens apte, quater abdita vulgat inepte;
   tam bene nec celat, quam male deinde refert.

furiously. No one bothered to shout encouragement; each one urged himself on, for fear that by urging on anyone else he might divert energy from his own activities. As tongs crunch iron under a hammer blow, so the exulting goose pinched and squeezed his tail. As a handy ax, dexterously wielded, hacks out a plank, so the cock tore out hairs and flesh right down to the bone. And yet the wolf couldn't even feel such ravages as these, so furiously did Reynard's savagery rage.

When the prelate had swallowed this dose of hospitality, and the whole group, their strength exhausted, sat down again in a stupor, then Joseph ordered the door to be closed. The ass obeyed, dropping a few murmured words into the wolf's ears: "You've been escorted this far on your way by your dear friends; now, if you put any trust in your legs, friend, leap for it!—and put your back into it! Leap now, if you ever did! The hour of day is even now calling the choir together for Nocturns. But don't bound away before you've said thank you. A little gratitude is enough to repay big services. We've allowed food and drink to be given you for nothing—the produce of the fields is for the communal good—but we require thanks because we've all acted as your escort. Beware of giving us any cause for offense; when the guest who showed no gratitude for what he was given earlier comes back for more, one keeps one's hand tightly closed."

Ysengrimus restrained his threats and took refuge in a superior silence, holding back what he planned to do until the time for it had come. But of what use is it to a fool to have learned prudence on one occasion? After showing a little wisdom, he carries on being even stupider. For every twice that he keeps quiet at the right time, he will four times

Quid prodest asino siluisse et dicere vulpi?
  Vicisset celans, vincitur ipse loquens.
675 Audierat vulpes verba irridentis aselli,
  quod matutini carminis hora foret,
atque cor indagare volens abeuntis, iturum
  lusuris patruum vocibus usus ita est:
"Bulgifer imprudens, alios, quam diximus istic,
680   hunc matutinos dicere velle putas?"
Restitit haec ad verba senex hostique perito
  ludificandus, avens ludificare, refert:
"Cantasti, Reinarde, tuos; ego differo nostros;
  nondum cantandis suppetit hora meis.
685 In lucem suspendo meos multumque diurnos
  cogito nocturnis dissimilare tonos.
Diximus obscuros istic, octavaque lecta est
  lectio, servatur nona legenda michi.
Nunc habet iste suam, nunc parvulus ille placentam,
690   et ratis in portu plena diebus adest.
Non bene servo vicem cantores solus in octo,
  alterius partis cras scola maior erit.
Matutina mei venient ad carmina fratres,
  qui laudes secus ac hircus et anser agant!"
695 "Patrue," rethor ait, "(patruus—cur vera negarem?—
  hactenus ut fueras, tu michi semper eris)
nonne potest munire deus quem somnia terrent?
  Iurgia sunt leges ad dirimenda datae.

blurt out secrets at the wrong one. And his success in con-
cealing something at one moment is not as striking as his
blunder in revealing it later. What was the good of his keep-
ing quiet to the ass, but speaking to the fox? He would have
had the upper hand by keeping quiet, but lost his advantage
when he opened his mouth.

The fox had heard the words of the mocking ass, that it 675
was the hour for Nocturns, and wishing to plumb the feel-
ings of the departing guest, he had recourse to the follow-
ing speech, in mockery of his uncle as he went: "Stupid pack
carrier, do you think he wants to say any other Nocturns 680
than the one we've recited here?" At these words, the old
man stood still, and, wishing to jeer, but destined himself
to be made mock of by his cunning enemy, replied: "You've
sung *your* Nocturns, Reynard; I'm putting off mine until
later. The hour for singing mine hasn't yet arrived. I keep 685
mine for the daytime, and I think there'll be a great differ-
ence between the music of day and of night. We've recited
here the appropriate chant for the dark, and the eighth Les-
son has been read; the ninth is reserved for me to read. One
little boy gets his sugarplum at one time, and another little
boy at another; after many days' voyaging a ship eventually 690
gets to port. I don't make a very good response alone against
eight singers, but tomorrow there'll be a bigger choir on the
other side. My brothers will attend my Nocturns, and will
recite Lauds in a different manner from the goat and the
goose!"

"Uncle," said the speech maker, "(why should I deny the 695
truth?—as you've been my uncle up to now, so you always
will be) isn't it true that although prophetic dreams may ter-
rify a man, God can protect him? The laws are enacted for

265

Quod si iudicio nostros commiseris actus,

700   hic, quod ames, factum est; unde querare, nichil.

Quamvis ipse neges, ob qualem nescio causam,

    lustra tibi certum est octo fuisse quater.

Omnis eo veniens aetatis oportet ut isto

    more salutetur, si iuvenescere avet;

705 ergo ut, qualis eras dictus te teste, redires,

    antidotum pietas hoc tibi nostra dedit.

Talibus obsequiis debentur flagra minaeque?

    Par Satanae est, qui vult impius esse pio.

Si vis, pro reduci nobis gratare iuventa;

710 istud ave ex nostra sedulitate refers.

Lentior extiteras annis quam temo bilustris;

    ianua nostra tibi est omine visa bono.

Nunc fore coepisti tener, ut faba trima, catellus.

    Pax tibi sit! Quo vis, vade, catelle tener!

715 Pax tibi! Vade alacer! Quotiensque redisse senectam

    senseris, hic semper parta iuventa tibi est.

Ob quod ad ista novum cantasti limina carmen,

    nunc tibi sit simplum, post erit usque duplum!"

Praesul ad haec: "Hic laureolum tibi currit, ut optas;

720 iusta refert meritis hora quibusque vices.

Multa in vasa quid hoc fundam? Servistis honeste;

    taliter, haut aliter, vos amo, sicut amor.

Nec michi servitum satis est, offertis agendum;

    cladibus hoc deerat ius synodale meis.

the settling of quarrels. Suppose you were to submit every- thing we've done to a judicial trial—what's taken place here has been what you should relish; there's no basis for any complaint. Although you yourself deny it (for what reason I don't know), you're certainly one hundred and sixty years old. It's necessary that anyone reaching that degree of age should be given this kind of salutation, if he wants to grow young; for this reason we gave you this medicine out of kindness, so that you might go back as what you were said, by your own testimony, to be. Are blows and threats what is due for such service? Whoever is willing to return cruelty for kindness, is equal to the devil himself. If you wish, thank us for bringing back your youth; this is the kind of farewell exchange you are taking away with you, thanks to our atten- tiveness. You were slower, because of your years, than a ten- year-old cart; it was lucky for you when you set eyes upon our doorway! Now you've begun to be a puppy, soft as a three-year-old bean. Peace be with you! Go wherever you want, young puppy!—Peace be with you! Go quickly! And any time you feel old age return, you can always be given youth again here; what has given you cause to sing a new song at our doors, may now have been performed once, but will in future be repeated with an encore!"

The bishop replied: "The game is going your way at the moment, but the hour of justice brings a due reward for ev- eryone's deserts. Why should I spell this out in detail? Your ministrations have been nobly performed; my love for you is of just the same kind as yours for me, and not a bit different. Nor have you done enough for me; you offer to do more! Synodal justice hasn't played a part in my destruction so far.

725 Olim non fuerat legis michi cura sequendae —
    nescio quis statuet nunc michi legis onus?
    Candidiore novo veterem non cambio callem;
    tardum est annosos discere vincla canes.
    Lege mea potior, sum praesul ego atque decanus;
730 cras synodum mando, conveniemus item.
    Quam michi vestra fuit pietas accepta, docebo,
    cum fuerit synodi contio lecta meae.
    Si non reddidero sumptis aequalia saltem,
    perfidior Suevo iudicer atque Geta!"
735 Exilit inde senex, vetuissent repere plagae,
    praebebant vires ira dolorque recens.
    Tunc iubet excubias caute Reinardus agendas,
    hostica ne subitas inferat ira manus.
    Ter stadium senior discesserat, elicit alto
740 murmure fautores pone proculque suos.
    Iam brevis undenos conflaverat hora sodales:
    ante alios omnes Gripo Triventer adest,
    abbatis socer ille fuit, cursuque rapaci
    Ysengrimigenae tres comitantur avum:
745 magna salus ovium, Larveldus Cursor, avique
    cum facie nomen Grimo Pilauca tenens,
    et numquam vel paene satur Septengula Nipig;
    Griponis subeunt pignora deinde duo:
    Guls Spispisa prior, post natus Guulfero Worgram;
750 hos inter sequitur Sualmo Caribdis Inops
    et proles amitae Griponis, Turgius Ingens
    Mantica, quo genero Sualmo superbus erat,

Being subject to the law was never of any concern to me in the past, and is someone now to bring the law to bear upon me? I won't swap an old road for a new one, even if it's more beautiful; it's a bit late to teach old dogs to wear chains. I administer my own law; I'm both bishop and dean. Tomorrow I'll summon a synod, and we'll meet again. I'll let it be known how welcome your kindness was to me, when I've got my synodal assembly together. If I don't return at least the equal of what I've received, let me be judged more treacherous than a Goth or a Vandal!"

Then the old man leaped out; his wounds should have prevented him even from crawling, but his anger and fresh-smarting grief lent him strength. Then Reynard ordered careful watch to be kept, in case the enemy's malice might produce a sudden attack. When the old man had traveled three furlongs, he called forth his adherents from far and near with loud howls. Already a short space of time had brought together eleven comrades. Before all the others, Gripo Three-Bellies arrived, who was the abbot's son-in-law, and with rapid pace three little Ysengrimi accompanied their grandfather: Larveldus the Runner, the great refuge of sheep; Grimo Goose-Snatcher, who resembled his grandfather in name and appearance, and Seven-Throated Nipig, who was rarely, if ever, satiated. Then there arrived two of Gripo's children, Greedy Dindins, the elder, and Gwulfero Sheepchoker, the younger. Among them, there followed Sualmo the greedy Whirlpool, and the son of Gripo's aunt, Turgius Great-Sack, whose father-in-law Sualmo was proud

Sualmonisque nepos, Stormus Varbucus, et audax
    privignus Stormi, Gulpa Gehenna Minor,
755 hinc patruus Gulpae, Sualmonis avunculus idem,
    Olnam cognomen Maior Avernus habens.
His mala, quae tulerat, lupus auctoresque malorum
    detegit et queritur, poena vovetur, eunt.
Paulo luce prius prorumpitur, armaque clamant,
760 tam male laturi, quam bene ferre rati.
Profuit arte malum, cessit victoria victis;
    invia robusto munia cautus adit.
Hospitis irati praesenserat excuba pernox
    terribilem reditum praemonuitque suos.
765 Gallus, cervus, ovis, caper, anser, caprea, vulpes
    alta petunt, solita mobilitate leves.
Consedere super celsi pinnacula tecti,
    eventusque suos operiuntur ibi,
at tam mole sui quam consuetudine deses,
770 ad cumulum faeni stabat asellus edens.
Assiliunt hostes coniuratamque ruinae
    unanimi stipant obsidione domum.
Sero fere metuens, asinus faenile per altum
    tendit, ubi socios suspicit esse suos.
775 Antera iam tectum tenet ungula, postera faenum,
    unde salus fieret sive ruina semel;
nec miser ascensor nec felix esse videtur,
    perdere tam facilis quam retinere fugam.
A pluteo tecti, suspenso corpore quantum
780 occupat interstans, subter acervus erat.
Tunc asinus magno se proripit impete sursum;
    calx obiter labens postera lusit eum,

to be, and Sualmo's grandson, Storm Scare-Belly, and Storm's brave father-in-law, Gulpa Little-Hell, and then Gulpa's uncle, and Sualmo's too, Olnam, nicknamed Hell-Itself.   755

To them the wolf made his complaint, revealing what he had undergone, and who was responsible for his injuries. They vowed revenge, and set off. They got under way a little before dawn, calling for battle, but doomed to fall short   760 of success to the same extent that they thought themselves sure of it. Their evil was turned to advantage by artfulness, and victory was the lot of the vanquished; cunning can pierce defenses which are impenetrable to strength.

The night watchman, foreseeing the terrifying return of their enraged guest, had warned his friends; the cock, stag,   765 sheep, goat, goose, roe and fox made for the heights, nimble through their customary agility, and perched on the gables of the high roof, there waiting for their fate. But the ass, who was sluggish by reason both of his size and of his habits, still stood eating by the pile of hay. The enemy attacked, and   770 together they surrounded the house they had sworn over to destruction. Turning frightened almost too late, the ass clambered over the piled-up hay to the place where he saw his friends to be. Now his front hoof held on to the roof, and   775 his back one the hay, from which position it would be safety or disaster once and for all; the mountaineer seemed neither unlucky nor successful, since it was as easy for him to retain the possibility of escape as to lose it. The heap was at such a distance beneath the slope of the roof that his outstretched body filled the space between them. Then the ass hurled   780 himself upward with a great rush, but immediately his back

succidit ille labans retro, saltusque supinans
    non asinum attollens in sua terga rotat.
785 Ut mons ille ruit, sub cuius pondere vasto
    illiduntur humi Turgius atque socer.
Vertit in auxilium iacturam provida vulpes
    taliter: "O demens, iussimus ista tibi?
Muribus his opus esse putas? Quin arripe primum
790   archilupum turbae totius hucque rota!
Inde tene seriem, maioribus adde pusillos,
    donec compereris non superesse pilum.
Me miserum, quod non plures huc appulit error!
    Hos penitus geminum lambimus ante diem.
795 Iussa facis, demens, Gerardus an irruet anser?
    Nec sinet hic caudam nec remanere caput!"
Anser deinde cavum proflans et fortiter alas
    concutiens gestum paene volantis habet.
Diriguere hostes, porro consurgere necdum,
800   qui ruerant, poterant, fit timor atque tremor.
Nec mora, quot capitum, tot circumquaque viarum;
    primum, cuius amor moverat arma, fugit.
Venerunt pariter, multum rediere dirempti;
    quo versi steterant, posteriora ruunt.
805 Turgius et Sualmo tandem consurgere nisi
    vix sua digesto membra tulere solo;
utque iter arreptum est, omnes post terga relinquunt,
    qui nisi fuerant praecelerasse diu.
Sic asinus victus Reinardi vicerat astu,
810   unius et clades omnibus egit opem.

foot slipped and betrayed him. He sank back and fell, and the leap which failed to take him upward rolled him over on his back. He toppled like a mountain, and beneath his vast weight Turgius and his father-in-law were flattened to the ground. 785

The fox, with foresight, turned this disaster into an advantage, saying: "Madman, is that what we ordered you? Do you think we have any use for these mice? First go and seize the leader wolf of the whole pack, and toss him over here! 790 Then proceed in order, adding the little ones to the bigger, until you find there's not a hair left over. What a pity that more of them weren't led here by their ramblings! We'll polish off this lot for dinner before two days are out. Are you 795 doing what you're told, madman, or shall Gerard the goose attack? He won't allow a tail or a head to remain intact!" Then the goose blew out the hollow of his throat and beat his wings so vigorously that he looked almost as if he was flying.

The enemy stiffened with fear, but those who had fallen 800 still couldn't get up. Fear and trembling broke loose, and immediately there were as many directions of escape as there were wolves. He on whose behalf the battle was being fought was the first to flee. They had arrived together, but they went back on widely separated paths; away they went, their backs turned in the direction they'd been facing. Fi- 805 nally Turgius and Sualmo tried to get up, but could hardly drag their limbs out of the cratered earth; once on their way, however, they left way behind them all those who had had longer to try and get ahead. Thus the ass, although beaten, nevertheless won the victory by Reynard's cunning, and the 810 misfortune of one brought relief to all of them.

Crastina lux aderat, mirantur gallus et anser
    tot vulpis victos arte fuisse lupos,
iamque retractantes sollertia facta, futuri
    oderunt socium suspicione doli.
815 Disponens igitur leni facienda susurro,
    Sprotinus socium format ita atque monet:
"Versutus nimis iste michi, Gerarde, videtur,
    nec nos in fatua simplicitate sumus.
Exiguum non est, ubi sit fallacia, nosse;
820   cognita vitatur vel minus anguis obest.
Ad nostram redeamus humum, quaesita profecto
    sat loca sanctorum credo fuisse michi.
Transmutemus iter, nichil aestimo sanius esse,
    nam mora suspecta est, demptaque causa morae.
825 Coniugium expletum est, cui decrevere necari;
    altilium domini quadrupedumque mares,
nec portanda foco Carcophas ligna veretur.
    Omnia sunt isto percelebrata die;
res igitur finem, quae nos praestrinxit, ut huius
830   Reinardi comites efficeremur, habet.
Quem bene si novi, non nostra ex stirpe quis umquam
    longa pace fuit nec comes eius erit.
Nec, quia iurarit, veracior esse putetur;
    iurant multa, quibus creditur usque parum.
835 Frangere fraus citius, quod iurat fortius, audet;
    iurandi non est indiga vera fides.
Iuravit nobis Reinardus, crede fidelem!
    Vult tibi, quod voluit patribus ante tuis.
Servat adhuc farto iuratum foedus omaso;
840   foedus obit, postquam desinit esse satur.

The dawn of the next day had arrived, and the cock and the goose were expressing amazement that so many wolves had been overcome by the artfulness of one fox, and now, going over the tricks he had performed, they conceived a dislike for their companion, through suspicion of his future cunning. So, outlining what they should do, in a gentle whis- 815 per Sprotinus directed and advised his companion as follows: "He seems too clever by half to me, Gerard—and we're not foolish simpletons. It's of no small importance to be aware where deception lies; a snake can be avoided once it's 820 been noticed, or at least it does less harm. Let's go back to our country; I really think there's been enough exploration of the saints' shrines as far as I'm concerned. Let's change our itinerary; I think nothing could be more sensible, for delay is dangerous, and the reason for delaying has disap- peared. The marriage is over for which our masters ordered 825 the slaughter of male birds and quadrupeds, and Carcophas isn't afraid of having to carry wood for the fire. All the cele- brations for that day are over; so the event which con- strained us to become companions of this Reynard has 830 reached a conclusion. And if I know him well, none of our kindred was ever at peace with him for long or will be his friend. Nor should he be thought more truthful just because he's taken an oath. People in whom little trust is to be placed swear a lot of things. The more vigorously deceit swears 835 something, the quicker it finds the confidence to break it. Real loyalty doesn't need to express itself in oaths. Believe Reynard faithful because he has taken an oath! His wishes for you are just the same as his wishes for your fathers be- fore you. So far he keeps the alliance he has sworn because his belly is full; when he is no longer well stuffed, the alliance 840

Ad libertatem peccandi surgit egestas;
    esse nichil crimen praeter egere putat.
Nec, sibi dum prosit, curat, quam pluribus obsit;
    hac timor atque pudor consiliante cadunt.
845 Clam rapienda fuga et subito est; si noverit hostis,
    propositum insidiis anticipabit iter."
Ille susurrantes attendens prodit et infit:
    "Unde timor, socii? Nonne abiere lupi?"
Cogitat hic gallus: "Tu nondum, frater, abisti,
850 tu michi vis sane quod lupus esse tibi!"
Addidit astutus rethor: "Quae causa pavendum
    suadet, ubi gaza est, relligio atque favor?
Stultus tuta timens fit tutus, quando timendum est,
    at sapiens trutina pendit utrumque sua.
855 Este penes socium tuti, coram hoste pavete;
    non me vos aliqua fraude notastis adhuc.
Septima cras lux est, nunc sexta, nec utor in istis
    carne domi, nedum cum loca sacra petam.
Qui caret ipse fide, nullum putat esse fidelem;
860 si bona vestra fides, et mea nota foret.
Comiter errantem sapiens supportat amicum;
    non vos pro modico crimine trudo foras.
Nunc iterata sacris habeat concordia pondus,
    ut duplicem culpam foedera fracta trahant.
865 Neve viam sacram, quamvis sit dura, timete;
    dulce nichil meruit, qui nichil acre tulit."

will be a nuisance to him. Necessity assumes the freedom to sin, and thinks nothing is wrong except being in need. It doesn't care how many people may be hurt while its advantage is being served; under the dictates of need, fear and shame are discarded. We must take flight secretly and quickly; if our enemy knows of it, he'll forestall the journey we plan with his tricks." 845

The fox, picking up their whispers, came forward and said: "Why are you afraid, friends? Haven't the wolves gone away?" The cock thought to himself: "You haven't gone away, brother, and you, indeed, want to be to me what the wolf is to you!" The cunning orator added: "What reason is there to be afraid, when profit, religious duty and interest are on your side? The fool is nervous in a situation of security, and is confident when fear is called for. In contrast, a wise man can size up both situations accurately. You should relax with your friend, and be nervous with your enemy! So far you haven't observed any deceitfulness in me; tomorrow is the seventh day of the week, today the sixth, and I don't consume meat on those days when I'm at home—let alone while I'm making for religious shrines. It's someone who is himself untrustworthy who thinks that no one else is honest; if your fidelity was valid, mine would be obvious to you too. A wise man puts up with the errors of a friend in a friendly fashion, and I won't thrust you out of doors for a trivial fault. Now let the repetition of our agreement, on holy relics, take on additional weight, so that if the alliance is broken, it may incur twice as much blame. And don't be afraid of the holy pilgrimage even if it's difficult. Whoever hasn't borne any hardship doesn't deserve any pleasure." 850 855 860 865

Gallus ad haec: "Nosti, quae dicebamus, et ac si
    verum nescieris, cetera fingis," ait.
"Iactabamus enim, quod nostris protinus herbis
870   exhibuit iuvenem ianua docta lupum.
Ergo quod simulas nos velle recedere mirum est,
    nam nos non dubitas velle coesse tibi—
quin, ne nos famulos tibi dedignere, veremur,
    nec tua mens nobis, sed tibi nostra patet.
875 Ne spes nostra labet, iuretur utrimque secundo,
    et grates, si nos non reprobaris, habe!"
Quamvis crediderat repetito foedere lusus
    dictator socios velle manere suos,
ieiunare minus rupto pro foedere gallum
880   terret, quam certa morte carere iuvat.
"Nunc propera, Gerarde comes, fortasse manemus
    incolumes hodie, cras comedemur," ait.
"Eia mox, dum nulla fugam cautela cohercet!"
    His dictis celerem corripuere viam,
885 sed cervus simul atque asinus, vervexque caperque
    hi nondum dominam destituere suam.
Sentit abisse duos nec curans fracta fuisse
    foedera Reinardus dampna uterina dolet.
Tunc baculum secum peramque prehendit abitque,
890   quaesitumque diu non reperire potest,
denique plena videns intra granaria gallum,
    insidias cassa calliditate parat.
"Heus!" inquit, "Sprotine comes, cur solus abisti
    omnibus ignaris sollicitisque tui?
895 Debueras saltem, licet incomitatus abires,
    dicere, ubi sociis inveniendus eras!

The cock replied: "You know what we were really saying, and you're inventing all this as if you didn't know the truth. We were talking about the learned qualifications of that doorway, which, with the aid of our medicine, so quickly turned the wolf young. So it's amazing that you should pre- 870 tend that we want to leave, because you're in no doubt of our desire to be associated with you—rather it's we who are afraid you might scorn to have us as your servants; your thoughts aren't clear to us, although ours are to you. Let the 875 oath be taken over again by both of us, lest our hope is disappointed, and accept our thanks for not rejecting us!"

Although their leader was fooled by the repetition of the oath into believing that they wanted to remain his companions, the cock's terror at the idea of fasting as a penance for the broken compact was less than his relief at escaping 880 certain death. "Now be quick, friend Gerard," he said, "today, perhaps, we survive unharmed, but tomorrow we'll be eaten. Ah, quickly, while no trick checks our flight!" This said, they quickly set out. But the stag and the ass, the sheep 885 and goat—these didn't yet desert their mistress.

When Reynard realized that the two of them had left, he wasn't bothered about the broken compact, but he was very sorry for the loss to his stomach. Then, taking with him his scrip and staff, he went off, but for a long time couldn't 890 find what he was looking for. At last, he saw the cock inside a full granary, and he prepared a trap for him, with fruitless cunning. "Hi, friend Sprotinus! Why did you go off on your own, with everyone in the dark about it and worrying about you? You ought at least, even if you went off unac- 895 companied, to have said where your friends could find you!

En egomet longo quaesitum tempore tandem
    vix isto potui te reperire loco."
Ille refert: "Frustra quaerebar, sponte redissem,
900   cum reditum nossem profore posse michi."
Intulit hostis: "Ita est, sed solum miror abisse—
    heu meruit nostrum nemo tibi esse comes?
Me taceo, quem semper amas te semper amantem;
    cetera se spretis te dolet isse phalanx,
905 sacraque vota nimis per te dilata queruntur,
    et nullo, donec veneris, ire volunt.
Nunc, nostri dum cura deum movet, accipe peram
    cum baculo, et sacrum perficiamus iter!"
Cristiger obiecit: "Scio, te duce tutus ego essem,
910   et cuperem semper te comitante gradi,
sed baculum peramque tuam refer, illa profecto
    Gutero, qui tenus hac haec dabat, usque dabit!
Accipe, si rogitas, causam: fidissimus esse,
    diceris esuriens, sed satur absque fide.
915 Non igitur tecum nisi ieiunante viabor,
    nil fidei stomacho luxuriante tenes."
Subridens vafer haec replicat: "Sociabimur ergo!
    Esurio, quantum credere nemo queat;
quoque fame crucior graviore, fidelior hoc sum."
920   Penniger econtra: "Tempora perdis, abi!
Per sanctos, quos quaeris, abi, Reinarde! Manebo;
    sit fas, sive nefas, nolo coesse tibi.
Gutero decrevit meliores visere sanctos,
    atque suus consors suasit ut esse velim.

See, I myself, having sought you out for a long time, have only with difficulty been able to find you in this place."

He replied: "It was silly to look for me; I'd have come back of my own accord, if I'd thought that my return would have been of any benefit." His enemy commented: "True, but I'm surprised that you went off alone—ah, why wasn't any of us worthy to be your companion? Not to mention myself, for whom you have a constant affection, just as I do for you, the rest of the company is hurt by your having gone off and rejected them. They complain about their sacred vows, which have been postponed too long on your account, and they don't want to go on until you come. Now, while God is on our side, take the scrip and staff, and let's finish our pilgrimage." The comb bearer objected: "I know I'd be safe under your leadership, and I'd always be willing to travel in your company—but take back your staff and scrip. Gutero the hare, who has bestowed them on me up to now, will continue to hand them out. If you ask, you can have the reason: you're said to be very trustworthy while you're hungry, but unreliable when full. So I won't travel with you unless you eat nothing; you have no loyalty when your stomach is indulged." Smiling, the traitor answered thus: "We can be companions then! I'm so hungry no one would believe it, and the more severe the hunger that tortures me, the more trustworthy I am."

The wing bearer countered: "You're wasting your time, go away! By the saints you're seeking, Reynard, go away; I'm staying here. Right or wrong, I don't want anything to do with you. Gutero has decided to visit better saints, and he has persuaded me into a wish to be his companion.

900

905

910

915

920

925 Suasit, eroque, redi! Nil nugis proficis istis;
 alterutrum nobis noscimur ambo satis."
His velut iratus responso vocibus apto
 obviat, ypocrita fallere fraude volens:
"Compater o nunc usque tuus, Sprotine, ferebar,
930 effestuco dehinc teque genusque tuum!
Muribus esto comes! Gallorum nullus haberis,
 et penitus patria nobilitate cares!"
Artibus ars cunctis respondet nulla vicissim;
 ille vafer subito ludificatus ait:
935 "Unde meo videor despectior esse parente?
 Coniugibus bis sex impero solus ego,
quaelibet et minimum non audet tangere granum,
 me nisi mandetur praecipiente prius."
Fictor ad haec: "Sprotine, tace! Tam vilia tanti
940 stirps patris ostentas? Proh pudor, opto mori!
Vilior hoc fore quisque solet, quo clarior ortu
 eximiis proavis inferiora facit.
Nam tuus ille parens uno pede functus et unum
 praecludens oculum carmen herile dabat."
945 Exultans Sprotinus idem despondet agitque,
 seque refert magno cedere nolle patri.
Addidit ille: "Tui generis nunc aemulus esse
 incipis, at patrem plus valuisse ferunt.
Fama nichil de te perhibet, nec scimus, iniquo
950 an iusto fuerit semine foeta parens.
Egregiam prolem maiorem patribus esse
 sive parem, sed non degenerare decet.
Ecce meo multum placuit tuus ille parenti,
 et titulis omnes nobilitabat avos:

He's persuaded me, and that's what I'll be, so go back! You 925
get nowhere with these idiocies; we both know each other
quite well enough." As if angered by these words, he made
an apt objection in reply, wishing to take him in by hypo-
critical deceit: "Up to now I was known as your godfather,
Sprotinus; henceforth I utterly renounce you and your fam- 930
ily! Go and associate with mice; you're not to be reckoned a
cock, since you're completely lacking in your father's excel-
lence."

No cunning is a match for every piece of cunning from
the other side; all at once the crafty cock was taken in,
and said: "Why should I seem more contemptible than my 935
sire? I enjoy sole mastery over twelve wives, and none of
them dares to touch the least little grain of corn unless she's
first ordered to do it by my say-so." The deceiver replied:
"Enough, Sprotinus! Do you, the son of such a father, boast 940
of such trivialities? Ah, the shame of it. I could die! The
more distinguished in birth one is, the baser one becomes in
failing to act up to one's outstanding forebears. Now that fa-
ther of yours, supporting himself on only one leg and closing
one eye, used to pour forth music that showed his lordly na-
ture." This Sprotinus happily promised and performed, pro- 945
claiming his reluctance to fall short of his mighty father. The
fox added: "Now you're beginning to emulate your family—
but they say your father was of even greater prowess. Fame
has nothing to say of you, nor do we know whether your 950
mother was made fruitful by licit or illicit seed. A distin-
guished offspring should be greater than his fathers, or equal
to them, but he shouldn't be worse. Now, your father was
very much to the taste of mine, and by his glory he ennobled

955 orbi quadrifido resonum fundebat, in uno
    stans pede, pupillam clausus utramque, melos,
qua deus usque potest aliquid, vox dulcis, et ultra
    audiri poterat milibus octo quater!"
Gallus idem iurans canit, utraque lumina clausus,
960   quem citius medio subripit ille sono,
irrisitque suo suppressum poplite: "Namque
    omnis agens, ut vult, se probat esse, quod est!
Egregie, Sprotine, canis! Sic postera cantet
    stirps michi cotidie, sic cecinere patres.
965 Porro quid optabas cantando dicere? Novi:
    foedera iuraras et violasse doles.
Dicere sed nimium clara hoc michi voce volebas,
    nescius insidias pluribus esse locis.
Quid si quis latitans audisset probra seorsum,
970   qui tibi, cum nolles, improperaret adhuc?
Idcirco vetui cantum prodire parantem.
    Intrandum est nemus, ut clam fatearis ibi,
iniungenda tuis est poena reatibus illic,
    et, tua qui prodat crimina, nullus erit.
975 Neglectam debere fidem maiore piari
    comperies nisu quam potuisse geri—
non quia te cupiam consumere quemve tuorum;
    hoc facerem invitus, sat tibi claret idem.
Esurio, servabo fidem, nil vendico de te,
980   ni quod, si sapias, sponte michi ipse dabis.
Non plumas comedo, pennas utrobique relinquo,
    integra perstabunt candidiora tui.
Hoc, quod vile tui est, esu quod inutile nosti,
    quod muscis alitur vermiculisque, molam."

all his predecessors. Standing on one foot and closing *both* 955
eyes, he poured out his echo-raising tones to the four cor-
ners of the world—and his sweet voice could be heard as far
as God's power extends, and thirty-two miles further!"

The cock, swearing to do the same, and closing both his
eyes, sang. Swiftly the fox seized him in the middle of his 960
song, mocking him while holding him under his paw. "Truly,
everyone shows what his nature is when he acts according to
his desire! You sing excellently, Sprotinus! Thus sang your fa-
thers, thus may your offspring sing daily for me. But what 965
did you want to express in your singing? I know: you swore
to the alliance and you repent of having broken it. But you
wanted to tell me this too loudly, unaware that there are
dangers in all kinds of places. What if some skulker over
there had heard your shameful acts, and were, besides, to 970
taunt you with them some time when you wouldn't like it?
So I stopped you from going further when you were getting
ready to sing. We must go into the wood, so that you may
there confess in secret. There the penance for crimes must
be imposed upon you, and there will be no one to betray
your wickedness. You will find that your broken faith must 975
be expiated with a greater struggle than was necessary to
keep it. Not because I'd want to devour you or any of your
family; I'd do it against my will, as is quite clear to you. I'm
hungry, so I'll keep my faith; I claim nothing from you but 980
what you yourself will give me of your own accord, if you
have any sense. I won't eat the feathers, and I'll leave both
wings, so that your more beautiful parts will remain intact.
But that which is vile in you, and that you know to be useless
for food, that which is nourished for flies and worms, I'll re-
duce to pulp."

985 Taliter irrisus reticebat, fraudibus hostem
     tempora lusuris commodiora legens.
   Reinardum tardasse piget, raptaque rapina
     supplebat cursu concitiore moras.
   Mensus iter medium fuerat, prospexit euntem
990   confuso strepitu rustica turba furens:
   "Aspice, quid portet Reinardus! Prende! Relinques!
     Quo nunc, fur? Quo sic? Prendite! Curre! Feri!"
   Senserat arrepto Sprotinus tempore fraudem
     posse refraudari sicque profatur ovans:
995 "Heu generis mansura mei confusio semper!
     A studio capitis libero fata mei;
   me generis prisci tangit pudor atque futuri,
     quorum nobilitas omine laesa meo est,
   quod sub degeneri captivus deferor hoste,
1000   a decies nono nobilis ortus avo.
   Olim praeda forem, vulpesque tulisset honorem,
     collatis generi patribus orta meo.
   Fur me foedus habet, mala me vulpecula portat!
     Cur dicam, rogitas, ista?" (rogabat enim)
1005 "Si possem, loquerer graviora decentius in te;
     vis credi probus, et quid probitatis habes?
   Exprobrasset enim turba haec tibi rustica gratis,
     si tibi, quod iactas, esset herile genus?
   Materiam, si vis laudari, praestrue laudis;
1010   absque operum titulis irrita verba volant.
   Ha quaeris, quid agas?" (etenim quaerebat) "et extas
     vulgatus sapiens? Disce, docebo quidem.
   Tu me visus eras sapientior usque dierum;
     te ferar hic saltem doctior esse semel.

The object of these jeers was silent, choosing a more suit- 985
able time for stratagems which would make his enemy look
foolish. Reynard regretted having wasted time, and seizing
his plunder, made up for his delay by a faster pace. He had
covered half the distance, when a crowd of peasants caught
sight of him as he went, and vented their rage in confused 990
outcry: "Look what Reynard's carrying!" "Catch him!" "Let
it go!" "Where now, thief?" "Where are you off to like that?"
"Catch him!" "Run!" "Kill him!"

Sprotinus had perceived that deceit could be deceived by
seizing the moment, and happily said: "Alas for the shame 995
which will settle on my race forever! I release the Fates from
any concern for my life; I'm concerned for the shame
brought on my ancestors and my children. Their nobility
suffers from my disgrace, in that I'm led away captive by a
lower-class enemy, I whose nobility goes back ninety genera- 1000
tions—whereas in the old days, had I been a prey, the tri-
umph would have been won by a fox born of ancestors com-
parable to mine! A dirty thief has hold of me, a nasty little
fox carries me off! Do you ask why I say that?" (as he did) "If 1005
I could, I'd with complete propriety speak far worse things
against you. You want to be thought respectable, and yet
how much respectability do you have? Would this crowd of
churls have got away with insulting you in this way if you'd
been of an aristocratic family, as you boast? If you want to be
praised, you should provide the material for praise; words fly 1010
about emptily without the deeds which substantiate them.
Are you inquiring what you should do?" (he was indeed) "—
and you have a reputation for wisdom? Well, learn, and I'll
certainly instruct you. You seemed wiser than me up to now,
but on this one occasion at least I'll be recognized as being

1015 Sic igitur facies: tu me depone—manebo,
     quid fuga prodesset? Mors patienda michi est!—
Et me deposito dic: 'Plebs insana, silete!
     Si porto, cuius rem nisi porto meam?
Sic pater est a patre meo portatus, et iste
1020   nunc feodum patriae conditionis habet.'
Te sin esset, ut est, melior pars septima lendis,
     destruere hoc posses rustica probra modo."
Deponens spolium, Reinardus inania clamat;
     depositus celeri mobilitate fugit,
1025 concutiensque alas super alta rubeta resedit.
     "Sum, domine, hic! Grates, galliger," inquit, "habe!
Hic, quamvis alibi mallem, vel me tamen esse
     grator, ubi sine te sero futurus eram.
Solvisti patriae bene vectigalia sortis;
1030   portatus genitor sic meus ante tuo est.
Sed quia tam subito solvisti tamque libenter,
     optima, si iubeas, hinc tibi mora dabo."
Dixerat et variis instigans cantibus hostem
     Ungarice et Graece Caldaiceque canit.
1035 Rettulit elusus simulato foedere lusor,
     responsum falsa sic pietate linens:
"O generis, Sprotine, tui tutela decusque!
     Nobilis et prudens, pulcer opumque dator!
Non miror, si mora michi socialiter offers,
1040   grandius obsequium cum michi saepe geras.
Sed non nunc michi mora placent; tu vescere, donec
     digrediar visum, paxne sit anne pavor.
Nolo iterum nobis insultet rusticus exlex
     aut nostrum impediat quilibet hostis iter."

the better instructed. So this is what you shall do: put me 1015
down and I'll wait—what use would flight be? I'm doomed
to die!—and when I've been put down, say: 'Stupid people,
be quiet! If I'm carrying him off, what am I carrying except
my own property? His father was thus carried by my father,
and he is now enfeoffed with his father's status.' If it wasn't 1020
that the seventh part of a louse's egg was better than you—
as it is—you could wipe out these plebeian insults in this
way."

Putting down his plunder, Reynard shouted empty noth-
ings—but the cock, when laid down, flew away with agile
swiftness, and beating his wings, settled on a high thicket of 1025
brambles. "Here I am, sir!" he said, "Thank you, cock bearer!
Even though I'd rather be somewhere else, yet I'm happy to
be where I wouldn't have been for a long time without your
cooperation. You've provided the services due from your fa-
ther's status very well; my father was carried by yours in just 1030
the same way. But because you've fulfilled them so speed-
ily and willingly, I'll give you the best blackberries from here,
if you ask." He ended his speech, and crowed in Hungar-
ian, Greek and Chaldean, taunting his enemy with different
screeches.

The beguiled beguiler replied with a pretense of friend- 1035
ship, coloring his answer with pretended affection. "O Spro-
tinus, preserver and glory of your race! Noble and wise, re-
splendent giver of treasures! I'm not surprised if you offer
me blackberries out of friendship, since you often do me 1040
even greater service. But I don't want any blackberries now;
you eat them, while I go off to see if there's a peace or a civil
disturbance! I don't want the lawless peasant to insult us
again, or any enemy to impede our journey."

BOOK FIVE

Insipiens quandoque rapit sapientis, itemque
    praeventus sapiens insipientis opus.
Vix aliquis semper sapienter, et omnia nullus
    quamlibet insipiens insipienter agit.
5 Reinardus per multa sagax cessavit in uno,
    utile dum laxo dente reliquit onus.
Deposuit gallum pro nobilitate tuenda;
    fastus et utilitas non simul esse ferunt.
Sed minus amissae tristis de sorte rapinae
10   quam de tam stolida credulitate fuit.
Plus semel eludi, qui fallere callet avetque,
    quam decies simplex innocuusque dolet.
Sed dampnum reparare vafer spe fisus inani,
    nulla palam tanti signa doloris habet;
15 scilicet ereptus laqueis, ne rursus eosdem
    aut similes sapiens incidat, usque cavet.
Ille igitur similis laetanti fruge carentes
    tendiculas alia calliditate novat.
Protinus obliquo digressus calle seorsum,
20 expertum credi, paxne sit, isse cupit.
Dum graditur, veterem speculatur forte coturnum,
    hunc rapit immerso dente diuque premit.

Sometimes a fool takes on the role of a clever man, and in the same way a clever man, when outwitted, takes on the role of a fool. Hardly anyone acts shrewdly all the time, and no one, even if he's a fool, does everything foolishly. Reynard, acute in so many matters, lapsed in one, when with slackened jaw he let go of his profitable burden. He put down the cock to defend his high birth; pride and profit are uneasy bedfellows. But he was less sorry for his bad luck in losing the spoil, than he was for having been so stupidly credulous. Anyone who relishes deception, and is skilled in it, is more upset at being tricked once, than a simple and harmless soul is at being tricked ten times. But the cunning creature, buoyed up by a vain hope of making good his loss, betrayed no signs outwardly of this great distress; a prudent man who's been set free from a snare is always on the watch that he doesn't fall into the same snare or one like it. So, as if he was quite happy, he re-laid his so far unsuccessful snares with another stratagem.

Without delay, he made off across country, wanting to have it thought that he had gone to find out whether there was a peace. As he went, he saw by chance an old shoe, which he seized, and sinking his teeth into it, gnawed at length.

Fel rabidum solvens in saevas denique voces,
    devovit dentes taliter ille suos:
25 "O dentes Satanae, non dentes vulpis honestae,
    vix scio, quid vobis imprecer atque velim!
Vos ebete exterebret culica, quem compede forti
    alligat invidiae nona Gehenna, Satan!
Concrepite in putri corio!" (ter namque quaterque
30   incussos dentes concrepere ipse dabat).
"Sic vos collidi, sic vos strinxisse decebat,
    subdita cum vobis carnea praeda foret.
Taliter in pinguem gallum mordere negastis,
    nunc veteres soleas rodite! Gallus abest,
35 prendite! Certe abiit, quidni? Mordere nequistis,
    mordendi gnaros ut sibi quaerat, abit.
Quid sperasse teri sub stultis dentibus illi
    profecit misero? Spes ea cassa fuit.
Non licuit, vetuistis enim, quid debuit ultra
40   quam venisse rapi? Quam voluisse teri?
Scilicet expectandus erat, quoadusque rogasset,
    quatinus a vobis se sineretis edi!
Ille, ubi vos segnes, ubi sensit stringere nolle,
    esca abiit cupiens dentibus esse bonis,
45 imprimere edoctis captique tenacibus atque
    morsuris subito; talibus ille favet.
Vos dentes fore? Vos gallum mordere? Meumne
    amplius os tales dedecorare feram?
Hiscere, non claudi, non stringere, solvere nostis;
50   hiscite iam, quantum vultis! Hiare licet!
Hiscere nossetis, non forsan gallus abisset;
    iamque revertetur gallus, hiate bene!

At last, releasing his bitter rage in savage words, he cursed his teeth in the following manner: "Oh, teeth of the devil, not of an honest fox! I hardly know to what fate I should curse you! May Satan, who is bound with a mighty chain in the ninth hell of malice, drill you out with a blunt chisel! Grind away on this rotten leather!" (for he had three or four times made his teeth grind as they met together). "That's how you ought to have been clashed together, that's how you ought to have pressed yourselves tight when the meaty prize was in your power. You refused to bite like that on the plump cock, so now you can gnaw old shoes! The cock's not here—first catch your cock! Of course he's gone off—why not? You were incapable of biting, so he's gone off to find teeth which know how to bite. What hope did the poor wretch have of being chewed by such incompetent teeth?— a futile hope that was! It wasn't allowed, you prohibited it. What more should he have done, besides coming to be seized? Besides showing a desire to be chewed up? Of course he was to be kept waiting until he had asked that you would allow him to be eaten by you! When he felt you to be lazy and unwilling to press together, he went off, wishing to be food for worthy teeth, those that have learned to dig well in, and hold on to what they've caught, and are ready to bite without more ado—that's the kind he likes. *You're* teeth? *You* bite a cock? Shall I allow your sort to disgrace my mouth any further? Gaping open, not being clamped shut, relaxing, not gripping, is what you're expert at—now you can gape as much as you want! It's all right to hang open! If you had known how to gape before, perhaps the cock wouldn't have gone away; if the cock comes back now, you must gape wide.

Si vos praenossem nil scire nisi hiscere tantum,
   mansisset vestrum nullus in ore meo.
55 Quid quod eum vestri saltem non contigit unus?
   Ludibrium vobis, non quasi praeda, fuit.
Grator ei gratis vos non lusisse, relusit;
   ludibrii dignam reddidit ille vicem.
Dicite, velletis reducem nunc stringere gallum?
60   Lectio sat lecta est anne legetur item?
Plus valet empta semel quam bina industria gratis.
   Doctrix mordendi vos scola nescit adhuc,
non didicistis adhuc, at vos mordere docebo—
   non ego, sed certe fida magistra fames.
65 Quid modo nobilitas vobis defensa rependit?
   Nunc opus est vobis, quid dabit illa boni?
Nobilitas melior nostro recitatur in aevo,
   quam: 'Pater illius hic, illius iste fuit.'
Mos faciendus erat, qui nostro tempore pollet;
70   saecula plus dampnum dedecore ista timent.
Dedecus est unum, nam non est dedecus ullum
   praeter egestati supposuisse caput.
Nobilis est locuples, ignobilis omnis egenus;
   divitiae tuta nobilitate nitent.
75 Mors opibus natisque patres rapit, urnaque claudit;
   convivunt vivis et dominantur opes.
Nobilitas veterum taceatur, nonne sepulta est?
   Quaeratur vivis auxiliare genus:
'Hic pater heredi pondo centena reliquit,
80   rem patris hic duplo transiit, ille triplo.'

If I'd known beforehand that you were no good at anything but gawping, not one of you would have kept a place in my mouth. How is it that at least one of you didn't grab hold of him? You treated him like a plaything rather than your prey! I congratulate him that you didn't play about with him for nothing—he played with you in your turn. He paid you back with a trick worthy of your fooling. Tell me, if the cock were to come back, would you now be willing to hold on to him? Have you learned your lesson well enough, or is it to be learned a second time? One piece of wisdom which is paid for is worth two acquired for free. So far you've not been put through the school that teaches biting; so far you haven't learned to bite, but I'll teach you—or rather, not I, but hunger, who is a very reliable instructor. What recompense does the honor you safeguarded give you now? Now that you've need, what good does it provide you with? A better kind of nobility is celebrated in this day and age than 'So-and-so was his father, his father was such-and-such.' I should have followed the custom which prevails these days; this generation is more afraid of loss than of dishonor. There's only one sort of dishonor, since there is none other than having bowed beneath the yoke of poverty. The rich man is noble, while every poor man is base; riches dazzle with their self-evident nobility. Death snatches ancestors away from their wealth and their children; the funeral urn closes on them, while riches live on with the living and wield their power over them. Don't mention the nobility of one's predecessors—it's dead and gone, isn't it? It's the kind of family that's some help to the living that should be sought after. 'This father left his heir a hundred pounds, he passed on double his father's goods, while the next passed them on threefold.'

Quid michi nobilitas, quae non ieiunia tollit?
Census alit viles, census obumbrat avos;
denique gaza iuvat pravo sub divite multos;
prodigus haut refert an sit avarus inops.

85 Ergo homines sapiunt: periit respectus agendi,
dummodo divitias illaqueare queant.
Lucrum iustitiae, lucrum praefertur honori,
nil nisi divitias non habuisse pudet.
Fraus, labor, insidiae, periuria, furta, rapinae,

90 bella, duella, cruces, ira, querela, minae,
proditio, caedes, ergastula, vincula, flammae,
obsequium, laudes, fictio, dona, ioci,
blanditiae, promissa, preces, iniuria iusque,
iudicia, usurae, faenora, cura, favor,

95 quaeque his adicias, et quae contraria dicas,
omnia iocundi sunt alimenta lucri.
Omnia constabunt summis leviora duobus:
'venit homo argento, venit et ipse deus.'
Primitus hoc populi decretum, denique cleri,

100 non modo pontifices, papa quoque ipse dicat.
Piscator Cephas et Beniaminita magister
fecissent eadem, sed sapuere nichil.
Innumeras marcas, animas piscantia paucas
retia piscator caelicus iste iacit;

105 non curans homines meritis sed pendere censu,
plura locat dantes in meliore polo.
Tutus apostolicae contempnit frivola vocis,
archisophi Symonis forfice tondet oves.

What use to me is the nobility that doesn't take away hunger? Money advances wretches, money eclipses a man's grandfathers; in short, money does good to a lot of people even when it's in the hand of a rich man who is wicked; with a poor man, the question of whether he's generous or mean doesn't even arise. So people show good sense; any regard 85 for how they behave has disappeared, so long as they can net a lot of money. Money is placed before justice, money is placed before honor; there's nothing shameful except having no money. Deceit, toil, plots, perjuries, theft, rapine, wars, combats, tortures, anger, accusation, threats, treach- 90 ery, murder, penitentiaries, shackles, flames, service, eulogies, pretense, gifts, jokes, flatteries, promises, prayers, justice and injustice, trials, interest, profits, concern, favor —whatever one may add to these or whatever opposites to 95 them you may mention, they are all fodder for beautiful money. All are of less weight than the double principle: 'Man is sold for money; for money God himself is sold.' First the laity, then the priesthood, and now not only the prelates but 100 the pope himself sanction this rule. The fisherman Peter and the schoolmaster Paul would have done the same, but they didn't have any sense. This heavenly fisherman casts his nets to fish up numberless marks, but very few souls; con- 105 cerned to weigh up men, not according to their merits, but according to their wealth, he places those who make bigger gifts in a better heaven. With serene contempt he treats the apostolic word as a bagatelle, and shears his sheep with the shears of the arch-trickster Simon.

Tornacum Romam studio virtutis in isto
110   transilit, Anselmo praesule fausta polis.
Interius vivo Tornacus vellera pastor
      decutit ipse ovibus, decutit ipse capris.
O utinam foret ille meis ex dentibus unus!
      Mordendi legem fratribus ille daret.
115   Ecclesias veluti leo saepta famelicus ambit,
      nil linquens nisi quod non reperire valet.
Dona, queat nequeat, qui iusso parcius offert,
      strictus obeditu mystica sacra tacet.
Quot gerit hic dentes, quasi tot praedonibus horrens,
120   vellera nequaquam rapta recresse sinit.
Praevolat et raperet, si posset, plura repertis—
      proh dolor! Inventis tollere plura nequit.
Hunc non posse modum rapiendi vertere plangit,
      hoc solum praedae certus inesse nefas.
125   Hunc ego pontificem vobis propono sequendum.
      Quid Claraevallis pannifer ille sapit?
Connectit paleas, nodum vestigat in ulva,
      decoriat calclos—mulgeat ergo grues!
Praesulis egregios mores imitaminor huius,
130   qui rapit ut Satanas utque Gehenna tenet!"
Dum ferus improperat dentes dementer hiasse
      neve iterum dubitent stringere prensa monet,
affore fagineus cortex spectatur ibidem
      ad formam cartae missilis atque modum.
135   Non bene cessuro fidens Reinardus in astu
      arripuit librum moxque reversus ait:
"Pax, Sprotine comes, iuratur! Ubique locorum
      (siste metum) tuti possumus ire, veni!"

In the pursuit of this virtue, Rome is outstripped by Tour- 110
nai, the city blessed with Bishop Anselm. This good shep-
herd of Tournai himself shears off the fleeces from sheep
and goats alike down to the living flesh. If only he were one
of my teeth! He'd give his brothers a lesson in biting. He 115
prowls around the churches as a hungry lion does the sheep-
fold, leaving only what he can't find. Whoever offers him
gifts less generously than he is told to (whether it's within
his power or not) is compelled on his obedience to leave off
reciting the holy offices. It's as if he bristles with as many
robbers as he has teeth, and he doesn't allow the shorn 120
fleeces to grow again; he gets in first, and would take, if he
could, more than he finds—what a pity that he *can't* take
more than he finds! He is sorry that he can't alter the limit to
taking, and is sure that this is the only thing wrong with
plunder. This is the bishop I hold up to you for imitation. 125
What does that rag wearer from Clairvaux know about any-
thing? He's a straw plaiter, someone who looks for knots
in sedge, a pebble peeler—let him go and milk cranes! You
should imitate the excellent behavior of this bishop, who 130
devours like Satan and holds like Hell!"

While he savagely castigated his teeth for having fool-
ishly opened, and told them that another time they shouldn't
hesitate to close on what they had seized, he saw lying there
the bark of a beech tree in the shape and form of a letter
patent. Reynard, trusting in his cunning (which was, how- 135
ever, to have no success) seized the bark, and returning with
all speed, said: "A peace, friend Sprotinus, has been sworn!
Forget your fear and come along!—we can go anywhere in

Repplicat ille: "Ratum est fortasse, sed ambigo paulum;
140   res nescit subitam rara movere fidem.
Dicere tu nolles forsan, nisi nosse putares,
     sed, quaecumque putas, dicere certa cave!
Unius et fraudis deprenditur inclitus auctor,
     postera credulitas curaque vocis obit.
145 Credere quo plures optat sibi quisque loquendo,
     hoc, quicquid loquitur, firmius esse decet.
Credendi faciles capiunt audita repente;
     difficiles animos insuperata trahunt."
"Indice me," ille refert, "dubitas? Ego dico tibi ipse!
150   Dicere me certum, quod puto, velle putas?
Ut de te taceam, frustrarer memet ego ipsum?
     Tam michi nativum quam trepidare tibi est.
Inter iurantes egomet iurare rogabar;
     vix spatium extorsi, dum comitere simul.
155 Expectamur enim, cursim properemus oportet;
     gressibus impavidis nos scio posse frui.
Aspice signatam, si non michi credis," (et offert
     quam tulerat) "cartam, nuncia pacis adest!
Nolebam monstrare tamen, quoadusque probassem,
160   an velles ultro credulus esse michi;
et veluti credas tibi me desisse favere,
     sic me nescio qua suspicione fugis.
Accipe et hac in teste fidem scrutare sodalis!"
     Taliter instanti reddidit ille vafer:
165 "Laicus, ut nosti, sum gallus, nescio cartas
     inspicere, et quidam falsa sigilla ferunt.

safety." He replied: "It may well have been settled, but I'm a bit doubtful; an unusual event cannot win credence immediately. Perhaps you wouldn't say so unless you thought you were certain of it, but be careful not to retail your imaginings as certainties! When the perpetrator of one deception is caught and acquires a reputation, what he says afterward is not given much credence or attention. The more people anyone wants to believe him when he speaks, the more reliably he ought to speak in every instance. Those who are easily credulous accept at once what they hear, while only the incontrovertible convinces skeptical minds."

"Are you in any doubt, when it is I who am your informant?" he replied. "I'm telling you myself! Do you think I would tell you as a fact what I merely conjecture? Never mind about you—would I deceive myself? Fear is as much a part of my nature as it is of yours. I myself was asked to swear along with the oath takers. With difficulty I won from them a delay until you should come along as well. We're waited for; it's necessary for us to hurry along with all speed. I know that we can proceed without fear. Look at this sealed letter, if you don't believe me," (and he offered what he had brought). "Here's the announcement of the peace! But I didn't want to show it until I'd tested whether you'd be willing to believe in me of your own accord—and as if you imagine I had ceased to be your friend, you run away from me like this under the influence of some suspicion or other. Here, take it, and examine the trustworthiness of your companion in the light of this evidence!" The shrewd cock replied as follows to his urgings: "As you know, I'm an unlettered cock, I don't know how to decipher charters—and some people bear forged seals.

Tu satis es verax, sed te fortasse fefellit
   qui bullam tribuit, terra repleta dolo est."
Callidus hic credens astutum fallere, falso
170   bullifer obiecit dura favore minax:
   "Bacharis, Sprotine Satan! Mortem incidis ultro?
   Vis, vesane, mori? Quin resipisce, miser!
Curia si sciret, quod cartae credere nolles,
   vix fierem vitae tutor ego ipse tuae!
175 Audi versiculum perlecta pace sequentem:
   'nolentes cartae credere teta trahit.'
Istius edicti viget incassabile pondus;
   carta tibi ostensa est et recitata palam.
Si potes aut audes, procerum decreta refelle;
180   credideris, vives, rennue, curre mori!
Si legere ignoras, at ne diffide relatis,
   credetur coram vindice sero nimis.
In dominum peccat, qui servum audire recusat;
   quid, dominus credi cum iubet ipse sibi?
185 Crede michi, iubeo, baronum scilicet uni
   sub quibus haec pax est: par michi praetor eris!"
Fallere multiloqua conantem fraude retundit
   laicus hac cantor calliditate iocans:
"Suspicio, Reinarde, perit michi, vera videris
190   dicere, nimirum qualiter usque soles.
Eminus incanum videor michi cernere quendam;
   aestimo, quod multas viderit ille nives.
Undecies denis plures barbae eius Apriles
   impendent, specta, sabbata quanta ferat.

You're truthful enough, but perhaps the person who gave you the document deceived you—the world is full of treachery." The crafty bearer of the document, thinking to deceive the astute cock, aggressively hurled back harsh words with a 170 false appearance of concern for him: "You're raving, Sprotinus, you devil! Are you incurring death of your own free will? Do you want to die, you fool? You should come to your senses, idiot! If the court were to know that you were unwilling to believe in the charter, I myself would barely be able to safeguard your life! Listen to the line which follows 175 when the bit about the peace has been read: 'Death is the punishment for those who refuse to put trust in the charter.' The weight of this edict is of unshakeable power; the charter has been shown and clearly repeated to you. Reject the decree of the nobles if you can or dare; if you put faith in it, 180 you will live; if you deny it, go quickly to your death! If you don't know how to read, at least don't be mistrustful of what's reported to you—it'll be too late to believe it when you're faced with the judge! Whoever refuses to listen to a servant, sins against his master—what when the master himself commands belief? Have faith in me, when I issue 185 the command, as one of the barons under whom this peace is created, and you'll be a court official like me!"

The fox's attempts to deceive with this treacherous spate of words were mockingly parried by the following ruse from the unlettered chanter: "My suspicion is gone, Reynard; you seem to be telling the truth, as you are only too well ac- 190 customed to do. Far off I see, methinks, a greybeard; many a winter do I judge him to have seen. More than a hundred and ten Aprils hang on his beard—see, what a wealth of

195 Illius a collo curvum, quae tibia fertur,
      pendet, et est album, quod sedet ipse super.
    Quin etiam nigri, speciem pietatis habentes
      nec dubie dulces, ante retroque ruunt.
    Accelerant cursim, non nos fortasse requirunt,
200   sed velut huc agili strennuitate volant.
    Cernis, ut illorum quisque aestuat utque vaporat?
      Nescio quid rufi pendet ab ore piis;
    vultus ut insontes notat, ut promucida blandos!
      Non agitat tales insita cura mali.
205 Curia nonne potest hos pacis mittere testes?
      Nam, veluti pacem testificentur, eunt.
    Quid nocet? Expecta! De pace rogentur, an illam
      tantum compererint, anne iubere velint."
    Non fuit hoc vulpi nimis acceptabile verbum;
210   quattuor hic nummos non meruisse putat.
    Incidit affectus geminos, cui pareat, haerens,
      spe prohibente, metu praecipiente fugam.
    "Utquid ab externis," ait, "amens galle, requires,
      quod nosti socio testificante ratum?
215 Propositum pacis, sicut cognosco, retexi;
      forsan et hi veniunt, ut fateantur idem.
    Adice, quod tibi sum carta quoque teste locutus,
      claudicet ut nulla suspicione fides.
    Utque nichil veri testetur carta (quod absit!),
220   annua cras ingens festa Machutus habet;

Sundays he bears! From his neck hangs something curved, 195
which is called a horn, and what he is sitting on is white.
What's more, black figures hasten before and behind him,
having an appearance of gentleness, and doubtless mild in
nature. They are advancing swiftly—perhaps they are not
looking for us, but it's as if, with vigorous haste, they are rac- 200
ing toward us. Do you see how hot and sweaty each of them
is? Something red hangs from the mouths of these gentle
creatures. How innocent their faces, how gentle their muz-
zles show them to be! No inward drive to evil animates crea-
tures like these. Isn't it possible that the court is sending 205
them to us as witnesses of the peace?—for it's as if they are
traveling about in order to testify to its existence. What's
the harm? —Wait! Let them be questioned about the peace,
whether they have merely learned about it, or whether it's
their job to enforce it."

This speech wasn't very acceptable to the fox; he wouldn't 210
have given four pence for it. He fell prey to twofold im-
pulses, doubting which one he should obey—the hope
which forbade flight, or the fear which encouraged it. "Why
should you ask outsiders, stupid cock," he said, "about some-
thing you know, on the testimony of your friend, to be set-
tled? I've announced the decree of peace as I know it; it may 215
be that this lot are coming to make the same disclosure. Add
to that the fact that my speech was backed up by the char-
ter as well, so that your faith might not waver through any
suspicion. Even suppose—which heaven forbid!—that the
charter contained no evidence of truth, tomorrow the great 220
Saint Malo has his yearly feast day. Listen, the bell has just

en comitante pari nonam modo clanga profestam
    tinnit, ut ipse audis, quid tibi tester ego?"
(Et tunc forte duo, sed non ob id, aera sonabant.)
    "Efficiunt tutas festa verenda vias.
225 Credis adhuc mecum securus pergere posse?
    Sed te non adeo diligit usque deus,
namque inter proceres pacem iurasse mereri
    nonne foret generi gloria magna tuo?
Ergo ego paulatim saltus enitar in istos;
230   elogium pacis curia sanxit ibi."
Econtra Sprotinus ait gratanter, ut hostem
    astibus exiguis succubuisse videns:
"Quin, Reinarde, mane, dum nuncius iste loquatur!
    Crediderim vanis nuncia tanta nolis?
235 Tuque bene acciperes, si mallem credere cupro
    quam tibi? Dum veniat nuncius iste, mane!"
Hostis ad haec: "Potius condensa frutecta revisam,
    nam michi nequaquam nota rogare libet;
coniuransque altae conscribar patribus aulae,
240   at te rusticitas dedecorosa premat!"
Intulit elusor: "Pax est iurata, comesque
    primatum pacis diceris, unde times?
Tu michi non metuenda times, et tantus haberis?
    Sta, miser, hic modicum, protinus ibo simul!
245 Venimus huc ambo, solus paterere reverti?"
    Taliter urgenti reddidit ille pavens:
"Iuratam fateor pacem, Sprotine, fuisse,
    sed nondum populis notificata patet."
Gallus item dixit: "Iurata pace vereris?
250   Sed 'Non est populis notificata' refers;

rung, followed by one just the same, for the Nones of the
vigil to the feast—as you hear yourself, why should I tell you
about it?" (And two bells were then by chance ringing, but
not for that reason.) "The honor due to the feast makes all
roads safe. Now do you believe that you can travel with me   225
in security? God isn't always so kind to you—for wouldn't it
be a great honor to your family to be found worthy to have
sworn to the peace among the feudal lords? So I shall in
leisurely fashion make for those woods—that's where the   230
court ratified the declaration of peace."

Sprotinus, happy to see that his enemy had fallen into his
little trap, replied: "No, Reynard, wait until this messenger
speaks! Shall I believe such important news on the basis of
some silly bells? I mean, would you yourself take it well if I   235
were to put my trust in some old copper rather than you?
Wait until this messenger arrives!" His enemy answered:
"No, I'll go back to those thick bushes, because I don't care
to seek information about what I know perfectly well. As
one of those taking the oath, I shall be enrolled with the
leaders of the noble court—but you can remain bogged   240
down in the state of an ignoble commoner!" His mocker re-
plied: "The peace has been sworn, and you say you're an as-
sociate of the nobles involved in it—so why are you afraid?
Are you reckoned so powerful, when you're afraid of things
that shouldn't even frighten me? Stay here a little, you
wretch, and I'll go with you in just a minute! We came here   245
as a pair; would you now be happy to return alone?" Timo-
rously the other replied to his urging: "Granted the peace
has been sworn, Sprotinus, but it isn't yet clearly publi-
cized to the people." The cock said again: "Are you afraid,
when the peace has been sworn?—But you reply that 'it isn't   250

309

ergo per hos testes et te vulganda per ipsum est.
    Hostis ob hoc forsan rex abeuntis erit!"
Cartiger agresti devictus turpiter arte
    effatur timida talia voce rogans:
255 "Ha, Sprotine, quid hoc, quod collo pendet ab alto,
    curvum portendit? Res ea pace venit?
Et canus nigrique doce quid quaerere possint,
    quorum dependens illud ab ore rubet!"
Ille refert: "Pax est primatibus agnita magnis,
260   quorum consilio fungitur aula potens,
sed conflare venit vulgares buccina turmas,
    quas accire negat curia docta rudes,
canaque collectis populis persona loquetur
    decretum celso regis ab ore datum.
265 Porro plebs hilaris comperta pace viritim
    transmittit regi dona venusta canes.
Quid me teste, miser, dubitas?" Ea quippe loquenti
    credere non audens bullifer infit item:
"Si verum esse potest, Sprotine, quod asseris, esto!
270   Ast ego in haec meditor ferre frutecta gradum,
et licet illorsum sit eundi parva cupido,
    ibo, velis nolis; manseris, ibo tamen,
gallicule infelix. Ut princeps inclitus ibo,
    tuque in perpetua rusticitate manes.
275 Forsitan hi pacem veniunt perhibere, quid ad nos?
    Nota foret nobis pax sine teste satis.
Nunc vero edictum pacis mora longa tenebit,
    contio dum populi tota coisse queat.

publicized to the people.' Well then, it shall be bruited abroad by these witnesses and by you yourself; it may be that the king, for this very reason, will be angry with anyone who leaves this spot!"

The charter bearer, shamefully outwitted by this rustic cunning, timidly put the following question: "Ah, Sproti- 255 nus, what does that curved thing hanging from his tall neck portend? Is that something to do with the peace? And the greybeard, and the black ones, tell me what they could be looking for—with that red thing hanging down from their mouths!" He replied: "The peace is known to the great no- bles whose counsel is followed by the mighty court, but the 260 horn comes to assemble crowds of ordinary people—the hoi polloi whom the well-bred court declines to summon, and when the people have been gathered together, the gray- haired person will read out the decree given from the noble mouth of the king, and afterward, the people, happy at the 265 news of the peace, will all send dogs to the king, as hand- some presents. Why are you in doubt, wretch, when you have my authority for this?"—Indeed, the seal bearer, not daring to believe what he said, began again: "If what you as- sert can be true, Sprotinus, so be it! But I am thinking of 270 taking a walk into these bushes. Although *your* desire to go there is small, *I* shall go whether you like it or not; even if you stay, I'll go, you miserable little cock. In going, I shall be a noble lord, while your staying keeps you in lasting obscu- rity. Perhaps they *are* coming to announce the peace—what's 275 that to us? The peace would be sufficiently well known to us without anybody to vouch for it. Now, however, a long de- lay will hold back the proclamation of the peace, until the

Sed quia consuescunt multos offendere multi,
280 saepe suos hostes turba gregata videt;
quod si pellicium alterius quis scinderet ante
  auditum pacis, tu quererere parum.
Ergo, licet morereris, eo, mortemque mereris,
  quod me nugosa garrulitate tenes."
285 Lusor ad haec: "Ergo remane! Venit aulicus hospes,
  si qua tibi est in me causa, sequester erit.
Emendabo libens aut excusabo, quid ultra?
  Praecipuis iras hostibus ista fugant.
Nescio, post ubi me videas, dirimamur amici!"
290 Vocibus his trepidans subdidit ille suas:
"Non huc me procerum timor aut reverentia banni
  traxit, nec placita est hic ad agenda locus."
Tunc sic improperans hosti Sprotinus ovanter
  respondit pavido: "Turpiter ergo fugis!
295 Turpiter hinc certe fugis ut vulpecula nequam,
  et pervado meo corpore ego ipse tuum.
Nobilitas cecidit, si non contenderis istic,
  pro qua te puduit rustica probra pati.
Fur michi tu deprensus abis, appello duellum;
300 si potes, haec collo probra repelle tuo!"
Intulit ille: "Diem forsan spectabo locumque
  quo defendendi suppetat hora michi."
Evolat inde ruens, ut qui non esse rogandos
  cogitat, an possint accelerare, pedes.

whole assembly of the people can come together. But because it's not unusual for many people to do harm to others, an assembled crowd often contains mutual enemies—and if anyone were to make a rent in anyone else's coat before hearing of the peace, you wouldn't complain too much about it. So I'm going, even if you were to die for it—and indeed you deserve to die, for holding me back with this frivolous chatter."

The trickster replied: "Wait then! The visitor from the court is coming. If there's a case against me, he'll be the arbitrator. I'll willingly make reparation or exculpate myself. What more do you want? These things assuage anger in one's greatest enemies. I don't know when you may see me again, so let's part friends!" To these words, the other tremblingly brought out his answer: "Neither fear of the nobles nor reverence for their proclamation brought me here, nor is this the place for conducting lawsuits." Then Sprotinus exultingly replied with taunts to his frightened enemy: "So you run away in disgrace! Yes, in disgrace you flee from here like a wicked fox. I challenge you, body to body; unless you enter into battle on the spot, your nobility, for the sake of which you were ashamed to endure the peasants' insults, is lost. You take to your heels, like a thief I've caught; I challenge you to combat—throw the weight of this insult from your neck if you can!" The other replied: "Perhaps I'll see a time and a place when the moment for defending myself will come." Then away he flew in a rush, like someone who thought that his feet shouldn't be asked whether they could

280

285

290

295

300

305 Post profugum ille alacer convicia clamat acerbe:
 "Heu michi, quam foedum est curia passa nefas!
 Iure suo regem spoliat Reinardus abitque
 liber, adhuc leviter consequeremur eum.
 Regis adeste, precor, proceres! Accurrite cursim!
310 Fur salit hic, furem pendite! Debet enim—
 aut agite huc! Si vos hunc taedet pendere, pendam;
 passus idem pater est a genitore meo."
 Respicit ille parum, nil praeter currere curans,
 laetior hoc, quo plus inde remotus erat;
315 spem turbante metu, spe consolante timorem,
 invia pensabat lance viasque pari.
 Et iam per casus nemorum amfractusque petrarum
 cursio lassarat quatriduana vagum,
 tempore nec tanto quicquam libasse ciborum
320 dicitur aut pausa se recreasse brevi;
 congestoque simul cursusque famisque labore
 officium fessi deseruere pedes.
 Tunc primum remeasse canes tutosque viarum
 circuitus posito credidit esse metu.
325 Postquam depulsa potuit formidine liber
 circumspectandi sedulitate frui,
 cuius ab incursu patrui defenderat agnos
 in campo quendam cernit adesse cocum.
 Utile multotiens sine dampno impensa recurrunt;
330 Reinardo est probitas auxiliata semel.
 Quem cocus ut vidit ieiunia longa viasque
 perpessum tremulo paene labare genu,
 pinguibus artocreis, quot lanx cumulata tenebat,
 officii veteris pro vice donat eum.

go any faster. The other one eagerly shouted harsh insults   305
after the fugitive: "Alas, what a foul wrong the court has suf-
fered! Reynard deprives the king of his right and goes off
free—but we could still overtake him with ease. Come here,
I beg you, nobles of the king! Hasten here quickly! The thief   310
is bounding off this way; hang the thief! He's guilty enough
—or bring him here. If you can't be bothered to hang him, I
will; his father got the same treatment from mine."

The other didn't look back, intent only on running, and
the happier, the further removed from that place he got.
With fear unsettling his hope, and hope allaying his fear, he   315
counted paths or open country as of equal value. And now,
four days of running through the wooded slopes and the
winding paths of the rocks had exhausted the wanderer, and
it is reported that in all that time he had not tasted any food
or refreshed himself with a little rest. Worn out with the ac-   320
cumulated hardship of running and hunger, his feet aban-
doned their office; then for the first time, laying aside his
fear, did he believe that the dogs had turned back, and that
the surrounding roads were safe. After he had shaken off his   325
fear, and could freely devote his attention to looking around
him, he saw a certain cook, whose lambs he had once saved
from an attack by his uncle in their field. Services which
cost one nothing often come back to one in the form of
profit—for once Reynard's honesty was of use to him. When   330
the cook saw that his trembling legs, having endured the
journey and the long fast, were almost giving way beneath
him, in return for the old favor he gave him as many rich
pies as a heaped-up plate would hold.

335　Ignotum est, ubi forte suum quis viderit hostem;
　　　Reinardus sollers praemeditatur idem.
　　Octo reservat, edens reliquas, capitique coronam
　　　postulat irradi, rasus it atque satur,
　　artocreasque ferens, patruum si viderit, ipsum
340　　cogitat oblato pacificare cibo.
　　(Mos illius erat quaecumque tulisse dolentis
　　　irarum viso non meminisse lucro.)
　　Nec fortuna animum praecustodita fefellit:
　　　obviat in mediis saltibus ille seni.
345　Ysengrimus ovans conspecto longius hoste
　　　quanta recalfacto gaudia felle gerit!
　　Euax saepe tonat saliens, mox vero resistit
　　　et victus placidae clamat odore dapis:
　　"Quo, Reinarde Satan? Quis te faustissimus istuc
350　　(vivere si scirer . . . sed sciar!) error agit?
　　Procide! Ne certe noceat protractio mortis,
　　　accipies subitam, non patiere, necem!"
　　Irruere aspiciens patruum sibi nolle repente,
　　　Reinardus victum novit et orsus ita est:
355　"Patrue, tam fandi quam congruit ordo silendi
　　　fratribus; ut mandat regula, disce loqui!
　　Reinardus Satanas non sum, sed dicor, ut exto,
　　　'Reinardus frater'; dicere mitte 'Satan.'
　　Nonne vides hic signa mei certissima voti?
360　　Frater ego; hoc produnt hinc cibus, inde caput.
　　Aspice, qui sapiat! Nostri cibus ordinis iste est,
　　　aspice!" et artocreas eminus ipse rotat.
　　Quas cadere in terram prohibens cum lance volantes
　　　praeripit, et nulla masticat ille mora;

One never knows when one might by chance see an en- 335
emy; the crafty Reynard took due thought for this. He kept
back eight pies, eating the rest, and asked to have a tonsure
shaved on his head. Off he went, shaved and stuffed, carry-
ing his pies; if he saw his uncle, he intended to appease him 340
by offering the food. (It was the wolf's custom, when be-
moaning whatever he had suffered, to forget his anger if he
glimpsed any profit.) Nor did the chance for which these
precautions had been taken deceive his expectation; he met
the old man in the middle of the woods. With what great 345
rejoicing, born of rekindled animosity, was Ysengrimus
filled when he joyfully spotted his enemy in the distance!
Leaping forward, he roared out repeated greetings—but
suddenly he halted, and overwhelmed by the smell of the
delicious food, cried out: "Where are you off to, Reynard
you devil? What most fortunate wanderings bring you here?
(Had you been aware that I was alive . . . but you'll be aware 350
of it all right!) On your knees! To avoid torturing you by a
long drawn-out death, you'll meet a sudden end, you won't
suffer!" Reynard, seeing his uncle was not going to fall on
him immediately, knew him to be defeated, and began thus:
"Uncle, there is a rule about talking for monks, as well as a 355
rule about keeping silence; learn to speak as the rule dic-
tates! I'm not 'Reynard you devil,' my name, in accordance
with my status, is 'brother Reynard'—so leave off the 'devil.'
Don't you see here the most indubitable signs of my vow?
I'm a monk; my head, on the one hand, and my food, on the 360
other, make this obvious. See what it tastes like! This is the
food of our order, see!"—and from a distance he tossed over
the pies. Not allowing them to fall to the ground, the other
caught them, dish and all, in midflight, and didn't waste time

365 sed quo tipsanas dentato femina ligno
      inverrit dentes dentibus ipse modo,
   et collisa semel moluisse minutius illum
      polline triticeo vasque cibumque ferunt,
   glutieratque prius, quam se libasse putaret,
370   fercula per latam praecipitata gulam.
   Ammirans igitur veluti spectabile monstrum,
      quod sibi contigerat, talia laetus ait:
   "In somnis, Reinarde, sumus? Fantasmate rerum
      fallimur, an vera est res quasi vana tamen?
375 Dulcia nescio quae michi iacta fuisse recordor;
      iactaras equidem, quis michi iacta tulit?"
   Atque huc dicendo circumspiciebat et illuc,
      nescius in baratro vincta iacere suo.
   Adiecitque: "Ego iacta videns prensurus hiabam,
380   atque fere labiis prensa fuere meis.
   Evasere tamen, quorsum volitasse putentur?
      Nam, nisi dormierim, iacta fuisse liquet.
   Intus adhuc aspirat odor, quem faucibus hausi,
      sed miseri dentes nil habuere boni.
385 Infortunati ceperunt aera dentes;
      proh, satis atque ultra rebar hiasse miser!
   Inglutisse solum ventusne efflata tulisse
      credatur, dubito, sed periere michi.
   Quaere, sit hic, in quod quierint cecidisse, foramen;
390   quaerere" (quaerebat scilicet ipse) "veni!"
   Stans procul ille refert monachus quasi tangere segnis
      mansueti metuens ora redunca senis,

chewing them, but in the same fashion as a woman pounds 365
barley kernels with a spiked pestle, he ground his teeth
against each other, and they say that he at once ground the
pulverized dish and food finer than wheat flour. He had dis-
patched the dish into his broad gullet and swallowed it be- 370
fore he thought he had tasted it. So, marveling at what had
happened to him as if at some amazing prodigy, he cheer-
fully spoke as follows: "Are we in dreamland, Reynard? Are
we deceived by the phantasm of things, or is this seeming
illusion true? I recall that some sweet things were thrown 375
to me. You certainly threw them; who snatched them away
from me after they'd been thrown?" And he looked here and
there on all sides as he spoke, unaware that they lay penned
in his belly. And he added: "Seeing them thrown, I had my
mouth open to grab them, and they were almost seized by 380
my lips. But they've escaped—where can they be imagined
to have whizzed off to? For, unless I've been asleep, it's evi-
dent that they were thrown. The smell of them, which I in-
haled through my jaws, still lingers inwardly, but my poor
teeth got nothing of any use. My unlucky teeth closed on air; 385
ah, wretch that I am, I thought I had opened my mouth
more than wide enough! It may be thought that the earth
has swallowed them or the wind has blown them away—I
don't know, but they're lost to me. Look and see if there's
any hole here into which they could have fallen—come and 390
look!"—and indeed he was looking himself.

The lazy monk, standing at a distance, as if afraid to make
contact with the yawning mouth of the gentle old man,

"Patrue, non clare video, fumosa culina
    obsuit et calidus lumina nostra vapor.
395 Denique quid prodest, ubi non cecidere, requiri?
    In rictus recolo iacta fuisse tuos.
Nonne tibi dentes vehemens immorsus edendo
    ferculaque oblisos dura cavasse queunt?
Quamlibet in criptam camerati lapsa molaris,
400   perdita quae quereris, delituisse reor.
Dividuos dentes interflua lingua pererret,
    oblique illambens scrupula quaeque proba!"
Reddidit ista senex: "Amissa perisse feramus;
    post strepitum sero porta pudenda coit.
405 Pristina pensentur profectu dampna futuro;
    frater, ubi his epulis vivitur, esse velim!
Nil me terret ibi nisi lex imposta vorandi,
    quod solet illabi leniter esca nimis,
nil faciunt dentes; hiscant, cibus incidit ultro,
410   tamque exit leviter, quam patienter init.
Sicque fit, ut venter persistat semper inanis;
    relligio vacui pessima ventris erit."
"Patrue," subiecit monachus, "depone querelam!
    Quamvis fluxa vorent, usque vorare licet,
415 usque vorare quidem!" Dictis his ille subinfert:
    "Ha, Reinarde Satan, ut profiteris, edunt?
Sufficiens uni saltem datur esca duobus?
    Non oberit parci dentibus, usque vorem."

replied: "Uncle, I don't see clearly. The smoky kitchen and the hot steam have closed up my eyes. And then, what use is 395 it to look for them where they never fell? My recollection is that they were thrown into your jaws. Isn't it that while you ate them, the violence of your bite and the hardness of the dish have made a hole in your teeth as they snapped together? I think that the lost property you're complaining 400 about has fallen into some cavity of a hollowed-out molar, and has gone to ground there. Let the tongue that lies between them run over the separate ranks of teeth; test every obstacle, poking your tongue in every direction!" The old man gave the following reply: "Let's accept the fact that these lost things have disappeared. Once the fart's got out, it's too late to clamp your arse together. Let initial losses 405 be counterbalanced by future profit—I should like to be a monk in the place where they live off these goodies! Nothing there terrifies me except the law imposed about gulping, because the food as a rule slips down too easily; the teeth do nothing. If they stand wide, the food slips down of its own accord, and makes an exit as gentle as its entrance was 410 smooth. The result is that the stomach remains empty all the time—and the religion of an empty stomach is the worst imaginable." "Uncle," interjected the monk, "Forget your objection! Although they guzzle mush, they're allowed to guzzle it incessantly, yes, guzzle incessantly!" The other re- 415 joined: "Ah, Reynard, you devil, do they eat in the way you claim? Is each one of them given food sufficient for two at least? It won't hurt my teeth to be let off lightly, if I guzzle incessantly!"

Intulit his frater, quasi quaedam dicta retundens:
420   "Patrue, deliras! Dicar ego usque Satan?
Frater es ipse fere, fraternis utere verbis,
   nec timeas praeter posse vorare parum!
Sufficienter edunt omnes, sed dulce canentes
   praecipue, satis est unius esca tribus.
425 Tu cui, si velles cantare, imitabilis esses?
   Expensam duplicem vox tibi pulcra daret.
Ne vox notitiam tollat suppressa canentis,
   erige clamosae faucis ad astra melos."
Laetus ad haec senior: "Nisi memet nescio, frater,
430   cantorum nulli blandior; aequa refers.
Hunc michi, qui nunc est, usum deus annuat illic,
   ultra speratum cantor herilis ero.
Inveniam nullum fratrem, cui latius hiscant
   guttura, vel cuius clarius ora sonent."
435 Tunc alacer Reinardus ait: "Quod saepe poposci,
   patrue, cerno: tibi regula sacra placet.
Nil igitur restat tibi nunc nisi dicere, cuius
   officii malis esse magister ibi."
Ysengrimus ad hanc submittit lumina vocem,
440   verbaque respondet qualia corde tenet:
"Frater, ego officium postremae vendico sortis
   (scis bene, cur teneat Lucifer ima nocens).
Dum meliore loco me provehat agnita virtus,
   lixa vel opilio comiter esse feram.
445 Nunc, quae claustra petam, refer, et praefinge coronam,
   ne qua perfidiae suspicione fuger."
Continuo iussus Blandinia claustra subire,
   vadit adusque aurem tonsus ab aure senex,
et facile est intrare datum, sed triste reverti.

The monk answered to this, in a fashion to blunt the edge of his remarks: "Uncle, you're demented! Am I still to be called 'devil' all the time? You're almost a monk yourself, so use the language of the cloister—and don't be afraid of anything except being able to eat too little. They all get plenty to eat, but especially those who sing sweetly—the food for one of them is enough for three people. If you were willing to sing, who could match you? Your beautiful voice would endow you with double rations. Lest the concealment of your voice deprive you of fame as a singer, raise the melody of your powerful throat to the stars." The old man cheerfully replied: "Unless I'm deceived about myself, brother, I need bow to no singer; you say but justice. If God grants me in that place the skill I have now, I'll be a chorister nobler than anyone hopes for! I'll find no brother whose throat gapes wider or whose voice rings out more clearly." Then Reynard said eagerly: "What I have often desired, uncle, I now see: you are favorably inclined to holy orders. So nothing remains to you except to say what office you would like to fill there." At this speech, Ysengrimus lowered his eyes and gave back the words he had in his heart: "Brother, I claim the office of lowest rank; you know well for what reason the wicked Lucifer occupies the lowest depths. Until my excellence may be acknowledged and advance me to a better place, I'll willingly put up with being a kitchen boy or a shepherd. Now tell me which cloister I should go to, and make me a tonsure beforehand, in case I should be chased away under suspicion of treachery."

The old man was immediately ordered to enter the cloister of Blandinium, and went off, shaved from ear to ear. He was granted an easy entrance—but painful was his exit.

450　Omnibus intrando dat recipitque vale.
　　　(Dat commune "vale," nondum "benedicite" doctus
　　　　dicere fraterne, discere coepit ibi.)
　　　Vota relata placent, admittitur, atque professum
　　　　continuo fratrem sumpta cuculla tegit.
455　Rumor is undenos abbates traxerat illuc,
　　　　in quibus abbatum Lucifer unus erat.
　　　Nomine vel numero unus erat sed nullus eorum,
　　　　vivendi studiis et pietate manus;
　　　quo super Egmundi fratres abbate beatos
460　　ius viget, augescit census, habundat honor,
　　　gaza venit cumulo, cumulataque prostat honesto,
　　　　et reditura datur, dandaque dupla redit.
　　　"Da dabiturque tibi" sapiens intelligit abbas,
　　　　certus id implentes fallere nolle deum.
465　Recta malos quam nosse piget, tam dicere taedet,
　　　　at michi recta quidem nosse loquique libet.
　　　Hoc alios inter refert abbatas et istum:
　　　　fas rapere est aliis, huic retinere nefas.
　　　Quos rapuisse pudet, lappas imitantur et uncos,
470　　ut dubites alia stirpe fuisse satos.
　　　O famosa viri famaque industria maior!
　　　　Percurso similes vix habet orbe duos.
　　　Paupera claustra patres opibus fecere retentis;
　　　　undique diffusis hic opulenta facit.

On entering he gave everyone a hello and got one back from 450
them. (He gave a general "hello" because he had not yet
been taught to say "benedicite" like a monk; that was where
he began to learn to do so.) The wishes he made known
found favor; he was admitted and straightway the cowl was
donned and enveloped the professed brother.

The report of this had brought eleven abbots to that 455
place, among whom one was the morning star of abbots; he
was one of them in name and number, but not one of them
in the pursuits of his life or the generosity of his hand. While
he is abbot over the fortunate brothers of Egmond, justice 460
reigns, wealth increases, honor flourishes. Riches are at-
tracted in heaps, and when heaped up they are sold for a no-
ble return, and are given away in order that they may come
back again, and come back to be given away again twofold.
"Give and it shall be given unto you"—this the wise abbot
understands, certain that God will not deceive those who
practice it. The wicked are as sorry to recognize right con- 465
duct as they are reluctant to speak about it, but I find de-
light both in recognizing and in describing what is right.
This is the difference between other abbots and this one;
for the others, grabbing anything is quite proper, whereas to
him, even keeping what he has is wrong. Even those who are
ashamed to carry anything off, at least stick to what they've
got like burrs and hooks, so that you'd doubt their being 470
born of any other race. Oh, the celebrated wisdom of this
man, even greater than it is famed to be! Were you to tra-
verse the world, you would hardly find two men like this
one. His predecessors made the monastery poor by hoard-
ing wealth; he makes it rich by scattering wealth on all sides.

475 Praedia quid clament? Ipsa ornamenta luerunt!
     Perditaque hic redimit plurimaque addit adhuc,
   implet in hoc et in his dominus promissa minasque:
     "Perdet egenus, et est plus habiturus habens."
   Hi sibi deficiunt, multis satis iste sibique est;
480   rebus egent parci, largus is auget eas.
   Hi perdunt clausas, hic, quando excludit, adunat;
     hi tentis inopes, affluit iste datis.
   Pellit utraque manu gazas, pulsaeque recurrunt,
     quotque viro redeunt, dividere ipse nequit.
485 Cuius si refici positis virtutibus ardes,
     haec est eximii secta verenda viri:
   se facere affatu medium, tractare perite
     seria causarum, reddere quaeque suis,
   conciliare iras populi, frenare tyrannos,
490   non curare minas blanditiisve capi,
   non pretio flecti, non inclinare favori,
     volvere multa, loqui pauca, silere diu.
   Personas dirimit meritis, non ponderat aere,
     recta docens, eadem, quae docet, ipse gerit.
495 Illius haec mundus, deus autem cetera novit;
     auditis paucis pluribus adde fidem.
   Talibus ornato comitem deus addidit unum,
     quem Lesburna cupit non petere astra cito.
   Hunc tibi, dignus enim est, hunc unum admitte sodalem,
500   ruderea reliquos cum strue verro foras.

Why should they lament their lost estates? The very church 475
ornaments had gone to pay debts! He wins back what had
been lost, and adds further increases. In him and in the
other abbots God fulfills both his promises and his threats:
"To him that hath shall be given, and from him that hath
not, even that he hath shall be taken away." *They* don't have
enough even for themselves, but he has enough for himself
and many others. Their miserliness lacks wealth; his gen- 480
erosity accumulates it. They lose what they lock away; he
amasses while he hands out. They are impoverished through
what is kept; he is affluent through what is given away. He
thrusts wealth away with both hands, and when it's thrust
away, it bounds back again, and returns to him every time,
so that he can't get rid of it. If you wish to be reformed on 485
the model of his virtues, this is the rule of life of this ex-
traordinary man which you must follow: to make yourself a
mediator in colloquy, to conduct the weighty business of le-
gal disputes with skill, to give everyone his due, to soothe
popular rancor, to restrain tyrants, to pay no attention to 490
threats and not to be lured by flattery, not to be swayed
by bribery nor to bend to influence, to reflect a great deal
but to speak little, and to keep silent much of the time. He
judges people according to their merits, he doesn't weigh
them up in money terms, he teaches what is right, and him-
self practices what he teaches. This is as much as the world 495
knows of him; God knows the rest. When you've heard
these things, you can add to them a belief in much more.

To the man who is endowed with such qualities, God
has joined a single companion, one whose entry into heaven
Liesborn wishes may be long delayed. Admit this one friend
for yourself, for he is worthy of it; the rest I sweep out with 500

Pace tua, Galtere, pater carissime, tester—
   non poterit tanti te puduisse paris—
ille tuis aliquid virtutibus adicit in se;
   optima cum facias, adicit ille tamen.
505 Impresso nimis ungue, pater, tu singula limans
   abbatem immodica te gravitate probas.
Utquid fronte riges? Utquid sermonibus horres?
   Cur michi non rides, nil michi dulce refers?
Largum laeta decet facies et lingua suavis,
510   ne rear iratum dona dedisse michi.
Solius ergo tenes exempla Catonis, at ille
   fit vicibus certis Tullius atque Cato,
utraque digna gerens abbate, remissus et asper,
   ambulat alterutram sed sine labe viam.
515 Quos se commansore fovet, quos hospite donat,
   hos necat egrediens, hos beat ipse redux.
Aspera sic laetis privato intercalat astu,
   ut nichil accuset livor amorve tegat.
Tu quoque, ne qua tuae probitati portio desit,
520   exhilara frontem, dic sine labe iocos!
Debes ecce deo, debes michi, solve vicissim;
   tam sua vult Caesar, quam deus, ambo ferant!
Haec duo virtutum deus exemplaria mundo
   reddidit, ut revocent, quas pepulere pii;
525 scilicet hinc iactas superae ad penetralia pacis
   pluribus aerumpnis hic vetuere premi.

the pile of rubbish. With your permission, Walter, dearest father—you can't be ashamed of so great a companion—let me record that he in his person adds something to your virtues. Although your excellence is superlative, yet he adds something. You, father, paying too meticulous an attention to details, show yourself an abbot by your untempered gravity. Why is your forehead so stern? Why is your conversation forbidding? Why don't you give me a laugh? Or make some pleasantry? A cheerful face and a sweet tongue are good things for a generous man to have, so that I shouldn't think that it vexes you to give me a present. So you follow the example of Cato only, but he is both Cicero and Cato by regular turns, adopting both types of behavior fitting for an abbot, relaxed and stern. He treads both paths without stumbling. Those who are cheered by his presence, and who enjoy the gift of his company—they are downcast when he leaves them, and made happy again when he returns. Thus he interweaves sternness and merriment with a skill of his own, so that malice has nothing to accuse nor affection anything to conceal. So you, too, lest there be any element lacking to your virtue, should brighten your face, and indulge in innocent jokes! See, you have a duty to God and a duty to me—discharge each in turn. Caesar wants his due, as well as God; render it to each of them!

These two models of the virtues God gave to the world, that they might bring back the virtues which the saints had taken into exile; that is, they had snatched them away from here to the sanctuary of peace in heaven, refusing to allow them to be oppressed by more hardships here. These

Hi duo virtutes peccasse videntur in ipsas,
    quas a pace dei rursus ad arma trahunt,
quas graviora adeo toleratis bella fatigant,
530   saecula quam priscis saevius ista furunt.
Sed quibus huc redeunt vivis, auctoribus hisdem
    de medio comites astra sequentur item.
His coram trepidanto alii profugique latento
    post archam, pudeat nominis atque loci,
535 nec modo se ignaris sese iuranto vocatos
    abbates, sed nec sponte fuisse sua.
Vivite quaeso diu, praeclari vivite patres!
    Vivite subsidio pluribus atque michi!
Ut sit sufficiens onerato sarcina collo,
540   addite me, in tanto fasce gravabo parum!
Ysengrimus erat frater, dudumque sepulti
    sumere presbiteri poscitur ipse locum.
Ille rogat, quod opus soleat patrare sacerdos?
    Pascere berbices anne parare dapes?
545 At typice fratres ovibus dixere tuendis
    praefore presbiterum; paruit ille libens.
Continuo "Dominus vobiscum!" dicere iussus,
    Ysengrimus ovans "Cominus," inquit, "ovis!"
Et "cúm!" teutonice accentu succlamat acuto,
550   nolens grammatica dicere voce "veni!"
(Compererat crebro Scaldaeas ille bidentes
    non nisi Teutonicos edidicisse modos;
quas ad concilium mandatas voce latina
    convicit simili non bene nosse loqui,
555 duraque nullorsum iactans in vincula, donec
    grammaticam scissent, pertulit ire reas.

two seem to have sinned against the virtues themselves, by
leading them out to combat again, away from the peace of
God, and wearying them with battles harder than they have
so far endured, inasmuch as these times are more turbulent   530
than those gone by. But they return while these two live, and
at their command they will again leave us and accompany
them to follow the stars. Trembling before these men, let
the others flee, and henceforth forswear monastic life,
ashamed of their name and position, swearing not only that   535
they were called abbots without their knowing it, but also
that it was against their will. Live long, I pray, live long, ex-
cellent fathers! Live to my benefit as well as that of many
others! So that the burden may be enough for your loaded
neck, add me to it; I won't weigh much in so great a bundle!   540

Ysengrimus, now a monk, was asked to take the place of a
priest who had just been buried. He asked what task a priest
customarily performed. Pasturing sheep or preparing food?
The monks said, speaking figuratively, that the priest was in   545
charge of looking after the sheep; so he willingly obeyed.
Promptly instructed to say "Dominus vobiscum!" Ysengri-
mus cheerfully repeated "Lambus-here-come!" interpreting
"cum" as the vernacular word, with a sharp accent, in prefer-   550
ence to the Latin word "veni." (He had often found that the
sheep of the Schelde had learned no speech but the vernacu-
lar; when he called them to a council in the Latin tongue, he
had clear proof from them that they didn't know how to
speak in a similar way so he threw them into cruel bondage,   555
and refused to allow the criminals to go anywhere before

Claustricola hic ideoque pius, qua noverat illas
    fungi, Teutonica voce venire iubet.)
Dumque docent "Amén" quasi Graecum, accentuat "ágne."
560   Pars illum melius dicere nosse negant,
pars ultro dixisse ferunt; strepit undique murmur:
    "Verba, quid hic monachus cogitet, ante notant.
Hic tondere gregem studet intra vellera; frater
    tollere, quod lanam non sapit, iste parat!
565 Dissimulat fraudem, non alterat, altera vestis;
    non habet, ut spondet, nigra cuculla fidem."
Murmure comperto socios non vera putasse
    insinuans, monachus convenienter ait:
"Fratribus ut caris assensi, nempe rogatus,
570   presbiter ut fiam, non prior ipse rogans.
Presbiter, ut credo, non optassetis ut essem,
    ni dignus tanto noscerer esse gradu.
Ergo ovium pastor quia dicitur esse sacerdos,
    praetaxo officii sacra gerenda mei.
575 Presbiter idcirco quia sum pastorque futurus,
    ante saluto meos elicioque greges,
ut pastoris oves oviumque attendere pastor
    indubia possit cognitione sonum.
Ne dubitate meae sub conditione salutis
580   credere servandas (mancipo fidus) oves!
Explorate fidem, quam vobis spondeo, fratres;
    ars mea, quod fertis, grande levabit onus.
Sim licet a silua rudis et quasi frater agrestis,
    doctus in hoc ego sum vosque docere queo.

they had learned Latin. This was why this kind monk or-
dered them to come in the vernacular tongue he knew them
to use.) When they taught him to say "Amén" in the Greek
fashion, he stressed it "Lámb-en." Some said that he was in-   560
capable of saying it any better, others that he had said it in-
tentionally. On all sides buzzed the comment: "This monk's
words give prior warning of his intentions. He is plotting to
shear the sheep of more than their fleece; this monk is pre-
paring to take away something that doesn't taste like wool!
A new set of clothes disguises treachery, but it doesn't   565
change its nature. The black cowl doesn't carry with it the
trustworthiness it leads one to expect."

Learning of this comment, the monk made a suitable re-
ply, explaining that his companions had imagined some-
thing untrue. "It was at your request, my dear brothers, that   570
I agreed to become a priest; I didn't ask first. You wouldn't
have wanted me to be a priest, I believe, unless I'd been
known to be worthy of such a position. So, because the
priest is said to be the shepherd of his sheep, I'm practicing
the rites that belong to my office. Because I am a priest and   575
shall be a pastor, I greet my sheep and call to them before-
hand, so that the sheep may respond to the voice of the
shepherd, and the shepherd to those of the sheep, with un-
faltering recognition. Don't doubt that the sheep will be
kept safely so long as I'm alive and kicking; you can rely on   580
me to keep them well penned in! Put to the test the faith I
pledge you, brethren; my skill will lighten the great burden
you bear. Even if I am a hick from the backwoods, and a rus-
tic sort of monk, I'm learned in this matter, and capable of

585 Ut meditor, sic dico: licet bene multa geratis,
    non habet arbitrium regula tota meum.
Arguere aestivum post prandia nolo soporem,
    quodque tenet sanctus tempora longa canor;
ver, aestas, autumpnus, hyemps aut carmine vellem
590   unius aut possent lege soporis agi.
Has autem meliore dapes abolebimus usu:
    artocreas nimium creditis esse bonas.
Artocreas utero limphamque infundere cribro
    proposita refert utilitate nichil.
595 Vixque, quot artocreas ambiret follis ovinus,
    viginti solidis posse videtur emi.
Septenae fortassis oves hoc aere parentur;
    cur igitur pluris vanior esca notho?
Artocreis cumulate michi coria octo bidentum,
600   omnibus ebibitis vix tetigisse putem.
Nam deus his numquam dentes insevit edendis;
    ut nothus in ventrem, pandite labra, volant!
Quod si quinque ovium det nostri cuique diatim—
    cena duas, totidem prandia, nona suam—
605 tunc taedere sui non accidit ordinis ullum.
    Viscera ventoso ne temerate cibo;
sunt solidi dentes, quid aquis vescantur et aura?
    Gaudet carne caro, dentibus ossa placent!
Gangaque pro faeno lanam constrata suavem
610   accipiat; faeno est non spolianda bidens.
Legitimi ferimur, nullum spoliemus oportet;
    sic sit, ne titubet qualibet ordo sacer.
Denique nostrarum ne fiat abusio rerum,
    nunc, quae praecipue sunt facienda, loquar.

instructing you. I speak as I think; although you manage a 585
lot of things well, your Rule doesn't have my approval in its
entirety. I don't want to quarrel with the after-dinner sleep
in summer, or with the fact that the sacred chant takes up a
lot of time. I could wish that spring, summer, autumn and
winter were got through with singing from a single monk, or 590
with a regulation for a nap. This food of yours, however, we
shall do away with, in the interests of a better custom; you
have too high an opinion of pies. Pouring pies into the stom-
ach, like pouring water into a sieve, does no good at all. And 595
it seems that the number of pies that a sheepskin bag would
contain could hardly be bought for twenty shillings; seven
sheep, perhaps, could be got for this price—so why do you
want a food that costs more, and is emptier than the wind?
Stuff the hides of eight sheep with pies—when they've 600
all been swallowed, I'll think I've hardly touched anything.
For God never planted teeth for the sake of eating these;
open your mouth and they fly into your belly like the
wind! So that if each of us were given five sheep daily—two
for dinner, two for lunch, and one for an afternoon snack
—then no one would ever grow tired of his order. Don't de- 605
file your innards with airy food. Your teeth are solid, why
should they eat air and water? Flesh enjoys flesh, bones
are what teeth like! Let the latrine be scattered with soft
wool instead of hay—the sheep shouldn't be deprived of 610
its hay. We are known to be law abiding, we shouldn't rob
anyone—so let it be, lest the holy Rule be weakened in any
way. Finally, lest there be any abuse of our goods, I shall
now describe the most important practices to be followed.

615 Qui minus oblato fuerit convictus in alvum
    traicere, auriculas cauteriatus eat;
  inque duas partes praebenda soluta secetur,
    quas probat aequato pondere rectus apex,
  ut lepidus frater, stomacho venerabilis amplo,
620   pauperiem biduo suppleat inde suam.
  Consilium, fratres, quis vobis tale dedisset?
    Res variae, quanti sit sapuisse, docent.
  Tempora contentus quaestu transire diurno,
    non studui magnas condere cautus opes.
625 Non vestra intererit confratres pauperis esse;
    consilio solvam, quod dare cista nequit."
  Consilium cupidi fratris pavefecerat omnes,
    sicque refert abbas:—verba referre parat,
  pendula signa sonant, canturas nocte sequente
630   personas puero vix recitare vacat.
  Ysengrimus in his frater, cui clarior aetas,
    sortitus decima est in statione vicem.
  Ille putabat oves dici responsa necandas,
    octo quater malens quam iugulare novem,
635 sed geminis numerum cantorum sensibus aptum
    credens, fert dubia mente refertque vagus.
  Cogitat apponi tot fercula nocte solere
    fratribus unius tempore danda cibi,
  quot puerum audierat legisse, et lecta profecto
640   cantorum fuerant nomina terna quater;
  seu quotiens idem signaverat esse canendum
    cantorum numero testificante puer,

Whoever is found guilty of transporting into his belly less 615
than he is offered, let him have his ears branded. And let the
now redundant daily ration of pies be divided into two parts,
which an accurate scale shall prove to be of equal weight, so
that the amiable brother, awe-inspiring in his ample girth,
may make good any needs he feels over a two-day period. 620
Who else, brethren, would have given you such advice?
Many different things teach you how valuable wisdom is.
Content to pass the day with the day's profit, I haven't tried
to be farsighted and to lay aside great wealth. But it won't 625
matter that you are fellow brethren to a poor man; my ad-
vice is worth more than anything the money chest can give."

The advice of the greedy monk had horrified them all,
and the abbot replied thus:—or rather he prepared to make
a speech in reply, but the swaying bells gave the signal, and 630
there was hardly time for the boy to recite the list of people
who were to sing during the night that was to follow. Among
these, Brother Ysengrimus, distinguished by his age, had
been allotted a place in the tenth position. He thought that
the Responsories named were sheep to be killed, and would
rather have slaughtered thirty-two than nine of them, but, 635
believing that the number of singers was capable of a double
interpretation, he vacillated this way and that in perplexity
of mind. He thought that the number of dishes which were
usually set before the brothers at one meal during the night
was the same as he had heard the boy read out—and, of
course, the names of the singers which had been read out 640
numbered twelve. Or, he thought that the number of times
that the boy had indicated the singing was to be done, by
making known the number of singers, was the number of

accitis totiens iterari fratribus esum,
 qui melior longe mos foret atque sacer.
645 Spe meliore tamen mox audet utrumque futurum
 credere, quo fieret regula firma satis,
plura die sperans ac saepius esse voranda
 fercula, dum somnus rarior esse solet.
"Quicquid," ait, "iubeor, fratres, implebo libensque
650 responsum decimum quindecimumque canam.
Tardus obedierim, totiens ubi nocte quoque estur
 felicemque uterum fercula tanta replent?
Gemma sit abbatum, qui primus sanxit in orbe
 tale cuculliferae relligionis onus!
655 Ha miseros homines, quos talis regula terret!
 Qui dubitat, dubitet, non revocabor ego.
Nunc certe video, quia me deus egerit istuc;
 nunc scio me iunctum fratribus esse bonis.
Ter tantumque die libanda cibaria rebar,
660 quadruplicem hunc numerum nocte dieque datis."
Interea ridens surrexit coetus et ibat,
 quippe diu signum tinnula vasa dabant.
Exclamans monachus revocatis taliter infit:
 "State parum, fratres, optima fabor adhuc!
665 Ne quid deficiat virtutis in ordine nostro,
 edicam breviter digna vigere diu:
vos ego miror opes, quas expetit aequoris usus,
 cocturis epulas evacuare focis.
Scite meum genus hoc numquam curasse, sed omnis
670 cruda solet plus quam cocta iuvare caro.
Primitus, ut coctas spoliarent unguine, lixae
 versuti carnes instituere coqui;

times that the brethren would be assembled for repeated eating—which would be by far the better custom, and a pious one. But with an even better hope, he soon dared to believe that both would be the case, by which the Rule would be very solidly established, hoping that more dishes would be devoured, and more often, in the daytime, when sleep is usually less frequent. "Whatever I am commanded, brothers," he said, "I shall fulfill, and I shall willingly sing the tenth, nay the fifteenth Responsory! Shall I be slow to obey when you eat so many times at night, and so many dishes fill your lucky stomachs? Call him the gem of abbots, who was the first in the world to sanction such a burden for the cowled order! Ah, wretched are the men who are terrified by such a Rule! Whoever doubts, let him doubt; I shan't be turned back. Now truly I see that God has brought me here; now I know that I have joined a goodly company. I thought that food was tasted only by day, and three times, whereas you give four times this number by day and night as well."

Meanwhile the company, laughing, had risen and was leaving, for indeed the ringing bells had long before been giving the signal, but the monk cried out to call them back, and spoke as follows: "Stay a little, brothers, now I'll say something wonderful! So that our order lacks nothing which is right, I'll outline in a short time some things that are worthy to be kept in force for a long one. I'm surprised that you use up the material needed for the sea trade in fires to cook food. Know, that my family has never bothered about this, but enjoys all its meat raw rather than cooked. In times gone by, cunning servants instituted the cooking of meat, so that when it was cooked they might steal the fat from it.

at nunc relliquias, inflati corda rapinis,
    dignantur dominis vix adhibere suas.
675 Elicit ergo adipem cocus, aridiorque trilustri
    caseolo infaustum strangulat esus herum.
Scit sapiens paucis, quorsum sententia tendat;
    sponte mea nullum, qui mea tollit, amo.
Ligna, focum, patinas, cacabos, ollasque cocosque
680   in sua proiciat posteriora Satan!
Quod quibus expendi solet aes et inania frugis
    plurima, quae superant, arte locate mea:
thuribula, et calices, et clangas, scrinia, capsas,
    candelabra, cruces, ostra, tapeta, libros,
685 omnia nos faciamus oves crudasque voremus,
    optima ne pereat pars rapiente coco.
Cumque ovibus constanter oves epulemur ovesque;
    vellem, quicquid habet mundus, ovile foret.
Vos etiam excipio non clare, ignoscite, fratres;
690   me solum excipio, cetera nulla quidem.
Me sibi non favisse putant monstra inscia veri —
    falluntur; quotiens cernor adesse, dolent.
Sit durum, sit molle quidem, nisi profore vellus
    dentibus insolitum, diligo, quicquid habent.
695 Quid vero typicat, quod non michi vellera prosunt,
    me nisi lanifica non fore matre satum?
Non mea me mater calatho incunavit Iprensi!
    Quid genus et referam? Nonne probabo fide?
Septimus a magno dicor quater esse Lovone,
700   viscera cui fudit sus sua, fusus ei;
illud in Hebraeis et Graecis atque Latinis
    codicibus scriptum mundus ubique legit."

But now, their spirits puffed up by their plunder, they hardly deign to use their own leftovers for their masters. So the 675
cook skims off the fat, and the food, dryer than a fifteen-year-old cheese, chokes the unfortunate master of the household. The wise man knows from little signs which way the wind is blowing; of my own accord I love no one who takes away my property. Wood, fire, pans, pots, cauldrons and cooks—let Satan stuff them all up his arse! You should 680
follow my plan for disposing of the money which is normally spent on these things, and the many things that are superfluous and without use: censers, chalices, bells, shrines, reliquaries, candelabra, crosses, vestments, hangings, books— let's make them all into sheep and eat them raw, in case the 685
best part is lost to the thieving cook. And let us dine constantly with sheep, on sheep and more sheep. I could wish that whatever the world contains were mutton—I don't even except you entirely, brethren, pardon me! I except my- 690
self alone, but nothing else at all. The monsters, ignorant of the truth, think that I am no friend to them, but they are deceived. When I am seen to be in the vicinity, they are unhappy. But be it soft or hard, I love everything they possess, unless it's their hide, which doesn't usually bring any profit to my teeth. But what, indeed, does it signify, that 695
their fleeces are of no use to me, but that I was not born of a mother who was a wool worker? My mother didn't cradle *me* in an Ypres basket! But why should I recount my family tree? Shan't I demonstrate it by my good faith? I am said to be the twenty-eighth descendant of the great Lovo, at 700
whose hand the sow poured forth her entrails, as his were poured forth for her; the world reads of this everywhere, written in Hebrew, Greek and Latin manuscripts." The

Contio tota iterum risit, fratremque locutum
    omnia silvestri simplicitate ferunt.
705 Interea duro Reinardus liber ab hoste
    partis ad obliquae devia flectit iter,
invisumque larem subit, Ysengrimus ubi ingens
    a quater undecimo lustra tenebat avo.
Ysengrimigenas lupulos invenit in antro;
710 parte alia gemitus hospita lassa dabat.
Tunc sic "Quo, lupuli, vos ortos patre putatis?
    Quove ierit pater hinc, sciscitor?" hospes ait,
"Et quando rediet, vel quando rursus abibit?
    Dicite, sum verax, dicite vera michi."
715 Respondent lupuli: "Nos ludere nolumus ullum.
    Ysengrimigenae dicimur atque sumus;
en cubat ex nobis, quos est enixa recenter,
    mater, adhuc etenim languet, ut ipse vides.
At pater ipse cibum perrexit quaerere nobis;
720 mane revertetur, vespere perget item.
At tibi, si quid habes genitori dicere nostro,
    quisquis es, o senior, lar patet iste, sede!"
Repplicat hostis: "Et hic patuit michi, gratia vobis!
    Quam primum, ut cupio, notificarer ego!
725 O quam felici vos edidit omine mater,
    ne careat fidum posteritate genus!
Maturus pater est nec longum posse putatur
    vivere; vos eritis, quod pater ante fuit.
Huc ego cum graderer, flebant vervexque caperque
730 de breve victuri debilitate senis.
Sic rogo vos, dampnum patris pensate sepulti;
    vos forma similes, moribus este pares!

whole assembly laughed again, commenting that their brother had said all this in rustic naivety.

Meanwhile, Reynard, free from his cruel enemy, bent his 705 course to the remote parts of an out-of-the-way region, and entered the home which was the object of his hatred, where the mighty Ysengrimus had had his lair from the days of his forty-fourth grandfather. In the cave he found some little Ysengrimian wolves; in another part the weary mistress 710 of the house was uttering groans. Then their visitor said this: "Of what sire, wolflings, do you believe yourselves to be born? And where has your father gone, I ask? And when will he come back, and when will he leave again? Tell me; I'm truthful, so tell me the truth." The wolf cubs replied: "We 715 don't want to deceive anyone. We're said to be Ysengrimus's children, and so we are. See, our mother is in bed from having recently given birth to us, and is still ill from it, as you yourself see. But our father went in person to find food for us. He will return in the morning, and leave again in the eve- 720 ning. But if you have anything to say to our father, whoever you are, reverend sir, this house is open to you, be seated!" The enemy replied: "And it was open to me, thank you! Would that I may instantly become as well known to you as I wish! How lucky it was that your mother bore you so that 725 your loyal family might not lack posterity! Your father is of ripe age and it is thought that he cannot live long; you will be what your father was before you. While I was on my way here, the sheep and goat were weeping over the weakness of 730 the old man, who has not long to go—so I beg you, make up for the loss of your father when he is buried. You are like

Hortabor, ne triste patrem senuisse querantur;
   ante suam genuit pignora fausta necem.
735 Me caper et vervex anserque errare timebunt,
   cum vos usuros dixero lege patris.
Quod vos laudarim frustra, dubitantibus illis
   obsecro, ne possint improperare michi."
Tunc sua crura levans et utroque foramine largus
740   intulit: "Hoc mixtum est, nonne suave sapit?
Sugite, dilecti patrueles, sugite! Vobis
   traditur haec natis mulsa retenta meis.
Non me subsidium vobis impendere taedet;
   vos estis patrui pignora cara mei.
745 Pro patris obsequio, quod non permitterer illum
   poscere, si praesens esset, habete meum!"
Ingemuere illi; gemitus quae causa, requirens
   mater ut agnovit, prosilit aegra licet,
procurritque foras, sed spe privata sequendi est,
750   aspiciens hostem praecelerasse nimis.
"Cur," ergo inquit, "amice, paras sic currere furtim?
   Non sequeris morem, tu meus hospes eras!
Turpiter hospitii grates furatus abisti;
   hospita te revocat, fare, resiste parum!
755 Ante michi gratans et commendatus abito,
   nunciaque affectus basia sume michi!"
Ille precans "Hera, suffer," ait "me solvere sero;
   faenore solvendi conciliabo moram.
Exieram minctum et redeo" (simulatque redire,
760   iratam cupiens elicere arte lupam).

344

him in appearance; emulate him in character! I will urge them not to lament sadly over your father's growing old; he has engendered a blessed progeny before his death. The goat, the sheep and the goose will be afraid I was wrong, when I say that you will fulfill the role of your father. I shall beg those doubters not to charge me with having sung your praises without foundation!" 735

Then, raising his leg and pouring forth a stream from both orifices, he said: "Here's a milk-soaked rusk—doesn't it taste good? Lap it up, dear little cousins, lap it up! I present this tidbit, which I was keeping back for my own children, to you. Far be it from me to be reluctant to give you a present; you are the beloved children of my uncle. If your father were present, the question of my asking him for his services wouldn't even arise; in return for your father's services, accept mine!" 740 745

They moaned and groaned; their mother sought the reason for their groans, and when she found out, leaped up, despite her illness, and ran outside—but she had no hope of pursuit, seeing that her enemy had got too far ahead of her. So she said: "Why, friend, are you preparing to run away on the sly? You were my guest, but you don't follow the rules of etiquette. You've gone off, boorishly robbing me of thanks for your entertainment. Your hostess invites you back, speak, stay a little! You should thank me and receive a farewell before you go, and take from me the kisses which are signs of affection." "Lady," he begged, "allow me to pay them belatedly; I'll make up for the delay by paying them with interest. I'd gone out to piss and I'm coming back." (And he pretended to return, wishing to lure out the angry she-wolf 750 755 760

"Nilque," inquit, "peccasse reor, cur debeat obdi
    porta michi; culpae conscius esto pavens."
Illa intro properans latitat post ostia sollers,
    ante domo natos interiore locans,
765 ad quorum stratum Reinardo introrsus eunte
    cogitat insidiis anticipare fores.
Hostis idem meditans fieri potuisse minatur
    incursum, calcans limina, seque refert,
et dominam grassans caeno impetit atque lapillis.
770   Non patitur fraudem dissimulare dolor;
exilit illa furens; ille expectare sequentem,
    comprensu facilis, si voluisset, erat,
moxque cucurrisset velocius illa, sed inde
    munia non longe, quae peterentur, erant.
775 Sublimis scopulus cono petit aethera, quantum
    it spatii funda parva rotante silex.
Hinc rupis: strepitus per saxa tenentia frustra
    serpere nitentis dulce susurrat aquae.
Illinc: florigero vultu blandissima Tempe
780   hospitium proprio ver sibi iure dicat.
Ante: iacet nulla tortus vertigine trames.
    Post: avium vario silva canore sonat.
Munia panduntur geminis adeunda fenestris,
    sed maior gravida vulpe subire nequit.
785 Per septem cubitos intrato limine primum
    ducit inoffensos semita plana pedes,
ulteriusque utrobique aditum nitentibus intro
    ter gradibus denis scansile praebet iter.
Congrandis furno testaque rotundior ovi
790   lar mediastina planus in arce sedet.

through his trickery.) "I'm not conscious," he said, "of having committed any fault for which the door should be closed to me; let someone who's aware of having done wrong be fearful." She hurried indoors and craftily lurked behind the entrance, having first placed her children in the inner part of the house, thinking that as Reynard went into the place 765 where they were lying, she would ambush him and get to the outer door first. But the enemy, thinking that this was what might have happened, pretended to enter, setting foot on the threshold, and then drew back, and the scoundrel pelted the mistress of the house with dirt and stones.

Her misery didn't allow her to conceal her trick; out she 770 sprang in a fury. He was easy to catch—that is, if only he'd been willing to wait for her pursuit, and she'd soon have outrun him, but that the place of refuge for which he was making was not far away. A high rock thrust its point toward the 775 heavens, as high as the distance that a pebble flies from the whirling of a little sling. On one side of the rock, the noise of a river, striving to creep through the stones which in vain held it back, murmured gently. On the other side was a most attractive valley, flowery of face, which Spring by due 780 right set apart as a dwelling for herself. In front lay the path, free from any bend. Behind, a wood rang with varied birdsong. The refuge was open to approach by two entrances, but anything bigger than a pregnant fox was unable to enter. When the threshold was crossed, the feet 785 were first led along a level path that offered no resistance, for a distance of seven ells. For those trying to go further in, it offered on both sides a staircase of thirty steps. The living room, as big as a chimney-opening and rounder than an eggshell, was right in the middle of the fortress. In it, 790

Intus olent dulces diversi nectaris herbae,
   frondeaque implexum fulcra cubile dabant.
Huc rapido cursu fugiensque fugansque ruerunt;
   ille sui leviter pervolat ora laris.
795 Dum temere illa sequens artum nimis incidit, haesit,
   nec proferre potest nec revocare gradum.
Nec magis in latum remeat, quam prodit in artum,
   ianua sic captum stringit adacta canem.
Sic haeret cuneus, qui decipiente relictus
800   malleolo nondum robora tota fidit.
Spe modici fructus in maxima dampna salitur,
   dum mala non astu praeduce vota ruunt.
Dum stultus temere petit hostem, traditur hosti;
   absque modo noli quaerere, quicquid amas.
805 Quae quaeris, potius quam te quaesitaque perdas;
   quoslibet ad ludos est sapuisse bonum.
Praeteriit stultus magno quaesita labore,
   atque eadem sapiens absque labore tulit.
Non bene conveniunt stultus simul atque dolosus;
810   subdolus incautum ducit in omne malum.
Dum cadit in laqueum stultus ducente doloso,
   ludus inaequalis luditur inter eos.
Ut videt haerentem nullo luctamine solvi
   posse, per oppositam desilit ille forem,
815 et male compatiens incommoda tanta ferenti,
   in faciem miserae ludicra probra iacit,
circumquaque salit, gestu sua gaudia testans,
   ut magis haerentis cresceret inde dolor;

sweet herbs of diverse scents exuded fragrance, and beds of leaves, matted together, provided a couch.

Hither rushed both pursuer and pursued in rapid flight— the latter swiftly hurtled through the living-room door. As the pursuing female dashed into the too narrow passage, she stuck fast, and was unable to advance or retreat a step. She couldn't retreat to the wide bit any more than she could advance into the narrow one. The narrowed doorway wedged the bitch tightly, just as a wedge sticks fast when the hammer fails it and leaves it before it has split through a whole block of wood. In the hope of a little gain, people rush into great losses, when hostile impulses race ahead without the precaution of cunning. When a fool rashly attacks his enemy, he gives himself into his hands. Whatever you desire, don't pursue it beyond reason! You should rather lose what you're aiming at, than lose your aims and yourself as well. Whatever the game, it's a good thing to keep your head. The fool fails of the things he's striven for with great effort, and the wise man carries them off without difficulty. The fool and the trickster aren't well matched; the cunning man leads the reckless one into all kinds of disasters. When the fool is led by the trickster to fall into a trap, the match between them is a very uneven one.

When he saw that the wedged she-wolf couldn't be freed by any of her struggles, he sprang through the door on the opposite side, and, not showing much pity for her subjection to such great discomfort, he hurled derisive insults in the wretched female's face, and bounded about, revealing his joy by his behavior, so as to increase the chagrin of the

795

800

805

810

815

818.1 atque parum curans patruelis foedera lecti,

818.2   assilit in fixam pravus adulter heram.

818.3 "Alter," ait, "faceret, si non ego; rectius ergo

818.4   hoc ego, quam furtim quis peregrinus, agam.

818.5 Si consanguinei minor est externus amore,

818.6   sum generis serie proximus atque fide.

818.7 Clareat obsequio pietas mea; nolo quis ausit

818.8   sospite me patruum zelotipare meum.

818.9 At tu, domna, subi tectum! Quasi vincta quid haeres?

818.10   Hospitis hic mores experiere boni."

818.11 Illa iocum cupiens "Reinarde, facetius," inquit,

818.12   "Publica quae de te fama fatetur, agis.

818.13 Si tibi, qualis inest industria, robur inesset,

818.14   verna penes dominas assererere probus.

818.15 Vix egomet cogenda tuos intrare penates,

818.16   ianua si paulum latior esset, eram!"

818.17 Gavisam scriptura refert his lusibus illam

818.18   et moechum patruum zelotipasse suum.

      Sic sua Reinardus demonstrans gaudia lusit,

820   sed monachus lusit tristia fata miser.

      Finierat decimus lector, signumque canendi

    silvigenae fratri supprior asper agit.

      Indoctus frater veneranda silentia rumpit:

    "Nescio, quid signes, tu michi verba refer!"

825 Mox uno, binisque dehinc, tribus inde monetur

    flantibus, ut sileat, non tamen ille silet.

      "Cur fletis, fratres, intelligo, parcite flatu!

    Accimur pransum, flatus id iste notat.

wedged creature. And then the base adulterer, showing little concern for the bonds of his uncle's marriage bed, mounted the immobilized lady. "Someone else," he said, "would do this, if I didn't; it's better therefore that I should do it than some passerby on the sly. If the love of a stranger is less than that of a relation, I'm closest to you, in terms of both kindred and friendship; let my affection appear in my services. I don't want anyone else to have the cheek to cuckold my uncle while I'm alive. But, lady, go into the house! Why do you stick here as if you were chained down? Here you'll experience the ministrations of a good host." She, warming to the game, said: "Reynard, you give a polished demonstration of that with which your public reputation credits you. If you had as much strength as skill, you'd be declared a trusty servant with the ladies; I'd hardly have to be urged to enter your house if only your doorway were a little wider!" History relates that she enjoyed the sport, and so the adulterer cuckolded his uncle.

818.1

818.5

818.10

818.15

818.18

So Reynard played out his game, showing his enjoyment, while the wretched monk played out a destiny of a miserable sort. The tenth reader had come to an end, and the stern subprior gave the brother from the backwoods the signal to sing. This unschooled brother broke the silence which was supposed to be observed: "I don't know what you're gesturing about; speak to me in words!" Immediately he was admonished to be silent by hisses from one, then from two, and finally from three of them—but he didn't shut up. "I know why you're hissing, brothers; hold your breath! We're summoned to breakfast, that's what that hissing means.

820

825

Si tempesta quidem, lex esset ydonea flandi;
830   iam flatum decies debuit esse diu!
Nunc, nisi nil sapio, paenultima cena daretur;
     horologa immersit tardus aena latex.
Acta nocte fere primam conflamur ad escam;
     orbata est multo regula iure sui.
835   Irascor, consurgo tamen; benedicite multum!
     (Sero venire potest consule nemo deo.)
Sanctificet potum atque cibum, qui fecit utrumque,
     augeat et larga munus utrumque manu!"
Fratris ad hanc vocem fit perturbatio grandis,
840   undique tunc naso flatur et ore simul.
Flatibus innumeris aedes procul icta reflabat,
     ut volucrum noctis milia terna sibi.
Tunc, quo more molens accitur, cuius in aurem
     edita non veniunt verba tonante mola,
845   sibila dante choro procul usque resibilat echo,
     atria quam muro circueunte patent;
stridula sic urgente notho canneta queruntur.
     Iam metuit vulpis prodier arte lupus;
aestimat in templo Gerardos flare trecentos
850   atque efflata suo claustra movenda loco,
seque pati stando tot flatus posse perhorret,
     flante uno pridem se cecidisse memor.
Flatibus attactae subitis obiere lucernae;
     fit pavor, et quidam caelitus acta putant.

If only it came at the right time, the custom of hissing would be a very welcome one; the time has long gone by when you should have hissed for the tenth time. Now, unless I'm a complete fool, the last meal but one should be given; the slow-dripping water has covered the bronze that tells the hour, and we're wafted into the first meal when the night is almost over. The Rule is being subjected to too much irregularity. I'm cross about that, but I'll rise anyway, and for what we are about to receive I'm truly thankful. In the eyes of God, the eleventh hour is not too late. Let him who made the food and drink bless them both, and let him increase both gifts with a generous hand!"

At this speech from the brother there was a huge commotion, and hissing from nose and mouth together broke out on all sides. The building, penetrated to its corners by countless hisses, gave them back again, like three thousand night birds to each other. Then, in the same way as one shouts to a miller, whose ear isn't reached by the words uttered, because of the thundering mill, as the crowd gave out its hissing, the echo hissed back again, to the very edge of the wall-encircled churchyard; just so do the whispering reeds shiver as the wind whistles through them. Now the wolf was afraid that he had been betrayed by the fox's cunning; he thought that three hundred Gerards were hissing away in the church, and that the cloisters were to be blown out of their place, and he despaired of being able to stay upright under the onslaught of so many hisses, when he remembered that he had previously succumbed to the hissing of one alone. The lamps, assailed by the sudden gusts, went out; terror ensued, some of them thinking that it was an act

830

835

840

845

850

353

855 "Te deum" rapitur, clanga ilico bombilat ingens,
　　et maior tonitrus altera more molit.
　　Signa pavet senior: cum parvum sueverit unum
　　　praetinnire cibos, magna tonare duo;
　　nam nisi fors ideo, quia parvam parva duasque
860　exigat ingentes grandior esca nolas.
　　Tunc sparsim fratres per candelabra, per alta
　　　scamna ruunt, libros, vasa crucesque rotant.
　　(Ast aetate rudes septem latuere tapetis,
　　　tres aulaea quater, scriniaque octo tegunt.)
865 post aram sub scamna ruunt, sub pulpita fusi,
　　　hic birrum labiis imprimit, ille manum,
　　viscera fissuro non imperat ille cachinno,
　　　terque cachinnantur quinque quaterque novem.
　　Iam conante cavas zirbo transponere fauces
870　affuit hic abbas, qui lupus alter erat,
　　non nisi quinquimum docilis glutire Falernum,
　　　pauca aliis tribuens plurimaque ipse vorans.
　　Tam bene se poterat quam sex portare molares,
　　　vermibus auxilium grande futurus adhuc.
875 Scotigenum crustas mollisset flamine terno
　　　atque saginasset (tam fuit ipse macer)
　　non secus in crassum quam si iacerentur aenum,
　　　sic creber pateris proveniebat adeps.
　　Quam macidum atque olidum ructabat mane fere escis
880　hic pater hesternis ebrius atque satur!
　　Unius haut noctis residebat crapula somno,
　　　quamvis solstitium mane nivale foret.

of heaven. The service was brought to an abrupt conclusion, 855
and a great bell instantly boomed out; another one, even
bigger, set off in thunderous fashion as well. The old man
trembled at these bells: when one little one had been used to
tinkle out before meals, now two huge ones thundered away
(unless, perhaps, it were to be because a little meal calls for a
little bell, and a bigger meal for two huge ones). Then the 860
monks rushed here and there, through the candelabra and
the high benches, and sent books, holy vessels and crosses
flying (but seven of tender years hid under the carpets,
twelve took cover under the tapestries, and eight in chests).
They rushed under the benches behind the altar, they scat- 865
tered under the pulpit. One pressed his robe to his mouth,
another his hand, a third failed to control the laughter that
threatened to split his belly, and all fifty-one of them burst
out laughing.

Here now, with his guts straining to burst out of his hol-
low jaws with laughter, was the abbot, who was a second 870
wolf, receptive to no teaching other than how to gulp down
five-year-old wine. Giving little to others, and himself de-
vouring a great deal, he could lug himself about with as
much ease as he could six millstones; he was destined to be a
great boon for the worms one day. Three breaths from his 875
mouth would have softened any Scottish rusks and plumped
them up again just as if they'd been thrown into a pan of
fat—that's how lean he was!—so much grease flowed out of
his dishes. How rich and reeking were the belches that came
from last night's dinner to this drunk and satiated abbot, 880
nigh on morning! His drunkenness didn't subside with the
slumber of a single night, even if the next day was the winter

Praedia quis vasta tot condere novit in alvo
   ovaque quis fratrum sic piperare suis?
885 Ut caper hic sapiens, et vocis ut ardea clarae,
   tamquam leproso gutture pingue sonat.
Unguento verbis intercrassante refractis
   dimidium stridet dimidiumque fremit:
"Ysengrime comes, canta, cantare iuberis!"
890 Hoc puto dicturus, si potuisset, erat.
Illius audito fratres stridore quierunt:
   "Cantatum, frater, te petit hora, veni!"
Silvigena inconsultus adhuc, cantare quid esset,
   rettulit irato fratribus ore suis:
895 "Non est hoc aliud, cur tanto turbine flastis?
   Heu potuit 'Canta' dicere nemo michi?
Debita iam video subduci prandia nobis,
   cantatum iubeor currere, quicquid id est.
Si saltem bibere est cantare, feremus omitti
900 prandia; si secus est, en bibiturus eo.
Triste fames cantat, sitis importunius urit;
   in caelos animam plena cuculla vehit."
Iussit eum placidus pater in cellaria duci;
   constitit ante fores datque redire ducem.
905 Solus init crumeram, tonnis pincerna duciclos
   detrahit, ut prodat quaeque, quod intus habet.
Singula vasa probat, sed quaeque probata recusat
   claudere, tam cupido corde probanda petit.
Et sibi sic dicit: "Scriptura teste probate
910 omnia, sic scriptum est, atque tenete bonum!

solstice. Who knew how to stow away such vast heaps of farm produce in his belly, or which of the brethren could spice eggs for his fellows as he did? He spoke with a rich sound, as if from a leper's throat—like a wise old goat, or a loud-voiced heron; with his words broken up by the oiliness oozing between them, he half squeaked and half growled: "Friend Ysengrimus, sing! You're being told to sing!"—that's what I think he was going to say, if he had been able to. Hearing the noise he made, the brethren fell quiet: "The office requires you to sing, brother; come!" The backwoodsman, still ignorant of what singing was, replied to his brethren in angry tones. "Is that all it is, the reason for your blowing such a whirlwind? Good heavens, couldn't anyone say 'sing' to me? Now I see that the meal due to us is withdrawn, and I'm ordered to hurry up with singing, whatever that is. If singing at least means drinking, I'll put up with dinner being forgotten, but if not . . . well, I'll go and have a drink. Singing is a miserable business for the hungry; it makes one's thirst rage all the more fiercely. It's a well-stuffed habit that gets your soul to heaven."

The long-suffering abbot ordered him to be led to the cellars. He stopped before the door, and dismissed his guide. The butler entered the wine store alone, and pulled out the bungs from the barrels, so that whatever was inside might pour out. He sampled each cask, but conducted the tasting in so greedy a spirit that he neglected to turn off the ones he had tried. And he said to himself: "Scripture is a warrant for it: try everything, hold fast to that which is good. That's

885

890

895

900

905

910

Abstinet usque bonis, quibus affluit, aeger avarus.
Cui vinum servas? Fac semel ipse bibas!"
Stantibus in cantu visa est mora longa bibentis;
it, qui dux fuerat, reddere iussus eum.
915 Invenit in vino collotenus ille natantem,
sicque inquit: "Frater, balnea pulcra facis!
Crede michi, hic caput est, quod cras intrabit in archam,
balnea sed dorso sunt adhibenda foris!
Prima nocte nimis largus pincerna fuisti;
920 alter in officium substituendus erit.
Artior ergo sitim nequiit compescere crater?
Saepe parum melius quam nimis esse semel!"
Potor ad haec: "Ad quid tua cista, cucullifer amens,
intranda est, nisi sit forsitan intus ovis?
925 Cur nisi propter oves cistam dignarer inire?
Quattuor est cistis amplior iste locus;
nonne locum teneo capitis dorsique capacem?
Quid me dimidias? Integer esse volo!
Quam subito offendit fratres, quod diligo legem;
930 quam cito me, quia sum rectus, adesse dolent!
Meque fugare venis, ignoro, iussus an emptus,
ut commune minus te sit agente malum.
Par facit auctori scelerum praeceptor et emptor;
efficit impuram mens scelerata manum.
935 Suggere deceptis, quia vivo sicut et ipsi;
non ego sum, quantum iudicor esse, rudis.
Regula vult, ni fallor, habetque infracta reatum,
ut superet mediam Bachus adusque gulam.

what is written. The wretched miser always holds back from using the possessions in which he abounds. Who are you keeping the wine back for? You should drink it yourself all at one go!"

To those who were standing in the choir, the drinker's delay seemed a long one. The one who had been his guide went off under orders to bring him back again. He found him swimming in wine up to his neck, and spoke thus: "Brother, you're making a lovely bath! Believe me, here's a head that will be going into a cell tomorrow—but as for your back, a cold shower will be administered to it outside. You have been too generous a butler on your first night; someone else will have to be substituted for this duty. Couldn't a smaller vessel slake your thirst? Little and often is better than too much at one go." The drinker replied: "Why should I enter your cell, you mad cowl wearer, unless perhaps because there's a sheep inside? Why should I deign to enter your cell unless sheep were the reason? This place is roomier than four cells; haven't I got a place big enough for my head *and* my back? Why should you divide me in half? I want to stay whole! How suddenly it offends the brethren, that I love the law! How quickly they are irritated by my presence, because I am just! And I don't know whether you have been ordered or bribed to come and get rid of me, so that the communal wickedness should be the less by your executing it alone. The one who commands or bribes is as responsible as the one who carries out crimes; the criminal intent creates the guilty hand. Say to those misguided ones that I live as they do; I'm not as uncultured as I'm thought to be. The Rule, unless I'm mistaken, desires that wine should slake a moderate thirst, and entails guilt if it is broken. This

915

920

925

930

935

Hoc variae clamides sectantur idemque cucullae;
940   multa bibunt fratres, plus tribus ipse pater.
Displicet abbati, quod moribus aemulor ipsum?
      Quid nocet insano me sua facta sequi?
Ordinis esse mei non ipsum conqueror, et cur,
      quos sequitur mores, invidet ille michi?
945 Deterius nichil est, quam quod sibi plaudit et in me
      detrahit exemplo perfida turba suo.
Nemo suae socium debet contempnere sortis;
      consimiles simili relligione sumus.
Abbas noster edax bibulusque ut fratribus alto
950   nomine, sic stomachi relligione praeest.
At michi non suffert abbas imitabilis esse,
      ergo sequi vetitus moliar ire prior.
Abbatem fratresque simul virtute praeibo,
      si, qui plura vorat, sanctior esse potest.
955 Me vino potuisse refers moderatius uti—
      non scis, me saturo quid superare queat.
Praeceleras nimium, postquam satiatus abibo,
      argue me, si quid videris esse super.
Sufferres misere, si perdita vina fuissent;
960   ecce vides coram stantia, tuque furis?
Vescerer et biberem cum fratribus, offer edendas
      cotidie, quantas censueramus oves.
Dum tenuem guttam de qua scrobe lingere possim,
      hic equidem noctes, hic habitabo dies."
965 Ille patri rediens et fratribus omnia narrat,
      quique ea laudaret, vix erat unus ibi.
Unanimes miserum iurant expellere fratrem;
      omnibus armantur, quae reperire queunt,

the frocked and the cowled practice alike. The monks drink 940
a great deal, and the abbot himself more than three of them.
Is the abbot cross, because I copy his behavior? How can it
hurt the idiot for me to imitate his actions? I don't complain
because he's of *my* order; why then does he grudge me the
practices *he* follows? Nothing is worse than for the hypocrit- 945
ical mob to applaud itself and at the same time criticize its
own example in me. No one ought to despise his companion
in destiny; we're all members of the same religious order.
Just as our eating and drinking abbot takes precedence of
his brothers in his exalted title, so he takes precedence of 950
them in the religion of the stomach. But the abbot won't al-
low me to imitate him—so since I'm forbidden to follow, I'll
try to lead, and to surpass in virtue abbot and brothers at
once, if it's the case that the one who devours more is the
more holy. You say that I could have consumed the wine 955
more temperately, but you don't know whether there may
be something left over when I've had my fill. You're in too
much of a hurry; after I've gone away full, then accuse me if
you see anything remaining. You'd take it hard if the wines
had disappeared; as it is, you see them still in front of you, 960
and you're angry? I should like to eat and drink with the
brethren, if only you offer as many sheep to be devoured
daily as we agreed on. While I can lick up a tiny drop from
any runnel, I'll live here night and day."

The other went back to the abbot and told the breth- 965
ren everything; it was hard to find one of them who ap-
proved of it. They all swore together to get rid of this dis-
graceful colleague, and armed themselves with everything
they could find. And so as not to lose time, they took up the

neve moram faciant, prius occurrentia prendunt:
970 ecce caballinum corripit ille caput;
hic faeno gravidam fertur rapuisse lagenam,
   in qua sese abbas mungere suetus erat;
quaeque ferebatur quintae mediana diei,
   dimidium fissae vendicat ille nolae;
975 hunc veteris redae pars tertia munit; at abbas
   ipse molendinum grande sinapis agit.
Talibus atque aliis irrumpunt ostia freti,
   qua securus erat frater adhucque bibens,
nilque nisi grates monachum meruisse putantem
980 talibus obiurgat noxia turba minis:
"Huc, vesane, foras! Satana insatiate, repente
   huc ad nos, aliter nec bibiture parum!"
Armatam ut rabiem videt Ysengrimus et audit,
   esse illic monachus non vovet ipse diu.
985 Tunc, quod spissus erat paries solideque cohaerens,
   non amat; hinc lapides devovet, inde fabrum.
Mox velut audacter, ne formidasse putetur,
   procedit, fratrum cominus arma notans.
"Quo, stolidi fratres," ait, "haec vexilla feretis?
990 Quis populus demens ista sequenda putet?
Nam nec recta quidem nec sunt conformia rectis,
   et melius poterant delituisse domi.
Non vos consilium sine me sapienter inistis;
   cur hodie non sum quam bene doctus heri?
995 Ergo domum redeant partis vexilla sinistrae,
   ingenium vobis notificabo meum.
Ordinis ex nostri coetu plerique leguntur
   pontifices, quorum est vita probata palam,

first things they came across. One of them snatched up a 970
horse's head; another is said to have seized the jar, laden
with hay, into which the abbot was accustomed to spit; an-
other appropriated the half of a cracked bell which was
called the "Thursday half-bell." A fourth was armed with a 975
third of an old horse collar, while the abbot himself wielded
a mighty mustard grinder. Relying on weapons like these,
and others besides, they burst through the door to where
their brother, free of care, was still drinking, and the danger-
ous crowd attacked the monk (who thought he had deserved
nothing but thanks) with the following threats: "Come out 980
here, lunatic! Insatiate devil, come quickly to us—you'll get
a different sort of drink, and plenty of it!"

When Ysengrimus saw and heard their armed fury, he
didn't want to remain a monk there for long. Then, he wasn't 985
too pleased that the wall was thick and solidly held together;
he cursed the stones on the one hand, and the workman on
the other. But soon he went forward boldly, so he shouldn't
be thought afraid, and seeing the brothers' weapons at close
quarters, he said: "Where are you taking those banners to,
my simpleminded brethren? What mad set of people thinks 990
they should be followed? For they are not of the right kind,
nor similar to the right kind, and they could have better lain
tucked away at home. You weren't wise to adopt this plan in
my absence—why should I not be as wise now as I have been
in the past? So let the banners of this topsy-turvy army go 995
home, and I'll tell you my idea. From the company of our
order the majority of bishops are to be chosen, men whose
life is publicly approved, and who shall demonstrate with

qui, quanta tueantur oves pietate deumque
1000   quam timeant nuda relligione, probant:
quae populus, quae clerus habet, quae claustra, licenter
         omnia constituunt diripienda sibi
vi, prece, iudiciis, ornatu, fraude, minisque
         et quibus ordo caret mosque modusque modis.
1005   Praesulibus sumptis de clero haec regula partim
         noscitur, et partim, ceu didicere, tenent;
omnia non sorbent, parco bachantur hiatu,
         seducti raptis plura manere sinunt.
Eligit idcirco pars cleri provida sanctos
1010   claustricolas, quorum est linquere norma nichil,
qui primum rapiant, tunc scalpant, denique lingant—
         vere his virtutum regula tota patet.
Antistes fieri sperans ego moribus hisdem
         praevulgo studium: devoro, praedor, hio.
1015   Innumerosque dies una virtute redemi,
         effuso vacuans omnia vasa mero.
Confestim lateque solet discurrere rumor,
         materies quotiens ardua solvit eum.
Propterea volui facinus committere clarum,
1020   ingluviem subito notificare volens,
ut, si praesul ob hoc fuerit quis forte fugatus,
         quod parce rapiat, subroger aptus ego.
Si quid adhuc sapitis, laudabitis acta, probeque
         fratribus atque michi consuluisse ferar.
1025   Quod si dampna movent vanum lucrosa furorem,
         hoc veniale meae sit probitatis opus.
Amodo nil perdam, nisi sit, quod perdere possim,
         quamquam non liceat paenituisse boni.

how much tenderness they care for their sheep, and with 1000
what pure reverence they fear God. They shall decide that
everything possessed by the people, the clergy, or the clois-
ter, is legitimately to be seized for themselves, by force, by
persuasion, by lawsuits, by simulation, by deceit, by threats,
and whatever means are alien to order, morality, or mod-
eration. This rule is only partially familiar to the bishops 1005
chosen from the secular clergy, and they observe it only par-
tially, as they have learned it. They don't gulp down every-
thing, but sip in half-mouthfuls; appeased by what they have
grabbed, they allow many things to get away from them. So
the more foresighted section of the clergy must elect holy
monks, whose practice is to leave nothing, and who may 1010
first gobble, then scrape, and finally lick. Truly, to them is
the whole rule of virtues disclosed. I, hoping to become a
high priest of these rituals, am giving an advance demon-
stration of my zeal: I devour, plunder, swallow. I have ac- 1015
complished the work of numberless days in a single heroic
act, in emptying all the vessels of their gushing wine. Ru-
mor usually travels far and fast once some notable subject
matter has set it going. Therefore I wanted to commit an
outstanding deed, desirous of making my greed known at 1020
once, so that if any bishop is perhaps to be got rid of because
his ravages are too restricted, I might fitly be appointed in
his place. If you still retain any sense, you'll praise what I've
done, and I'll be said to have taken good care of my own in-
terests and those of my brethren. But if it's the financial loss 1025
that incites your groundless anger, let this action, whose
motive was virtuous, be counted venial; from now on, al-
though it isn't permissible to be sorry for something good,

Peiores dici quam laica turba potestis,
1030   si luero primae crimen inane vicis;
et commissa semel villanus daemone peior
       donat, vos acies lenior este precor!
At quocumque trahat sententia, nolo fugari;
       saltem, ubi nulla potest esse cupido, locer,
1035 et michi praeposito domus infirmaria subsit,
       quamvis consilio discrepet illa meo.
Nam cum desiero rapere obtuleritque voranti
       exigua positas assecla lance dapes,
tunc, quod erat certe praeda ingluvieque merendum,
1040   exspes officii pontificalis ero."
Pravior Angligena caudato partis iniquae
       quidam rufus ad haec dogmata clamat ovans:
"Frater, tende foras! Optata paratius instant
       tempora quam speras! Hora beata venit!
1045 Hora beata venit, qua consecrabere praesul;
       festus adest nobis iste tibique dies,
teque his vexillis introductura sacratum
       contio fraterni tota favoris adest."
Poscitur actutum cunctis e fratribus unus,
1050   ungere pontificem dignus, adestque celer;
aedituus plenam pulicum producit acerram,
       auriculas meriti fratris utrasque replens.
"Hoc aspergo sacri caput," inquit, "semine olivi;
       deficit uncturus timpora sacra liquor.
1055 Sanctius est semen, vita est in semine, transit
       in cerebrum saltu sanctificante vigor.
Infula, ne capiti benedictio decidat, assit!"
       Faeniferum gestans fictile frater adit,

I won't destroy anything except what I'm able to. If I'm to 1030
be punished for the first footling blunder, you can be said to
be worse than the mass of the laity; even the peasant, who
is worse than the devil, forgives isolated offenses—I beg
you to be a milder adversary! But whichever way judgment
sways, I don't want to be expelled; at least let me be placed
where there is no temptation, and let the hospital be put in 1035
my charge, although it doesn't tally with my plan. For when
I have given up stealing, and the servant has brought me
food to eat, placed on a little dish, then I'll lose all hope of 1040
the bishop's office, which I would certainly have merited by
my greed and plunder."

A certain redhead from the evil band, one who was more
vicious than a tail-bearing Englishman, cheerfully called out
in response to this doctrine: "Brother, come outside! The
time you long for is at hand, sooner than you hope. The
blessed hour has arrived! The blessed hour in which you will 1045
be consecrated bishop has arrived; this day is one of celebra-
tion for you and for us, and the whole company of your af-
fectionate brethren is here to lead you with these banners
to the consecration." Immediately, one was summoned who
out of all the brothers was worthy to anoint the bishop, and 1050
he quickly came up; the sacristan produced an incense cas-
ket full of fleas, and filled both ears of the worthy brother
with them. "With the seed of the sacred oil," he said, "I
sprinkle this head; there isn't any liquid for anointing the sa-
cred temples. Seed is holier; there is life contained in seed, 1055
and its power passes into the brain in one sanctifying leap.
Let the miter come, lest the consecration fail to take effect on
the head!" The brother carrying the hay-filled earthenware

et faenum excutiens stolpato verberat orbe
1060 pontificis frontem, "Sume," ait, "alme pater!
Hanc etenim Artacus mittit tibi papa tyaram."
 Bombilat hic grossum ventre lagena cavo,
percussorque refert: "Felici tempore mitram
 apposui, praesul iam modo signa facit;
1065 scilicet, ut sacrum tetigit caput, infula clanxit."
 Percutitur rursum pontificale caput,
clanxerat in primo, sed verbere fracta secundo
 dissilit in testas octo lagena quater.
Pontificis capiti ter inhaerent fragmina quinque,
1070 unius in testae continuata modum.
Intulit ergo sagax percussor voce iocosa:
 "Aspicite huc, fratres, quam bene mitra sedet!
Nulla umquam melius mitra absque ligamine sedit!
 Nunc stola quaeratur, vincta tyara bene est."
1075 Redifer exclamat: "Stola adest, ut credo," suique
 pontificis collum terque quaterque ligat.
Munerat hic dorsum pius abbas caute molari
 et "Mea gratanter munera," dixit, "habe!
Istud (crede michi, vulgaris nominat usus),
1080 quod tibi do, libum suscipe, dono libens!"
Nec mora, gestator mediani provolat aeris,
 pontificem cunctis plenius ille sacrat.
Procumbit decies antistes verbere deno
 et resilit totiens, undecimoque iacet.
1085 Tunc ferus irridens ioculenta voce sacrator
 ludicra nequitiae protulit ista suae:
"Aeger ut appares, nisi fingas esse, magister
 ut super infirmos constituaris, eges;

pot came up, and tossing out the hay, he struck the bishop's   1060
forehead with the upturned pot. "Accept this, beneficent fa-
ther!" he said. "The bishop of Artois sends you this miter" —
here the pot resounded dully from its hollow belly, and the
one who struck with it went on: "In a happy hour have I
placed the miter in position; the bishop is already working
miracles, in that when it touched his blessed head, the miter   1065
made a sound." Again the bishop's head was struck; the pot
had resounded at the first blow, but at the second it broke,
and flew into thirty-two fragments. Fifteen of the pieces
clung to the bishop's head, side by side in the manner of a   1070
single piece. So the clever striker of the blow said, in joking
tones: "Look here, brothers, how well this miter sits! No mi-
ter ever sat better without being tied on! Now let the pal-
lium be fetched, since the miter is well fastened on." The   1075
bearer of the horse collar cried out "The pallium's here, I
believe," and wrapped it seven times round his bishop's
neck.

Now the kindly abbot diligently administered the mill to
his back, saying: "Receive my gifts thankfully! Take the piece   1080
of cake I offer you (believe me, that's the name given to it
in common parlance); take it, I give it gladly!" Without de-
lay, the one who carried the half-bell rushed forward, and
consecrated the bishop more thoroughly than all of them.
For the tenth time, under the tenth blow, the prelate fell; as
many times he got up again, but at the eleventh he lay still.
Then the savage consecrator, out of his wickedness, mock-   1085
ingly brought out these jeers in a bantering tone: "As you ap-
pear to be ill—unless you're putting it on—you need to be

haec igitur fratres invitatura comesum
1090 infirmos media cimbala pende domo."
Vix miser antistes respiret, durus equini
  vector adest capitis consiliumque dedit:
"Si sapis, Ysengrime, cave fallacibus istis
  credere, non recte consuluere tibi.
1095 Esse potes praesul meritis et nomine debes,
  sed non officium nosse videris adhuc.
At tua te gnarum ioculandi dextera naris
  indicat aspectu; fungere sorte tua!
Hanc tibi dono gigam, pagana est utpote porrum
1100 osseaque ut dominus Blitero, sume, vide!
Dum nimis optatum facinus concedit amicus,
  debetur dono gratia magna brevi.
Haec giga donatur gratis tibi, sume!" Nec unum
  verbere iam verbum prodiit absque suo.
1105 Verba nimis praesul sed parce verbera curans,
  gallus ut in prunis, per medium agmen abit.
Lixa malus revocans non expectare volentem
  dicitur ignitum praeripuisse veru.
"Frater, frater," ait, "modicum expectare memento!
1110 Oblitus plectri quo cupis ire tui?
Accipe! Quid faceres sine plectro?" Interque loquendum
  candenti ferro colla humerosque fodit.
"Arsque tibi," adiecit, "nondum est bene nota gigandi,
  cum cordas plectro sumpseris absque suo.
1115 Quam primum cuperes modulari, nonne puderet
  ante oculos plectro te caruisse tuo?"
His donis studium exagitant; erratque pavetque,
  sicut in externis per loca nota viis,

370

put in charge of our sick. So hang these half bells in your   1090
building, to call the sick brothers to their food."

Hardly could the wretched prelate breathe again before
the stern bearer of the horse's head came up and gave his
opinion. "If you are wise, Ysengrimus, beware of putting any
faith in these deceivers; they haven't advised you right. Your   1095
merits fit you to become a bishop, and your fame makes it
your due, but you don't seem to know yet what your duties
are. On the other hand, the right side of your nose indicates
by its appearance that you are an expert in minstrelsy, so ful-
fill your appointed role! I give you this fiddle—it's as com-
mon as a leek and as bony as master Blitero. See, take it!   1100
When a friend grants a much longed-for favor, great thanks
are due even for a little gift. This fiddle is given to you for
free; take it!"—and not one word came forth without its ac-
companying blow.

The bishop, caring a lot for his words, but little for the   1105
blows, dodged through the midst of the crowd like a cock on
hot coals. The wicked cook called back the wolf, although
he was unwilling to wait, and, they say, snatched up a glow-
ing spit. "Brother, brother," he said, "wait a little! Where do   1110
you want to go without your bow? Take it! What would you
do without a bow?"—and while speaking, he bored into his
neck and shoulders with the glowing iron. "The art of fid-
dling," he added, "isn't yet very familiar to you, since you
would have laid hold of the strings without their bow. At the   1115
moment you wanted to play, wouldn't you be ashamed in
front of everybody to be without your bow?"

With such gifts they urged him on. Terrified, he blun-
dered through places he knew well as if he was on unfamiliar

et non ante sui meminit, quam staret, ubi uxor
1120   haerebat, medio corpore vincta tenus.
Extraxit miseram, referunt iurantque vicissim
        crimina Reinardi morte pianda gravi.
Tot tamen offensas (scit enim Reinardus, ubi et qui
        divisus) fertur conciliasse baco.—
1125 Erubuit vulpes dici tam saepe quiisse
        nunc falli gallo, nunc ioculante lupo.
Senserat hoc subito vocemque erumpere promptam
        cetera lecturi supprimit ursus apri.
Desierat Bruno, lausque astrepit undique dictis;
1130   tunc epulas alacer rex iubet atque iocos.
At misere interea miser Ysengrimus in agro
        luserat ac tulerat fercula dura satis,
usque profunda fere corium detractus ad ossa,
        regia dum linquens ad sua tecta redit.
1135 Corvigarus sonipes, eunuchus fortis et ingens,
        cernitur in ripa stare paludis edens.
Qui paulo ante cibum sumpturus in amne palustri
        constiterat, medias mersus adusque iubas.
Pone legens pisces ibis sua crura videbat
1140   pressa caballino sub pede posse parum.
Non multum poterat, sed credi posse volebat;
        vim pellit cautis vis simulata minis.
"Corvigare, hic, frater, densa," inquit, "stamus in ulva;
        non oculi hic possunt observare pedes.
1145 Est imperspicuus gurges, quisque ergo suorum
        esto pedum custos, en ego servo meos.

372

paths, and didn't come to himself until he stood where his wife was stuck fast, wedged tight up to the middle of her body. He got the wretched woman out, and they recounted Reynard's crimes to each other, swearing that they should be expiated by a cruel death. These were the outrages which, as the story relates, were avenged by the bacon (for where and how it was divided, Reynard knows). 1120

The fox blushed to have it related that he could be deceived so many times—now by the cock, now by the jeering wolf. The bear perceived this at once, and put a stop to the boar's voice as it was ready to break forth and read the rest. After Bruno's interruption, applause for the narrative resounded on all sides. Then the king gaily called for food and entertainment. 1125 1130

Meanwhile, however, the wretched Ysengrimus, having had his skin taken off almost right down to the bare bones, on leaving the king's house and returning to his own had had a wretched enough game of it out in the field, and had swallowed some rather rough medicine. On the edge of a marsh, Corvigarus the horse, a huge and strong gelding, was to be seen, standing eating. A little earlier, he had been standing in the marsh water, submerged up to halfway up his mane, to get food. A stork, catching fish nearby, perceived that his legs could be somewhat crushed by a horse hoof. His strength wasn't great, but he wanted it to be thought so; a show of force wards off force by means of cunning threats. "Corvigarus, brother, we're standing here in thick sedge," he said, "and our eyes can't keep watch on our feet in this place. The pool is muddy, so let each of us be caretaker of his own feet; see, I'm taking care of mine. I'm afraid that I might 1135 1140 1145

Ne tibi deculcem talos, ne qualibet artus
    quasseris, timeo, sis memor ipse tui!
Qui minus optat habere pedes quam perdere, votis
1150   talibus hic aptum noverit esse vadum.
Hanc igitur mortem quia me spectante subisti
    grator; adhuc spero tutus abire potes.
Si michi post tergum venisses, nulla profecto
    reddere te sanum fors potuisset agro.
1155 Dum potes incolumis meque hinc insonte salire,
    (fuscinulas Satanae porto) memento fugae!
Si tibi messuero coxas ignarus et armos,
    quid nisi dampna refers meque dolere facis?
Te potius sanum, ut vellem, retinere nequisse
1160   admissum membris quam spoliasse querar."
Tunc madidas alis vehementibus ille papiros
    verberat et multo perluit imbre iubas.
Terretur sonipes nec deteriora timetur
    facturus, fieri quam sibi posse timet.
1165 Mox volucri saltu perlatus ad arida, pedit,
    volvitur, est, cursat, gaudia mille furit.—
Ut lupus hunc vidit, plagarum oblivia fiunt;
    pelle sua pluris censet adesse lucrum.
Incipit omnino fortunae ignoscere, quoque
1170   exita quove inita est curia, tempus amat.
Tardius aut citius nollet pro pellibus octo,
    qualem perdiderat, regis abisse domo;
tam fors cornipedem non invenisse reversum
    quam mala venturum praecelerasse fuit.
1175 Corvigarus viso non cogitat esse pavendum,
    solus enim in solum sufficiebat eum.

tread on your heels, or that you might break one of your legs somehow—look to yourself! If anyone is less keen on preserving his feet than on losing them, he will recognize that these shallows are just made to suit his wishes. So I'm glad that you ran the risk of this death while I was around to see—and I hope that you can still come off safely. If you'd come after me, I'm willing to bet that no chance could have made you fit for the field again. Mind you run away while you can gallop safe, and without my having hurt you! (I bear the devil's own claws!) If I were unwittingly to shear away your hip or shoulder, what would come of it except injury to you and regret to me? I would be more sorry for having been unable to fulfill my wish to keep you safe, than for having deprived you of your limbs by allowing you to proceed." Then he beat the dripping reeds with his vigorous wings and splashed the horse's mane with a great shower. The horse was terrified, and what the stork feared he was about to do was no worse than what he feared might be done to him. Immediately, with a flying leap he was carried on to dry land; he farted, wheeled about, chewed grass, galloped, and whinnied his joy a thousand times.

On seeing him, the wolf forgot his wounds, thinking that here was a bonus of greater value than his skin. He began to pardon Fortune completely, and blessed the time at which he left the court, as well as the time at which he entered it. He wouldn't, for the sake of eight such skins as he had lost, have left the king's house any later or any sooner—it would have been as bad luck not to have come across the horse because he had gone, as to have got there before he arrived. Corvigarus didn't think it necessary to be afraid at the sight of him, since he alone was a match for a lone wolf. He who

1150

1155

1160

1165

1170

1175

Arte lupum vicit, qui cesserat ibidis arti;
    ars scit nulla vices artis in omne genus.
Tunc quasi conqueritur: "Domine Ysengrime, quid hoc est?
1180   Nonne cucullatae relligionis eras?
Quis tibi diripuit vesanus latro cucullam?
    Atque tibi est intro dempta cuculla nimis!"
"Corvigare, ex multis," ait, "o michi care diebus!
    Me veluti laesum conspicis atque doles.
1185 Me nisi diligeres, non te mea dampna moverent,
    dampna sed haec magnus conciliavit honor.
Non haec insidiis et viribus acta latronum;
    sors melius cecidit, quam cecidisse putas.
Saepe brevi impenso lucratur maxima prudens;
1190   grande brevi nostri cessit utrique bonum.
Gesturus nostri praeclara negotia claustri,
    legatus subii moenia regis ego;
interea nostrae rex aeger pellis egebat,
    quam subito exutam rege rogante dedi.
1195 Non fuit hoc magni, donassem iniussus, et omnis
    curia cum magno rege petebat eam!
Quippe tuam noram michi te hic astare paratum
    sponte dare atque illud proposuisse diu,
sed deerat, cur maestus eras, occasio dandi;
1200   nunc desiderio suppetit hora tuo.
Pone cutem; reddam, cum nostra recreverit, utram
    malueris; merces optio fito datae!
Et de carne tua, nam tunc quoque crassus et ingens
    sat remanes, detur cena pusilla michi.
1205 Non hoc quaero michi, tu mole iuvaris obesa,
    ocius ut curras—vix modo membra moves.

had succumbed to the stork's cunning defeated the wolf by his own; no cunning is ever wise to every twist and turn of cunning. Then he said, in mock lament: "Dom Ysengrimus, what's this? Weren't you one of the cowled order? What mad thief has robbed you of your cowl? And in fact, rather a lot of what was inside it has been taken away with the cowl!" 1180

"Oh Corvigarus, dear friend of many days! You see that I appear to be hurt, and you grieve; unless you loved me, my injuries would not affect you. But a great honor has made up for these injuries; they haven't been inflicted by the violence or treachery of bandits. A better fate has befallen me than you think. A shrewd fellow often makes great gains for a little outlay; a great good, in return for little, has come the way of both of us. I entered the king's palace as an emissary, to carry out some important business of our monastery. During this time, the king was sick and in need of my skin, which I straightway removed and handed over at the king's request. This wasn't much; I'd have given it without being told to, and the whole court, together with the mighty king, was asking for it! Of course, I knew you were standing here ready to give me yours of your own accord, and that you had for a long time intended this, but the occasion for the gift was lacking—for which you were sad. Now the time for your wish has come. Take off your skin! When mine has grown again, I'll give you back whichever of the two you prefer; let the choice be your reward for the gift! And let me have a little dinner off your flesh, for you'll still be large and fat enough afterward. I don't ask it for my own sake; it will do you good to have some of your fat eaten up, so that you can run more swiftly. At the moment, you can hardly stir your 1185 1190 1195 1200 1205

Non costas aut ossa velim tibi tollere, paulum
    cedarum clunes vendico pone popas.
Efficit herba tibi carnem, sine vescar habunde,
1210   fasciculo herbarum pars tibi dempta redit.
Non dico, quia te dubitem quaesita daturum—
    quin avidum dandi longa loquela gravat—
quem prius inventum titulis elegero tantis,
    rex pretium pellis reddidit ipse meae,
1215 quasque michi grates rex danti scripsit et illi
    obstanti dempta conditione necem."
Corvigarus fallax "Pellem petis," inquit, "et escam;
    non sunt a sociis ista petenda diu.
Sponte sequens non est iniecto fune trahendus;
1220   esse queror tanto dignus honore parum.
Sed sine consilio nichil est prudente gerendum.
    Hic tibi suspecta est undique turba canum,
nec duce te silvas ausim confisus adire,
    ut capias illic tutus ab hoste cibum.
1225 Rapta cuculla tibi est, nimiumque corona recrevit;
    te species fratrem nulla fuisse docet.
Truncandas submitte comas, redolabo coronam,
    in nemus ut possim te duce tutus agi.
Nescio, si nosti, privatim tondeo fratres;
1230   pauperis officii me pudet esse palam.
In talis aptata meis rasoria porto."
    Cui lupus: "Hoc nichil est, ne nisi vera refer!
Nam quotiens paulisper ebent rasoria, cautus
    inverrens corio tonsor acuta facit.

limbs. I wouldn't want to take your ribs or bones away from you; I only claim a little of your hide, in the vicinity of your fat rump. Grass makes flesh for you, so let me feed plentifully; a bundle of hay will suffice to bring back the portion you've lost. It's not because I doubt that you will give what's asked (rather, you're so eager to make the gift that my lengthy speech irritates you) that I tell you that the king himself gave me, as a reward for my skin, the first person whom I should choose for such great honors, and what thanks the king decreed for anyone who made me the gift— and a merciless death for anyone who refused."

The deceitful Corvigarus said: "You ask for a coat and for food; you don't have to ask friends for a long time for such things. One who follows of his own accord needn't be dragged by a rope thrown around him. I'm sorry only to be unworthy of so great an honor. But nothing should be done without wise planning. All round here there's a pack of dogs which holds danger for you. Nor would I dare to go to the woods, trusting in you as my escort, so that you might consume your food there, safe from any enemy. Your cowl has been taken away from you, and your tonsured hair has grown too much; nothing in your appearance indicates that you were a monk. Allow your hair to be cut; I shall refashion your tonsure, so that I can safely be brought to the wood under your escort. I don't know if you were aware that I'm a private barber for monks; I'm ashamed to be publicly known to be of a poor trade, so I carry my razors fitted into my hooves."

"This is nonsense; don't tell me untruths!" answered the wolf. "For whenever razors get a little bit dull, a careful barber makes them sharp by rubbing them on leather,

379

1235 Nulla tibi pendet corrigia, detege, si qua est!"
  Corvigarus penem nudat aitque: "Vide!
Subligar hoc acuit rasoria nostra, secantque,
  aspice!" ferratos exhibuitque pedes.
Aspicit ut ferri spiras in calcibus hospes,
1240   quaeque vetat dici cetera saepe pudor,
fallere cornipedem facili deliberat astu:
  "Corvigare, indoctos credis ita esse lupos?
Sed suit ex duro crepidas tibi subula ferro.
  Vis procul hinc sanctos quaerere sicut ego,
1245 estque viae baculus, quod subligar esse fateris;
  fallere me nulla calliditate potes.
Quod durum est, ostendis, et est corrigia molle;
  hunc baculum voti contuor esse tui.
Elapsum est ferrum, contemplor inane foramen,
1250   ferratum fuerat; perfice vota, miser!
Tonsa corona michi satis est, fidenter eamus;
  quolibet optaris, dux tibi fidus ero."
Ille refert: "Non nugor, adest corrigia praesens
  et, si vis, capiti tonsor et arma tuo.
1255 Quoque michi corium quam fratrum spissius extat,
  fratribus officii tam super arte feror."
Postquam nil senior verbis profecerat illis,
  sermones alia condidit arte suos:
"Corvigare infelix, esse haec rasoria dicis,
1260   imbannite quater quindeciesque Satan?
Inter sacrilegas lichnis stolulisque Gehennae
  devovere tuum bis caput octo patres!
Quod foribus nostris omnes detraxeris anos,
  accusabo nefas; hic tua furta patent."

whereas there's no strop hanging on you—reveal it, if it's 1235
anywhere." Corvigarus unsheathed his penis and said:
"Look! This leather strap sharpens my razors, and they can
cut—have a look!"—and he proffered his iron-shod hooves.
When his visitor saw the iron curves on his heels, and the 1240
other thing which shame forbids being frequently named,
he resolved to deceive the horse with a simple trick. "Corvi-
garus, do you think wolves are so uninformed? The awl has
stitched shoes out of hard iron for you. You want to seek out
saints, far from here, as I do, and what you say is a leather 1245
thong is a staff for the road; you can't fool me with any de-
ceitfulness. You show me something hard, and a strop is
something soft; I see that this is a staff for accomplishing
your vow. Only the iron tip has fallen off; I'm looking at the
empty socket which was iron tipped. Carry through what 1250
you've vowed, you wretch! My tonsure's shaved well enough.
Let's set off with confidence. I'll guide you reliably wherever
you want to go." He replied: "I'm not joking, there's a razor
strop here, and if you want them, a barber and his imple-
ments for your head. Moreover, just as my bit of leather is 1255
thicker than that of the monks, so I'm reputed to outdo
them in the skill of my trade."

The old man, having got nowhere with these words,
shaped his speech according to another stratagem. "Misera-
ble Corvigarus, do you call these razors, you devil nineteen 1260
times accursed? Sixteen priests, with stoles and candles,
have condemned you to hell as one of those guilty of sac-
rilege. I'll denounce your crime of stealing all the rings
from our doors—your act of robbery is as clear as daylight!"

1265 Tonsor ad haec: "O parce reo, domine abba! Quid horres?
       Es monachus, parca tende flagella manu!
       Qui miser esse potest, miseros mediocriter angat;
          qui sibi vult parci, parcat et ipse reis.
       Vel tulimus lapsum vel labi possumus omnes;
1270   quisque sui, dum quem corripit, esto memor!
       Peccavi, peccasse piget, nec me abnego sontem
          esse nec excuso, detrahe furta michi!
       Cominus huc propera; senui tumbaeque propinquo;
          in banno vereor flagitiisque mori.
1275 Dedo pedes," talumque levans praecolligit horam
          obliquis oculis, quando ferire queat.
       Prensa calce putans facilem Ysengrimus abactu
          ilicet accedit sicque sibi inquit ovans:
       "Tres male sustentant tabulata quadrangula postes,
1280   nec tribus incedit firma quadriga rotis."
       Ut satis aptatus stetit Ysengrimus ad ictum,
          Corvigarus talum promovet atque ferit.
       Si scit, quidque ferit, medioque intervenit ictu
          auriculas; retro funditur ille procul,
1285 moenia non aliter quam iactus in alta molaris,
          officiumque aures osque oculique negant.
       Talus equo rediit, sed spira in fronte remansit;
          os penetrant clavi, spira retenta sedet.
       Nec transire potest nisi quatenus acta volando;
1290   illaeso formam presserat osse suam,

382

The barber replied: "Oh, spare the guilty, lord abbot! Why 1265
are you so outraged? You're a monk; apply the scourge with a
sparing hand. Let anyone who is liable to misfortune refrain
from harassing the unfortunate too much. Whoever wants
to be spared himself, let him spare the guilty. We have all ei-
ther made a slip or else are liable to do so in the future. Let 1270
everyone have a mind to his own case when he is scolding
someone else. I have sinned, I am sorry for my sin. I don't
deny that I am guilty, or excuse myself. Take from me what I
have stolen. Come near to me quickly; I am old and hasten-
ing to the grave, and I am afraid of dying in my sins and un-
der excommunication. I surrender my feet to you." — And 1275
lifting up his foot, with a sidelong glance he selected in ad-
vance the moment when he could strike. Ysengrimus, think-
ing he would be easily mastered once his foot had been
grasped, immediately went over, jubilantly saying to him-
self: "Three legs don't hold up four-cornered boards very
well, nor does a cart move steadily on three wheels!" 1280

When Ysengrimus stood in the appropriate position for
the blow, Corvigarus moved his hoof forward and struck.
He hit him as fairly and squarely as he knew how, and landed
a blow right between his ears. The wolf was hurled backward
a long way, just like a heavy stone catapulted at high bat- 1285
tlements. His ears and mouth and eyes refused to perform
their functions any more. The hoof came back under the
horse, but the horseshoe remained on his forehead. The
nails sank into the bone, and the shoe was held on and re-
mained, nor could it move without being in some way forced
into flight. It had impressed its shape in the unbroken bone, 1290

namque relecta super ferrum membrana coibat
   vix oculo plagae percipiente locum.
Corvigarus monachum ferro feliciter ictum
   aspiciens dulci voce iocatur ovans:
1295 "Unum, frater, habes, hunc offer fratribus anum;
   vester an extiterit, consule quasque fores.
Si sublatus ibi fuit hic, mea prata revise,
   substituam socios, fixus ubi iste modo est.
Surge, quid expectas?" (immotus namque iacebat)
1300   "In capite est, palpa, circulus haeret ibi.
Invenies in fronte tua, quod quaeris in herba;
   cum gradiere, cave ne cadat, haeret adhuc.
Figere, da veniam, potui non firmius illum.
   Perge, tuis nostrum fratribus infer ave!"
1305 Denique paulatim motis prorepere membris
   cum crebro gemitu nititur ille miser.
"Eia, care comes, modo Romam! Quodque sigillum
   fronte tua fixum est, effice papa legat.
Dic papae, quia Corvigarus, qui vescitur herbis,
1310   cum Romam peteres, hoc heremita dedit.
Tutus eris, me pontifices, me papa veretur,
   nominis et vitae conditione meae.
Corvigarus dicor, sic nullus papa vocatur.
   Papa quis est herbas? Est cibus herba michi.
1315 Plus me papa potest, sed sedis iure beatae,
   sed merui vita nomineque esse prior.

for the peeled-off skin drew itself together over the iron so that the eye could hardly make out the location of the wound.

Corvigarus, seeing the monk had been most beautifully hit by the iron, happily joked in a pleasant tone: "You've got one door ring, brother, offer this to your brethren—or ask all the doors whether it's yours. If this is one that was taken from there, come back to my fields, and I'll put its fellows in the place where that one's fixed now. Get up, what are you waiting for?" (for he was lying motionless). "It's in your head; feel, the ring is stuck fast there. You'll find that what you're looking for in the grass is in your forehead. Take care it doesn't fall off when you walk; it's still clinging fast. Pardon me, I couldn't fix it any firmer. Go, and carry my greeting to your brethren!"

At last the wretch moved his limbs and tried to crawl forward with frequent groans. "Now, dear friend, go to Rome! and let the pope see the seal which is fixed on your forehead. Tell the pope that Corvigarus the hermit, who feeds on herbs, gave you this, since you were making for Rome. You'll be taken into protection; the pope and prelates revere me because of my life and name. I'm called Corvigarus—no pope has a name like that. What pope feeds off herbs? Herbs are my sustenance. The pope has more power than I, but through the right of his holy see; I, on the other hand, have deserved to take precedence by my life and name. That's

Idque sigilla notant, etenim sunt plumbea papae,
    cerea pontificum, ferrea nostra quidem.
Quam ferro plumbum, quam plumbo cera rigore,
1320   tam praesul papae, tam michi papa subest.
Protinus ergo, simul spectarit papa sigillum
    Corvigari, claustro restituere tuo!"

what the seals mean. The pope's are of lead, the bishop's of
wax, while mine are of iron. Just as lead is inferior to iron,
and wax to lead in hardness, so the bishop is inferior to the 1320
pope, and the pope to me. So, as soon as the pope has seen
Corvigarus's seal, you'll be restored to your cloister."

BOOK SIX

Talibus expletis sano gavisa tyranno
   curia dispersa est, ad sua quisque redit.
Transibat Reinardus, ubi Ysengrimus adempta
   pelle parum gaudens et caput ictus erat,
5 sed nimium muscas aegrum pietate parantes
   visere concussis dentibus ire rogans—
quorum exauditur longe collisio, tamquam
   lanilegus pecten pectine crebra sonans.
Ictibus auditis Reinardus clamitat alte:
10   "Regia quis socius robora caedit ibi?
Quis, domine, es, caesor, qui sic, nisi me ante rogasses
   caedendi veniam, regia ligna secas?
Defensore putas silvam, vesane, vacantem,
   cum sit tutelae credita silva meae?"
15 Ysengrimus item feriens horrebat, at ille:
   "Et quis bannitum caedit itemque nemus?
Quisquis es, hic linques dolabram, nisi caedere cesses,
   si sum silvituus regis, ut esse puto.
Cum sua villani pacare salicta sinantur,
20   cur requiem lucus regis habere nequit?
Tam cave, ne exilem violaveris amodo brancum,
   quam, tecum ut redeat tuta securis, amas!"

When all this was over, the court dispersed, rejoicing in the king's health, and each one went to his own home. Reynard passed by the place where Ysengrimus, with a battered head, was bemoaning the loss of his skin, and was clashing his teeth together, so as to beg the flies which, in an excess of charity, were preparing to visit him in his sickness, to go away. Their clashing could be heard for a long way, echoing repeatedly, like the noise of one weaver's comb against another. Hearing their snapping, Reynard called out loudly: "Friend, who is that cutting down the king's oaks there? Who are you, sir woodcutter, to fell the king's wood like this without having first asked me for permission to cut? Do you think, you fool, that the wood lacks a keeper, when it is entrusted to my care?" Ysengrimus gnashed his teeth once more in fright, and the other said: "And who is felling protected woodland yet again? Whoever you are, unless you stop cutting, you'll leave your ax here, if I'm the king's forester, as I think I am. When even peasants are allowed to protect their plantations, why can't the king's forest remain unmolested? Take care you don't harm even a teeny little branch from now on, if you want your ax to go away with you safe!"

Taliter irritat, donec prope constitit illum;
    "Hiccine, noster," ait, "patrue dulcis, ades?
25 Succisum silvas aliquem venisse putabam.
    Da veniam, ignarus noxia verba dedi!"
Ysengrimus humo poterat consurgere necdum,
    sed quod non poterat viribus, arte parat;
"Huc, cognate, veni! Silvam sub rege tueris,
30 tu meus es sanguis, ne vereare, veni!
Ignosco spolium pellis, servire tyranno
    te decuit; regi, non tibi, triste velim.
Hinc succido nemus, caesori tolle securim,
    regia ne officium transferat ira tuum!"
35 "Appropiare tibi non possum, patrue dulcis,
    tam doleo trabeae perditione tuae.
Cur sine pelle tua tot amicis fultus abisti?
    Nam quicumque mei, nonne fuere tui?
Sed malus hoc fecit Ioseph tibi; pendat acerbe.
40 Hic modo bis sena prole superbus ovat;
si quid adhuc virtutis habes, proficiscere mecum,
    reddat pro corio seque suosque tuo.
Nec tenebrae metuantur, habes in vertice lunam,
    haec nobis rectum praevia pandet iter.
45 Si triduana fuisset adhuc, iam plena coiret,
    aut triduum rediit, post ubi plena fuit."
Hanc lupus ad vocem redivivo robore surgit,
    ignoscit vulpi, mitia verba refert;
Corvigari totam detexit in ordine fraudem.
50 Mox stabulum Ioseph nil metuentis adit.
(Praedocuit vulpes vervecem regis in aula,
    fallere qua posset calliditate lupum.)

In this way he chivvied him until he had come up to him. "Oh, is it you that's here, my dear uncle?" he said. "I thought someone had come to cut down the wood. Forgive me—I said those nasty things in ignorance!" Ysengrimus still couldn't rise from the ground, but he tried to accomplish by cunning what he couldn't manage by force. "Kinsman, come here! You guard the wood under the king; you're of my blood; don't be afraid, come here! I pardon the removal of my skin; you had to comply with the king. It's not to you but to the king that I bear ill will. I'm cutting down the wood here, so take the ax away from this woodcutter, in case the king, in anger, changes your job!" "I can't come near you, sweet uncle, I'm so sorry for the loss of your coat. Why did you go away skinless when you had the goodwill of so many friends? For weren't all my friends yours? But the wicked Joseph did this to you—let him pay for it severely! He is now proudly rejoicing in a family of twelve. If you still have any strength, come with me, and he will hand over himself and his family in return for your hide. Don't let the darkness scare you; you've got a moon on your head which will go before us and show us the right way. It's either got three days to go before it rounds out completely, or else it's three days on the wane after having been at the full."

At this speech the wolf's strength revived and he got up; he forgave the fox and answered with gentle words, explaining Corvigarus's whole trick from start to finish. Soon he was at the pen of Joseph, who had no apprehensions. (The fox had previously instructed the sheep, in the king's court, on a piece of trickery by which the wolf could be deceived.)

"Patrue, pone minas et praeblandire parumper;
qui simulat pacem, certius ense ferit.
55 Ne subito effugiant, patrem natosque saluta!"
"Pax vobis, fratres! Hic bonus hospes adest;
quem totiens optastis, adest; procedite laeti!"
"Quis nobis pacem tempore clamat in hoc?
Pace precor careat, qui debuit obdere caulam!
60 Non michi clamata pace opus esse reor.
Rus habito, numquid silvalem debeo censum?
Hinc procul indictor foederis huius eat!"
"Haec, frater, michi verba subintendisse videris."
"Nil ego, domne, tibi praeter honesta loquar;
65 quilibet externus, qui nobis profore nollet,
clam potuit nostras insiluisse fores."
"Et quid, amice, putas? Potuitue externior hospes
deteriorque tuos ullus inisse lares?"
"Care pater, potuit, si non michi nequior optas
70 esse, tuus genitor quam fuit ante meo."
"Nec melior nec peior ero; si comiter illud,
quicquid erit, tuleris, scis bene ferre iocum.
Iugera nunc solves, quot sum tibi mensus; ego istos
tres quater usuram, te capitale peto.
75 Ergo minas omnes laxatae redde crumenae!"
"Mallem villano quam cibus esse tibi?
Nil michi sive meis contingat tristius agnis;
vix michi tam rebar velle favere deum.
Si me dumtaxat totum consumere posses!
80 Sed polus aurora progrediente rubet,
hic homines oriente die patiere canesque;
si petimus silvas, stirps nocitura tua est.

"Uncle, lay threats aside and first flatter a little; the man who feigns peace can strike more surely with his sword. Greet the father and his children, in case they run away immediately!"—"Peace be unto you, brethren! Here is a welcome guest! The one you have so often longed for is here; come forth and rejoice!"

"Who cries peace to us at this time? I pray that whoever it was who should have fastened up our sheepfold may have his peace taken away from him! I don't think I need a greeting of peace. I live in the open country; do I owe forest dues? The promulgator of a peace like that can get lost!" "You seem to be getting at me in this speech, brother!" "To you, sir, I'll utter nothing but civilities; it's some stranger, who wished us no good, who could secretly have slipped in through our gates." "And what are you imagining, friend? Is it possible for any worse or more alien guest to have entered your house?" "Dear father, it is possible, if you don't wish to be any more harmful to me than your father once was to mine." "I'll be neither better nor worse; if you'll put up with whatever takes place in a friendly fashion, then you know how to take a joke well. Now you'll make payment for all the acres I measured out for you. I ask for you as the capital, and these twelve children as the interest, so open up your purse and pay up all the money!" "Would I prefer to be food for a peasant rather than for you? Nothing worse could befall me or my lambs. I hardly imagined that God's will would be so favorable to me; if only you can manage to eat me whole! But the sky is reddening with the advancing dawn; here, as the day approaches, you'll be exposed to men and dogs. If we go to the woods, your family will spoil everything.

395

Est opus arte nova; pars nostri corporis opto
    nulla tibi pereat; fac mea dicta, sapis:
85 ad terram reside retroque innitere posti,
    atque bene impressos in scrobe fige pedes,
inde michi tota protende voragine fauces—
    quam late valeas pandere labra, vide!
Rumor ubique refert, quam sis Bernardus hiandi;
90 nunc parebit, utrum noris hiare bene.
Integer ingenti ferar in tua viscera saltu;
    buccellam talem fors tibi nulla dedit.
Nil formido nisi in stomachos discurrere plures.
    Hiscere si nosti, deprecor hisce semel!
95 Si bene laxaris buccam michi, funditus intro;
    hoc tibi consilium proderit atque michi.
Tunc non sollicitabor, ubi superantia condam,
    cancellosque uteri quosque replebo tui!"
Imprimit ille pedes scrobibus postique retrorsum
100 appodiat, furno laxius ora patent.
Impete si recto vervex in labra ruisset,
    intrasset medio guttura ventre tenus.
Assilit ergo hostem sublatis cornibus alte;
    fixerunt superum cornua bina labrum,
105 bina cavas nares, frontem duo, bina palatum.
    Excutitur senior sensibus atque loco.
Conqueritur Ioseph: "Domine Ysengrime, rogaram,
    firmiter ut stares, tamque repente cadis?
Aut cadis aut titubas; sta firmiter, esca parata est.
110 Vescere constanter, cerne, diescit enim.

A new stratagem is needed; I don't want any part of my body to be lost to you, so if you're wise you'll do what I say. Sit on 85 the ground and brace yourself from behind against the doorpost, and plant your feet in a hole, firmly entrenched. Then stretch open your jaws for me to the full extent of their chasm. See how wide you can open your mouth! Rumor everywhere relates that your jaws gape as wide as Bernard's— now it will become clear whether you know how to open 90 wide. With one mighty leap I'll be carried whole into your entrails; good luck has never given you such a mouthful before. I fear nothing except being dispersed into lots of different stomachs; if you know how to open wide, I beg you to open up this once! If you stretch your cheeks apart prop- 95 erly for me, I'll go right in. This plan will benefit both you and me: I won't be worried about where I'll store any leftovers, and your stomach will be filled to its very boundaries by me."

He pressed his feet in some holes and leaned back against the doorpost, his mouth open wider than an oven. If the 100 sheep had hurtled between his lips with a straight charge, he would have gone down his throat as far as the middle of his stomach. So he charged at his enemy with high-raised horns; two horns pierced his upper lip, two his hollow nostrils, two 105 his forehead, and two his palate. The old man was jolted from the spot and from his senses as well.

Joseph complained: "Dom Ysengrimus, I asked you to stand firm—are you falling over so soon? You're tottering or falling; stand firmly, your food is ready. Eat steadily— 110 look, day is coming! Once upon a time, you used to eat

Sex ovibus quondam sumptis illectus ad esum
  et plus dimidio ventris inanis eras.
Vix libata tibi hic una est, effetus abisti;
  plus quam dimidius resto superstes adhuc.
115 Nunc fugis, ut dantur tibi fercula prima; cibusne
  moverit, ignoro, taedia sisne satur.
Hoc sapit ante diem caro vervecina; redibis
  vespere, quid sapiat tunc quoque, nosse dabo.
Efficiam, ne non toto scribatur in orbe,
120   perlepide ludum me didicisse pati.
Sive satur sive insipidam pertaesus es escam,
  nolo michi parcas, do satis atque super.
Scrabonis vetuli penna paganior essem,
  tantillae vellem si dapis esse tenax.
125 Dic patruo, Reinarde, tuo, vescatur habunde."
  Namque aderat vulpes, festa cupita gerens.
"Grates, frater, habe! Satur est, dormire sinatur.
  Nil audit, dextro poplite (dormit) abi!"
His dictis abiit Ioseph comitantibus agnis;
130   ut potuit demum, repsit et ille domum,
et donec misero virtus coriumque recrerunt,
  nullorsum a propria prodiit aede foras.
Convaluisse lupum fama perhibente renidet
  vulpes, ut nitido noctua furva die.
135 Tunc tendit laqueos ad callida vota valentes;
  robore diffidens fraude capescit opem.
Difficilem veniam scelerum ratus esse priorum,
  tertia disponit praenocitura lupo.
Non dubitat recto praependere lucra leonem
140   et leviter motum, quo vocat ira, sequi;

six sheep to work up an appetite for food, and half your
stomach still remained empty; now you've barely tasted one,
and you've turned away exhausted, while more than half of
me still remains alive. Now you're running away when the   115
very first course is given you. I don't know whether the food
has turned your stomach, or whether you're just full. This is
what mutton tastes like before daybreak; if you come back
in the evening, I'll let you know what it tastes like then as
well. I'll take care that it's put on record for all the world
that I've learned to take a joke very pleasantly. Whether   120
you're full, or whether you're nauseated by the insipid food,
I don't want you to spare me—I give enough and more. I'd
be shittier than the wing of an old dung beetle if I wanted
to hang on to such a little snack. Tell your uncle, Reynard,   125
that he should eat plentifully!"—for the fox was present, rel-
ishing the kind of delicacies he hankered after. "Accept his
thanks, brother! He's full; let him be allowed to sleep. He
hears nothing, he's sleeping; go, while the going is good!" At
these words Joseph left, accompanied by his lambs, and the   130
other crawled home when at last he could. And until the
wretch's skin and courage had renewed themselves, he didn't
go anywhere outside of his own house.

When rumor reported that the wolf had recovered, the
fox was as glad as dusky owl is at the shining day. Then he   135
laid traps adequate to his cunning purposes; mistrustful of
strength, he tried to enlist the aid of deceit. Judging that
pardon for his former crimes was hard to come by, he made
provision for giving the wolf the kind of dues that would do
him no good. He had no doubt that the lion valued profit
before what was right, and was easily induced to follow   140

scitque lupum nescire inter duo dura petendum,
    unde sit eniti pronius, esse magis.
Saepe malum sapiens fert pro peiore fugando;
    stulti vana timent inque timenda ruunt.
145 Esuriens ibat raptum leo, cautus eunti
    obviat hospes, humi stratus adorat eum.
"Rex domine, obnixe tuus Ysengrimus, ut illuc
    pransurus venias neve morere, rogat,
expectaris enim." Facilis leo paruit, itur.
150   Cominus accedunt, ostia clausa vident.
"Patrue, nonne semel saltem tua vota peregi?
    Nunc saltem grates promeruisse sinar?
Per me parta tibi est haec gloria—forsan honore
    vix isto gaudes, tam sapis usque parum.
155 Exultes, tristeris, adest, quod saepe petisti:
    progredere, adventum suscipe regis ovans!
Rex tuus hospes adest, tuus hospes! Nunccine nosti
    me favisse tibi? Rex tuus hospes adest!
Ergo epulum accelera, quod heri te rege daturum
160   hospite iactabas; rex properare cupit."
His senior verbis stupet erumpitque probatum
    haeccine Reinardus dixerit anne Satan.
Viso rege silens trepidat, detracta recesse
    conqueritur, rursum tergora danda timens.
165 "Patrue, mandatus rex ad tua prandia venit.
    Ipse petitus adit, non tua dona petens,

where anger summoned him, and he knew that the wolf was
unaware that of two evils, the one to be chosen is the one
which it is easier to escape from. A wise man often bears
an evil for the sake of avoiding something worse; fools are
afraid of trifles, but nevertheless rush into things they
should be afraid of. The hungry lion was prowling in search   145
of prey; the prudent visitor met him on the way and, pros-
trated on the ground, paid him reverence. "Lord king, your
Ysengrimus earnestly beseeches you to come and dine with
him, and not to delay, for you are awaited." The lion readily
acquiesced, and off they went. As they approached, they saw   150
the door was shut.

"Uncle, haven't I fulfilled your wishes this time at least?
Now, at least, mayn't I be allowed to have deserved thanks?
Through me has this distinction alighted upon you! Perhaps
you're not very happy at this honor, you're always so lacking
in sense. Whether it makes you happy or sad, what you've   155
often asked for is at hand: come forth, and joyfully welcome
the king's approach! The king is here as your guest—as your
guest! *Now* do you recognize the favor I've done you? The
king is here as your guest! So speed up the banquet which
yesterday you were boasting you would lay on when the king
was your guest; the king is in a hurry."   160

At these words the old man was astounded and rushed
out to see if Reynard, or the devil, had spoken them. When
he saw the king, he trembled in silence, and regretted that
the skin which had been removed had grown again, fearing
he would have to make a present of it for the second time.
"Uncle, the king comes by invitation to your dinner. He is   165
here at your request, he doesn't request your gifts himself—

et promissa negas? Nobiscum rura require;
  nil tibi promisit rex epulumque dabit.
Inveni vitulam, sed vis abducere aventi
170   defuit, et regem praepedit ecce pudor;
tu medius nostri, tu fortis et absque pudore.
  Curramus! Nemori rura propinqua sedent.
Tu deductor eris praedae, rex tutor, ego index,
  et fore communem rex patietur eam."
175 Vulpe loquente leo reticet, non antea pontem
  quam capras habeat praefabricare volens.
Mens aliter versat; fortuna dante iuvencam
  non dubitant vulpes et leo, cuia foret.
Annuit Ysengrimus, eunt, reperitur, abitque
180   in nemus arreptis bucula ducta toris.
Ut tenuere locum, quem rex praeceperat escis,
  tunc patuit, quanti sit sapuisse, palam.
Bos cadere est morsu, non verbo, iussa caditque;
  non moriens ausa est dicere "Nolo mori."
185 At lupus insipiens, vix rege rogante, quis illam
  divideret recte, "Partiar," inquit, "ego."
(Tam praeceps fatuus quam non est gnarus agendi;
  expectat sapiens, dum sapienter agat.)
"Ergo partifica, domine Ysengrime, decenter!"
190   "Partiar egregie, rex here, nonne leges?"
Assilit ergo bovem, semota est, membra tripertit;
  partibus aequatis inspicit acre leo.
"Ysengrime, putas, est bos divisa facete?"
  "Rex, bene divisa est et sine fraude, proba!"
195 "Experiar paucis, an sit divisa perite;
  si bene divisa est, utile dico tibi.

402

and are you going to refuse what has been promised? Come with us to the fields; the king has not promised *you* anything, but he will give you a banquet. I have found a calf, but I lacked the strength to carry it away as I wanted to, and 170 shame, you see, hinders the king from doing so. You supplement both of us, being both strong and shameless. Let's hurry! The fields lie near the wood. You'll carry the booty, the king will protect it, and I will show the way to it; the king will allow it to belong to us all." While the fox was 175 speaking, the king was silent, not wanting to count his chickens before they were hatched. He had other ideas in mind; if fortune delivered up the calf, there was no doubt in the minds of the fox and the lion as to whose it would be.

Ysengrimus agreed, and off they went. The heifer was found, her flesh seized, and she was dragged into the wood. 180 When they had reached the spot which the king had ordained for the meal, then the value of wisdom became evident. The cow was ordered to fall—ordered with the teeth, not with the tongue—and fall she did, not even daring to say "I don't want to die" as she died. But the stupid wolf, almost 185 before the king asked who should divide it up properly, said "I'll divide it!" (The fool is as rash as he is ignorant when it comes to action; a wise man holds his fire until he can act wisely.) "Well then, divide it up properly, Dom Ysengrimus!" "I'll divide it splendidly, lord king; would you like to take 190 your pick?" So he leaped on the cow, jointed it, and divided its members into three portions. The lion grimly surveyed the equal portions. "Ysengrimus, do you think the cow has been properly divided?" "King, it's been divided well and honestly—have a look!" "I'll find out soon enough if it's 195 been expertly divided; if it's been well divided you'll hear

Pars haec prima trium cuia est?" "Tua, maxime mi rex."
 "Et cuius media est?" "Rex, ego sumo michi hanc."
(Rector adhuc sed vix inscissa bile tacebat.)
200 "Tertia pars cuinam cedat, amice, iubes?"
"Reinardo vulpi"; rabies tunc tota movetur,
 nec motis animis imperat ille diu—
a scapulis pellem caudatenus excutit illi.
 "Qui, patrine, dein? Partificata bene est?"
205 Territus ille fere retro salit atque seorsum
 coctana vendentis more resedit anus,
oblitusque suam partem, indignatus an ira
 nescio, si meminit sumere, liquit ibi.
"Patrue, nunc claret, quanto consuescat honore
210 aula secutores glorificare suos.
Serviit ante ursus, modo rex tibi; parce faventi!
 Gratulor auspiciis invideoque tuis!
Quod si me pateris verum tibi dicere, rector,
 hunc pudet officium sustinuisse tuum.
215 Non potuit coram primatibus absque ministro
 exuvias alba ponere fronte suas.
Hoc fortuna loco nos tres dumtaxat adegit,
 rexque licet consors tu quasi noster ades.
Hic, sua si placitura tibi velamina nosset,
220 ipsemet iniussus depositurus erat."
"Me prior hic, Reinarde, tuus vestire volebat,
 qualiter expediit non tolerare michi.
Sero fere sensi, sensi tamen; ipse lucelli
 si quid habet, bursae condat in ore suae!

something to your advantage. Whose is the first portion of the three?" "Yours, my mighty king." "And whose is the middle one?" "King, I'll take that for myself." (So far the king held his peace, but it was with difficulty that his anger had not broken forth.) "And to whom do you advise that the 200 third portion should go, friend?" "To Reynard the fox." Then his whole fury was let loose, and his spirit having been roused, he didn't control it for long—he tore off the other's skin from his shoulder blades to his tail. "How about it now, godfather? Has it been well divided?"

The wolf, quite terrified, jumped backward, and squatted 205 down some way off like an old woman selling quinces. Whether he forgot his share, or whether, if he remembered, he was too much displeased by the king's anger to take it, I don't know, but there he left it. "Uncle, now it's clear with what great honor the court is accustomed to magnify its fol- 210 lowers. Before, it was the bear who put himself at your service, now it's the king; don't give your helper too much trouble! I congratulate you on your good luck, and am envious of it.—King, if you will allow me to speak truth to you, he is ashamed that you have performed this office. In front of 215 the barons, he would have blushed to take off his clothes without a servant to help him. Chance has brought us three alone to this place, and although you are the king, you are here equivalent to our companion. If he'd known that his garments would please you, he would have taken them off 220 himself without being told to."

"This prior of yours, Reynard, wanted to clothe me in such a way as wasn't fitting for me to tolerate. I caught on quite late, but I did catch on. If he has any gain from it, let

225 Me, cui vult, iubet esse parem, coniudico, quidni?
    Solus ego hic, quid rex? Unus ut unus agit."
"Anne tibi externo potius, rex docte, favere
    quam consanguineo debuit atque sibi?
Denique nescio quae perpessum incommoda iactas;
230   ferre potes grates, unde tibi ira placet.
Ominis ille boni credit vestire superbum
    induviis regem bis meruisse suis;
vera tamen dicam, nisi mitis sontibus esses,
    pendere praesumptus debuit acta sui."
235 "Ysengrimus, ut est, partitur et eligit, ut vult;
    hoccine tu saltem participare potes?"
"Dividere ignoro, nullus mea foedera curat,
    quaeque acquiro, mei solius esse solent.
Tu solus vitulam, prout ad me spectat, habeto;
240   offensam patrui nolo movere mei."
"Improbe, rex ego sum natus punire rapaces —
    suggeris, ut michimet iura aliena petam?
Perdita conciliem potius, quam dicar inique
    eripere externas et violenter opes!
245 Divide, communis praeda est, nil vendico sane
    praeter quod merito dixeris esse meum."
"Incidit ammissum patruus meus atque luendi
    aestimat eventum, partiar ergo iubes?
Quicquid vis, facito; quoadusque ignoveris illi,
250   quod male divisit, partificabo nichil."
"Omne nefas illi pariter poenamque remitto,
    et tibi do veniam; divide sicut aves."

him bank it. He lays it down that I should be the equal of 225
whoever he likes—well, I assent, why not? I am only one
here; I may be king, but so what? One counts as one."
"Should he have shown favor to you, a stranger, oh wise king,
rather than to his kinsman and to himself? What's more, I
don't know what these inconveniences are that you claim
you've suffered; you might as well be thankful for what you 230
choose to be angry at. This lucky fellow thinks himself wor-
thy of clothing the proud king with his own garments for
the second time. However, to tell the truth, unless you were
being lenient to the guilty, he ought to pay for his presump-
tuous acts."

"Ysengrimus makes the division according to his nature, 235
and makes his choice according to his wishes. Can't *you*, at
least, share this out?" "I don't know anything about division,
no one seeks for my partnership. Whatever I win is usually
mine alone. You can have the calf all to yourself as far as I'm
concerned; I don't want to cause any harm to my uncle." 240
"Reprobate, I'm the king, born to punish robbers; are you
suggesting that I should go after someone else's rights for
myself? I should rather repair losses than be said to have
seized other people's wealth wrongfully and by force! Make 245
the division, the booty belongs to all; of course I claim noth-
ing except what you shall say is rightfully mine." "My uncle
has done the wrong thing and is reflecting on the conse-
quent penalty—and so you order me to make the division?
Do whatever you want, but until you've pardoned him for 250
dividing badly, I'll share out nothing." "I release him from
every crime and from punishment likewise, and I give you
leave to divide as you want."

Tunc itidem ternos aequans Reinardus acervos
    constituit, sed non utilitate pares:
255 pinguibus ex frustis spissisque et paene sine osse
    portio prima aliis pluris utrisque valet;
crassaque non adeo, quamquam carnosa, secunda est;
    est ossosa parum tertia carnis habens.
Tresque pedes demum perfectis partibus addens,
260   seposuit quartum partibus ille procul.
"Qualiter intendas, dubito, sed dividis apte;
    quem cuiusque velis nescio partis herum.
Mutabisne aliquid? Vis quid cui demere parti?
    Addereve? An, quales esse videntur, erunt?"
265 Nil variabo quidem, divisa est bucula prorsus.
    Elige, quam malis de tribus esse tuam."
"Tu lege pro cunctis, pars cuius quaeque sit, edic!
    Proposui, quicquid dixeris, esse ratum."
"Hanc tibi (summus enim libare potissima debet)
270   quam carnosa onerant crassaque frusta, lego.
Proxima reginae dabitur, cura eius agenda est;
    illa domi recubat foetibus aegra novis.
Crescentes nati tibi sunt ideoque voraces,
    inque tuas epulas et genetricis hiant;
275 his nisi quid demus, quod saltem rodere possint,
    nec tibi nec dominae pars sua tuta meae est.
Ossibus indomitos his exercento molares;
    castigent cupidam fercula dura gulam."
"Et pes cuius erit, qui solus secubat illic?"
280   "Sit meus aut parti suppetat ille tuae!
Sic ego divisi, sic quaeque locanda putavi;
    qui melius norunt, aptius illa locent."

Then Reynard formed three piles all over again, making them equal, but not the same in quality. The first part, of fat, thick and almost boneless chunks, was worth much more than both the others. The second was not so fat, although meaty, and the third was bony, having little meat. Finally he added three feet to the completed portions, and laid the fourth one aside, some way off from them.

"I don't know what your intentions are, but you make division in the right way, although I don't know who you want to take possession of which portion. — Or will you change anything? Do you want to take something away from any portion? Or add anything? Or shall they be as they appear now?" "Certainly I shan't alter anything; the calf is divided up sure enough; choose which of the three you'd prefer to be yours." "You choose for all of us; say which portion shall be whose. I have decided that whatever you say will be approved." "This portion, weighed down by fat and meaty pieces, I choose for you (for the highest ought to eat the best). The next is to be given to the queen. She ought to be taken care of; she's lying at home, weak from her new offspring. And your growing children are so ravenous, and gape after your food and their mother's — unless we give them something they can at least gnaw, neither your share nor my mistress's will be safe. Let them take the edge off their eager greed by exercising their unblunted teeth on these bones."

"And whose will be the foot which is lying by itself over there?" "Let it be mine or let it do for your share! That's how I've made the division; that's how I thought everything should be disposed. Let those who know better dispose of

255

260

265

270

275

280

"Debetur iure o tibi pes, tuus esto! Videris
   ut fidus dominis verna favere tuis.
285 Quisnam te docuit partiri taliter? Ede!
   Per michi quod debes et tibi foedus ego."
"Me docuit docturus adhuc non pauca, quod istic
   quodque alias sapui, patruus iste meus."
"Et cum divideret, cur non sibi novit id ipsum?"
290   "Propter Belvacos non fuit ausus idem."
"Ergo, quod edocuit, misere intellexerat ipse,
   teque aliosque docens ipse docentis eget?"
"Rex miser, ignoras letargo saecula laedi?
   Saepe valens aliis non valet ipse sibi. —
295 Patrue, quid prodest, quod te castigo frequenter?
   Quo te plus moneo, stultius usque facis.
Stulte aliena petens sua seque petitaque perdit.
   Nescis, quid vulgi mystica dicta notent? —
Frania putrescunt melius quam poma vorentur;
300   vas plenum recto, qui tenet, orbe ferat.
Patrue, nos inter tres tantum sermo vagetur:
   tu nimis in partem regis avarus eras.
Lingere debueras ubi, nam mordere parabas;
   librat bufo tenax atque relibrat humum.
305 Curia dissimulat lingentes, morsa remordet,
   et repetunt proceres faenore morsa gravi.
Sospes, si saperes, et regis amicus abisses,
   sed tibi, quae multis, pessima plaga nocet.

them more fittingly." "Oh rightly is the foot due to you, let it
be yours! You seem to look after your masters' interests like
a faithful servant. Who taught you to share things out like 285
this? Tell me, by the faith you owe to me, and I to you." "He
who has still many lessons of this sort to give me, taught
me the wisdom I have shown here and elsewhere—my uncle
there." "And why didn't he know how to do it himself when
he was making the division?" "It was the example of the citi- 290
zens of Beauvais that meant he didn't dare to do it." "So
what he taught he only dimly understood himself, and al-
though he taught you and others, he was himself in need of a
teacher?"

"Poor king, don't you know that the world is crippled
by inertia? Someone who is of use to others is often of no
use to himself.—Uncle, what good is it for me to reprove 295
you so often? The more I warn you, the more foolishly you
always behave. Someone who foolishly aspires to someone
else's property loses what he aspires to, what's his own, and
himself as well. Don't you know what the people's cryptic
phrases signify? 'Royal apples should go rotten before you
dare to eat them; let anyone who holds a full bowl carry it 300
with a level rim.' Uncle, let the discussion be confined to the
three of us alone: you were too greedy of the king's share, for
you were ready to bite where you should only have licked.
The toad measures out in its grasp one lot of earth to eat,
and only then measures out another. The court takes no no- 305
tice of those who lick, but when bitten, it bites back, and
the nobles seek to have back what's been chewed off, with
a heavy interest. If you had been wise, you'd have left this
place unharmed and on good terms with the king; but the
worst kind of handicap cripples you, as it does many others

Non simul ingluvies discretioque esse sinuntur;
310   liberior victrix debilioris erit.
Servares aliena, tuis consuetus abuti?
    Cuius erit custos, qui negat esse sui?
Venit egestati venter, qui vendit agellum;
    venter egens vendit fasque nefasque cibo.
315   Idcirco partemque tuam regisque petebas,
    et rex continuo motus utramque tulit.
Non adhibere potes nisi pleno vincula folli;
    dum superest aliquid, nil tetigisse putas.
Sumere praestabat modicum quam perdere totum;
320   'multa ubi, sat' fertur 'quod iuvat, esse bonum.'
Utilis est oculus, cui profore desinit auris;
    subsidium parce, dat tamen usque deus.
Ecclesia est ingens, cantatque in parte sacerdos;
    multa oculus capit, sed manus aequa praeest.
325   Tonsa bidens melior quam decoriata, iuvatque
    decoriata aliquid, perdita tota perit.
Mortuus aut esses aut regia iura tulisses;
    rex tua teque tenet sub dominante iugo.
Ius sub rege tuum non est sed regis, at illi
330   gratia, si quicquam liquerit esse tuum;
cum quo si quid habes, quod uti commune feratur,
    optima des illi, ne tua teque premat.
Aspera sors misero sese est cognoscere nullo:
    non regum comites, rustica turba sumus.
335   Luxuriant reges, et rustica turba laborat.
    Quid regum est? Aether, flumina, terra, fretum;
villanus cribro pronascitur atque galastrae,
    rex Cereri et piperi, carnibus atque mero.

besides. It's not possible for greed and discretion to coexist; the more unbridled of the two will overcome the weaker. 310 Should you take charge of other people's property, when you're in the habit of mishandling your own? How can anyone look after someone else, when he refuses to look after himself? The stomach that sells the land that feeds it is itself sold into the power of want; the hungry stomach sells right and wrong for food. So you tried for your own share 315 and the king's, and the king was immediately roused and took both. You can't put any fetters on your stomach unless it's full; while there's still anything left over, you imagine you've touched nothing. It was better to take a moderate amount than to lose everything. It's said that 'Where there's 320 abundance, it's a good thing to be content with a sufficiency.' The eye is useful to someone whose ear has ceased to give any help; God gives assistance sparingly, but unfailingly. The church is huge, but the priest sings only in part of it. The eye wants a lot, but a moderate handful is the best. A sheep is 325 better sheared than skinned, and even when skinned is some good, but is utterly useless when destroyed. You should have submitted to the royal decrees on pain of death. The king holds you and yours under the yoke of his rule. Under the king, the law is not yours but the king's, and it's a favor in 330 him to have left anything for you. If you have anything which is supposed to be common property, you should give the best to him, lest he injure you and your goods. It's a hard fate for a wretch to recognize his own worthlessness: we're not the companions of kings, but the peasant masses. Kings 335 take their ease, while the crowd of peasants toils. What belongs to kings? The air, the rivers, the earth, the sea. The peasant is born to the sieve and the milk pail, the king to

Rusticus e sulco producit regibus ostrum,
340   stuppeaque ipsius sagmata corpus arant.
Qui sua dementer vastant, externa capescunt;
     servans parta potest sumere, quando libet.
Suppetit ingluvies aulae, cui cuncta creantur;
     sobrietas miseras stringit egena casas.
345 Pauperis ingluvies exhausta protinus archa
     prodit, quam noceat deseruisse modum.
Legem pone gulae, ne fias pauper abusu
     et male mendices aut male rapta luas."
His siluit dictis rimansque procacibus irquis
350   dilecti patrui singula membra notat—
pars autem, nisi pelle carens, in corpore toto;
     iudice Reinardo nulla decora fuit.
Tunc parat ornatu patruum meliore beare,
     quadrupedem metuens currere posse nimis,
355 rem miseram repetens et paucis profore credens
     cuique lupo innatas quattuor esse bases.
Maluit ergo uno nullum pede sive duobus
     quam dulcem patruum rite carere tribus.
Aestimat ausurum pedibus quam plurima tantis,
360   quae nimio nequeant absque labore geri.
"Non oberit cuiquam, prosit, si profore possit,
     si fuerit saltem qualibet arte tripes."
Tunc constante fide senis ista susurrat in aurem:
     "Patrue, non nobis hoc bene cessit iter.
365 Nil nobis cum rege; potest nimis ille, feroxque
     viribus intendit; nil pietatis habet.

wheat and spices, meat and wine. The peasant produces pur-
ple cloth for kings from his furrow, while his own body is   340
plowed by smocks of coarse tow. Those who stupidly squan-
der their own property lay hold of other people's, whereas
the man who stores up what he's acquired can consume
it when he wants. Greed is all right for the court, for which
everything is produced, but a needy frugality cramps the   345
houses of the poor. In the case of a poor man's greed, the
speedy emptying of the money box makes clear how harm-
ful it is to abandon moderation. Put a curb on your greed,
lest you become poor through prodigality, and lest you
should miserably beg or steal and miserably pay for it."

With these words he fell silent, and examined every limb   350
of his beloved uncle, surveying him with an insulting gaze—
although in Reynard's opinion, no part of his whole body
was beautiful unless it was skinless. Then he prepared to
make his uncle happy with a better getup. He feared that,
with four feet, the wolf was only too able to run, and think-   355
ing over this unhappy state of affairs, he believed that it was
not of benefit to many people that any wolf should be born
with four legs. So, he would rather that his dear uncle should
duly lose three legs, than that anyone else should lose one or
two. He thought that with so many feet he would venture
on all sorts of things which couldn't be borne without exces-   360
sive hardship. "It won't hurt anyone—and let it do what-
ever good it can—if by some stratagem he becomes three
legged."

Then with his usual trustworthiness he whispered in
the old man's ear: "Uncle, this journey hasn't turned out
well for us. We shouldn't take up with the king; he is too   365
powerful, and brutally relies on force; he has no mercy.

Res a rege tuas non vi, non arte tueris;
 sunt tibi mutata lucra petenda via.
Balduinus senior, 'Bona' qui 'Fiducia' fertur,
370 pellicium patri debuit ipse tuo,
reddere quod blande monitus cum saepe negasset,
 denique censores constituere diem.
Debitor interea mortem exactorque tulerunt,
 causaque maiori cessit inacta minor.
375 Carcophas patriis successit rebus ut heres,
 sic quoque solvisset debita rite patris.
Poscere nec veniam nec solvere curat, eamus!
 Convictum facili calliditate tenes.
Non didicit causas Galla tractare loquela;
380 praeposuit Franco Danubiale solum.
Teutonicus miser et rudis est ut papa salignus,
 stridula Bavarico gutture verba liquans.
Ore michi Franco causam committe tuendam;
 indiget ille suae compositore vicis.
385 Reddere pellicium primo clamore coactus
 exuet; incautum me duce fisus adi!
Quid dubitas?" (dubitabat enim) "Semel obsecro tempta,
 quam sine versuta sit meus arte favor.
Si res ista tuo fuerit contraria voto,
390 me glutito tuae curva catasta gulae."
Ille ratus verum, quod cogitat esse lucrosum,
 incidit audita conditione plagam.
"Nescio, te, Reinarde, parem cui suspicer esse;
 tu meus es fautor, tu meus hostis item.
395 At monitis ubicumque tuis obtempero, laedor;
 cedo tamen, veluti sis michi fidus adhuc.

You won't protect your property from the king by skill or strength; you should seek for profit by a different route. Baldwin the elder, who was nicknamed 'Good Faith,' owed 370 his hide to your father, and since he had often refused to hand it over when requested politely, finally the judges appointed a day of settlement. In the interim, both debtor and creditor fell prey to death, and the lesser matter, unsettled, gave way to the greater one. Carcophas succeeded as heir to 375 his father's property, and so he ought also duly to have paid his father's debts. He doesn't take the trouble either to pay or to ask for a release. Let's go! With a little cunning he'll be defeated, and in your power. He hasn't learned how to conduct cases in the Gallic tongue; he has preferred the land of 380 the Danube to that of France. He's a wretched German, and as crude as a willow-wood pope, squeezing out guttural words from his Bavarian throat. Commit your case to the care of my French tongue. He has no advocate on his side. He'll be forced to take off his coat and hand it over at the 385 first outburst. Rely on my guidance and catch him unprepared. Why are you hesitating?" (for hesitating he was) "I beg you to make trial just once of the extent to which my friendship is devoid of cunning trickery. If this affair goes contrary to your wishes, let the curved gallows of your 390 throat swallow me up!"

The other, imagining that anything that seemed to him profitable was true, and having heard this condition, laid himself open to injury. "I don't know, Reynard, into what category of persons to put you. You're my protector and you're also my enemy. And whenever I comply with your advice, 395 I come to harm. But I consent, as if you were still loyal

Indice, ni fallor, fama michi debuit ille
    pellicium, et fraus est hac michi facta tenus."
"Patrue, fama meae concordat ydonea voci,
400   dicere tam nosti me tibi vera magis.
Hac iter est, mora segnis obest; succede, praeibo,
    et, qua continuant lucus et arva, mane,
(hostibus horret ager!) ne nobis triste quid obstet.
    Ad silvas asinum qualibet arte traham."
405 Protinus invento vulpes praedixit asello
    propositum fraudis, nec dolet ille sequi.
Invenere senem silvarum extrema tenentem,
    Carcophas rauco ter sonat ore vale.
"Frater, ave hoc falsum est! Si me salvare cupisses,
410   iam michi venisset res mea missa domum.
Nunc tam redde libens, quam commodus exigo, facque
    denuo ne repetam! Nunc repetisse feram."
"Nil tibi me recolo, domine Ysengrime, tulisse.
    Debita do; quod lex publica mandat, agam."
415 Consilio vulpes accitur, itemque reversi
    constiterant, vulpem bis iubet ille loqui.
Iussa locuturum paucis praevenit asellus:
    "Nequaquam placita hic rebar agenda michi,
inconsultus ob hoc feror huc; opus ergo tuente
420   si fuerit, vocem consiliumque peto."
"Utquid consilium, frater, vocemque requiris?
    Quaeruntur patruo debita certa meo:
pellicium reddi, quod tanto tempore debes
    et tu cuius eum cernis egere, iubet."

to me. Unless I'm deceived, the general report of it is a witness that he owes me the hide, and up to now I've been the victim of a fraud!" "Uncle, the general report agrees very aptly with my words, so you recognize even better that I'm 400 telling the truth. This is the way; no use in lazy dawdling. I'll go first, you follow, and stop where the wood and the fields join (the open country is bristling with enemies), in case anything unfortunate should harm us. I'll bring the ass to the woods by some stratagem."

When he'd found the ass, the fox immediately told him 405 his plan for a trick, and the other was not sorry to follow. They found the old man occupying the borders of the woods, and Carcophas three times brayed out a "how d'you do" in his harsh voice. "Brother, this address is deceitful! If you'd cared about my well being, my own property would 410 have come back to me, sent to my home. Now give it up as willingly as I am accommodating in claiming it. See that I don't ask a second time, and I'll overlook the fact that I've had to claim it this time." "I don't remember, Dom Ysengrimus, having taken anything from you; I pay my debts, and I shall do what the public law demands." The fox was called 415 aside for a consultation, and when they had come back again, the wolf twice ordered the fox to speak; the ass, however, got in a few words before he spoke what he'd been ordered to. "I had no idea I'd have to conduct a lawsuit here; because of this I've come without legal advice. So if there's any need for an advocate, I request counsel and the right of 420 reply." "What would you want counsel and the right of reply, brother? My uncle is claiming evident debts; he orders the return of the hide which you have owed for such a long time—and which, as you see, he has need of!"

425 Tunc seriem causae a fundo perstrinxit et addit:
   "Taliter haec retines debita tamque diu.
   Quot tu pensus oves (hoc dampnum ponderat horno)
   hanc massam dampni mittit amore tui.
   Laetius ac citius tam solvere iusta memento,
430   quam superas sensu divitiisque patrem.
   Dedecet ingenuos patria probitate carere;
   obprobrium pravis stirps generosa parit.
   Pauperior tota meus anteritate suorum
   patruus hoc anno bis sua texta novat;
435 est quater undenis haec larva tibi insita lustris,
   nec tu credis adhuc hanc senuisse satis?
   Exue! Fructus erit duplex tibi: debita solvis,
   et nova succrescens dat tibi cappa decus.
   Et quam ferre diu potuit, scis leniter illum
440   supportasse; suae nunc eget ipse rei.
   Credita qui reddit, rursus debere meretur;
   redde nec excusa nec tibi quaere moram!
   Ditior es genitore tuo meliusque videris
   solvere posse tuus quam potuisse parens.
445 Mater Ybera quidem, genitor tibi Francus, et ipso
   ditior atque ortu clarior illa fuit;
   at tibi nobilitas amborum cessit opesque,
   astu praeterea quod tibi crevit, habes."
   Haec ubi Burgundo vulpes expresserat ore,
450   consilium et vocem poscit asellus item.
   Ysengrimus itemque negans ait: "Improbe, debes!
   Hoc est consilium, rem michi redde meam!
   Quis tibi consuleret melius? Mea, quaero, secusne
   ac michi solvendo conciliare putas?"

420

Then he sketched the outline of the case from its founda- 425
tion, and added: "In this way, and over so long a period, have
you withheld these dues. As for all the sheep that have
added to your weight (he estimates this loss by his annual
drop on profits), he remits the amount of this damage
through affection for you. Take care to pay what is due just
so much quicker and more cheerfully as you surpass your fa- 430
ther in wealth and wisdom. It's shameful for noblemen to
lack their ancestors' honesty; a noble family brings disgrace
to its wicked members. My uncle, though poorer than all his
ancestors, has renewed his clothes twice this year; has this 435
ugly costume been stuck on you for two hundred and twenty
years, and you still don't think it's old enough? Take it off!
There will be a double profit for you: you'll pay your debts,
and your new cloak, when it grows, will lend you charm. You
know that he meekly put up with it as long as he could toler-
ate it; now he needs his property. A man who pays back what 440
is lent to him earns the right to be allowed a second debt.
Pay it back, and don't make excuses or ask for a delay for
yourself! You're richer than your father and you seem bet-
ter able to pay than your parent was. Your mother of course 445
was Spanish, your father French, and she was richer and of
higher birth. But the nobility and wealth of both passed to
you, and you have besides the increase due to your cunning."
    When the fox had made this speech in the Burgundian
tongue, the ass again asked for counsel and the right of reply, 450
and Ysengrimus, again refusing, said: "Scoundrel, you owe a
debt! This is your advice: give me back my property! Who
could advise you better? Or, I ask you, do you think you
can compensate me any other way than by paying me what's

455 "Patrue, parva aliquando solet res profore multum.
     Cominus huc aures arrige, pauca loquar."
(Arrigit ille aures) "Omnino cepimus istum.
     Perdere nil poteris, iusta querela tua est;
consulturus eat meque oratore loquatur—
460   deterit hic nullo forma colore prior.
Ille vafer nimis est, fortassis voce negata
     altius appellans vim sibi clamet agi.
Debita, ni caveas, reddet, sed reddita vendet
     forsitan, et quaestu quaestio pluris erit.
465 Aucupis ut laqueo non evasura tenetur,
     unguibus et pennis improba saevit avis."
"Ite! Feram, sed quae posuisti, fixa manento!"
     Consultu redeunt. "Patrue, recta sapis,
nec michi Carcophas nisi rectum velle videtur.
470   Te quoque, si verum est, quod profitetur, amat.
Dicit enim, quia, quicquid habet pretiosius, ultro,
     si tribui peteres praeciperesve, daret;
poscere si praesens nolles, per quemlibet illi
     mandasses miserum, praesto fuisset ovans.
475 Sed quia pellicium fertur debere nec offers
     legitimam turbae testificantis opem,
te putat, ut bonus es, non hoc ab iure petisse,
     sed se nil meminit iuris habere tui,
nec tibi se, quot dicis, oves minuisse nec unam,
480   si fuerit solvens cetera quoque modo.
Suspicionis agit tam sera exactio causam;
     contigit hoc rerum mentio prima die.

mine?" "Uncle, sometimes a small thing can prove very use-   455
ful. Prick up your ears in my direction, I want to say a few
things." (He pricked up his ears.) "We've got him completely
trapped. You can't lose anything, your complaint is a just
one. Let him go away and seek advice, and let him speak
through my advocacy; his present appearance won't deterio-   460
rate in complexion in the meantime. He's all too cunning
and perhaps if he's denied a voice he will appeal to a higher
court and complain that force was brought to bear on him.
If you're not careful, he may repay his debt, but perhaps sell
the repayment dearly, and the lawsuit will cost more than it
brings in. When a pest of a bird is caught without hope of   465
escape in a fowler's net, it wreaks havoc with its wings and
claws." "Go! I'll allow it—but let what you have stipulated
remain unchanged!"

Back they came from their consultation. "Uncle, you
know what's right, and Carcophas too seems to me to want
nothing but what's right. And also, if what he claims is true,   470
he loves you. For he says that he'd willingly give you what-
ever he has that's most valuable, if you were to request or
order it to be handed over, and if you had been unwilling to
ask for it in person, but had commanded him by any kind of
wretch, he'd cheerfully have been at your service. But be-   475
cause he is said to *owe* a hide, and you don't produce numer-
ous witnesses as legal support, he thinks, as you're a worthy
man, that you wouldn't have requested it without just cause,
but he doesn't remember having any of your property, nor
having deprived you of as many sheep as you say—in fact,
not of one—even if he were to pay the rest of the debt in   480
some fashion. So tardy a claim gives rise to suspicion; it was
only today that the first mention of these things cropped

Te tua iura putat (totiens extranea tollis)
  non dilaturum sponte fuisse diu.
485 Aut igitur testes, quis possit credere, quaerit,
  aut ut praeiures pignora sacra super,
et de stirpe sua cum lectis ipse refellet
  aut legem auxilio deficiente feret.
Sed modo nil debet nec vult debere quid umquam;
490 mos malus est hodie et cras quoque sicut heri.
Se tibi formidat numquam persolvere posse,
  reddere si tulerit iussa tributa semel,
rusticus ut solvens debet tamen usque tyranno
  nec fiscum papae Gallia trina replet."
495 "Huc, Reinarde, veni!" (venit) "Quid consulis actu?"
  "Solvere si vellet, rectior ille foret;
quaerit recta tamen." "Vis iurem?" "Patrue, quidni?
  Audacter iura, perdere turpe tua est.
Scit bene Carcophas, quod non evadere possit;
500 quaerit cancellos, solvere taedet eum.
Non habet auxilium; si sic sineretur abire,
  pellicium vellet dimidiare volens.
Protinus abstabunt, quoscumque elegerit, illi,
  sciris enim praeter recta movere nichil.
505 Denique quid paulum tibi periurasse nocebit?
  Tot fratrum pro te postulat usque chorus."
"Desiperem, toto si pars michi carior esset.
  Quis michi relliquias afferet? Aequa velim."
"Patrue, relliquiae, gradiamur, cominus assunt!"

up. He thinks that (so often do you take what belongs to others) you wouldn't of your own accord have deferred claiming your own property so long. He asks, therefore, either for witnesses in whom he can trust, or that you should first swear an oath on holy relics. And he will refute you with the help of selected members from his family—or, in the absence of such help, will pay the penalty. But as for now, he owes you nothing and has no wish ever to do so—it's a bad habit, always has been and always will be. He's afraid that he'll never be able to pay you off, if he once allows the exacted tribute to be handed over, just as a peasant who pays up is nevertheless always in debt to his king, and the three divisions of Gaul are not enough to fill the treasury of the pope."

"Reynard, come here!" (He came.) "What action do you advise?" "If he were willing to pay, he'd be acting with more propriety, but what he's asking for is within his rights." "Do you want me to take the oath?" "Uncle, why not? Swear boldly; it's shameful to lose what's yours. Carcophas knows well that he can't escape. Being reluctant to pay, he wants to go to law. He has no support—he'd willingly agree to giving up half his hide, were he to be allowed to get off in that way. Whoever he chooses, they'll quickly dissociate themselves from him, for you'll be known to be promoting nothing but justice. Anyway, what harm will it do for you to perjure yourself a little bit? Such a huge choir of monks prays for you constantly!" "I'd be foolish if a part was worth more to me than the whole. Who shall bring me the relics? I want justice!" "Uncle, let's go, the relics are near at hand!"

485

490

495

500

505

510 Ventum est ad pedicam. "Patrue, fige gradum!
 Prospice, quid iures! Capitur, qui peierat istic,
  nec sinit hic sanctus gratis abire reos.
 Debita si nosti te iusta requirere, iura!"
  Quicquid avet, rectum cogitat esse lupus,
515 impositumque pedem coeuntia robora prendunt.
  "Patrue, iuratum est sufficienter, abi!
 Iurandi reverens Carcophas solvere praesto est,
  porro sine emenda solvere posse rogat.
 Sacramenta quidem, te malle remittere partem
520 quam iurare ratus, dixit agenda sibi.
 Periurasse tamen convictus debita perdis,
  pignora si moris sacra; movere cave!
 Immotis digitum sacris subducere tempta!"
  Attonitus casu stat lupus atque silet.
525 "Patrue care, quid hoc? Captivus paene videris,
  relliquias mosti!—Culpave maior obest:
 debuerat nummus tua iuramenta praeisse
  placandis sanctis, nec datus ille fuit!
 Pignus ob hoc temet sanctus sibi vendicat ipsum.
530 Me quoque ne capiat sanctus, abibo, mane!
 Non poteris redimi, plus nummo pignus amatur;
  pes vadium nummi vel pede maius erit.
 Mancipium sanctis collo corioque dicarer,
  si vadium vellent credere, nempe negant.
535 Verum multa solent contingere, patrue, fures,
  raptoresque hodie saecula docta sacrant.
 Pontifices rapiunt, sectantur furta decani,
  namque hi, si raperent, praeda repente forent.

They came to a trap. "Uncle, halt your steps. Consider   510
what you are to swear. Anyone who commits perjury here is
caught, and the saint doesn't allow criminals to leave with
impunity. If you are conscious of having requested your le-
gal dues, take the oath!" The wolf thought that whatever
he wanted was just, and so he laid his foot on the pieces   515
of wood, which sprang together and seized it fast. "Uncle,
you've sworn enough; depart! Out of respect for the oath,
Carcophas is ready to pay, and asks besides that he be al-
lowed to pay without a fine. In fact, he said that the oath
was to be made to him because he thought you would give
up part rather than swear. But you'll be convicted of perjury   520
and forfeit the debt if you disturb the sacred relics; take care
not to disturb them! Try to take your hand out without mov-
ing the holy objects."

The wolf, stunned by what had happened, stood silent.
"Dear uncle, what's this? You almost seem to be a prisoner.   525
You've moved the relics!—or there's some greater guilt act-
ing as an obstacle. Money ought to have formed the pre-
lude to your oaths; you didn't give any money to placate the
saints! Because of this, the saint claims you yourself as a
surety. I'm off, in case the saint seizes me as well—you stay   530
here! You can't be ransomed; a surety is generally preferred
to money. Your foot, or something more valuable than your
foot, will be the pledge for your money. I'd become the
saints' property, neck and hide, if they were willing to rely
on bail—but of course they won't accept it. Truly, thieves lay   535
their hands on a lot of things, uncle, and these days the en-
lightened times consecrate thieves. Bishops pillage, and
deans practice pilfering, for if they were to pillage openly,

Raptor eras, sanctique suum novere sodalem;
540   nunc raptum comitem semper habere volunt.
Sanctificant subito sancti, quodcumque prehendunt,
    incipit idcirco pes tuus esse sacer.
Intrasses utinam sanctorum scrinia totus!
    Nunc de te tantum pes modo sanctus erit.
545 Atque utinam sanctis omnes caperentur ab hisdem,
    a quibus es captus, quos tua vita tenet!"
Tunc duo discedunt; ubi nollet, tertius haeret.
    Tunc male deceptum se lupus esse videt.
Pertaesus tardare malis peiora redemit,
550   abmorsumque suo deserit ore pedem.

they'd quickly become a prey themselves. You were a grab-
ber, and the saints have recognized their colleague; now   540
they want to have their compeer firmly in their grasp for
good. The saints instantaneously consecrate whatever they
lay hold of—so your foot has taken on a quality of sanctity.
Would that you had entered entire into the reliquary! As
it is, your foot will be the only part of you to be sanctified.
And would that all who live like you were seized by the same   545
saints that you are now held by!"

Then the two of them left, while the third remained fixed
where he didn't want to be. Then the wolf realized that he
had been wickedly deceived. Unwilling to linger, he bought
off the worse with the bad, and chewing off his foot with his   550
mouth, he left it there.

BOOK SEVEN

Hos tandem finire volens fortuna labores
    proiecit miserum mortis in ora senem.
Ereptus pedicis in guttura dira Salaurae
    incidit; ad lucum venerat usque miser,
5   illic scropha, papae! glandes, quot quinque ter, ultra
    miserat annoso ventre Salaura vorax.
Callida vel solo rerum, quas viderat, usu
    vafrior abbatum pontificumque novem,
saecula sex tulerat Reingrimi dira trineptis,
10   ne vindex prisco debita deesset avo.
Tunc, ut saepe alias, miser Ysengrimus et illam
    cogitat ingenio fallere posse suo.
"Pax tibi, pax, matrina, tibi, carissima! Quantum
    temporis est, ex quo vexor amore tui!"
15 Ut venisse senem vidit pedis unius orbum,
    despicit irridens: "Quomodo, frater, ita est?
Anterius dudum (nimirum antistes et abbas)
    candelabra duo ducere suetus eras;
pars unius abest, id cuius in aede locasti?
20   Corporis at moles alleviata parum est!"
Ille suos narrans casus sibi robora abesse
    cladibus et senio, ne metuatur, ait:

At last Fortune, wishing to put an end to these sufferings, hurled the wretched old man into the jaws of death. After he had been wrenched free from the trap, he fell into the dreadful jaws of Salaura. The wretch had got as far as the wood where the greedy sow Salaura had, heaven help us, dis- 5 patched to her aged stomach more than fifteen times as many acorns as the rest of her kind. She was cunning, and merely by virtue of her experience of the things she had seen, she was craftier than nine abbots or bishops. The dreaded great-great-great-granddaughter of Reingrimus had lived six centuries so that her first ancestor should not be 10 without a fitting avenger. Then, as on other occasions, the wretched Ysengrimus conceived the idea of tricking her by his cunning. "Peace be unto you, peace be to you, dearest godmother! How long a time it is that I have been troubled by a desire to see you!" When she saw the old man had ar- 15 rived minus a foot, she mockingly made fun of him: "How has this happened, brother? Previously you used to carry two candlesticks before you (for you are of course a bishop and an abbot), and part of one of them is missing. In whose church have you left it? The weight of your body is a little 20 bit lightened, at any rate!"

He related his adventures, and so that she shouldn't be afraid of him, told her that his strength had left him through

"Nunc, matrina, nichil nisi solam cogito pacem,
    cerno michi modicum temporis esse super.
25 Proximus ergo neci, quid agas, praerimor et opto
    iungere matrinae basia iusta meae.
Offero, tuque refer pacem!" Iamque ibat ad illam
    paulatim, veluti basia fida gerens.
"Sta penitus, sta, frater, ibi! Tua cognita forsan
30   est tibi, sed nondum regula nostra patet.
Tu monachus caperes, si ferrem, basia nonnae,
    quae timet ad missam iungere nupta viro.
Adde, quod et nondum primae nola nuncia tinnit,
    orta recens lux est!" (luxque erat orta recens)
35 "Missa solet pacem, non pax praecedere missam,
    ergo prior fiat missa, futura prius!"
"Claudico, non possum missam celebrare, nec alter
    presbiter est nobis; quis celebraret eam?"
"Quis celebraret eam, nisi summa magistra suillae
40   abbatissarum relligionis ego?
Abbatissa feror nonnis praelata trecentis,
    vox tamen illarum nullius aequa meae est.
Transabiit mea fama Dacas, nec pone manenti
    abbatissa tibi nota Salaura fuit?
45 Silvestrem missam, quam tu mireris et ipse,
    (debita, fer, donec venerit hora) canam!"
"Ius didici, matrina, tuum, nunc accipe nostrum
    (ridendo redeant praestita liba domum):
carnea clanga michi, non aerea nunciat horam;
50   non nola me signum, sed gula lata docet.
Fit michi non Phoebus, sed venter temporis index;
    sit fors, quod didici, cum iubet ille, cano.

his injuries and old age. "Now, godmother, I have nothing in mind but peace; I see that only a little time is left to me. Near to death, I am first discovering how you are faring, and I want to give my godmother dutiful kisses. I offer the kiss of peace; do you return it!"—for he was gradually moving up to her, as if to administer friendly kisses. "Stand quite still, brother, stand there! You are familiar with the rule of your own order, perhaps, but mine hasn't yet been made clear to you. You, a monk, would, if I were to allow it, take kisses from a nun—kisses which even a married woman hesitates to give a man at Mass. Besides, the bell which is the signal for Prime is not yet ringing; the sun has just risen!" (and the sun had indeed just risen) "Usually the Mass precedes the kiss of peace, not the kiss of peace the Mass. So let the Mass which is to precede it take place first." "I'm lame, I can't celebrate Mass, and we have no other priest; who should celebrate it?" "Who should celebrate it but I, the high mistress of the porcine order? I am, as is reported, an abbess in charge of three hundred nuns, but none of them has a voice equal to mine. My fame has spread beyond the ladies of Denmark, and has the abbess Salaura remained unknown to you, who live nearby? Wait until the right hour arrives and I'll sing a woodland Mass that you yourself will marvel at!"

"I've heard about your rule, godmother; now listen to mine. (One good turn deserves cheerful repayment by another!) It's a bell of flesh, not of brass, that tells me the time. The signal is not given me by a bell, but by my capacious gullet. My stomach, not the sun, is my indicator of time; should it happen that it gives the order, I sing what I have learned. If I were willing to rely constantly on the sky for the times

Credere si vellem semper mea tempora caelo,
    quando sub inductis nubibus hora foret?
55 Nunc nox atque dies aequato examine pendent,
    defaecat nimium prodigus exta sopor;
visne ministerium celebrem tam luce modo alta,
    quam propter sancti festa Iohannis ago?
Aestivae lucis nocte hac michi tertia visa est,
60   cum canerent galli carmina prima senes.
Taliter arguerent tua tintinnabula tempus?
    Omnia servo intus nullaque signa foris.
Tam meus iracunda movet michi cimbala venter,
    nocte quoque ut media, ni pudor obstet, edam;
65 nec fuit horarum clanga experientior usquam,
    etsi fudisset papa Suavus eam.
Incipe, quod nosti, non curo carmen agreste
    an silvestre canas, si placet hora tibi;
pace data faciam, ne nostro discrepet usu.
70   Sin autem, dico tempus adesse meum.
Papa parum, maneas missam abstima pransane, curat;
    sobrius en ego sum, pax mea labe caret.
Ergo, michi dilecta simul matrina sororque
    (praeter enim missam singula nosco satis),
75 tantum lene ferens quantum lucrare reluctans,
    nostra tibi pax est experienda semel.
Sed quid verba iuvat pacem praeeuntia nosse,
    si dederit misere lator ineptus eam?
Si cui iactari probitas sine crimine posset,
80   edidici pacem ferre decenter ego.
Tanta meae pietas et tanta peritia pacis
    (hoc infra medium notificabo diem),

of day, when would the service be sung if the sky were over-
spread with clouds? At the present time, night and day are   55
evenly balanced in length, and a lengthy sleep empties out
one's innards to a quite excessive degree—and do you want
me to celebrate divine office only when the sun is as high as
it is when I do so on Saint John's day? Tonight, when the old   60
cocks were crowing Prime, it seemed to me the equivalent
of Terce in summertime. Would your bells tell the time in
this way? I keep all my alarm bells inside and none of them
outside. My stomach rings such angry bells inside me that
I'd eat in the middle of the night too, if shame didn't forbid
it. No bell was ever more active in telling the hours, even   65
one cast by a Swabian prelate. Begin on what you know—I
don't care if it's a Mass of the woods or the fields—if the
hour suits you; once the kiss of peace has been given, I'll see
to it that it isn't out of line with my own practices. If you   70
won't do it, I declare it to be time for *my* Mass. The bishop
does not care whether you remain fasting before Mass or
eat, but as for me, I haven't eaten anything, and my kiss of
peace is without taint. So, my beloved godmother and sister
too, just try my kiss of peace once (for I am expert in lots of
things besides how to celebrate Mass), submitting to it as   75
meekly as you are reluctant to take it. But what use is it to
know the words that preface this kiss, if its clumsy of-
ferer gives it badly? If it were possible for anyone to boast
of his own virtues without incurring reproach, I could say   80
that I have learned to implant the kiss of peace very ele-
gantly. So great is the warmth and the expertise of my kiss
(as I'll make known before the day is half over) that I bestow

ut mea matrinis et neptibus oscula figam,
    saepius exiguis grandia frusta trahens.
85 Experieris idem, neu quartum deesse queraris,
    candelabra super sto tria firmus adhuc!"
"Quandoquidem, frater, scis tempus adesse, canatur,
    sed nequeo cantum promere sola gravem.
Huc ades immorsamque michi preme fortiter aurem,
90   ut tua concussis dentibus ora crepant.
Confratres quorum spissa ac promucida dentes
    occulit elata voce vocabo meos;
oscula sacra quibus securo astringere labro,
    cum dandae pacis venerit hora, queas.
95 Oscula praebenti vereor tibi reddere morsum;
    vix inhibent dentes tenuia labra meos."
"O veniant fratres, quorum est promucida pinguis!
    Spissum aliquod sequitur pinguia labra latus."
Haec tacitus secum; prensa mox aure Salauram
100   fortiter angebat, sus levat acre melos.
Sus super aequa levans monacordum iura canebat
    altius et falso sex diapente sono;
Allobrogas pretium si speret carminis omnes,
    clangere tam nequeat tenuiter ipse Satan.
105 "Officium, matrina, probo, sed scandis inepte;
    deficies media voce, remitte fidem!"
"Hospite te, frater, festivius organa clangunt;
    rarus es hic, ideo clarior oda sonat.
Officium laudas, aliter graduale sonabit;
110   donec conveniat contio nostra, mane!

my kisses on godmothers and granddaughters, and get from them large mouthfuls more often than small ones. You'll 85 find this yourself. And don't be sorry that I lack a fourth candlestick, I still stand firm on my three!"

"Since you are certain that the hour has arrived, brother, let the singing begin—but I can't produce the strenuous chant all on my own. Come here and seize my ear in a bite so strong that your mouth clatters with the clashing of teeth, 90 and with raised voice I'll summon my brethren, whose snout is thick and covers their teeth. On them, you can press your sacred kisses without any danger to your lips, when the time comes for giving the kiss of peace. I'm afraid that I might 95 give you a bite when you offer your kisses, since my thin lips hardly constitute a guard on my teeth." "Oh let your brethren, whose snout is plump, come! Fat lips are accompanied by a plump flank"—this he said silently to himself. Without delay he seized Salaura's ear and squeezed it violently. 100

The sow raised a harsh melody; tuning her vocal chords above the proper level, she sang in a cracked voice six fifths higher. If he were hoping for all Burgundy as a prize for a song, the devil himself couldn't sing more shrilly. "I ap- 105 prove of your introit, godmother, but you are singing improperly high. You will falter in midvoice; slacken your strings a bit!" "Brother, the polyphonic song takes on a specially festive character when you're my guest. You're a rare visitor here, and so the song rings out more splendidly. You praise the introit, but the gradual will sound different; wait until our company has assembled. And we don't, if by 110

Nec, si forte roges, comitamur cantibus Anglos.
　　Musica ter ternos fertur habere modos,
bisque plagis binis distinguitur ordo tonorum—
　　nescio quis legem rusticus hancce dedit—
115　at vetus in nostro iam musica viluit usu.
　　Terminat undenis musica nostra tonis;
armoniam quandoque damus ter quinque modorum,
　　isque solet nostri carminis esse tenor:
Becca michi cantum sesqualterat, inde Sonoche
120　　vocis epytritae pondera subtus agit.
Baltero vero baco, pronepos meus, Anglicus ybris,
　　quid, villane, putas, qualiter ille canit?
'Cunctipotens' quotiens poscunt encaenia sive
　　'Alleluia' petit festus herile dies,
125　hic grossum diapente tonat sub voce Sonoches,
　　et modulos Beccae duplicat ore gravi.
Dum sic organici damus intervalla melodis,
　　alternat dulcem contio mira liram,
cetera turba modos confusa lege vagantes
130　　ordine Romano deprimit atque levat.
Eia nunc stringas, si quid sapis, acrius aurem;
　　proxima prosperitas, quam tibi quaeris, adest!"
Vix angente lupo vocem dabat illa secundam,
　　audiit infesti Becca magistra gregis.
135　"Proh, proceres! Proh, cara soror!"—nil addidit ultra.
　　Undecies senos concutit ira sues;
undique "Proh!" frendunt, "Proh! Proh!" Frendore iuvatur
　　cursus, agi penna, non pede, quemque putes.
Non aliter trepidum clamore ac turbine mundum
140　　proculcare ruent Gog comitante Magog.

chance you were to ask, follow the English in our singing.
Music is said to have nine intervals, and the system of modes
is embellished by four of the plagal sort. I don't know what
oaf laid down this rule, but the old music has fallen into con- 115
tempt in our practice: our music has finals in eleven modes,
and sometimes we produce a melody of fifteen intervals.
And this is usually the tenor of our chant: Becca sings a fifth
below me, and Sonoche sustains the part of the voice a 120
fourth below hers. As for the fattened pig Baltero, my great-
grandson, the English hybrid, what do you imagine, you ig-
noramus, is the way he sings? As often as festivals of dedica-
tion call for an 'Almighty God,' or a feast day demands a
special 'Alleluia,' he thunders out loudly a fifth below So- 125
noche's voice, and repeats Becca's notes at a lower pitch.
While we are thus diaphonically following the chant mel-
ody at our different intervals, our wonderful choir chimes in
with us in sweet song, the rest of the crowd singing the wa-
vering melodies at a higher or lower pitch in a totally undis- 130
ciplined order, according to the Roman rite. Now, if you've
any sense, you'll squeeze my ear more severely—the good
fortune you're seeking is at hand."

Hardly had she given voice for the second time at the
wolf's nip than Becca, mistress of the dangerous band, heard
her. "Oink, noble pigs! Oink, my dear sister!"—she added 135
no more. Anger stirred sixty-six pigs. "Oink!"—with teeth
gnashing on all sides—"Oink!" Their running was spurred
on by their grunting; you'd have thought each of them was
borne on wings, not feet. Just so will Gog and his compan- 140
ion Magog come stampeding with shouts and confusion to

Porcellus Cono, proles generosa Salaurae,
     ter septem iunctus fratribus ante volat;
utraque Cononis matertera, quinque Sonoche
     subsequitur natis Beccaque freta decem;
145 pignoribus septem fidens Burgissa subibat,
     quam dicunt amitam, Cono, fuisse tuam;
Baltero postremus ruit instigatque ruentes
     sex generos, fratres quattuor, octo nurus.
Hos lupus infelix ut vidit rictibus amplis
150   spumosam rabiem fundere, flare minas,
offendi terram fremitu, molirier ornos
     impete, diriguit, non stetit absque metu.
Esse sibi, qualem dare venerat ipse, daturos
     fingebat pacem; cessit ab aure parum.
155 Risit scropha nocens: "Utquid, vesane, relinquis
     officium? Persta, stringe parumper adhuc!
Pax perlata fere est; forsan, ni strinxeris aurem,
     me cantante nichil cassa caterva redit."
"Cantavit tua turba satis, didicere profecto
160   tollere clamose carmina prima nimis."
"Siccine tu credis nostros cantare sodales?
     Erras, frater, adhuc contio nulla sonat.
Comperies cantum, cum venerit hora canendi.
     Ut video, templum rarus inire soles.
165 In templis taciturna praeit confessio missam;
     rure licet positi, nos imitamur idem.
Murmure submisso sua nunc delicta susurrant,
     inde canent luco vix patiente sonum."

trample down the terrified world. The piglet Cono, the noble offspring of Salaura, flew ahead, accompanied by twenty-one of his brothers. Both Cono's aunts, Sonoche and Becca, followed after, Sonoche backed up by five of her children and Becca by ten. Burgissa, who is reported to be your great-aunt, Cono, came along, backed up by her seven offspring. Last of all galloped Baltero, urging on four brothers, six sons-in-law and eight daughters-in-law as they ran.

When the hapless wolf saw them, pouring forth foaming rage from their wide jaws, hissing threats, the earth shaken by their roaring and ash trees torn up in their charge, he stiffened, and found it hard to stay upright without fear. He imagined that they were about to administer to him just the same sort of peace that he had come to impart himself. He let go of the ear a little, and the malicious sow said mockingly: "Why are you abandoning your job, idiot? Keep going, carry on nipping it a little! The kiss of peace is almost delivered; if you don't nip my ear and I sing nothing, maybe the crowd will be disappointed and go home again." "Your congregation has sung enough; they've certainly learned to recite Prime over-noisily." "Do you think that's the way our fraternity sings? You're wrong, brother; so far the congregation hasn't uttered a note. You'll recognize the singing when the hour for song arrives; I see that you're not used to enter a church very often. In churches, a quiet confession precedes the Mass; although we're located in the countryside, we imitate this practice. At the moment they're whispering their sins in a subdued murmur; afterward they'll sing so that the wood will hardly hold the sound."

Vix bene finierat crudelis scropha loquelam,
170 Cono ferit miseri posteriora senis,
et frustum praegrande rapit de clune sinistra.
 Oscula iuravit prava fuisse lupus:
"Tam subito primae qui pacis repperit horam,
 devoveant illum Roma Remisque simul!
175 Ordine legitimo pacem rebamur agendam,
 sed nescit rectum rustica turba sequi.
Nonne magister eram vita senioque verendus?
 Aetatem superat sola Salaura meam;
rerum ergo series si vobis recta placeret,
180 ore meo primum pax tribuenda fuit."
"Si tibi rennuero pacem, Ysengrime, secundam,
 prima velim peius, quam michi poscis, eat!
Ne primam invidia ferar importasse vel ira,
 foederis haec nostri testis et obses erit.
185 Nec timeas! Ubi prima iacet, non figo secundam;
 accipient pacem singula membra suam.
Nescieram, donec prorupit mentio pacis,
 missa quod a nobis esset agenda tibi;
eia nunc audi, quid epistola sacra loquatur!"
190 Bisque fere, quantum dempserat ante, tulit.
Affirmant Britones dextra de clune putatum,
 quantum tresse solet vendere cerdo Remis.
"Lectio finita est, cantum modo fortiter omnes
 tollite, sit nullus, qui reticere velit!
195 Accipe quaesitum, frater carissime, carmen!
 Sic, ubi sacrantur templa vetusta, canunt;
hoc graduale boni nos edocuere Suavi."

Hardly had the cruel sow come quite to the end of her speech before Cono crashed into the rear end of the wretched old man and tore a great chunk out of his left buttock. The wolf swore that this was a lousy sort of kiss. "Let Rome and Reims together curse whoever it was who so abruptly pitched on the moment for giving the first kiss! I thought the kiss was going to be administered in the proper sequence, but this oafish crowd of peasants doesn't know how to perform anything right. Wasn't I a teacher, and should I not be revered for my age and my way of life? Only Salaura exceeds me in age, so that if you had complied with the proper order of business, the kiss of peace should have been given first from my mouth." "If I refuse you a second kiss, Ysengrimus, may the first one have worse consequences than you call down on me! Lest I be said to have implanted the first in envy or anger, this second one will be a testimony and pledge of our friendship. Don't be afraid! I won't place the second one where the first is situated; all your limbs will get their own kiss. I didn't know, until the mention of the kiss of peace came up, that we were supposed to conduct a Mass for you—but now listen to what the holy Epistle has to say!"—and he took off almost twice as much as he had removed before. As much, say the Britons, was lopped off his right buttock as is usually sold for three pence by a tanner in Reims. "The Lesson is finished; now let everyone raise a loud song; let there be no one willing to keep silent! Dearest brother, accept the song you have longed for. This is how they sing when old churches are consecrated; the virtuous Swabians taught us this gradual."

Protinus in monachum tota caterva furit.
Sed grex multus erat, dumque omnes vellere quaerunt,
200 iam medius lato stat lupus orbe procul,
circumstentque licet pressa statione coacti,
ad plenos ictus copia nulla datur.
Ultima divellit solos promucida villos,
praevalidi quidam frustula parva trahunt.
205 Incipit irasci monachus nec vulnera, quamvis
parva forent, laeto corde ferenda putat.
Pulsibus aspiciens offendi Baltero fratrem
semotus giro clamitat ista iocans:
"Quid facitis, stulti? Sapitis nichil, unde venitis?
210 Creditis hunc ludum posse placere michi?
Hospitibus caris sic vos cantare soletis?
Hostibus hoc vestris, non michi, debet agi.
Sic cantetur ei, qui sic graduale notavit,
gaudeat et cantor carmine sicut ego!
215 Luditis ut fatui, male luditis, iste profecto
ludus villanos vos probet esse reos.
Colligere egregie socios didicisse putatis,
colligitis sane sicut agreste pecus!
Quas super hoc ludo grates sperare potestis?
220 Ludus omittatur, dum liquet esse bonum.
Heu, genus illepidum, fugite hinc! Nisi protinus iste
desierit ludus, non ego lene feram.
Venimus huc, matrina, tuo, fidissima, ductu,
meque tibi recolis saepe fuisse pium;

Immediately the whole crowd let loose its fury on the monk. But the herd was numerous, and since they were all seeking to have a tug, the wolf stood in the middle of a wide-extending circle, and although, as they stood round, they were crammed together by the closeness of their positions, there was no scope for major onslaughts. The snout that was farthest away tore out only a few hairs, although some of the strongest pulled off a few little chunks. The monk was beginning to get angry, and although the injuries were only minor, he didn't think they were to be borne cheerfully.

Baltero, seeing that the brother was hurt by these jabs, moved out of the circle and playfully called out the following: "What are you doing, fools? Don't you have any sense where you come from? Do you think this sport can give me pleasure? Is this how you are accustomed to sing to your cherished guests? This treatment ought to be given to your enemies, not to me—let this song be sung to him who set the gradual to such music, and let the cantor have the same pleasure in his song as I do! You're playing around like fools; you're playing a nasty kind of game—in fact, this game proves you to be lower-class thugs. You think you've learned how to entertain your friends splendidly, but actually you entertain like wild brutes! What thanks can you expect for this game? Let the game be left off while it's clearly going well. Unmannerly race, get out of here! Unless this game comes to a stop right away, I won't take it lying down. We came here, most loyal godmother, under your guidance, and you remember that I have always been kind to you.

225 hos age Iudaeos, iocus hic malus incipit esse,
          ne peior fieri possit, abire iube!
     Nolo diu duret iocus hic, pro me anxior, ante
          quam scierint, possunt laedere me; oro, veta!
     Quando quid incipiunt ratione tenacius urgent—
230   pessima quae potuit monstra cacare Satan!
     Divide nos subito, propera intercurrere nobis;
          offensam ludus forsitan iste parit."
     Quo suus hanc pronepos intendit Baltero sannam,
          noverat in primo cauta Salaura sono.
235 "Suffer, amice, graves cruciatus corde quieto;
          constantes animas carnea poena beat.
     Fortiter et longum aedituus vasa aerea tundit,
          dum sperat plena lucra futura manu.
     Ut salves animam, tormentis subde cadaver;
240   verberat electos ira benigna dei.
     Nec furor hos saevire facit, dilectio suasit
          hoc opus, ut poenas hic patiare tuas.
     Si quid habes culpae, gauderes pendere vivens;
          post obitum cruciant longa flagella reos.
245 Denique venisti moriendi nescius istuc;
          hoc praeter solum cuncta peritus eras.
     Mors tibi discenda est, non delibabere morti—
          nolo feras mortem sed doceare mori.
     Discere nunc debes, qui doctor saepe fuisti;
250   virga aliis fueras, nunc tibi virga vacat."
     Suspensus senior, quis tam lugubre seorsum
          plangeret, haerebat mente oculoque vagus.

Call off these Jews! This is beginning to be a bad joke; order 225
them to go away so that it doesn't get worse. I don't want
this joke to last long; I'm worried for my own safety. They
could hurt me before they were aware of it—tell them not
to, I beg! When they begin on anything, they pursue it past
all reason—the worst monsters that Satan could shit! Sepa- 230
rate us at once, hurry up and come between us. Perhaps this
sport will lead to an injury!"

The wily Salaura had recognized at the first word where
her great-grandson Baltero was aiming this mockery.
"Friend, bear your heavy torments with serenity of spirit! 235
Bodily pain beatifies the souls that remain steadfast, and the
sacristan strikes the brass bells loud and long when he hopes
that profits in abundance will come of it. Subject your body
to tortures so that you may save your soul. The kindly wrath 240
of God chastises his elect, and it is not anger that makes
these people rage—it is love that prompted this action, so
that you might suffer your torments here. If you are guilty in
any way, you should be glad to pay the penalty while you're
alive; the wicked are tortured by lengthy scourgings after
death. And finally, you came here without any knowledge of 245
death; you were expert in everything except this alone. You
must learn about death, but you won't be given up to it en-
tirely. I don't want you to suffer death, but to be taught how
to die. You, who have often been a teacher, must now be
taught. You were a rod for others, and now the rod is applied 250
to you."

The old man was baffled, his mind and eye flitting about,
uncertain who had uttered such a doleful lament from a

449

Baltero suspicitur post Beccae terga, senemque
    respicit irridens: "Frater, ubi esse putas?
255 Hic tibi fautores sperabas affore paucos,
    speratis plures (ne verearis!) habes:
nempe ego nunc collega tibi fidissimus assum,
    Beccaque te multum, scropha fidelis, amat.
Distractus paulo ante tui meminisse nequibas;
260   quo tibi erat, pro te qui loqueretur, opus.
Hactenus ergo dabam verbum, quasi tutemet essem,
    clamque apud hos omnes Becca gerebat idem.
Quod si scire libet, cur convellaris ab istis,
    contendunt, primum quis tuus hospes erit.
265 Nescit iniquus homo panis meminisse comesti;
    nos opis acceptae non meminisse piget.
Saepe coegisti scisso velamine nostros
    currere cognatos in penetrale tuum;
ergo tuam mavult pars nostri scindere vestem,
270   quam, quo vis, si vis, ire sinare semel.
Elige, nobiscum maneas invitus an ultro;
    nil nisi te raro nos penes esse queror."
Talibus intento seniore subassilit atque
    eradit laevum callida Becca pedem.
275 "Gaudeo vosque velim michi congaudere, sodales!
    Non hodie quoquam noster amicus abit.
Arrabo, quam michi quaero, datur pes iste manendi;
    hunc dedit et plures sponte dedisset adhuc."
(Sus partim mentita fuit; dedit ille profecto
280   sponte pedem, sed non sponte manebat ibi.)
Ysengrimus humi velut oraturus in ora
    labitur, accedit dulce Salaura rogans:

distance. Baltero, having been spotted behind Becca's back, mockingly returned the old man's gaze. "Brother, where do you think you are? You were hoping that you might have a few supporters here, but don't be afraid, you have more than you hoped! For indeed I am here as your loyal associate, and Becca, the faithful sow, is very fond of you. You were torn this way and that a little while ago, and couldn't quite recollect yourself, so it was necessary for someone to speak for you. So up to now I've been speaking as if I were yourself, and without letting on, Becca did the same in front of everyone. And if you want to know why you're tugged about by this lot, they're quarreling about who first shall be your host. It's a wicked man who forgets the bread he's eaten; we are glad to remember the favors we have received. You've often forced our kindred to rush into your inner sanctum, their coats torn off their backs, so some of us prefer to rip *your* coat off rather than that you should on any occasion be allowed to go where you wish—if you do wish. Choose whether you'll stay with us under duress, or of your own free will; my only regret is that you are so rarely among us."

While the old man was attending to these words, the crafty Becca leaped on him and tore off his left foot. "I rejoice, and I want you to rejoice with me, friends! Our friend isn't going anywhere today; this foot is granted me as the pledge I wanted that he will remain. This he gave, and would willingly have given more." (The sow was lying in part; he certainly was willing to give up his foot, but it wasn't willingly that he remained.) Ysengrimus fell to the ground on his face, as if about to pray, and Salaura came up, asking

255

260

265

270

275

280

"Obsecro pro me etiam, domine abba, precare, merebor;
    matrinae veteris quaeso memento tuae!
285 Scilicet hoc saltem nostri memorabere signo,
    accipe!"—et invisum perfodit illa latus,
multifidumque extraxit epar. "Germana Sonoche,
    aspice, quod fecit perfidus iste nefas!
Glutierat librum, quo pax oblata daretur,
290 et michi latorem se fore pacis ait!
Inventus liber est, omnes admittite pacem!"
    Indubium senior sensit adesse necem.
"Illepidam rabiem, stulti, frenate, bisiltes!
    Mortiferum nostis vulnus inesse michi;
295 mors Mahamet patienda michi est! Ignobile letum
    unius indultu conciliate precis:
cedite dumtaxat, donec ventura prophetem.
    Effugere amisi, cedite quaeso parum!"
Ceditur, ille canit, plaudit fortuna canenti,
300 prona nocere aliis, non bene velle seni.
"En morior, nec vita potest michi longior esse;
    exequiis celebris nox erit ista meis!
Prospera mors misero numquam tardare roganda est;
    mors omnes miseros pensat honesta dies.
305 Octo dies pariter numquam laeto omine vixi;
    nunc pressere meum pessima fata caput.
Interitum turpem celebris vindicta secundat;
    turpiter emoriar, vindicer ergo probe.
Expleat hoc Agemundus opus, foris ille pudendae
310 arbiter est, mortem vindicet ille meam.
Hoc equidem non est ingens in daemone virtus,
    sed, quaecumque potest, perficit absque dolo.

meekly: "I beseech you to pray for me too, my lord abbot, and I'll deserve it; I beg you to remember your old godmother! Receive this token, so that by it, at least, you'll remember me!"—and she bored through his detested side and gouged out his ruptured liver. "Sister Sonoche, see what a crime this traitor has committed! He said he was going to offer me peace, and he'd swallowed the charter by which the offered peace might be granted! The charter has been uncovered, so now let everyone receive the peace." The old man felt that death was certainly upon him. "Put a stop to your loutish savagery, you stupid pigs! You know that I have my death wound; the death of Mohammed is to be my fate. Compensate for this shameful end by the granting of one prayer: draw back at least until I can prophesy the future. I've lost the power to run away; draw back a little, I beg!"

They withdrew, and Fortune smiled on his prayer, not out of benevolence to the old man but out of readiness to harm others. "Lo, I am dying, and my life can last no longer; this night will be consecrated by my funeral. One who is in misery has no reason to ask for the deferment of an honorable death; a splendid end outweighs all the days of wretchedness. I have never lived a week of good luck together, and now the worst of all fates has put an end to my life. But a glorious vengeance compensates for an ignoble death. I shall die meanly, so let me be nobly avenged. Agemundus shall fulfill this task; he is the ruler of the arsehole, and he shall avenge my death. Of course, there isn't a great deal of power in this demon, but he does whatever he can without

285

290

295

300

305

310

453

Dedecore ille novo genus impleat omne Salaurae;
    ultor in extremam saeviat usque tribum.
315 Hactenus admoto claudebat pollice portam,
    pollice semoto postmodo pandat iter,
turpibus ut ventis numquam impetus absit eundi;
    laxentur patulae nocte dieque fores.
Haec somnum, haec vigiles, aerumpna haec laedat edendo,
320 nec siliquam capiant hac sine labe brevem.
Flatibus ergo malis obstacula nulla resistant,
    nec tenui strepitu sibilet aura nocens,
ut caveant homines et, quem prope laeserit aer,
    verberet infidum devoveatque genus!
325 Pars hominum probro non inferiore prematur
    (moribus insignes excipiuntur herae).
Obsequa si fuerit stirpis quid nacta prophanae,
    segnities illam continuata premat;
nox hiberna brevis miserae videatur, ut orto
330 sole ter undecies surgere iussa neget;
saepe inter scapulas vestita recumbat itemque
    descendat toto semiparata thoro;
recidat in spondam, non excussura soporem,
    ter nisi sit dominae poplite pulsa suae;
335 brachia tunc costasque humerosque et crura femurque
    timporaque et collum strennuus unguis aret!
Inter mulgendum citra nimis usque vel ultra
    subsideat variam lacte tenente viam;
pars tunicae, pars stillet humi, pars influa multro,
340 imputet hoc sedi dissideatque loco;
tunc meus astringat fallaciter ostia daemon,
    pressa parum laxans et prope laxa premens,

double-dealing. Let him cover the whole race of Salaura with new shame, and let his vengeance rage against even the last of her tribe. Up to now, he stopped their orifices by holding his thumb over them; in future, let him take his thumb away and clear the exit, so that the power to go forth is never lacking to their foul gusts—let the exits stand wide open night and day. Let this nuisance harass their sleep, their waking, their feeding, and let them not consume so much as a little husk without this drawback. So, let no obstacles put a check in the way of these ill winds, and let the noxious air whistle with no small sound, so that men may be warned, and may anyone who has been near enough to feel the ill effects of the fumes beat and curse the treacherous race. Let a portion of human beings be afflicted by no less a shame (ladies of genteel behavior are exempted). If there is a maid who has picked up anything from this impious race, let continual torpor oppress her; let a winter's night seem short to the wretched girl, so that when the sun has risen she refuses to rise, although ordered to do so three-and-thirty times. Let her often lie down again once she's got her clothes over her shoulders, and then get off the bed again half-dressed in her shift, and again let her drop on to the couch, unable to shake off sleep without being repeatedly nudged by her mistress's foot. Then let her mistress's busy fingernails furrow her arms, her ribs, her shoulders, her legs and thighs, her face and neck! At the milking let her always sit too near or too far off, so that the milk comes in a wobbling stream; let part drop on her dress, part on the ground, part flow into the milk pail. Let her blame this on the stool, and move her position. Then let my demon constrict her orifices deceptively, opening them a little when closed, and shutting

315

320

325

330

335

340

ut, quotiens sellam demoverit obsequa, longo
    eruptu luctans horreat aura foras.
345 Rarescat butirum super illo lacte, levique
    attactu laedens ustulet ignis idem.
Mos suus emulcta bove saepe resopiat illam;
    excutiat plenum dum pede vacca cadum;
futile sit multrum, sit futilis obba, putrescant
350 lacte sinus, colae limus inesto iugis;
non expectata dormitum nocte recurrat,
    dormiat officii nullius ante memor.
In lare quodcumque est utensile sive supellex,
    esto vagans, sparsim singula iacta cubent:
355 straba supinetur, transversa cathedra iaceto,
    prodeat aut redeat sospite nemo genu;
urceus, olla, lebes, coclear, lanx, pelvis, aenum
    scrutaque diversae sparsa vagentur opis;
integra mane, eadem sint vespere fissa; reliquit
360 sana cadens Titan, fissa videto redux!
Haec dabit ille meae daemon solatia morti—
    amplius est illi non potuisse datum."
Finierat senior, verum fortuna prophetam
    illius auxilio daemonis esse dedit,
365 cuius ut accipitris rostrum, iuba sicut equina est,
    catti cauda, bovis cornua, barba caprae,
lana tegit lumbos, dorsum plumatur ut anser,
    ante pedes galli, post habet ille canis;
sub quo posteritas premitur dampnata Salaurae
370 et mulier stirpis quaeque quid huius habens.
"Audi, quid iubeam, domine Ysengrime propheta:
    nulla umquam nonna est nomine functa meo,

them when they are almost open, so that when the maid
moves the stool, the air may shudder forth, struggling, in a
long outburst. Let butter evaporate from that milk, and let   345
fire set it aflame, harmfully, at the slightest touch! When the
cow has been milked, let habit send her off to sleep again,
until the cow kicks over the full bucket with her foot. Let
the milk pail be leaky, let the bucket leak too, let her apron   350
front stink with old milk, let there always be dirt clogging
the strainer. Let her hasten back to sleep without waiting
for nighttime, and let her snooze without thinking of any
chores. In the house, let every utensil and piece of furniture
be out of place, and let everything lie tossed about in con-
fusion. Let the footstool lie on its back, and the chair re-   355
main overturned—let no one come or go without banging a
knee. Let water jug, pot, kettle, spoon, plate, basin, copper,
and the scattered debris of various objects swirl around. Let
those things which were intact in the morning be broken by
evening, and what the setting sun left whole, let him see   360
smashed on his return! These consolations will this demon
bring to my death—the power to do more is not granted to
him."

 The old man had ended, and Fortune allowed him, with
the help of that devil, to be a truthful prophet—that devil   365
whose beak is that of a hawk, whose mane is horselike, with
the tail of a cat, the horns of an ox, and the beard of a goat.
Wool covers his loins, and his back is feathered like a goose;
he has the feet of a cock in front, and those of a dog at the
rear. He it is who afflicts the cursed posterity of Salaura, as   370
well as every woman who has any features of that breed.

 "Listen to what I ordain, Dom Ysengrimus the prophet.
No nun has ever borne my name, and no prophet yours. So

nemo tuo vatum. Mutetur nomen utrimque:
  sis michi tu Ionas et tibi Cetus ego.
375 Ecce prophetatum satis est, tibi sicut amico
  dicitur: in musac proiciere meum.
Ingredere ergo meam felix alacerque tabernam;
  impensum sumptus omne remitto tui.
Nec, quibus hibernum possis expellere frigus,
380 defectura tibi ligna timebis ibi,
nec duce me vectus Niniveam tendis ad urbem;
  non in suspecta te regione vomam,
sed, donec securus eas ac sponte, quiesces,
  istud amicitiae pignus habeto meae!
385 Tam celeris nulli provenit gloria sancto,
  si crepere hunc probitas immoderata daret.
Primum sacra suis emergunt corpora tumbis,
  clarescunt signis, inde levantur humo,
denique vulgantur scripto commissa feretris.
390 Dissimiles meritis non decet unus honor:
hi post fata diu, tuque incassabere vivens;
  nec famam meritis praebet arundo tuis,
scimus enim, iam sanctus ades, iam dignus inire
  scrinia, iam pleno dignus honore coli!
395 Si scires, ratio quam congrua suadeat illud,
  ut vellem peteres, si facere ipsa negem,
nam scriptura refert quod amari debeat hostis,
  omnis amans hostem dignus amante deo est.
Hoc ago praeceptum; si quonam quaeris in hoste,
400 quis michi ventre meo verior hostis obest?
Me flagris, me saepe minis, me pulsibus infert;
  hunc, rea ne fiam perditionis, amo.

let there be a change of names in both of us: you can be my
Jonah and I'll be your whale. See now, that's enough prophe-   375
sying. I say to you as a friend that you are about to be thrust
into my collection box. So enter my inn joyfully and eagerly;
I let you off all charges for what you consume. And you
needn't be afraid that you will there lack wood with which   380
you can drive away the winter cold, nor that under my steam
you'll be carried in the direction of the city of Nineveh. I
won't spew you up in a dangerous country. On the contrary,
you shall lie low until you can leave safely and of your own
accord; accept this pledge of my friendship! Glory never   385
came so speedily to any saint, even if he were fairly bursting
with excessive virtue. First, the holy bodies emerge from
their tombs; they make themselves famous through mira-
cles, so they are raised out of the earth. Then they are placed
in reliquaries, and publicized in writing. One and the same   390
honor is not appropriate for those who differ in merit: they
are enshrined long after their death, you, while you are alive.
Nor shall the pen win renown for your merits, for we know
that you are a saint while you are still among us, that you
are already worthy to enter a reliquary, already worthy to be
honored with unstinting veneration! If you knew how fit-   395
ting is the reason that prompts it, you would request me to
be willing to do it if I myself were to deny it, for scripture re-
lates that one should love one's enemies, and everyone
who loves his enemies is worthy of God's love. This pre-
cept I fulfill. If you ask, in respect of which enemy?—then   400
who is a truer enemy to me than my stomach? Often does
it attack me, with scourges, with threats, with blows; it I
love, so that I may not be condemned to perdition. And

Namque hic cuncta mei devastat lucra laboris;
  quod vi, quod furtim, quod paro iure, vorat,
405 quodque magis dulce est, hoc offero laetius illi,
  ut plenum sacro pectus amore geram.
Sanctior hoc amor est, quo purius hostis amatur,
  nec michi te excepto carior hoste quis est.
Ergo ego proposui carum committere caro;
410 quam michi complaceas, experiare velim.
Tu michi dilectus dilectum intrabis in hostem,
  ut mea saepe hostem stirps tibi cara tuum.
Utque sacer discurrat amor, nos ibis in omnes;
  non mereor tanta sola salute frui.
415 Conditus ergo simul dignis donabere capsis;
  notitiam meritis hoc epygramma dabit:
  VNVM PONTIFICEM SATIS VNVM CLAVDERE MARMOR
    SVEVERAT. EX MERITO QVISQVE NOTANDVS ERIT.
  VNDECIES SENIS IACET YSENGRIMVS IN VRNIS.
420   VIRTVTVM TVRBAM MVLTA SEPVLCRA NOTANT.
  NONO IDVS IVNIAS EXORTV VERIS IS INTER
    CLVNIACVM ET SANCTI FESTA IOHANNIS OBIT."
Tunc epar ereptum crudelis scropha voravit.
  Irruit in reliquum turba cadaver atrox;
425 discindunt miserum, citiusque vorata fuisse
  frustula dicuntur quam potuisse mori.
Avellit diafragma simul cum corde Sonoche,
  fisa sigillatae pacis habere notam:
"Becca, quid hic habeo? Deus hoc dedit, amodo sane
430 pace sigillata fungimur, ecce vide!
Sorbuit ut librum pacis, sic iste sigillum."
  Elicuit guttur cardine Cono cavum;

moreover, it makes mincemeat of all the fruits of my labor; it devours whatever I get by force, by theft, or by right. Whatever is sweetest, I offer to it most willingly, so that I may bear a breast swollen with holy affection. This love is the holier, the purer the affection for the enemy; no one, you excepted, is dearer to me than this enemy. So I have decided to entrust one loved one to another; I want you to find out how dear to me you are. You, who are dear to me, shall enter my dear enemy, as my dear family often did into your enemy. And so that this holy affection may spread, you will come into all of us; I am not worthy to enjoy such great good fortune by myself. So you'll be buried and placed in worthy reliquaries all at the same time. And this inscription shall publicize your merits: ONE MARBLE TOMB USED TO BE ENOUGH TO ENCLOSE ONE BISHOP. BUT EVERYONE MUST RECEIVE THE DISTINCTION APPROPRIATE TO HIS MERITS. YSENGRIMUS LIES IN SIXTY-SIX URNS. THE MANY TOMBS SYMBOLIZE HIS MULTIPLICITY OF VIRTUES. ON THE NINTH IDES OF JUNE, AT THE BEGINNING OF SPRING HE DIED, BETWEEN CLUNY AND THE FEAST OF SAINT JOHN."

Then the cruel sow gobbled up the torn-out liver, and the savage herd rushed on the rest of the body. They tore the wretch to pieces, and the morsels are said to have been devoured quicker than he could have died. Sonoche tore out his diaphragm, together with his heart, confident that she had traces of the sealed charter of peace. "Becca, what have I got here? God has granted this—from now on we've got possession of the sealed document of the peace; look here! He'd swallowed the seal, just as he had the charter of peace." Cono pulled out the hollow gullet from its ligament.

"Glutierat, socii, flatricem pacis et ipsam,
    ne quid perfidiae deforet, iste tubam.
435 Cornicinor pacem, matertera, tuque sigillas,
    mater habet librum, pax modo plena viget."
Taliter interiit miser Ysengrimus; ego autem
    ut notam scripsi, credulus esto legens!
Vix michi, quam penitus periit, si dixero, credes;
440 ut michi credatur, vix memorare queo.
Parte minus minima porci superesse tulerunt,
    si fuerit partes sectus in octo pulex.
"Cana genas annis, sed mentem canior astu,
    omnes te sequimur, fare, Salaura soror—
445 dicitur hic abbas olim praesulque fuisse,
    quamquam noluerit pectoris esse boni;
qualibus impensis honor exequialis agetur?
    Nil prosunt animae dona precesque malae,
perdita namque anima est; sed honestas publica mundi
450 exequias celebres et sacer ordo petit!"
"Becca soror, michi crede, licet meus iste sit hostis,
    si semel implesset quod probitatis opus,
non me auctore foret privandus honore sepulcri!
    Hunc scelerum numquam paenituisse liquet,
455 ordinis ergo sacri pereat reverentia, postquam
    occubuit, cuius vita nefanda fuit.
Numquid, apostolici quod erat collega senatus,
    promeruit Iudas exequiale decus?
Quo magis alta tenet nequam, magis ima meretur,
460 et bonus ex humili surgit ad alta loco.
Extulit Ysaydes frontem diademate regni,
    disperiitque deo proiciente Saul.

"Friends, he had swallowed the very trumpet to blow for the peace, just so that no act of treachery would be missing. I'll trumpet the peace, aunt, you have the seals and my mother the charter; now the peace can have its full force."

In this way did the wretched Ysengrimus die; at any rate let the reader give credence to my record of the event! You'll hardly believe me if I were to tell how utterly he perished; I can hardly speak in such a way as to be believed. The pigs allowed less to survive than the least portion of a flea that has been cut into eight parts.

"Sister Salaura, your cheeks are hoary with age, but your mind is even hoarier with cunning. Speak! We all follow you. This man is said to have been at one time an abbot and a bishop, although he wasn't of a virtuous disposition; what should we spend on performing his funeral honors? Alms and prayers are no good to a wicked soul, for the soul is damned, but the public decency of the world at large, and his holy order, call for solemn funeral rites." "Sister Becca, believe me, although he is my enemy, if he had on any occasion performed a work of virtue, he wouldn't be deprived of the honor of a tomb at my instigation! It's clear that he never repented of his crimes, so let reverence for the holy order be extinguished, after the death of someone whose life was an abomination. Or do you think Judas deserved funeral honors because he was a member of the company of apostles? The higher a wicked man climbs, the more he deserves to be abased, while a good man rises from a humble position to the heights. The son of Jesse exalted his head to a king's crown, while Saul was destroyed, overthrown by God.

435

440

445

450

455

460

Perfidus hic itidem, non curo praesul an abbas,
    quam prius ascendit, tam modo vilis erit.
465 Has decet exequias illud, quo papa dolosus
    Christicolas Siculo vendidit aere duci—
proh pudor in caelo! Dolor orbe! Cachinnus Averno!
    Regna duo monachus subruit unus iners!
Eohe me miseram! Quam novi flebile verbum,
470   cur adeo linguae frena relaxo meae!"
"Cara, refer nobis, germana, nec occule tactum,
    quicquid id est, verum ne recitare time!"
"Cara soror, Boreas, Oriens, Occasus et Auster
    comperit ac deflet, nec tibi monstra patent?
475 Qui vos ergo lues, nisi non mansistis in orbe,
    quae nullum potuit clima latere soli?"
"Christicolae populi collectas novimus iras
    barbariem contra concaluisse procul;
hic satis est nostras rumor perlatus ad aures,
480   felicemque homines creditur isse viam.
Consilio et iussu papae sua seque dederunt
    casibus incertis arbitrioque dei.
Cur ergo perhibes, quia vendidit? Immo redemit
    Christicolas omni crimine papa bonus!"
485 "Cara soror, nimium clamas, reminiscere sexus;
    maereat exultet femina, clamor obest.
Rem tetigi, tetigisse piget, sed quaelibet ortum
    postquam res habuit, non habuisse nequit.
Incidit attonitam lacrimosa tragoedia mentem,
490   quam posset vates vix superare Maro.
Quod si me premeret penuria nulla loquendi
    parque modus calami materiaeque foret,

Just so, this traitor—I don't care whether he is bishop or ab-
bot—will now be as contemptible as he was previously ex-
alted. What would be right for his burial is the cash for   465
which the crafty pope sold Christians to the duke of Sic-
ily.—Oh, disgrace to heaven! Grief to the world! Laughter in
hell! One feeble monk has overthrown two kingdoms! Ah,
woe is me! How lamentable is the tale I have heard, which   470
is the cause of my loosening the bridle on my tongue in
this way!" "Dear sister, tell us, and don't conceal what you've
mentioned; whatever it is, don't be afraid to relate the
truth!"

"Dear sister, North, South, East and West know and weep
over these monstrosities, and are they unknown to you?
If you were living anywhere on earth, how could a disaster   475
which could remain secret in no corner of the world be
hidden from you?" "We know that the stored-up anger of
Christian people had become inflamed against heathendom
in distant lands. This rumor had indeed been brought to
our ears, and it is thought that some men had set out on a   480
blessed journey. By the pope's exhortation and decree, they
surrendered themselves and their property to uncertain ac-
cidents and to the will of God. Why then do you assert that
the good pope sold them? Rather, he redeemed the Chris-
tians from all sins!" "Dear sister, you're making too much   485
noise, remember your sex. Whether a woman is sad or
happy, noisiness isn't nice. I touched on this matter, and I'm
sorry to have touched on it, but once begun, an affair can't
be un-begun. My mind is numbed by a tearful tragedy, which   490
the poet Virgil himself could hardly master. Even if no pov-
erty of expression hindered me, and the nature of my pen

immemor esse suae non debet femina sortis;
   vincula naturae rumpere nolo meae.
495 Femina sit reverens, quamvis praeclara loquentem
   hunc sexum nimio non decet ore loqui.
Dissecor in bivium, non haec omnino taceri
   convenit, et non sum talibus apta modis.
Hoc igitur ritu, qui nobis competit, utar:
500   iure sibi innato femina flere potest;
materiam fletu, sexum sermone tuebor,
   et tenuis maesto planget avena sono.
Coniugis extincti sic fortia facta modeste
   flet referens coniunx strennua flensque refert."
505 Plancturae graviter cari pro morte Salaurae
   Reinardus veluti voce dolentis ait:
"Domna Salaura, tui singultus detege causam!
   Nescio cur, species sed tibi flentis inest.
An patruo violenta meo fors contigit usquam?
510   Si super hoc doleas, ede, dolebo simul.
Dic, Cono, reticet mater tua" (namque tacebat
   anxia, principium carminis unde trahat).
"Dic michi, Cono, precor, quid habet mea domna doloris?
   Evenit patruo quid nisi dulce meo?
515 Nil ego vos novi laturos tristius esse,
   ni fallor meriti vos meminisse putans."
(Sic, quasi nesciret Reinardus facta, rogabat,
   omniaque agnorat, cominus inde latens.)

were equal to that of my subject, a woman ought not to be forgetful of her lot. I don't wish to break the bonds of my nature. A woman is to be modest; it is not fitting for her sex to speak with too ready a tongue, however excellent the things it produces. I am torn in two directions: it's not good to keep completely silent about this, and on the other hand, I'm not fit for such activities. So I'll adopt that practice which suits us: according to the laws of her nature, a woman is allowed to weep. I'll pay respect to my subject matter in my weeping, and to my sex in my speech, and my little reed will quaver with a mournful sound. So a wife gently weeps as she relates the mighty deeds of her dead husband, and relates his heroisms as she weeps."

As Salaura was about to weep bitterly for the death of her loved one, Reynard said to her, in the accents of a mourner: "Lady Salaura, reveal the reason for your tears! I don't know the reason for it, but you look as if you are weeping. Has a violent accident of some sort befallen my uncle? If this is what you are grieving for, tell me, and I shall grieve with you. Speak, Cono, your mother is silent!" (for she remained silent, through doubt as to where she should begin her speech). "Tell me, Cono, I beg, what sorrow is it that my mistress suffers? Has something unpleasant happened to my uncle? I know that there is nothing you would take harder, unless I am mistaken in my belief that you were conscious of his merit." (Thus did Reynard inquire, as if he didn't know what had happened, but he had been lying hidden nearby and had seen everything.)

"Non hodie ad missam, frater Reinarde, fuisti?
520   Festa tibi curae debuit esse dies!
Quae te causa, miser, fecit tam sero venire?
    Missa hodie est patruo saepe iterata tuo.
Desiit esse malus, mores proiecit iniquos;
    nil sceleris faciet postmodo nilque doli."
525 "Ergo obiit? Certe? Proh, patrue dulcis, obisti?
    Heu tumulum sine me, patrue care, tenes?
Addite me patruo! Miseri subducite cippum!
    Commoriar patruo, vivus inibo lacum!"
"Frater, tumba prope est, accede, rotaberis intro:
530   exilem nobis praebuit ille cibum."
"Falsificabo prius, quaecumque Salaura loquetur;
    —nescio quae siquidem dicere falsa parat—
et cras ingrediar vivus patruelae sepulcrum;
    laude caret probitas immoderata nimis."
535 "Frater, si patruum, sicut testaris, amasti,
    nunc patruo dulci contumulandus obi.
Propositum felix dilatio saepe resolvit;
    libera sit virtus, prodeat absque mora.
Nil nisi non fieri virtus concepta timeto.
540   Incide, dum pietas aestuat alta, necem!"
"Non dicar furiis, sed amore in fata salisse;
    actio cor stultum praecipitata probat.
Mentibus in pravis virtus concepta tepescit,
    at michi mens eadem cras hodieque manet.
545 Tempore vera fides interlabente calescit;
    mens furiosa tepet, qua levitate calet."
Postquam conticuit vulpes et tota Salaurae
    contio, vox tristem solvit amara liram.

"Weren't you at Mass today, brother Reynard? A feast day 520
ought to be of some importance to you. What cause made
you come so late, you wretch? Today the Mass has been read
over your uncle many times. He has left off his wicked life
and cast away his evil habits; he won't do anything wrong or
treacherous from now on." "So he's dead? Truly? Alas, sweet 525
uncle, are you dead? Ah, dear uncle, are you in the tomb
without me? Unite me with my uncle! Lift the stone from
the wretch! I shall die with my uncle, I shall go alive into the
pit!" "Brother, the tomb is close by; approach and you'll be
tumbled into it. He has provided us with a little snack." 530
"First of all I'll prove wrong what Salaura is going to say—
since she's about to tell some falsehood or other—and to-
morrow I shall go, alive, into my uncle's tomb. Virtue is not
to be praised when it's carried beyond limits!"

"Brother, if you loved your uncle as you claim, die now 535
and be buried with your sweet uncle. Delay often weakens a
good resolution; if virtue is not obstructed, let it proceed to
action without delay. Let virtue, once initiated, fear nothing
except being unfulfilled. Embrace death, while your affec- 540
tion burns high." "Let me not be said to have leaped to my
doom out of frenzy, but out of love. A rash action gives evi-
dence of a foolish heart. In base minds, virtue cools after its
seed has been sown, but my mind remains the same from
yesterday to today. True loyalty grows warmer with the lapse 545
of time; a passionate spirit cools as easily as it kindles."

Then the fox, and the whole of Salaura's herd, fell si-
lent, and her mournful voice gave vent to this melancholy
song: "It's easy to attempt to find out, by sinning, how long

469

"Quam longum divina ferat patientia sontes,
550   peccando facile est quaerere, nosse grave est.
Iudicis asperitas magno anticipanda timore est;
   optima peccatis est medicina timor.
Ubere si laqueos proventu gratia nondum
   conterit, hoc saltem est allicienda modo.
555 Sint hodie sordes, metuatur poena Gehennae,
   et miser in vitiis horreat esse sini.
Qui metuit parce, pravos non diligat actus;
   nolle timere malum, peius amare mala est.
Qui non sponte cadit, miserabilis esse videtur;
560   labentes ultro sistere nemo cupit.
Protinus alternant certamen flebile, prave
   hinc transgressor agens, hinc deus acta ferens,
donec perversos ultra, quam parcere iudex
   devovet, in poenas exigat aequa dies.
565 Lis ea saepe habita est inter mundumque deumque,
   et quasi devicto pessima palma deo.
Quid referam Sodomae foetores atque Gomorrae,
   quod commisit Adam, quod iugulator Abel?
Quid Noe fluitantis aquas animosque gigantum,
570   Niliacas pestes et Pharaonis iter?
Impia quid Datan et Abyron factaque Choreque
   inque heremo varias agmina passa neces,
splendentis vituli scelus et male manna cupitum?
   Quid Balaam fraudes insidiasque Balac,
575 Amalechitarum, Iericho, Ismaelis et Assur,
   atque Philistaeos Antiochique manus?
Quid, cum saevierit fornax Chaldaea lacusque
   et quem non homines ut timuere ferae?

God's patience will suffer criminals—but difficult to know 550
the answer. The judge's severity is to be forestalled by the
operations of great fear; fear is the best medicine for sins. If
divine grace, in its abundant outpouring, does not yet set us
free from sin entirely, it is at least to be elicited by these
means. If the present times give evidence of depravities, let 555
the penalty of hell be feared, and let the wretch shudder to
be allowed scope for his vices. Anyone who has felt a little
fear shouldn't be fond of wicked deeds; unwillingness to be
afraid is bad, but to love wickedness is worse. Anyone who
falls unwillingly appears pitiable, but no one is willing to 560
catch those who stumble of their own accord. A lamentable
struggle is waged continuously—on one side, the sinner act-
ing wickedly, and on the other, God suffering his acts—until
the day of judgment summons to their punishment those
who continue to be evil beyond the point at which the judge
decides to spare them. This struggle between the world and 565
God has been waged from the beginning of time, and it
seems as if God is conquered, and comes off worst. Why
should I mention the foulnesses of Sodom and Gomorrah?
Or what Adam did, or the murderer of Abel? Or the waters
on which Noah floated, and the characters of the giants, the 570
plagues of the Nile and the expedition of Pharaoh? The im-
pious deeds of Dathan, Abiram and Korah, and the hosts
that suffered destruction of different kinds in the desert?
The crime of the glittering calf, and the manna wickedly
desired? The deceits of Balaam and the traps of Balak, of 575
the Amalekites, of Jericho, Ishmael and Assyria, the Philis-
tine and the hosts of Antiochus? Or the time when the fur-
nace and the lion pit of Chaldea wreaked their fury, and
him whom men did not fear so much as the wild beasts?

471

Quid torrens Cison, quid cladis comperit Endor,
580   pestibus hic populos, hic cecidisse fame?
Quid Canadae gemitus pravorumque ydola regum?
    Quis secuit vatem? Fataque tristis Heli?
Quid tulit Helias, altare quis inter et aedem
    et qui sub duplici vate ruere viri?
585 Et quae praetereo mundi portenta nocentis,
    ne desperato fine vagetur opus?
Finiit has tandem vindex sententia lites;
    noluit omnipotens saecula prava pati.
Mittitur humano discretor corpore saeptus,
590   qui paleas urat puraque grana legat.
Mittitur Emmanuel, quem si Iudaea sequatur;
    si minus, in tenebras, quas meruere, ruant.
Addictus post probra cruci est, diffunditur ergo
    blasphemae toto plebis in orbe furor.
595 Ex hoc dura manus punit, non sustinet hostes;
    haec est, quae miseros obruit, ira gravis;
numquam venturi cassa expectatio Christi,
    exilium, tenebrae morsque salute carens.
Plectuntur sontes nec, quem vicere ferentem,
600   iratum possunt exsuperare deum.
Immodice parcens manet immoderabilis ultor;
    quique diu tulerat, nunc sine fine ferit.
Non ergo Hebraeos miror gentesque perire,
    quos praeiudicii poena tenacis habet,
605 non secus in mundo quam daemones ante creari;
    insita confectos vindicat ira reos.

The slaughter to which the brook Kishon and to which En-
dor was witness, or the people falling now through plagues,   580
and now through hunger? The groans of Canaan and the
idols of the wicked kings? Who clove the prophet in two?
Or the fate of poor Eli? What Elijah suffered, or who fell be-
tween the altar and the temple, and what other men fell in
the times of the two prophets? And what other monstrosi-   585
ties of the cruel world do I pass over, lest my account should
ramble on in despair of a conclusion?

At last a punitive sentence put an end to this strife; the
Almighty was unwilling to endure the wicked world. The as-
sessor was sent, enclosed in human flesh, to burn the chaff   590
and gather in the purified grain. Emmanuel was sent, if Is-
rael was willing to follow him; if not, they were to plunge
into the hell they had deserved. After shameful treatment
he was given over to the cross, and so the frenzy of the blas-
phemous people was spread through the whole world. Be-   595
cause of this, his severe hand punishes, rather than toler-
ates, enemies; this is the weighty anger which casts down
wretches. The expectation of Christ's coming, entailing ex-
ile, captivity and death without salvation, will not prove a
vain one. The guilty are punished, and cannot triumph over   600
God now he is angry, although they overcame him when he
was patient. He who is merciful beyond measure is implaca-
ble as an avenger, and having long endured, he now strikes
back without ceasing. So I am not surprised that the Jews
and the heathen perish, subjected to punishment for their
obstinate offense, nor that devils are created in the world   605
just as they were once before; the wrath which has been im-
planted in God takes vengeance on the guilty by destroying
them. I lament the fact that those who have accepted the

Qui sumpsere fidem, quibus est baptisma tributum,
　　involvi prisca perditione queror.
Prima crucis satio messem dedit ubere fructu;
610　　vinea labruscas multiplicata tulit.
Paulatim reprobo coepit rarescere mundo
　　spiritus excessu corripiente sacrum.
Prorupit Satanas vitiosum liber in orbem,
　　omniaque in scelera est irreverenter itum.
615　Saecula dampnavit rursum polluta creator,
　　pura tamen bonitas usa tenore suo est:
noxia non subito zizania messuit ense;
　　horribiles longum praefremuere minae.
Praenorunt miseri, non excusare sinuntur.
620　Indicium mundi machina trina dedit:
transsumpsere suas elementa ac tempora leges,
　　deseruitque prior non loca pauca situs.
Aestive transivit hyemps, hyemaliter aestas;
　　intorsit tonitrus, fulminat udus Ilas.
625　Mulciber hibernus combussit templa domosque;
　　severunt hyemem Carchinus atque Leo.
Instar parmarum cristallos Saxo iacentes
　　repperit in campis obstupuitque suis;
extimuit glaciem, qui tutus staret in enses,
630　concutiente novo fortia corda metu.
Duruit in terram mare, terra liquatur in aequor;
　　piscibus accessit campus, harena satis.
Evasit discrimen aquae pro navibus utens
　　nantibus in fluctu plurima turba casis.
635　Prodigium refero, quod Fresia tota fatetur,
　　consolidatque agri sessor agerque fidem.

faith, and on whom baptism has been bestowed, have envel-
oped themselves in their primitive state of damnation. The
first sowing of the cross brought in a harvest of abundant
fruit; the vineyard, as it multiplied, bore wild grapes. Gradu-   610
ally, the Holy Ghost has absented himself from this wicked
world, and in departing takes religion with him. Freed from
his chains, Satan has burst forth into the depraved world,
and the road to all kinds of crime is shamelessly followed.
The creator has once again condemned the polluted times,   615
and yet his unsullied goodness has held to its usual course;
he has not cut down the harmful tares with a hastily wielded
blade. Terrible warnings have for a long time been rumbling
a prelude, and the wretches have had advance knowledge;
they are not allowed an excuse. The threefold structure of   620
the world has furnished a sign: the elements and the sea-
sons have transposed their natural laws, and many features
of the landscape have shifted their original position. Winter
has become summery and summer wintry; the watery Hylas
hurls down thunder and lightning. Vulcan has burned down   625
houses and churches in winter; Cancer and Leo have pro-
duced cold. The Saxon has found hailstones the size of
shields lying in his fields, and been terror-struck. The one
who would have stood confidently in the face of swords is
terrified by ice, and a new fear shakes brave hearts. The sea   630
has solidified into land, the land is dissolved into sea; the
field has given way to fish, and the beach to crops. Great
numbers of people escaped the peril of the water by using
houses, swimming in the flood, as boats. I'm recounting a   635
marvel which all Friesland speaks of, and whose truthful-
ness is confirmed by both the land and its possessor. When

Demolitus agrum cum possessore domoque
    protulit externi pontus in arva viri,
publica litigium tandem censura diremit:
640   incola, cuius humum nemo videbat, abit,
quique superficiem fundi vellusque superne
    vendicat, hic liber iudice plebe sedet.
(Hoc in iudicio non sensit Fresia rectum:
    qui dominus fundi, legitime esset agri.)
645 Excussit templis ingentia tigna trabesque
    et longinqua tulit ventus in arva furens.
Fugit inextincta populus sua tecta favilla,
    et repsit gemina vix ope tutus homo;
vix applosa solo tenuerunt corpora fortes,
650   horruit ingenti turbine terra tremens.
Nocte sub hiberna Phoebi radiantior ore
    cernitur arctoum flamma cremare polum.
Noctibus innumeri bello concurrere soles,
    sanguineus limphas horrificasse rubor.
655 Bis latuit taeter Titan, causamque latendi
    non soror aut nubes terreave umbra dabat.
Omnia dixerunt clades elementa futuras,
    nec tetigit tantus pectora dura pavor."
Coeperat abbatissa loqui lugubria flendo,
660   et lacrimae imbuerant milibus octo solum.
Auribus ut surdis foret intolerabile verbum,
    clamor ad undecimum venerat usque polum.
Excidium mundi plancturam triste Salauram
    corripuit vulpes: "Stulta Salaura, sile!
665 Praescio, quid penses: sceleris dampnare dolique
    pontificem Latium, perfida porca, cupis.

the sea destroyed the land and carried its possessor and his home into the fields of another, a public judgment finally put an end to the dispute. The farmer whose land was no 640 longer visible withdrew, and the one who claimed the building on the land, and its upper accouterments, remained in free possession, in the judgment of the people. (Friesland didn't understand what's right in this judgment; whoever is owner of the land, should legitimately be owner of its produce.) A furious wind tore down huge rafters and timbers 645 from churches and swept them into distant fields. The people fled their homes with the fire still burning, and men tottered along, hardly preserved by having the strength of two; the strongest could hardly sustain their bodies, stricken to the earth, when the trembling earth shuddered with the 650 mighty hurricane. In the winter's night, a flame brighter than the face of the sun was seen scorching the northern sky. At night, numberless suns clashed together in battle, and a bloodred color disfigured the waters. The hideous sun 655 twice disappeared from view, without the moon or clouds or the earth's shadow giving cause for his disappearance. All the elements proclaimed the destruction to come, and yet obdurate hearts were not touched by this great fear."

The abbess was weeping as she uttered her lament, and 660 her tears had wet the ground for a distance of eight miles. Her utterance would have been intolerable even to deaf ears, her wail having gone up to the eleventh heaven. The fox reproved Salaura as she was about to lament the sad decay of the world. "Shut up, stupid Salaura! I already know 665 what you're thinking: you want to condemn the bishop of Rome for wrongdoing and deception, treacherous swine.

Dicere vis, quia dux Ierosolmam Aethneus ituros
    Christicolas timuit per sua regna gradi;
papa ergo Siculi ducis aere illectus utroque
670   Argolicum populos carpere suasit iter,
casibus atque dolis Graiorum immissa famique
    regna duo monachus subruit unus iners.
Praeter quos pelagi rabies et pesticus aer
    et fraus Argolidum perdidit atque fames,
675 in convalle virum duo milia somnus et imber
    enecuere, altis undique saepta iugis.
Improba, tu nescis, hoc quare papa benignus
    fecerit! Ausculta, cognita dico tibi:
dimidiare solet nummos ignobile vulgus,
680   et dirimit sacram rustica turba crucem.
Hoc scelus est ingens, hic mundi pessimus error;
    taliter errantes papa perire dolet.
Qui secat ex nummis obolos, in frustula mille
    cotidie hunc Satanas dividat ense suo!
685 Scit bonus hoc pastor stolidasque in devia labi
    et per opaca trahi compita maeret oves.
Salvificare animas omnes vult papa fidelis;
    caelitus est illi creditus omnis homo.
Idcirco aes Siculi sumpsit, Francique tyranni,
690   Angligenae et Daci et totius orbis avet,
omnes namque animas hominum salvare laborat,
    quaque licet, dirum vult abolere nefas.
Non valet, ut vellet, totum delere reatum;
    qua sinitur, scindi stema salubre vetat.
695 Materiam minuit signum caeleste secandi,
    quamvis non valeat tollere prorsus eam.

You're going to say that the duke of the volcanic region was afraid to let the Christians pass through his realm on their way to Jerusalem, so the pope, seduced by the gold and silver of the duke, persuaded the people to take the road through 670 Greece, and one feeble monk overthrew two kingdoms, giving them up to hunger and misfortunes and the cunning of the Greeks. Besides those who were destroyed by the fury of the sea and the pestilence-laden air and hunger and the deceit of the Argolids, sleep and a storm killed two thou- 675 sand men, in a closed valley, surrounded by high hills on all sides. Impudent creature, you don't know why the benign pope did this! Listen, and I'll tell you what is known about it. The common people are in the habit of cutting pennies in half, and thus the ignorant multitude destroys the holy 680 cross. This is an enormous crime, this is the worst of worldly errors. The pope is sorry that those who err like this should be damned. May Satan with his sword daily split into a thousand pieces anyone who cuts pennies into ha'pennies! The good shepherd knows this, and grieves that his stu- 685 pid sheep wander astray and are led up darkened paths. The faithful pope wants to save every soul; heaven entrusts every man to him. So he took the money of the Sicilian, and would like that of the French king, the English, the Danish, 690 and of the whole world, for he labors to save the souls of all men, and wishes to destroy abominable evil wherever possible. He is not able to uproot all evil, as he would like to, but where he is allowed to, he puts a stop to the cutting up of the sacred image of salvation. He reduces the mate- 695 rial for cutting up the heavenly symbol, although he is unable to take it away completely. On this understanding he

479

Hoc tulit aes Siculum pacto et pietatis eodem
    totius immensas tolleret orbis opes.
Aes sibi non rutilum, non aes desiderat album;
700   vult sibi commissum salvificare gregem.
In sua quot librat thesauros scrinia, servat;
    non creat inde obolos, integra quaeque tenet.
Pontificem ergo pium cur proditione nefanda
    arguis? Ignoras, quod bene nosse putas!
705 Patrue care, iaces! Utinam efficerere superstes;
    obloquium fatuae non paterere suis.
Innocui papae fieres spontaneus ultor,
    stultitiam linguae penderet ista suae!"

took the Sicilian money, and on the same charitable under-
standing he would take away the vast wealth of the whole
world. He doesn't want money, whether gold or silver, for
himself; he wants to save the flock entrusted to his charge.   700
Whatever treasures he throws into his chests, he keeps; he
doesn't make ha'pennies out of them, he keeps everything
whole. So why do you accuse the merciful pope of an execra-
ble treachery? You are ignorant of what you think you know
all about!

Dear uncle, you lie dead! Would that you were made the   705
survivor of us two! You would not suffer the slander of this
stupid pig. You would become a willing avenger of the inno-
cent pope, and she would pay for the folly of her tongue!"

Appendix

Sources and Analogues

I include below brief indications of classical or early medieval sources for the individual episodes of *Ysengrimus,* as well as indications of their appearance in the *Roman de Renart* and the *Fables* of Marie de France, where applicable. References following the title of each episode are relevant classification numbers in vol. 3 of Adrados, *History of the Graeco-Latin Fable* (where H. = the section comprising fables in Hausrath's collection of Greek fables, not-H. = Graeco-Latin fables not in Hausrath's collection, and M. = medieval Greek and Latin fables), and in Dicke and Grubmüller, *Die Fabeln des Mittelalters und der frühen Neuzeit* (cited as DG). Both Adrados and Dicke and Grubmüller provide brief summaries of the fables and full bibliographical details of their occurrence in literary sources.

 1. *The Bacon-Sharing* (M.512)
  Predecessors: see Booty-Sharing, below
  Successors: *RdR* V 1–148; cf. XV 101–298
  —— *Fox Shamming Dead* (M.490; DG 206)
  Predecessors: Bestiary (see McCulloch, *Bestiaries,* 119–20); Isidore, *Etymologies* 12.2.29; Sedulius Scotus, *Carmina* 57

Successors: *RdR* 3.43–138, 7.750–70, 11.618–729, 13.868–89, 13.2264–309, 14.555–89; cf. 11.1093–1348

2. *The Fishing* (M.269; DG 224)
Predecessors: ———
Successors: *RdR* 3.377–510

3. *The Field-Division* (M.139, 245; DG 648)
Predecessors: cf. Avianus 18; Babrius 44
Successors: *RdR* 20

4. *The Court of the Sick Lion* (H.269; M.233; DG 599)
Predecessors: *Aegrum fama fuit; Ecbasis captivi* 392–1097
Successors: *RdR* 10.1–99, 1153–1704; Marie de France 69

5. *The Pilgrimage* (M.349)
Predecessors: ———
Successors: *RdR* 8
——— *Ass on the Roof* (not-H. 230)
Predecessors: cf. Babrius 125
Successors: ———

6. *The Fox and the Cock* (M.175; DG 187)
Predecessors: Alcuin, *De gallo; Gallus et vulpes;* Ademar Fable 30
Successors: *RdR* 2.1–664; Marie de France 60–61

7. *The Wolf in the Monastery* (M.257, 509; DG 634)
Predecessors: *De lupo; Ecbasis captivi; Fecunda Ratis,* Prora 1554–67
Successors: *RdR* 3.165–376; cf. 8.126–134, 6.704–30, 14.202–524; Marie de France 82
——— *Rape of the Female Wolf* (M.390)
Predecessors: ———
Successors: *RdR* 2.1027–1396; cf. Marie de France 70

8. *The Horse and the Wolf* (H.198; M.221; DG 393)
Predecessors: Babrius 122; *Romulus vulgaris* 3.2
Successors: *RdR* 19

9. *The Sheep and the Wolf*
Predecessors: ——
Successors: ——

10. *The Booty-Sharing* (H.154; M.464; DG 402)
Predecessors: *Romulus vulgaris* 1.6; *Fecunda Ratis,* Prora
1311–27; cf. Prora 1174–89
Successors: *RdR* 16.721–1506; cf. Marie de France 11A–B

11. *The Oath* (M.508)
Predecessors: ——
Successors: *RdR* 14.969–1088; cf. *RdR* 1b 2909–86,
10.369–522

12. *The Death of the Wolf* (M.510)
Predecessors: Embrico of Mainz, *De mahomete*
Successors: ——
—— *Mass Used to Call for Assistance* (M.104, 266; cf. DG
652)
Predecessors: ——
Successors: Marie de France 94

Works Cited

Ademar: *Ademaro di Chabannes, Favole,* ed. Ferruccio Bertini and Paolo
Gatti. *Favolisti Latini Medievali,* III, Università di Genova, Pubblicazi-
oni del Dipartimento di Archeologia, Filologia Classica e Loro Tra-
dizioni. Genoa, 1988.

*Aegrum fama fuit: Die Gedichte des Paulus Diaconus: Kritische und erklärende
Ausgabe,* ed. Karl Neff. Quellen und Untersuchungen zur lateinischen
Philologie des Mittelalters, 3.4, pp. 191–98. Munich, 1908.

Alcuin, *De gallo* ("Dicta vocatur avis"): *Poetae Latini Aevi Carolini,* vol. 1, p. 262, ed. Ernst Dümmler. Berlin, 1881.

———: translated in Ziolkowski, *Talking Animals,* 241.

Avianus: in *Minor Latin Poets,* ed. and trans. J. Wight Duff and Arnold M. Duff. Loeb Classical Library, rev. ed., 2 vols., 2:669–749. London, 1935.

Babrius: *Babrius and Phaedrus,* ed. and trans. B. E. Perry. Loeb Classical Library. London, 1965.

De lupo: ed. Ernst Voigt, in *Kleinere lateinische Denkmäler der Thiersage aus dem zwölften bis vierzehnten Jahrhundert.* Quellen und Forschungen zur Sprach- und Culturgeschichte der germanischen Völker 25, pp. 58–62. Strasbourg, 1878.

———: ed. Friedrich Walter Lenz. "Bemerkungen zu dem Pseudo-Ovidischen Gedicht *De Lupo." Orpheus* 10 (1963): 21–32.

Ecbasis captivi: Ecbasis cuiusdam captivi per tropologiam, ed. K. Strecker, Scriptores rerum germanicarum in usum scholarium. Hanover, 1935; repr. 1977.

———: *Ecbasis cuiusdam captivi per tropologiam. Escape of a Certain Captive Told in a Figurative Manner. An Eleventh-Century Beast Epic,* ed. Edwin H. Zeydel [with English translation]. University of North Carolina Studies in the Germanic Languages and Literature 46. Chapel Hill, 1964.

Embrico of Mainz, *De Mahomete: Embricon de Mayence. La vie de Mahomet,* ed. Guy Cambier. Collection Latomus 52. Brussels, 1962.

Fecunda Ratis: Egbert of Liège: *Egberts von Lüttich Fecunda Ratis,* ed. Ernst Voigt. Halle (Saale), 1889.

Gallus et vulpes: ed. and trans. in Jill Mann, *From Aesop to Reynard: Beast Literature in Medieval Britain,* Appendix 4, 318–25. Oxford, 2009.

Isidore of Seville, *Etymologies: Isidori Hispalensis Episcopi Etymologiarum sive Originum Libri XX,* ed. W. M. Lindsay, 2 vols. Oxford, 1911; repr. 1966.

McCulloch, Florence. *Mediaeval Latin and French Bestiaries.* Rev. ed. University of North Carolina Studies in the Romance Languages and Literatures 33. Chapel Hill, 1962.

Marie de France: *Marie de France. Fables,* ed. and trans. Harriet Spiegel. Toronto, 1987.

RdR: Le Roman de Renart, ed. Ernest Martin. 3 vols. plus supplement. Strasbourg, 1882–1887.

Romulus vulgaris: Der lateinische Äsop des Romulus und die Prosa-Fassungen des Phädrus, ed. Georg Thiele. Heidelberg, 1910.

Sedulius Scotus, *Carmina:* in *Poetae Latini Aevi Carolini,* vol. 3, ed. Ludwig Traube. Berlin, 1896.

Abbreviations

Blaise = Albert Blaise, *Dictionnaire latin-français des auteurs chrétiens* (Turnhout, 1954)

Du Cange = Charles du Fresne du Cange, *Glossarium Mediae et Infimae Latinitatis, auctum a monachis ordinis S. Benedicti, cum supplementis . . . editio nova* (Niort, Fr., 1883–1887; repr. Graz, 1954)

Lewis and Short = Charlton T. Lewis and Charles Short, *A Latin Dictionary,* rev. ed. (Oxford, 1907)

Niermeyer = J. F. Niermeyer, *Mediae Latinitatis Lexicon Minus* (Leiden, 1976)

OLD = Oxford Latin Dictionary (Oxford, 1968–1982)

PL = Patrologiae Cursus Completus, Series Latina, ed. J. P. Migne (Paris, 1844–1864)

Voigt = *Ysengrimus,* ed. Ernst Voigt (Halle a. S., 1884)

Note on the Text

There are five surviving manuscripts that contain a complete (or once complete) version of the *Ysengrimus,* as follows:

A = Liège, Bibliothèque de l'Université 160A

B = Paris, Bibliothèque Nationale de France lat. 8494

C = Brussels, Bibliothèque Royale 2838 (mutilated)

D = Pommersfelden, Schlossbibliothek 12

E = Liège, Bibliothèque de l'Université 161C

In addition, a number of florilegia contain excerpts from the poem, and other works preserve quotations of a few lines (see Voigt, Introduction, xv; Mann, *Ysengrimus,* 188–89; Yates and Rouse, "Extracts"). The *editio princeps* was produced by Franz Joseph Mone (based on manuscripts A B E) in 1832, under the title *Reinardus Vulpes.* In 1884 Ernst Voigt produced a full critical edition, with the more appropriate title *Ysengrimus.* Voigt's text was the basis for my own edition in the series Mittellateinische Studien und Texte, published by E. J. Brill in 1987, with an accompanying English translation, full introduction on the poem's literary and historical aspects, and commentary. That edition follows Voigt's closely, but occasionally I adopted different readings or altered punctuation in a way that affected the meaning of the text. The present edition reproduces the text and translation in my 1987 edition, and I am grateful to Brill for giving permission to use them; however, spelling and punctuation have been altered to bring both text and translation into line with the DOML guidelines, and I have occasionally taken the opportunity to improve phrasing or correct a few typographical errors. For fuller details of manuscript readings and problems of interpretation, the reader is referred to Voigt's apparatus criticus and notes and to my own Commentary in the Brill edition. Like Voigt, I follow the seven-book division of the poem found in manuscripts A and B, whereas Mone followed the division into four books and twenty-four fables found in D and E (see Voigt, introduction, xvii and xix, and for a discussion of the different divisions of the work in the various manuscripts, editions, and translations, with a summary in synoptic form, see Knapp, *Tierepos,* 48–54).

Notes to the Text

369   Voigt places a comma after *hic,* rather than after *esuries,* and treats the whole line after *cras* as a parenthesis. My punctuation follows Mone.

919–20 Voigt places a comma after *sabbata,* and would interpret "there could be two Saturdays [in a week] and the Rhine could become the Elbe before . . ." etc. My repunctuation is in line with the comic combinations of time- and place-references elsewhere in the poem (see 3.688, 7.421–22).

Book 2

412   *bonus*] The reading of MS A; other MSS read *bonos,* and this reading is adopted by Voigt.

439   I have added the brackets in accordance with my interpretation of the line. Voigt and Schönfelder both take "licet" to mean "it is allowed," rather than "although."

Book 3

252   I restore *est,* the reading of all MSS, in place of Voigt's emendation to *es.*

372   Voigt punctuates after *devoveo,* but the absolute use of this verb would be unusual, and *tamen* suggests a simple contrast based on *stellas.*

440   Voigt's comma at the end of this line has been changed to a full stop.

506   In MSS C D E, the following lines are added at this point:

> Inter pontificem Geroldum teque vicissim
> per consanguineam dic michi, quaeso, fidem . . .

The reference is to Gerard, bishop of Tournai (1149–1166), who succeeded Anselm and was, like him, an abbot before his election.

700   Voigt places a comma after *est,* and takes *dicto* to mean "I repeat." I punctuate as Mone, and take *dicto* to be an ablative.

775–76   Voigt phrases this differently, placing a comma at the end of line 775, rather than after *dubitans.*

BOOK 4

267–68   Voigt interprets *notitia* as "distinguishing mark" and punctuates after *donat* rather than after *notitiam* and *ovanter.* The sense would then be "whoever is awarding marks of quality, this one rejoices in possessing it!" (*herilem* because it is fit for Bertiliana, the mistress of the house).

319   I take *quid* to mean "why," and therefore change Voigt's exclamation point to a question mark.

403   Voigt's punctuation makes this line continuous with the following one.

933   Voigt makes this line part of Reynard's speech and translates, "while your father embodied all arts, you possess none." I follow MSS A B D (and Mone) in ending Reynard's speech with line 932.

992   Comparison with 5.310 might suggest that *prendite* should be emended to *pendite;* but since MSS C D E read *prendite* at 5.310, perhaps it is the latter that should be emended.

BOOK 5

391   Voigt takes *quasi* with *monachus segnis,* rather than with *metuens.*

563   In punctuating after *intra,* Voigt goes against the manuscripts and has to assume that *tollere* is the object of both *sapit* and *parat*

("he seeks to shear the flock at the inner level"; this monk is preparing to remove the fleeces, because he doesn't know how to remove the wool). I have restored the phrasing that seems to make better sense.

818.1–18   These lines are found in their entirety only in MS B, where they appear between lines 817 and 818. They are entirely absent from MS A (lines 809–19 are written over an erasure, but Mölk reports that examination under ultraviolet light shows that the recopied text is identical with the original, and the recopying aimed to adjust incorrect spacing; "Fuchs und Wölfin," 517). In MSS C D E, lines 818.5–6, 9–10, and 15–18 are missing, and the remaining ten appear between lines 814 and 815. Voigt thought that the whole passage was an interpolation, arguing that the female wolf's sudden switch from anger to sexual enjoyment is inconsistent, but he seems to have been unaware of the regrettable medieval myth that women can enjoy rape once it is in progress. It seems more likely that these lines were omitted from MS A because of their indecent content. The presence of the guest/host motif that pervades the whole poem is a feature that favours the presumption of their authenticity. Mölk ("Fuchs und Wölfin") defends Voigt's view, and adduces in support the versions of the rape in Marie de France Fable 70 and in the *Romulus "LBG"* (a Latin recasting of Marie). However his flat assertion that Marie knew neither the *Ysengrimus* nor Branch 2 of the *Roman de Renart* (which he admits must derive from *Ysengrimus*), and that her version must go back to an earlier source, is highly doubtful (see Mann, *From Aesop to Reynard,* 10 n. 48, and 244).

1044   Voigt punctuates after *tempora* and takes *quam* to be a relative dependent on *hora*. I have preferred to take *quam* with *paratius,* since it seems less appropriate here than it does elsewhere to assume that the comparative is being used as a positive.

1080   Voigt punctuates "Quod tibi do, libum; suscipe . . ." ("what I give you [is] a cake; take [it] . . ."). I assume that *libum* is the antecedent of *Quod* and the object of *suscipe.*

BOOK 6

324   oculus *con. em.*: culus *all* MSS (*cŭlus* does not fit the meter, and Voigt has to assume a change in quantity; see his introduction, xxvii).

461   Voigt punctuates after *fortassis* rather than after *est*.

BOOK 7

112   Voigt's punctuation links this line with the preceding one, presumably taking *musica* to mean "their [i.e., English] music" rather than a generalizing statement.

300   Voigt inserted a comma after *nocere* and interpreted the line to mean that Fortune was generally eager to do harm and to be benevolently inclined only to others, not to the wolf. I follow the punctuation of the manuscripts and take line 300 as having a causal relation to 299: Fortune for once favors the wolf, not because she is relenting towards him, but because in doing so she can inflict more harm on others.

524   Voigt follows MSS A B in reading *scieris* and *dolet* ("you are to know that he won't do anything henceforth, and he suffers nothing"); the C D E readings yield better sense, however, and I have emended Voigt's text accordingly.

669   Voigt assumes that Salaura interrupts at this point and speaks for herself up to the end of line 676 (since the *Improba* at the beginning of 677 must clearly be spoken by the fox). Mone placed a similar interruption at lines 671–76. Since, however, Reynard begins putting words into Salaura's mouth at 667, there seems to be no reason why he should not continue to do so.

Notes to the Translation

Glosses are supplied here for single instances of words or meanings not found in either *OLD* or Lewis and Short; unfamiliar words used more frequently in the poem are included in the Glossary (pp. 535–37 below). For further documentation, see the notes and glossary in Voigt's edition of the *Ysengrimus*.

BOOK I

1 *Ysengrimus:* the first three syllables are long, and the stress falls on "-grīm-."

20 A medieval superstition held that one's luck for the day was determined by what kind of man, animal, or thing one first encountered.

27 Obizo, physician of Louis VI of France and teacher of medicine in Paris; died in 1138/1140.

29 The Camenae were water nymphs who came to be identified with the Muses.

35 The prophet Jonah, who was carried in the whale's belly.

39 A reference to the beating that Ysengrimus received in the pilgrimage episode, which precedes this episode in the sequence of fictional events, although related later (4.1–810).

46 *eant = pereant.*

48–50 The "Slavic drink" is a beating; for the metaphorical equation of drinks and blows, see Schwab, "Gastmetaphorik," 220–23.

51–52	The incident in which the fox rapes the wolf's wife and urinates on their cubs is related in 5.705–820.
56	*deterere:* "to deteriorate, get worse."
58	*adhiscere = inhiare,* "to gape open for."
72	Arabian gold was proverbial.
75	*circinare:* "to circle, move around" (compare Ovid, *Met.* 2.721).
76	Literally, "confident of having the game secure in his fist."
94	Literally, "three times eight nights."
101	Alluding to the Roman idiom *paenulam alicui scindere,* "to tear off one's traveling cloak; to urge one to stay." Compare 4.204, 7.267, and notes below.
113	*pocula:* literally, "drinks."
124	Scythians, Saxons, and Suevi are cited as examples of hostile barbarians.
138	Voigt understands the line to mean "must a mutual leave-taking follow immediately [as a consequence of my refusing your invitation]? Would not a few friendly words be in order before our separation?" I have preferred to take *alternum ave* as meaning "the opposite kind of welcome"; that is, refusal of the polite invitation leads to its repetition in the form of physical force.
181a	Voigt puts this half-line in quotation marks, but I have been unable to trace it as quotation or proverb.
187	*praependere:* "to prefer."
191	Compare Ovid, *Ars amatoria* 1.443.
201	On the significance of these references to bishop and abbot, see Introduction, pp. ix–xii.
209	*sublegere tramitem:* "to move stealthily along a path."
227	The meaning of *liquaster* is uncertain; see the entry in Du Cange and the entries in Voigt's glossary for *liquaster* and *liquare* (for which see 2.10, 6.382).
229	"A Greek willow" and "a Danish nun" are two examples of impossibilities.
242	*insectans = si insectaretur.*
257	*repplicare vices:* "to retaliate, respond in kind"; compare the use of *reddere vices* in Ovid, *Met.* 14.36.

260 *reflare:* "to draw breath"; compare the entry in Du Cange for *reflatare.*

271 *varia ambage meandi:* formed on the model of Ovid's "variarum ambage viarum" (used of the labyrinth), *Met.* 8.161.

274 *vinculum = volumen,* "a coil or winding."

280 *oblongare = oblongum incedere.*

283 *diludia:* "varying tricks."

288 *par habere = instar habere,* "to be as, have the powers/functions of."

297 Reynard comes back on the peasant's left side because he is turned away from it, looking over his right shoulder.

331–32 *ter . . . ter. . . . ter . . . ter:* a parodic imitation of a Virgilian formula; see *Aeneid* 2.792–93; 6.700–701; 10.685–86, 885–87.

355 *quaestor:* "someone who procures food and the other necessaries of life" for a monastery (Du Cange 2); since the fox procures the bacon for the wolf, who is a monk, he is appropriately referred to by this term. *aedem:* either "a church, chapel" (compare 4.25, 5.841, 7.19) or "a house" (compare 6.132), perhaps a traveler's hospice in the woods, like the one where the animal pilgrims stay (4.102).

365 A reference to the phrase "requiescat in pace," which closes the burial service.

366 *retorta:* "twisted rope."

395 Literally, "where you would drag the rope." *funem ducere =* "to command" (see the entry in Lewis and Short for *funis* 2a); for vernacular expressions founded on this idiom, see Singer, *Sprichwörter,* 1:161.

416 Literally, "mine, hanging broadly, is roomy in its oblong hollowness."

417 The bishop's court, or synod, exercised jurisdiction over all clerics.

432–34 See *Regula S. Benedicti,* chs. 34.2–4 and 43.13–14.

438 Literally, "the shadow of a ham is present." The phrase has a biblical flavor (compare Psalms 17:8 [Vulgate 16:8]; 57:1 [Vulgate 56:2]; Canticle of Canticles 2:3; Isaiah 49:2, 51:16; Hebrews 8:5, 10:1), which my translation aims to capture.

441–42   See *Regula S. Benedicti,* ch. 33.

453   Matthew 6:34.

455   *torques = retorta* (compare 1.366), "twisted rope."

457   See *Regula S. Benedicti,* ch. 7.

462   Apparently a free interpretation of *Regula S. Benedicti,* ch. 40.

465   At 457b–65a, the wolf, who is already quoting his hypothetical defense lawyer, has the lawyer quote himself; in 465b–69a, we return to the lawyer's final comments, and at 469b, we revert to the outer speech of the wolf, addressed to the fox.

467   The diocese of Tournai, to which the author seems to have belonged (see 5.109–10), was part of the archdiocese of Reims; the archbishop's court at Reims was therefore superior to the bishop's, and the papal court at Rome was highest of all.

468   *apex:* "bishop" (Du Cange 3).

481   Literally, "according to measure."

505   Compare Ovid, *Tristia* 5.7, 47.

532   *blaesa:* literally, "stammering, lisping."

555–56   For the monastic prohibition against meat, see *Regula S. Benedicti,* ch. 39.

570   *his* refers back to *quaecumque* in 567.

658   Literally, "crooked, you are being stupid."

697   Literally, "when the bones, suddenly encountered, hurt my teeth."

741   The famous hymn of Venantius Fortunatus, "Salve, festa dies, toto venerabilis aevo," was sung as a processional hymn on Easter Sunday; its famous first line was borrowed or adapted in many other hymns sung on other dates in the liturgical year.

742   *kyri ole:* the Greek words "kyrie eleison" are garbled by the uneducated people.

768   *anhela:* the feminine ending may be understood as referring to *vulpes,* even though the fox is here designated as *raptor* (masculine).

799   A blending of two constructions: "non rebar captos tantos, quantos fore sentio," and "rebar captos tantos, quantis fore sentio plures."

816   *omen:* "good fortune." Compare 1.923.

862   The monastic *Consuetudines* of William of Hirsau (ca. 1080) specify that a sprinkling with holy water should precede the tonsuring of a novice (1.2; *PL* 150, col. 934).

865   *praestabilis:* "available, obtainable on request."

883   *sublegere* = *subducere,* "to draw up, raise."

884   *discidium:* "departure."

887   *emoliri:* here used intransitively.

919–20 Comic jumblings of time- and place-references occur elsewhere in the poem (3.688, 7.421–22); "Cos" therefore seems more likely to be taken as the name of the Greek island than as "whetstone."

927   "Tu autem domine miserere nobis" was used to conclude readings in church services and in the monastic refectory, and thus became used as a phrase to mark the end of anything.

933   See note to 1.467.

943   Literally, "less than bigger and bigger than smaller."

967–71 The wolf is accused of poaching in an area of reserved fishing rights. The poet may be thinking of the stretch of meadow known as "Muink-meersen" or "Prata monachorum," which lay between two branches of the Schelde, directly below the monastery of Blandinium and the next-door parish church of St. Mary's; the abbey of Blandinium possessed fishing rights in the Schelde all along the border of the "Muink-meersen."

972–73 As an abbot, Ysengrimus would want the sheepskins not only to provide parchment for the monastic scriptorium but also to provide the monks with warm clothing.

981–82 The ordeal was used as a method of establishing guilt or innocence in the medieval period.

1001   *legere et cantare:* "to celebrate Mass."

1004   A reference to the "pax," the kiss of peace given by the priest celebrating Mass to the members of the congregation, as a sign of Christian love and unity.

1009–14 The shepherd counts in the normal way, from one upward; the flock thus appears to "increase" as he counts. The wolf, in contrast, begins from the total number of sheep and counts downward, "subtracting" rather than adding, until he arrives at "none."

1041   Probably punning on two senses of *crispare,* "to brandish (a weapon)" and "to trill (musically)"; for the latter sense, see the entry in Du Cange for *crispatio.*

1043–46 A reference to the monastic feasts known as "caritates"; the abbot mixed and handed round the wine on such occasions.

BOOK 2

10   *liquare:* see note to 1.227.

11–12   *Gerardus . . . Teta:* traditional names for a goose and a hen.

27   *habitum = id quod habetur.*

47–48   A pun on two senses of *bulla,* "a swelling or bump," and "a boss or rounded ornament."

61–70   Excelsis, Osanna, Alleluia, and Celebrant are prominent words in the Latin Mass, which Aldrada ignorantly takes to be the names of saints. The rescue of Osanna from the gallows seems to be a confused memory of the story of the biblical Susanna (Daniel 13). Anna, the mother of the Virgin Mary, is confused with the prophetess Anna, daughter of Phan'u-el (Luke 2:36). The apostle Peter was married, but his wife was (of course) not Alleluia, and the archangel Michael was not his son; the mistake perhaps arises from a hymn that links Peter and Michael and ends with Alleluia as a refrain. Helpuara and Noburgis are perhaps travestied versions of Hilwara and Notburgis, both women who were revered for sanctity. Brigid, an Irish saint, had a chapel dedicated to her in Cologne. Saint Pharaildis was particularly venerated in Ghent; she is here comically confused with both the biblical Herodias and her daughter Salome, who brought about the decapitation of John the Baptist (Matthew 14:1–12; Mark 6:14–29). The story about the blowing head and Herodias's afterlife as a witch appears to be a piece of folklore that the *Ysengrimus* poet has mischievously attached to the perfectly respectable Pharaildis; see Mann, *Ysengrimus,* 32, 92–94.

63   *quam . . . Annam = Anna . . . quam. everrere de sura:* "to give birth to."

92   *carmina prima:* "Prime."

97–100 Aldrada reproduces in garbled form the following phrases from the Latin Mass: (1) *Pater noster,* (2) *Credo in [unum] deum,* (3) *Da [propicius] pacem [in diebus nostris],* (4) *Miserere nobis,* (5) *Orate fratres,* (6) *Pax vobis,* (7) *Deo gratias.*

121 At the end of the Introit of the Mass, the deacon says "flectamus genua," and the priest and congregation kneel.

128 Punning on *ănus,* "old woman," and *ānus,* "anus."

179–81 Saint Gereon was allegedly a soldier, who was martyred, along with fifty companions, for refusing to sacrifice to pagan gods. His column stood in St. Gereon's church in Cologne until 1794, when it was removed by the French; part of it was later found and reerected in the church (see Gompf, "Ysengrimus und die Gereonssäule"). Apparently it was believed that those who swore by it falsely would be rooted to the spot and unable to move. Compare 4.25–26.

215 *fictor:* "hypocrite."

247 *ferrum* refers to the surgeon's knife, *flamma* to the fire used for cauterization. The whole line is a parody of the methods that an abbot is advised to use (metaphorically) against recalcitrant monks: first, the "unguents" of exhortation; next, the "cauterization" of excommunication or beatings; finally, the "amputation" of expulsion from the community (*Regula S. Benedicti,* ch. 28).

249 A pun on two senses of *sapere,* "to taste, eat," and "to be wise."

267 *cuculla:* a monk's cowl. Sheepskins were worn by monks for warmth.

267–68 The wolf is recalling 2.199–200.

278–79 The implied etymology for Colvarianus is *calvus aures* ("earless") and for Belinus, *hyalinus* (interpreted as *vitreus,* "glassy" in medieval glossaries).

281 For the construction, compare 1.799 and note.

299–302 Belinus has two horns, Colvarianus four, Bernard six, and Joseph eight.

333 *vivum:* "tumult, war."

377 *at:* "even, at least."

399–402   Medieval proverbs imply that both dogs and pigs were fed on bran. These lines seem to imply a fable or anecdote relating a specific battle between a dog and a pig over their food, but it has not been identified.

429   *vorans:* "having devoured." The present participle is frequently used to express past action in this poem.

435   *prius viso = priusquam visus sum.*

439   *ausos = audentes.*

446   *tam:* a corresponding *quam meum mihi* is to be understood.

459   The title *dominus* is appropriate to Ysengrimus's role as a monk, and even more so to his role as an abbot; see Introduction, pp. ix–xii.

464   *disponere super re:* "to deliberate, make arrangements regarding (something)."

470   *dictare:* "to take counsel together."

476   *concidit:* literally, "has fallen into."

487   *stadium:* "boundary, goal," rather than "racecourse."

500   *doce:* used in the colloquial sense, "punish him for."

525   *bannus:* see Introduction, p. xiv.

530   Twenty is the total number of the sheep's horns (2 + 4 + 6 + 8), and is thus the number of blows (= "dishes") that the wolf will receive from their charge.

541–42   An allusion to the death of the wolf, which will be brought about by the sow Salaura (Book 7).

543–58   Joseph is afraid to charge directly at the wolf's mouth and so aims a little to the right; even so he would have penetrated both temples if the wolf had not flinched. His oblique attack means that Bernard's charge peters out before they meet in the middle. The other two sheep attack the wolf's sides but miss the region of his heart.

631   *expingere:* "to knock out."

650   *aliquid pacis = aliquid belli* (antiphrasis).

655–56   Reynard sets the sheep an arithmetical problem: given that they each have a different number of horns, they must work out how many charges will be necessary for them each to inflict the same number of blows. The sheep correctly deduce that the lowest number that they can equally inflict is 24: Joseph (eight horns) must make three charges, Bernard (six horns) four, Colvarianus (four horns) six, and Belinus (two horns) twelve (Schwab, "Gast-metaphorik").

pocula pietatis: a reference to the monastic "caritas" feasts (see note to 1.1043–46).

664   *propino tibi:* literally, "I offer you a drink."

678   *vina Boema:* refers to the legendary cruelty of the Bohemians.

685–86   Compare *Regula S. Benedicti,* chs. 4.30 and 7.35–36, 42–43.

BOOK 3

16   *quibus miseris* = *miseros quibus.*

38   When the sun is passing through the zodiacal sign of Cancer (mid-June to mid-July), it is at its highest point in the sky, and in consequence, this is the hottest season of the year.

62   *pax:* a legal "peace," declared and enforced by ecclesiastical or lay authority, which guaranteed the safety of people and property. Violation of such a peace incurred extra penalties additional to those prescribed for any crime. The counts of Flanders issued such declarations of peace, which protected specific categories of people, including travelers.

81   *promptu:* "speedily."

111   *discutere:* "to diagnose."

113   *status:* "the critical point in the course of a fever."

118   Medieval doctors distinguished four types of fever, with corresponding crisis points on the third (or fourth), seventh, fourteenth, or twenty-first day after its onset; Ysengrimus claims that the lion's fever is of the first type.

129   *te sospite facto* = *te sanando.*

169   *monachus atque sacerdos:* the earliest monks were laymen, but as time went on, ordination to the priesthood became more common.

185   The legal peace applied with special force to feast days.

195   Literally, "let profit be sought through right and wrong" (i.e., by any means whatever).

201   The lion was popularly believed to spare those who prostrated themselves before him; see Ovid, *Tristia* 3.5, 31–34, and Mann, *From Aesop to Reynard,* 280 n. 39.

213   *suppulsus:* "silent blow."

248   Luke 14:7–11. Compare Matthew 19:30.

309–10   *tribunus, praetor:* from Carolingian times onward, it was customary to apply the names of the public officials of the Roman empire to the legal officers of the medieval state. Thus, the officer who presided over a court, whether the count himself or the castellan who was his representative, was designated *praetor,* and the *scabini,* members of the subordinate tribunals presided over by the castellans, were designated *tribuni* (Mann, *Ysengrimus,* 99).

310   Literally, "evening will not pass for the fourth time."

315–16   *quamquam . . . carens:* "even if he were to lack."

323–24   The mole's soft body could have given rise to a popular idea that it had no bones.

375   Salerno was home of the leading medical school of the twelfth century.

379   The appeal to worn-out shoes as a fraudulent proof of a long journey is found in Joshua 9:13.

382   *Turce:* that is, Greek, the language of Turkey at this period.

419   *quam primum = cum primum.*

439   *venus:* "seemliness, decorum."

453   *Mulciber:* a surname of Vulcan, god of fire, and so used here as a synonym for fire.

473   Literally, "without the old man (i.e., the wolf)."

493–94   The fox is about to claim that the wolf is a mere child, and so suitable for the king's cure.

           sacris libris: perhaps referring to biblical genealogies, but perhaps to the genealogical records of important families which were kept by the monasteries of Flanders.

525   *rufum caput:* redheads were traditionally held to be deceitful tricksters.

529   *laborare* is used in the sense of French *travailler,* "to harass, pressurize."

535   *tene ferulam:* literally, "take the (teacher's) rod."

551–52   These lines are evidence that it was customary to recite in courts the genealogies of great families, and their most important deeds, as a social entertainment.

561   Compare Horace, *Od.* I 24.19–20.

579   *loquensve:* the *-ve* is superfluous and added for the sake of the meter.

590   The wolf's claim to be 160 years old is supported by the poet's own statement at 4.73.

591   A difficult line. *auspicium* elsewhere means "success," but the sense "leadership, authority, guidance" would have been familiar to the poet from Virgil (see *OLD* 4), and this sense best fits the rest of the line.

593   *fila trahere:* literally, "to spin."

599   *accidit = est accidens* ("accident" in the philosophical sense, opposed to "substance"; see Blaise).

607   *libertus:* Reynard is insultingly representing the wolf as a freedman, who still owes the king all or part of the payment for his manumission.

617–32   The fox is referring to the pilgrimage episode, which had taken place earlier but is not recounted until Book 4, in which the wolf tried to get himself out of trouble by claiming to be his own young godson (4.427–42).

643   *ordo datur:* for the sense "to give an order," compare 3.348.

655   A white crow = "no one."

659   It was a traditional joke or insult in the Middle Ages to claim that Englishmen had tails.

660   *nam = sed.*

666   An ironic reference to *Disticha Catonis* 3.3, which urges that anyone who is obliged to bear witness against a friend should conceal his faults as far as possible.

673   *quod amas:* sc. *lupum.*

685   The rhetorical topos of the *senex iuvenis* (old head on young shoulders) is here comically parodied.

687   Étampes was the scene of various important church councils in the first half of the twelfth century and was also the location of the meeting in early 1147 at which the Second Crusade was planned.

688   This absurd mix of time- and place-references is paralleled at 1.919 and 7.421–22.

690   *Cephas* is the Hebrew equivalent of "Peter"; in the Middle Ages *cephas* was thought to mean "head." Combined with the word *ars* (prefaced by "C," a "barking sound") it would mean "head/chief of learning." In actuality, the most natural derivation of "Carcophas" is from *carcare,* "to load" or "to carry a load" (compare 4.9–10), which would better fit the ass.

692   Literally, "may you be associated with my pupils."

693–94   *titulus:* "abbreviation mark." n̄c̄ is the usual scribal abbreviation for "nunc."

701   I have expanded the translation to make clear the metrical quality of *b.e.b.* in the Latin text.

705   Line 707 suggests that the implication is "you haven't sung Prime at all."

714   *tribulus:* "[a schoolmaster's] leather strap."

717   Saint Bavo was a seventh-century saint, a disciple of Saint Amand. One of the two monasteries of Ghent was dedicated to him (see Introduction, p. xvii).

742   Saint Martin, bishop of Tours, while still a Roman soldier was moved by pity for a beggar to cut his cloak in two and give the beggar half.

751–52   *quiris:* "[young, new] knight." A *quiris plebigena* is someone of plebeian birth who has won entry to the rank of knighthood, and so may be considered an upstart.

761   The sun is at its lowest point in the sky in the zodiacal sign of Capricorn and at its highest in the sign of Cancer; they therefore represent midwinter and midsummer.

787   *non procul a vivo:* literally, "not far from [i.e., near] the quick."

788   *probitas:* "kindness." Compare 3.853 and 4.390.

799   The Sarmatians were a Slavic people.

804   *quattuor:* that is, the fox, sheep, goat, and ass.

812   Literally, "a bird in the net is worth eight at liberty."

819   That is, [*si*] *vis,* [*es*] *iuvenis;* [*si*] *vis,* [*es*] *canus.*

850   The translation follows the interlinear gloss on *manzer avarus* in MS D (f. 103r): "genitus adulterio et dicitur flaminge vrec hoerenzone [greedy son of a whore]."

857 *sensio* = *senecio,* "old man." The meaning of "Aspice, quo iactes" is not self-evident; Voigt assumes that the phrase *lupum in vincula* is to be supplied ("Look around for where you are to cast the wolf in chains"), but I take *iactare* in the sense "to boast," and I supply *te.*

863–64 An ironic reference to the fox's role in getting the wolf's hide torn to ribbons in the fishing episode and the field-division episode.

869 *qua licet:* "as far as possible."

898 Literally, the horse is generous *(larga)* rather than a gift horse, but the familiarity of the proverb in medieval as in modern times suggests that this is the meaning.

912 *semare:* "to halve."

921 Literally, "the sweating king will melt in the four-holed skin."

932 On the satiric implications of this bizarre request, see Introduction, pp. x–xi.

939 Saint Botulph was a seventh-century Anglo-Saxon saint.
    quem saepe requiro: Compare the phrase *quaerere sanctos,* "to visit the saints' shrines," used at 4.477, 821, 921; 5.1244.

942 Literally, "you're acting worse than a tapeworm."

947 *Latiam loquelam:* literally, "the Latin language." *Latius* (adj.) = "Roman" (compare 7.666), but here, as 3.950 shows, *Latia loquela* means "Romance language," and specifically French, not Italian. See Voigt's note to 3.407.

952 *restrofare:* "to skin, flay." *ephot:* a term used as an equivalent to *superhumerale* or *amiculum,* to designate a linen cloth covering the priest's head and shoulders. It is the first of a series of terms denoting liturgical garments in this section of the narrative.

953 *altum medias* = *altas medium;* one of the frequent examples of hypallage in the poem.

957 *suralia:* a technical term referring to a bishop's hose, which formed part of his distinctively pontifical vestments (along with gloves, miter, staff, and ring).

959 *caudale:* the ribbon hanging down from the back of a miter.

968 *at* = *saltem, certe* (with a preceding "if not . . ." clause understood).

975 *phanaticus:* "priest."

977–78   The biblical Abel was a shepherd, and *abellus* means "lamb" in medieval Latin. The sheep is called *cappifer,* because his white fleece resembles a *cappa,* a liturgical garment worn by acolytes. As acolyte, his duty is to remove the *casula,* or chasuble, which was a sleeveless, circular overgarment worn by the celebrant at Mass.

981   Compare *Regula S. Benedicti,* ch. 4.32, 40, 51.

997   *balnea:* the anointing of a priest or bishop in consecration.

1000   *infula:* the bishop's miter.

1006   *tyara:* the term referred to the papal tiara, the bishop's miter, and an abbot's miter. Lines 1000–1001 make it clear that it is the bishop's miter that is meant here.

1028   Ivory was thought to get redder as it ages.

1029   The term *tunica poderis* was used of one of the two diaconal garments worn by the bishop, the *tunicella* or *dalmatica minor,* which was customarily scarlet.

1032   Literally, "the rich and the poor pull the rope in different ways" (presumably, one leads and the other is led).

1084   *pallia:* here and at 1091, not the archbishop's pallium, but an outer garment in general.

1097   The ribbon of skin on the wolf's head is now referred to as the nosepiece of a helmet, as if the wolf were an armed knight.

1119–20   Literally, "you wouldn't resort to your shocking impudence, *would* you?"—with heavy sarcasm, implying that this is just what the wolf *would* do.

1121   *duellum:* a judicial combat, used to settle a legal dispute.

1131   The fox interprets the skin on the wolf's forepaws as "gloves" that are "thrown" before the king as a proffered gage for battle.

1153   *caestus:* originally, "a boxing glove," here used for the gauntlets that formed part of knightly armor.

1156   That is, something that has to be requested is not given freely and does not earn gratitude.

Book 4

11   *dictatus:* "leadership."

25–26   On Saint Gereon's column and its miraculous powers, see note to 2.179–81.

31 *soli:* genitive of *solum,* "earth." The phrase is apparently formed on the model of *unde gentium. quid actum:* I take *actum* to be a supine with a verb of motion understood.

43 See Job 20:4–5, and compare 8:13, 13:16, 15:34, 27:8.

52 Literally, "a well-known path is trodden with an undeviating step."

55–56 Compare Philippians 4:12.

65–66 For the real reasons why some of these animals left home, see 4.825–28.

73 Literally, "four times eight *lustra*" (*lustrum* = five years); this confirms the wolf's claim at 3.590.

81 For *vertebrum* = "hip bone," see the entry for *vertebra* III in Lewis and Short.

86 A parody of Virgil's description of the death of Dido (*Aeneid* 4.690–91). Compare 1.331–32 and note.

96 Literally, "intended to do good to few."

98 *senex:* the name often given to Ysengrimus is here used as a simple synonym for "wolf."

102 The house seems to be one of the hospices provided for the accommodation of pilgrims on major pilgrimage routes.

108 *inescare:* "to equip with food, bait."

110 A reference to the wooden horse by means of which the Greeks gained access to Troy.

114 The human brain was thought to consist of three cells; memory occupied the rear position.

128 Literally, "let me be allowed to follow your orders without punishment."

141 *benedicite:* a greeting offered by monks (see 5.451–52). *pax vobis:* a formula used by the bishop in addressing the congregation at Mass, in place of the priest's *dominus vobiscum.*

163–64 Pilgrims to Jerusalem wore the sign of the cross in token of their mission; in the twelfth century the crosses were often blessed by a priest.

204 *inscissis pilis:* literally, "with his fur untorn," referring to the idiom *scindere paenulam,* "to tear off someone's cloak (in order to prevent them from leaving). Compare 1.101, 7.267, and notes.

219	Joseph assumes that the wolf, as a hermit who follows the monastic rule, will not eat meat.
228	Compare Titus 1:15.
240	*suppeditare* (with dat.): "to serve."
249	*vacare:* "to be available."
282	*plumeum:* "feather bed."
285	Sithiu is the original name of Saint-Omer, site of the abbey of Saint Bertin. *gravidus:* "weighed down."
286	*Atrebas sanctus:* "the saint of Arras"—that is, Saint Vaast, bishop of Arras at the turn of the fifth and sixth centuries and dedicatee of a local monastery.
311	*pungilis = fustis.*
318	Literally, "tied by what rope does the day hang back?"
319	*Quid* = "why?"
332	*Geticas nives:* The Getae were a Thracian tribe on the Danube; their territory is associated with cold by Juvenal, *Satires* 5.50.
335–36	The monastic rule prescribed rest in bed after dinner (*Regula S. Benedicti,* ch. 48.5).
346	*orator:* "pilgrim" (Du Cange 1; Niermeyer 2) rather than "(legal) advocate," as at 1.421 and 6.549.
363	*quintana febris:* the five-day fever was an extra type sometimes added to the usual four classes (see note to 3.118).
377	*abusio:* "consumption."
387	Literally, "he should have been asked to want what he asks of us."
398	*ter:* "often, repeatedly," not translated here, as the sense makes it redundant.
399	*discidium:* "departure."
405	*quaestor:* see 1.355 and note.
436	*praependere = praeponderare,* "to oppress with weight, weigh down."
439	*traditur archae:* literally, "is consigned to the chest (where valuables were stored)."
443	*annosi iuvenis:* a comic allusion to the rhetorical topos of the *senex iuvenis* (compare 3.685 and note).

449	Hypallage (exchange of cases): *hospitium* is the subject, and *ultimus tenor* the object.
483	Literally, "cease to flatter."
499	*poplite dextro:* translated literally, "with his right knee," rather than figuratively, "with fortunate steps" (compare 6.128), but perhaps a double meaning is intended.
503	The polders of Friesland were well adapted to the grazing of sheep and cattle.
508	*quam . . . avem = avis quam.*
531	*ob insignes oculos:* apparently calqued on the French idiom "pour les beaux yeux de [quelqu'un]," meaning to do something "for love, without reward."
559ff.	Sheep, stag, and goat are all at this point outside the door, while the fox, goose, and cock remain inside. The ass keeps the wolf wedged in the door; Bertiliana the roe apparently maintains a ladylike aloofness.
571	*hora:* that is, the canonical hour, which in this case is Compline (*Carmina completoria,* l. 557).
591	*affirmare:* "to practice saying something beforehand, *sotto voce*" (Du Cange 3). *verbum:* "utterance, speech."
592	Reims was the home of an important school at this period.
609	The Brabanters had a traditional reputation for violence and lawlessness. Part of the territory of ancient Brabant lay within the town of Ghent, and the monastery of Saint Bavo's was traditionally described as being "in pago Bracbantinse" (Mann, *Ysengrimus,* 86–87).
611	*trifurculare:* "to sound from triple-branched horns." The glossary in MS D (f. 185r) explains *trifurculo* as "drietackede" ("with three points").
612	The sounds produced from the goat's horns are a parody of three-part polyphony.
615	*tongus = phthongus,* "sound, tone."
620	*calices:* literally, "cups." My translation puns on "rounds" of drinks and "rounds" of a boxing match.
622	*macra iuventa:* literally, "lean youth," i.e., "young man's leanness" (to be interpreted sarcastically as "old man's fatness").

628   Literally, "have a taste of what this goblet may bring."

629–31   Pilgrims were invested with a staff and scrip (pilgrim's bag or knapsack) as well as the cross (see note to 4.163–64).

633–34   Literally, "may great Satan consecrate these drinks!" parodying a traditional form of grace before meals; my translation substitutes a traditional English form of grace.

638   *famulas* is an adjective qualifying *manus*.

639   *velle . . . nolle:* treated as indeclinable nouns, meaning "wishing" and "not-wishing" respectively. The sense appears to be that the wolf cannot complain that he has fewer drinks than he wants (*non . . . infra velle* = "not less than his wishing"), even though he cannot *not* complain that he also has more than enough of what he *doesn't* want (*ultra nolle* = "beyond the point of his not-wishing," with the preceding *non* negating the *non* of *non queritur*).

641   *mas:* the male genitals.

647   *astulare:* "to hew, hack."

658   *matutinum chorum:* this reference to Matins may seem to contradict the reference to the evening service of Compline at 4.557, but Matins was a night office (its three divisions are referred to as "Nocturns," and I have used this term in translation to make its timing clearer).

661   *discos paterasque:* "plates and bowls," metonymically for "food and drink."

664   *materiare offensam:* "to cause annoyance, offense."

665   Literally, "one's thumb is closed up in one's fist" (a proverbial expression meaning "to withhold generosity").

683–94   Reynard and his friends have sung Matins at night, as customary; the wolf threatens to follow it with his own *matutina carmina* in the daytime.

687–88   Matins contained nine Lessons or readings from scripture.

694   *laudes:* Matins was immediately followed by the singing of Lauds at break of day.

719   *laureolum:* literally, "discus." Apparently a reference to some kind of popular game in which a thick disk is driven toward a goal by means of a club.

721   Literally, "why should I pour this out into many vessels?"

734   On the Suevi, see note to 1.124; on the Getae, see note to 4.332.

760   Literally, "[they were] about to wage it as badly as they thought they were to wage it successfully."

763   *excuba:* glossed "vigilator" in MS D.

768   *operiri = opperiri.*

775   *anterus = anterior.*

825   The real motives behind the animal pilgrimage are here revealed.

841   The principle that need legitimated the overriding of law (*necessitas non habet legem*—"need has no law") was accepted in both Roman and canon law, and was familiar to medieval writers.

846   *anticipare:* "to thwart, forestall."

870   *ianua docta:* literally, "learned doorway."

930   *effestucare:* to throw back a straw *(festuca)* at someone was a sign of the formal rupturing of a bond of homage; here, in a more general sense, "to renounce, repudiate."

939   *fictor:* "hypocrite."

953   That is, the fox's father ate the cock's father.

1019–20 A reference to the feudal obligation known as "carriage" (*vectigal;* see l.1029), by which a vassal or tenant was obliged to provide transport for his lord.

BOOK 5

8   Literally, "pride and profit don't tolerate being together."

27   *culica:* the word is unattested elsewhere, and "chisel" is Voigt's guess at its meaning.

61   *industria:* generally "wisdom, cleverness" (as at 5.471), but here the specific piece of wisdom or "lesson" derived from an instructive experience.

97   *summa:* in the sense "the main thing, chief point."

101   *Beniaminita magister:* the apostle Paul was of the tribe of Benjamin (Romans 11:1; Philippians 3:5).

103–4   A reference to Christ summoning the fisherman Peter and his brother Andrew with the promise: "I will make you fishers of men" (Matthew 4:19; compare Mark 1:17).

110   *transilire:* "to surpass." On Anselm, bishop of Tournai, and his central role as target of the poem's satire, see Introduction, pp. ix–xii.

115   Compare 1 Peter 5:8.

118   *obeditus = obedientia.*

126   *Clarevallis pannifer:* Saint Bernard of Clairvaux. On the poem's references to Bernard, and their overall significance, see Introduction, pp. xiv–xv.

134   *missilis carta:* an open letter. The English term "letters patent" denotes a legal document open for general inspection, with the seal appended to the bottom, rather than folded and sealed shut.

136   *liber:* the word means both "bark" and "charter" (see Niermeyer).

137–284 On the legal peace that the fox pretends has been sworn, see note to 3.62.

176   A gloss in MS A makes it clear that *teta* is the Greek letter *theta* (θ) and explains that those who were condemned to death were branded with this letter (perhaps standing for θάνατος, "death").

191–208 Sprotinus conjures up the picture of a huntsman, riding on a white horse and accompanied by a pack of dogs.

220   Saint Malo was a seventh-century saint of British origin, who went as a missionary monk to Brittany. He was known and revered in Flanders.

224   See note to 3.185.

284   *nugosus:* "trivial, ridiculous."

291   *bannus:* a legally binding proclamation of peace, issued by secular authorities, which among other things guaranteed safe-conduct to travelers (Niermeyer 8).

296   *pervadere:* "to attack."

299   *duellum:* see note to 3.1121.

311–12 The hanging of a fox by a cock or a goose is a traditional motif illustrating the world upside down.

316   Literally, "weighed with an equal balance."

317   *casus nemorum:* "declivities of wooded mountains."

392 The word "gentle" is sarcastic.

397 *immorsus:* "bite."

442 The cause of Lucifer's fall was his pride.

444 The wolf volunteers for the two tasks that will cater to his greed: as kitchen boy he can steal food, and as shepherd he can devour the sheep.

447 *Blandinia claustra:* Blandinium was the domanial name of the Benedictine abbey of Saint Peter's, Ghent. See Introduction, pp. xvi–xvii.

449 Compare Virgil, *Aeneid* 6.126–29.

459 The abbey of Egmond was situated twenty-six kilometers north of Haarlem, in the county of Holland and the diocese of Utrecht. Walter was abbot from 1130 to 1161; he was a former monk of Blandinium and was chosen as abbot of Egmond by Arnold, abbot of Blandinium from 1114 to 1132. On the poet's praise of Walter, see Introduction, pp. xvi, xix.

461 *honesto:* an ablative of price. The word implies that the reward is both financial *and* moral.

463 Luke 6:38.

477–78 See Matthew 13:12, 25:29; Mark 4:25; Luke 8:18.

498 On Baldwin of Liesborn, see Introduction, pp. xvi, xix.

500 *rudereus = ruderarius,* "used for rubble."

511–12 The opposition between the sternness of Cato and the charm of Cicero is conventional.

522 A reference to Matthew 22:21; Mark 12:17; Luke 20:25.

534 *archa:* "monastic cell" (Blaise *arca* 2); thus "the cloister" and (by transference) "monastic life."

549 *teutonice:* the reference to the river Schelde makes it likely that this means "in Dutch" rather than "in German."

571–72 On monk-priests, see note to 3.169.

573–80 This passage plays on the two senses of *pastor:* "shepherd" and "priest."

574 *praetaxare = praedicere,* "to say beforehand."

577–78 Compare John 10:3–5.

580 *mancipare:* "to confine, imprison."

586 *arbitrium:* "approval."

587   On the monastic custom of sleeping after dinner, see note to 4.335–36.

588   Possibly an echo of Cistercian criticism of the elaboration of the liturgy at Cluny.

604   *nona:* none, the ninth hour of the day, which would fall at different times of the day as daylight lengthened or shortened, but was generally midafternoon. At none, one of the eight monastic offices (Matins, Lauds, Prime, Terce, Sext, None, Vespers, and Compline) was sung, and it was also at some times of the year a mealtime (see *Regula S. Benedicti,* ch. 41). Monks ate twice a day in summer and only once a day in winter, sometimes with the addition of a breakfast of bread and wine or ale.

609   *ganga:* "latrine." Hay was provided in the latrine to perform the function of modern-day toilet paper.

618   *apex:* "the pointer on a scale."

629–34   Matins (sung during the nocturnal hours) normally contained nine Lessons (readings from the scriptures) and the same number of Responsories (soloist's chants), but on Sundays and feast days, the number was increased to twelve. Each Responsory is here allotted to a different singer, and the wolf is given the tenth.

630   *puer:* an oblate, one of the children being trained for monastic life, whose regular duties included singing in the monastic offices and public reading.

659   *ter:* the Benedictine Rule mentions two meals a day (ch. 41), and this seems to have been the norm; the wolf may be including breakfast (see note to 5.604 above).

667   The wolf thinks that the wood should be used to build ships rather than to feed cooking fires.

677   Literally, "to which direction opinion declines."

681–86   The wolf's proposal burlesques the new emphasis on austerity characteristic of the Cistercians. See Mann, *Ysengrimus,* 117–19.

689   *non clare = non pure* (in the juridical sense of *pure,* "unconditionally, absolutely"; see *OLD* 6b).

697   Possibly a reference to William of Ypres, a claimant to the title of count of Flanders after the murder of Charles the Good

	(1127); William was illegitimate, born of a noble father and an ignoble mother who continued to card wool as long as she lived. Ypres was a center of medieval cloth production.
700	It is not clear whether this refers to copulation between the two animals or to a battle to the death.
701	Hebrew, Greek, and Latin are the three sacred languages used in the Bible.
740	*mixtum:* literally, "breakfast" (Niermeyer), which in the Middle Ages often consisted of bread dipped in wine.
755	*commendatus: commendare aliquem [deo]* = "to say farewell" (compare 3.1176).
779	*Tempe:* a beautiful valley in Thessaly. Here used for "valley" in general.
781	Literally, "twisted by no turning."
818.18	*zelotipare:* "to make jealous, to cuckold."
821	See note to 5.629–34.
823	*veneranda silentia:* monks were supposed to reserve silence as far as possible, and especially during the hours of night (*Regula S. Benedicti,* ch. 42). An elaborate system of sign language was used instead of speech.
831	Since the wolf equates Lessons with meals, and ten Lessons have been read, he is correct in surmising that it is time for the eleventh "meal" (out of the complement of twelve).
832	*horologus:* "telling the hours." The horological mechanism of a water clock is activated by the controlled release of water.
835	Since *benedicite* is a grace (compare 1.1029–30), I have substituted the appropriate English formula in translating.
836	Literally, "as far as God is concerned, no one can come too late," referring to the parable of the vineyard (Matthew 20:1–16).
855	The hymn *Te deum laudamus* would normally be sung as a conclusion to Matins (*Regula S. Benedicti,* ch. 11.8), and despite the fact that the service has not been properly completed, thanks to the wolf's disruptive behavior, the monks hurriedly bring it to a close.
863	*aetate rudes:* a reference to the *pueri* (see note to 5.630).
869	*zirbus:* "fat covering the intestines."

879   *macidum:* literally "lean, thin" = "rich" *per antiphrasim.*

882   That is, even if it were the longest night of the year.

883   *praedia:* literally, "farms," here used metonymically for the food that the farms produce.

887   *intercrassari:* "to intercalate with fat."

909–10   A reference to 1 Thessalonians 5:21.

917   *archa:* here used in the sense "prison cell" (Du Cange *arca* 2), rather than "monastic cell."

923   *cista:* "punishment cell."

933   *par facere:* "to do/be the same as."

937–38   The Benedictine Rule allows monks to drink wine but recommends that they do so sparingly (*Regula S. Benedicti,* ch. 40).

939   The two groups referred to may be Cluniacs, who wore the cowl as their outermost garment, and Cistercians, who wore the *froccus,* an ample garment with sleeves, over the cowl, or novices, who wore the *froccus* up to the time of their profession, and professed monks (i.e., "young and old").

970   Horses' heads were fixed to buildings to ward off evil spirits.

997, 1002, 1009   The present tense is used with imperative force in *leguntur, constituunt,* and *eligit.* The "new order" of monk-bishops that the wolf proposes to institute had in actuality a long history behind it by the twelfth century; see Mann, *Ysengrimus,* 14–15.

1035   The wolf wants to be put in charge of the infirmary because sick monks were allowed better food (*Regula S. Benedicti,* ch. 36).

1041–42   See note to 3.659 (on Englishmen) and 3.525 (on redheads).

1045–1104   Only certain elements of the episcopal consecration ceremony are reproduced in parodic form in the following action: the ceremonial procession to the church with banners (1047–48), the anointing of the episcopal candidate with oil (1049–55), the placing of the miter (*tyara,* 1061, 1074; *mitra,* 1063, 1072–73; *infula,* 1065) on his head.

1059   *stolpare:* "to turn upside down."

1061   There were three bishoprics in Artois: Terwaan, Arras, and Cambrai; it is not clear whether this is a specific reference to any of them.

1075   *stola:* since the bishop would already be wearing a stole for the consecration service, it seems that the word is here used in the sense of "pallium," the mantle bestowed by the pope on archbishops and especially important bishops.

1080   *libum,* "cake," here refers to the gifts offered by the clergy to the new bishop.

1085   *ioculentus = iocosus,* "joking."

1100   Apparently a reference to a twelfth-century poet named Blitero, who is probably to be identified with a canon of Bruges.

1125   At this point the inset narrative ends and the scene shifts back to the court of the sick lion. The outer narrative goes on to relate what happened to the wolf after he had left the lion's court without his skin.

1156   *fuscinula:* literally, "three-pronged fork," here used of the stork's three-pronged claws, similar to those of Satan.

1233   *paulisper:* used as an adverb of degree, "a little," rather than "for a brief while."

1237   *subligar:* "leather strap" (see Du Cange).

1248   The staff and scrip were the signs of a pilgrim (see note to 4.629–31).

1261   The wolf is threatening the horse with excommunication: priests carrying burning candles pronounce the anathema and then throw the candles to the ground and extinguish them.

1263–64   The wolf pretends that the horse's iron shoes are the rings used as door handles in his monastery. The monastic rule specifies that the abbot is responsible for the safekeeping of the iron tools *(ferramenta)* and all other monastery property *(Regula S. Benedicti,* ch. 32). The wolf, in his character as abbot, is rightly denouncing the thief.

1267–68   Compare Ecclesiasticus 28:2–5.

BOOK 6

5   Visiting the sick was one of the Seven Works of Mercy (compare Matthew 25:36).

12   *regia ligna:* kings and nobles jealously guarded their rights over forests (which they used as game reserves for hunting). The

counts of Flanders exercised such rights over large tracts of land, including a forest to the northeast of Ghent known as "Conincsforest," "the king's forest," which may be referred to here.

14 The fox is pretending to be a forester, an official charged with the protection of forest rights.

16 *bannire:* "to put under a ban, to prohibit any injury to a thing or any infraction of a place" (Niermeyer 8).

19 *pacare:* "to fence round" (Niermeyer 5).

43 *lunam:* that is, the horseshoe implanted in the wolf's forehead.

61 Forest tenants were obliged to render special services to their feudal lord.

62 *indicere* in classical Latin means both "to proclaim, publish" and "to impose, enjoin" (for the latter meaning, see also the entry in Du Cange for *indictor*). The reference here may be either to the person who authorized the peace or to the person who publicized it.

73 A reference to the field-division episode recounted in 2:271–688.

89 A reference to Saint Bernard of Clairvaux, but it is not clear whether it is a hit at his greed or at his being a loudmouth.

111 Literally, "when six sheep had been consumed you were tempted to eat."

123 *paganior:* literally, "more uncouth, boorish."

128 *dextro poplite:* see note to 4.499 above.

138 *tertia:* not only a literal third, but more specifically the name given to feudal dues payable to both secular and religious superiors, out of agricultural produce in the first case and church revenues in the second. The wolf could expect such dues in his role as bishop.

139 *praependere:* "to prefer."

175–76 Literally, "not wanting to build a bridge before he had any goats" (proverbial).

187–88 Compare Proverbs 29:11.

224 Literally, "let him put it in the mouth of his purse."

247 *incidit ammissum:* literally, "has incurred guilt."

290 Various scholars have advanced tentative explanations of this line, but none is entirely satisfactory; see Mann, *Ysengrimus,* 162–63.

299 *frania:* "belonging to a lord."

304 The toad was believed to feed off earth and to eat each day only as much as it can hold in its front paw, out of fear that the supply might run out.

311–12 Compare Ecclesiasticus 14:5.

313 I have spelled out the implications of this maxim by adding "that feeds it" in translation.

333 *nullo:* ablative of price.

340 *sagma:* literally, "burden, load," here used metaphorically for the coarse, heavy clothing worn by the peasant.

349 *irquus:* "corner of the eye," and thus "sideways (sneering) glance."

381 *papa salignus:* apparently a reference to the folk custom of keeping carved or earthenware figures in the house as "household gods."

409 The wolf puns on two senses of *salvare,* "to protect, safeguard," and "to salute, greet."

427 The implication seems to be that the ass has made inroads on the sheep while clothed in the wolf's skin; compare the fable of the ass in the lion's skin, Avianus, fable 5.

477 *ab iure: ab = sine,* thus "without legal grounds."

479–80 That is, even if the ass were to pay the hide, he does not admit to having deprived the wolf of any sheep.

485–88 Those who were accused of crime could defend themselves by a legal purgatory oath, usually made with the support of "oath helpers," who testified to the good character of the defendant.

500 *cancelli:* literally, "railings," here used for the bar in a court of justice.

Book 7

8 *abbatum pontificumque:* that is, she is nine times craftier than the wolf, who is both abbot and bishop (see l. 17).

18 The wolf's front legs are equated with the two candlesticks carried by acolytes at the head of the procession to the altar at the Mass.

27 *pax:* the kiss of peace offered by the priest to the congregation at Mass (see note to 1.1004).

48 Literally, "loans should be returned with laughter." Since this is a proverbial saying (see Voigt's note, and Singer, *Sprichwörter,* 1:156–57), I have adapted it to the corresponding English proverb.

58 The feast of Saint John takes place on June 24, when the days are at their longest and Mass can therefore be celebrated at a later hour.

66 Swabians appear as comic characters in medieval literature. If there is a more specific allusion in the phrase, it is now obscure.

71 *abstimus* = *abstemius.* Both celebrant and communicants were supposed to fast before Mass.

101 The monochord was a musical instrument composed of a soundboard with a single string; here the term is applied to Salaura's solo voice.

102 *sex diapente:* singing one fifth higher than the melodic line was a normal practice in medieval discant, but singing *six* fifths higher is an exaggerated absurdity.

107 *organa: organum* is a medieval term denoting a kind of polyphonic singing, in which the *vox principalis* is accompanied by a *vox organalis* singing at a different pitch. It was particularly based on intervals of a fourth or fifth. Salaura's account of the intervals adopted in the pigs' singing (ll. 119–26) is technically accurate. For a detailed account, see the notes to lines 107–27 in Mann, *Ysengrimus.*

112 The term *modus* is here used to mean "interval" rather than "mode" in the technical sense (see next note), as is confirmed by its use in a contemporary source, which agrees that there are nine intervals.

113 Gregorian chant employed eight modes, each of which is a scale consisting of the tones of the C-major scale, but starting or closing on d, e, f, or g (the "final"), and limited to the range of about

an octave. The four modes called "authentic" extended in range from the final to the upper octave, and the four called "plagal" extended from the fourth below the final to the fifth above it.

116–17 Salaura's system of eleven modes and fifteen intervals is a piece of comic absurdity. *Terminat:* for the importance of the "final" in defining each mode, see preceding note.

119–26 *epitryte:* a Greek term for *sesquitertia,* the interval of a fourth. The intervals of fourths and fifths that Salaura specifies in these lines correspond to those in *organum* singing (see note to 7.107).

123 Probably a reference to the well-known *Kyrie* trope "Cunctipotens dominator coeli et angelorum, terrae, maris et mortalium."

127 See note to 7.107.

140 For Gog and Magog as precursors of the end of the world, see Revelation 20:7.

174 *Roma Remisque:* that is, the pope and the archbishop (Ghent belonged to the archdiocese of Reims).

191 Breton storytellers specialized in the fabulous and the supernatural.

192 *Remis:* Reims was the site of an important annual fair.

197 In the introductory part of the Mass, the singing of the Gradual follows the reading of the first Lesson.

209–32 Baltero mockingly speaks as if he were the wolf.

225 Ysengrimus's "martyrdom" is presented as a macabre parody of Christ's Passion.

235 Salaura answers Baltero's speech as if the wolf had really uttered it.

237–38 The sacristan rings the bells for funerals, for which he is paid large fees.

240 Compare Hebrews 12:6.

247 A grotesque parody of the *ars moriendi.*

262 Baltero further confuses matters by attributing Salaura's speech to Becca.

267 *scisso velamine:* see notes to 1.101 and 4.204 above.

289 Since no book is involved in the giving of the kiss of peace at Mass, the peace referred to here must be a legal peace, guaran-

teed by a legal document (*liber* in the sense of "charter"). See note to 3.62.

295   According to medieval legend, Mohammed was eaten by pigs. In consequence, the wolf claims the right to imitate Mohammed's role as prophet (l. 297).

309   The name and attributes of the demon Agemundus are evidently a comic invention by the poet.

327   *obsequa:* "maidservant."

350   *sinus:* metrical quantity suggests that this is *sĭnus* ("bosom") rather than *sīnus,* the rare masculine form of *sīnum* ("bowl"). *cola:* the more usual form is *colum.*

391   *incassare:* "to place in a reliquary" *(capsa, cassa).*

397–98   Compare Matthew 5:44; Luke 6:27, 35.

421–22   This nonsensical mixture of time- and place references is like those at 1.919 and 3.688.

428   I take *nota* in the general sense of "sign, token" (the seal is evidence of the charter's existence), but it may be used in the sense "charter" (see the entries for *notula* in Du Cange and in Niermeyer).

433   The trumpet would summon an assembly of the populace, to whom the peace would be proclaimed.

438   *nota:* "memoranda, minutes" (see Lewis and Short I.B.4 and Du Cange 3), and thus "a written record of an event."

459–60   Compare Luke 14:11, 18:14.

465–84   The reference is to the disastrous Second Crusade (1148–1149), instigated by Pope Eugenius III, with the enthusiastic support of Bernard of Clairvaux, in response to the news of the fall of Edessa to Arab forces in 1144. The crusaders took the overland route to the Holy Land, through Hungary and the Byzantine Empire, and Salaura claims that this was because Roger, duke of Sicily, had bribed the pope to ensure that they did not pass through Sicily and travel thence by sea to their objective. In fact it seems that Roger had offered to provide ships to transport the crusaders to the Holy Land, but his offer was turned down.

468	*monachus:* Pope Eugenius III was a Cistercian monk. The "two kingdoms" are France and Germany, the two nations involved in the Crusade.
475	Literally, "unless you were not living in the world."
500	Compare the proverb: "Fallere, flere, nere, statuit Deus in muliere."
551	*anticipare:* "to thwart, frustrate, make void."
567	Genesis 18:20–19:28.
568	Genesis 3–4.
569	Genesis 6–9, and for the giants, Genesis 6:4.
570	Exodus 7–14.
571	Numbers 16.
573	Exodus 16 (manna) and 32 (golden calf).
574	Numbers 22–24.
575–76	These lines refer to tribes or nations who were constant enemies of the Israelites in Old Testament times.
577	Daniel 3 (furnace) and 6 (*lacus* = "lions' den"; Lewis and Short IV.c).
578	As a divine punishment, Nebuchadnezzar was driven out to live with wild beasts for seven years (Daniel 4:22, 5:20–21.
579	Judges 4–5; Psalms 83 [Vulgate 82]:10–11.
581	*Canada* possibly = *Canaan,* and this line refers to God's promise to dispossess the Canaanites in favor of the Jews (Numbers 33:50–54).
582	According to tradition, Isaiah was put to death by being sawed in two. For Eli's death, see 1 Samuel 4:10–18; he may be "sad" because of the behavior of his sons (1 Samuel 2:12–17, 22–25).
583–84	On Elijah, see 1 Kings 17–19; 2 Kings 1–2. The prophet who fell "between the altar and the temple" is Zechariah (2 Chronicles 24:20–21; Matthew 23:35; Luke 11:51). The "two prophets" are presumably Elijah and Elisha; on the murder of prophets during their lifetime, see 1 Kings 18:4, 13, 19; 19:10, 14.
598	Compare Luke 21:12, 16, 24.
603	A reference to the slaughter of German Jews instigated by the monk Rudolf under the influence of Saint Bernard's call to the

Crusade. This is represented here as punishment for the Jewish rejection of Christ.

604   *praeiudicium:* "wrong, offense" (Niermeyer 3–4).

610   Isaiah 5:4.

613   The loosing of Satan from his chains heralds the end of the world (Revelation 20:7).

620   *trina:* that is, composed of earth, sea, and sky.

624   Hylas, a Greek youth, was drowned by water nymphs who were enamored of his beauty. His name is used as a synonym for Aquarius, the zodiacal sign for January 20–February 20.

625   Mulciber is a name for Vulcan, god of fire, here signifying fire itself.

631–36 There were great floods in Friesland in the mid-1130s and in 1164, but the likeliest candidate here is the flood of 1143.

641   *vellus:* "the earth's covering" (compare Psalms 72:6 [Vulgate 71:6]).

651–52 Probably a reference to the comet whose appearance in late 1147 preceded the Second Crusade.

655   There was an eclipse of the sun in October 1147; the second eclipse referred to may be the eclipse of 1140, or the eclipse of 1133, which was said in contemporary annals to have taken place without the intervention of clouds or the body of the moon.

662   That is, as far as the Empyrean, abode of God and the angels.

667–72 See note to 7.465–84. *Aethneus:* "of Mount Etna," the Sicilian volcano; used here to designate Sicily.

669   *aere utroque:* literally, "by money of both kinds."

671   The Byzantine Greeks were understandably reluctant to worsen political relations with their neighbors by all-out support for the Crusade, and the crusaders became convinced that the Greeks were working against them. Greek treachery is a running theme in Odo of Deuil's chronicle of the Crusade.

673   *pelagi rabies:* many members of the crusading army suffered shipwreck on the return journey.

675–76 Huge numbers of crusaders were drowned in a flash flood while encamped at Cheravas on the Thracian plain.

BOOK 7

Bibliography

EDITIONS

Mann, Jill, ed. and trans. *Ysengrimus: Text with Translation, Commentary and Introduction*. Mittellateinische Studien und Texte 12, Leiden, 1987.

Mone, Franz Joseph, ed. *Reinhart Fuchs aus dem neunten und zwölften Jahrhundert. (Reinardus Vulpes: Carmen epicum seculis IX et XII conscriptum)*. Stuttgart, 1832.

Voigt, Ernst, ed. *Ysengrimus*. Halle a. S., 1884.

TRANSLATIONS

Charbonnier, Elisabeth. *Recherches sur l'Ysengrimus. Traduction et Étude Littéraire*. Wiener Arbeiten zur germanischen Altertumskunde und Philologie 22, Vienna, 1983.

van Mierlo, J. *Magister Nivardus' Isengrimus: het vroegste Dierenepos in de Letterkunde der Nederlanden*. Utrecht, 1946.

Nieuwenhuis, Mark. *Ysengrimus, uit het Latijn vertaald*. Amsterdam, 1997.

Schönfelder, Albert. *Isengrimus: das flämische Tierepos aus dem lateinischen verdeutscht*. Niederdeutsche Studien 3, Münster, 1955.

Stella, Francesco. *Nivardus Gandensis. Ysengrimus. Nivardo di Gand. Le Avventure di Rinaldo e Isengrimo: Poema satirico del XII secolo, Libro I*. Pisa, 2009. [with Latin text]

Sypher, F. J., and Eleanor Sypher. *Ysengrimus by Magister Nivardus*. New York, 1980. [unreliable]

SECONDARY SOURCES

van Acker, Lieven. "Parodierende Elementen in Nivardus' Ysengrimus." *Handelingen van de Koninklijke Zuidnederlandsche Maatschappij voor Taal- en Letterkunde en Geschiedenis* 20 (1960): 335–63.

Foulet, Lucien. *Le Roman de Renard.* 2nd ed. Paris, 1968.

van Geertsom, A. "Bruno, de Auteur van de Ysengrimus." *Verslagen en Mededelingen van de Koninklijke Academie voor Taal- en Letterkunde* n.s. 1962: 5–73.

Gompf, Ludwig. "Ysengrimus und die Gereonssäule." *Göppinger Arbeiten zur Germanistik* 492 (1988) (*Festschrift für Paul Klopsch,* ed. Udo Kindermann, Wolfgang Maaz, and Fritz Wagner): 56–66.

Jauss, Hans Robert. *Untersuchungen zur mittelalterlichen Tierdichtung.* Beihefte zur Zeitschrift für romanische Philologie 100. Tübingen, 1959.

Knapp, Fritz Peter. *Das lateinische Tierepos.* Erträge der Forschung 121, Darmstadt, 1979.

———. "Materialistischer Utilitarianismus in der Maske der Satire: Magister Nivards 'Ysengrimus.'" *Mittellateinisches Jahrbuch* 10 (1975): 80–99.

Mann, Jill. *From Aesop to Reynard: Beast Literature in Medieval Britain.* Oxford, 2009.

———. "On Translating the *Ysengrimus.*" *Revue canadienne d'études néerlandaises/Canadian Journal of Netherlandic Studies* 4 (1983): 25–31.

———. "Proverbial Wisdom in the *Ysengrimus.*" *New Literary History* 16 (1984–1985): 93–109.

———. "The *Roman de Renart* and the *Ysengrimus.*" In *A la recherche du Roman de Renart,* 2 vols., edited by Kenneth Varty, 1:135–62. New Alyth, Perthshire, 1988–1991.

Mölk, Ulrich. "Fuchs und Wölfin. Über eine Episode des *Ysengrimus* und ihre englische Quelle." In *Anglo-Saxonica. Beiträge zur Vor- und Frühgeschichte der englischen Sprache und zur altenglischen Literatur. Festschrift für Hans Schabram zum 65. Geburtstag,* edited by Klaus R. Grinda und Claus-Dieter Wetzel, 515–25. Munich, 1993.

Scheidegger, Jean. "Le conflit des langues: écriture et fiction dans l'*Ysengrimus.*" *Revue canadienne d'études néerlandaises/ Canadian Journal of Netherlandic Studies* 4 (1983): 9–17.

Schwab, Ute. "Gastmetaphorik und Hornarithmetik im Ysengrimus." *Studi medievali* 3rd ser. 10.2 (1969): 215–50.

Singer, Samuel. *Sprichwörter des Mittelalters.* 3 vols. Vol. 1, *Ysengrimus,* 143–78. Bern, 1944–1947.

Yates, Donald N., and Richard H. Rouse. "The Extracts from 'Ysengrimus' in Paris B. N. lat. 16708." *Mittellateinisches Jahrbuch* 22 (1987): 212–29.

Ziolkowski, Jan M. *Talking Animals: Medieval Latin Beast Poetry,* 750–1150. Philadelphia, 1993.

Glossary

For a full account of the poem's nonclassical vocabulary, with supporting documentation, see the glossary in Voigt's edition of the *Ysengrimus*.

adhuc: (1) still, now, 1.769; 3.856, 1000; 4.186; 5.225, 664 (2) some day, on some future occasion, 2.423; 3.596; 4.970; 5.874

ave: used as a salutation (on departure), 1.346; 2.676; 4.710; (on arrival), 3.98, 394; 4.30; 5.1304

conciliare: (1) reconcile, 3.1140; 5.489 (2) make acceptable again, 2.174 (3) compensate, make up for, offset, 1.178, 372; 2.296; 3.20; 4.140; 5.758, 1124, 1186; 6.243, 454; 7.296

debere: to be guilty, 1.56; 4.575; 5.310

gratari: (1) thank warmly, 2.386; 3.362; 4.709; 5.755 (2) be glad, rejoice, 1.39; 2.505; 3.933, 1157; 4.1028; 5.1152 (3) congratulate, 5.57

impensum: gift, something given, 1.515; 4.359; 5.329, 1189; 7.378

inverrere: rake with a crushing or grinding tool, 5.366, 1234

medius: common ("in the middle, between mine and thine"), public, general, 1.202, 561

nullo: nowhere, 1.65; 4.906

nullorsum: nowhere, 3.813; 4.520; 5.555; 6.132

obiter: quickly, 2.562; 4.101, 473, 782

obviare: (1) meet, 5.344; 6.146 (2) get in the way of, hinder, 1.682 (3) reply, 3.601; 4.575, 928; cf. *obvia verba,* 3.244

omen: fortune, luck, good/bad auspices, 1.133, 655, 816, 923; 4.712, 998; 5.725; 6.231; 7.305

partus: = *paratus* (1) prepared, 3.391 (2) ready, available, at (someone's) disposal, 1.148, 351; 2.13; 3.811; 4.247, 466, 716

pietas: (1) kindness, tenderness, affection (especially between relatives, guest/host, friends, or others who owe each other affection as a duty), 1.129, 405, 478, 643, 828–29, 833, 859, 917; 2.13, 656; 3.56, 672, 717, 725; 4.618, 706, 731, 1036; 5.197, 999; 6.5; 7.81, 540, 697; *see also* n. to 2.655–66 on *pocula pietatis* (2) mercy, 1.418, 510, 512, 570; 2.323; 3.439; 4.262; 6.366 (3) generosity, 5.458

pius: (1) meek, gentle, 2.376, 387, 686; 3.217; 5.202 (2) kind, 4.708; 5.557, 1077; 7.224 (3) virtuous, 5.524

pone: near (adv.), 2.237; 4.470, 740; 5.1139; 7.43; (prep.), 5.1208

praeire: (lit.) go before, precede, 4.467, etc.; (fig.) surpass, excel, 1.636; 5.953

quam primum: (conj.) = *cum primum,* as soon as, 3.419; 5.1115

quatenus: somehow, 1.295; 5.1289

repente: quickly, without delay (without suggestion of surprise), 1.18, 106, 122; 2.452; 3.411, 1181; 5.147, 353, 981; 6.108, 538; (with connotation of suddenness), 1.777; 2.47; 4.143

speculari: (1) look, 3.898 (2) see, 3.379; 4.545; 5.21

subito: (1) immediately, quickly, straightway, 1.849; 3.448, 457, 773, 1091; 4.445, 845, 934, 1031; 5.46, 1020, 1127, 1194; 6.55, 541; 7.173, 231, 617 (2) suddenly, all at once, 2.575; 3.369

subitus: swift, speedy, instant, 3.4; 4.214; 5.140, 352

super: (in addition to usual senses) in return for, on account of, 3.983; 7.219, 510 *suspendere:* (1) sacrifice, 1.387; 3.175 (2) put off, delay, 1.781; 3.363, 773, 1067; 4.685 (3) suspend (from office), 1.749

ungue impresso: = *ad unguem,* to a hair, to perfection, exactly, 3.324; 5.505

ungue, ungue infixo: tenaciously, with tooth and nail, 1.208; 3.431, 569, 718; cf. 3.811

vale: used as a salutation (on meeting), 1.438; 5.450, 451; 6.408; (on parting), 1.866

vendicare: claim, 1.90, etc., is sharply distinguished from *vindicare* (avenge, revenge), 7.308, etc.

viari: = *viare,* 4.38, 915

vocem rogare/petere/poscere, etc.: ask for the right of reply (as part of legal procedure), 3.887; 6.420, 421, 450

Index

This index is limited to the names of personages, fictional or historical, that appear in the narrative of the poem.